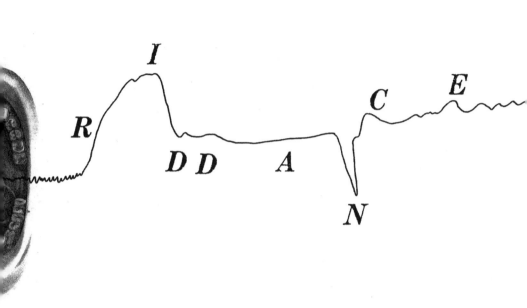

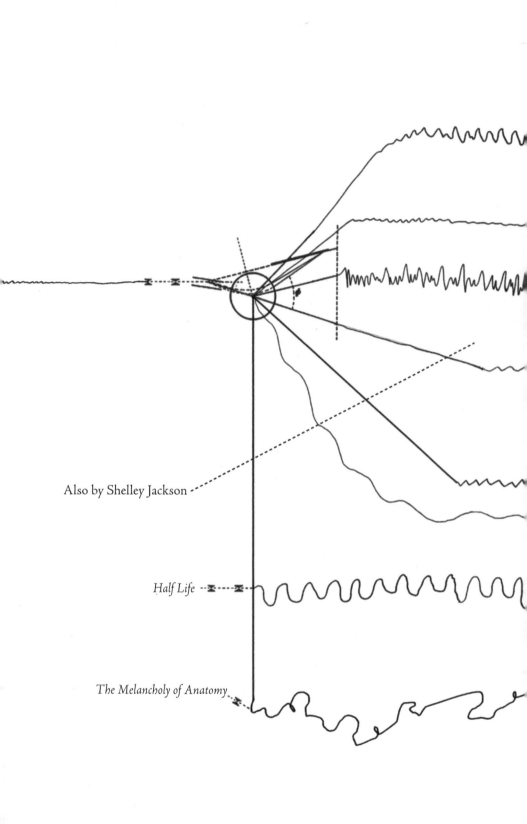

Also by Shelley Jackson

Half Life

The Melancholy of Anatomy

RIDDANCE

Shelley Jackson

(SHELLEY JACKSON)

BLACK
BALLOON
PUBLISHING

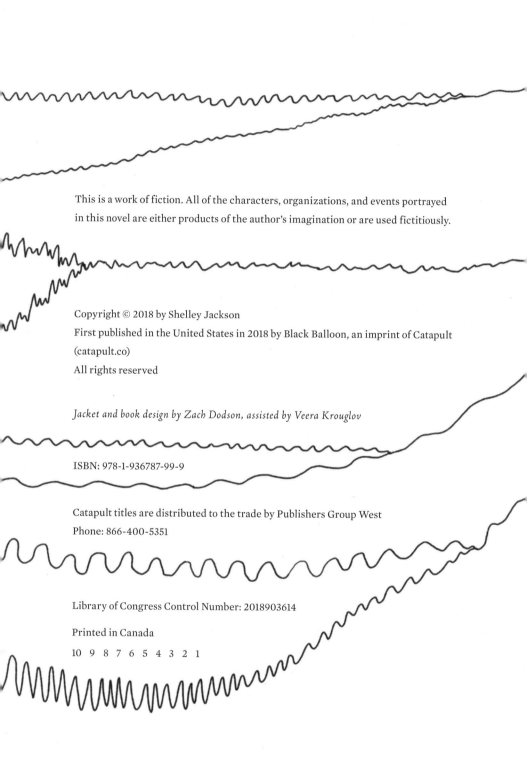

This is a work of fiction. All of the characters, organizations, and events portrayed in this novel are either products of the author's imagination or are used fictitiously.

Jacket and book design by Zach Dodson, assisted by Veera Krouglov

ISBN: 978-1-936787-99-9

Catapult titles are distributed to the trade by Publishers Group West
Phone: 866-400-5351

Library of Congress Control Number: 2018903614

Printed in Canada
10 9 8 7 6 5 4 3 2 1

For Shibire,
who will read it someday

Contents

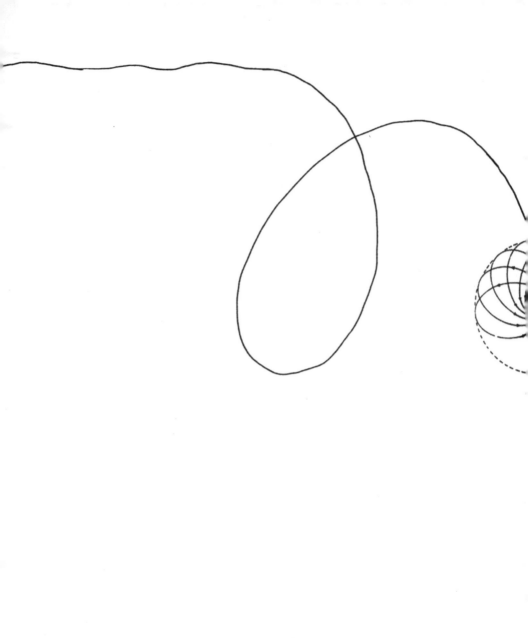

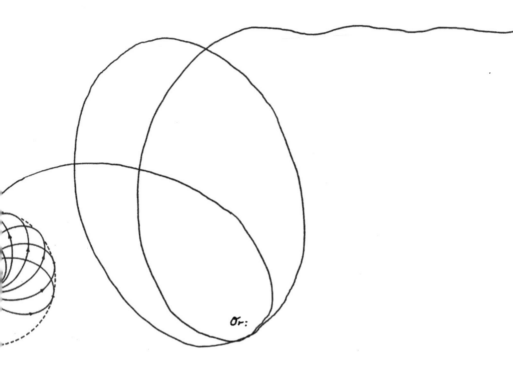

Or:

The Sybil Joines Vocational School
for
Ghost Speakers & Hearing-Mouth Children

RIDDANCE

SHELLEY JACKSON

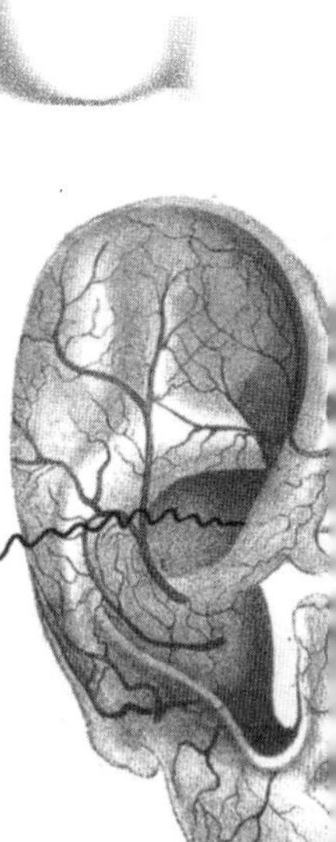

W. C. Times, Feb. 25

SHOCKING MURDER

Latest Death at School for Stammerers

MASS — *The Cheesehill, Massachusetts school for stammerers that has been so much in the news lately can add another death to its grim tally, and this time the verdict is murder.* --

It is our unpleasant duty to report the discovery of a charred body on the grounds of the Sybil Joines Vocational School for Ghost Speakers and Hearing Mouth Children, recently in the news for the accidental death of a student, the second this year. The victim has been tentatively identified as Regional School Inspector Edward Pacificus Edwards, who had been reported missing the previous night after his duties took him to the Vocational School, his vehicle having been discovered empty some hours after he had been believed to have gone home. An autopsy confirmed the police detective's opinion that the victim was already dead when immolated, having been struck with a blunt object from behind with enough force to stave in the skull. Observing no particular abundance of blood near the site, the police detective gave his opinion that the fatal blow was struck elsewhere, the body having been transported at some point during the night to this low-lying and densely wooded part of the school grounds and there set alight. The clothes and personal effects of the victim were presumably consumed by the fire. A bottle of paraffin was found beside the body.

To add to the macabre circumstances surrounding this grisly find, the Headmistress of the school, Miss Sybil Joines, was discovered deceased of natural causes in the early morning hours of the night in question. A representative of the school, Jane Grandison, stenographer, denied any knowledge of the Regional School Inspector's whereabouts after about 4 PM when he left the Headmistress's office to conduct a final inspection of the grounds.

Her offer to attempt to contact the deceased, employing the method of spirit communication taught at the school, was declined by the authorities, who called it a "tasteless publicity stunt."

The student who discovered the body was not available for interview but we have learned that her mother has withdrawn her from enrollment at the school, citing extreme emotional distress.

The police are interested in questioning a drifter seen loitering around the [...] the week.

Editor's Introduction

I owe my discovery of the Sybil Joines Vocational School to a bookstore and a ghost.

Afternoon in a then-unfamiliar city, some years ago—heavy, overcast sky—the almost continuous grumble of distant thunder. I was in town for an academic conference, but had slipped out of the warren of little rooms in the ugly and prematurely dilapidated "new building" where the conference was being held and walked rapidly off campus into the deserted streets of the business district, feeling a little guilty about missing my colleague's presentation, but unable to stand a moment more of our special brand of fatheadedness.

It was one of those melancholy downtowns not meant for walking, where the buildings take up whole blocks and there is nothing to be seen from street level except the stray sheet of paper listlessly turning itself over and over, or a street sign that suddenly starts vibrating and then as suddenly stops. It was with relief that I turned onto a block of small shops, though they were unprepossessing enough: a shuttered cigar store, a bodega in which an exhausted-looking man in a stained polo shirt consented to sell me a bottle of warmish water, and an unlit bookstore whose door yielded to an experimental push, revealing dark narrow aisles between leaning shelves, blocked here and there by jumbled landslides of books among which were many comfortable little hollows furry with what was probably cat hair—the place had an animal smell. A ragged floral towel curtained a doorway into the back of the shop, where something bumped and rustled.

I stooped to pluck out a book from a tightly packed bottom shelf, then withdrew my hand with a cry. A bead of blood was forming on the back of my finger. The impression that one of the books had *bit* me faded as the scrabbling sounds of a retreat made itself heard in the lower reaches of the shelves: the cat, no doubt, surprised in one of its hideaways. I stooped again and hooked a finger in the cloth binding at the top of the spine; the volume was stuck fast; I pulled harder and jerked it out, along with a neighboring book and a thin pamphlet, but felt the binding rip under my finger; guiltily I shoved it back in without looking at it, but had to get to my knees to retrieve the pamphlet (a 1950s-era educational brochure on hydroelectric dams) and the other book (an elocution handbook from the 1910s or '20s), which had fallen open to a page where a newspaper clipping must have been used as a bookmark, printing the pages it was pressed between with its phantom image. Ghosting, it is called in the rare-book business, and that is apt, for this image was only the first of the ghosts that from this moment on would throng to me.

The clipping itself had slipped out. I looked for it, found it, brown and brittle with age, under my own knee, replaced it against its fainter double, and only then saw what it was.

Shocking Murder Latest Death at School for Stammerers

The Cheesehill, Massachusetts, school for stammerers that has been so much in the news lately can add another death to its grim tally, and this time the verdict is murder.

It is our unpleasant duty to report the discovery of a charred body on the grounds of the Sybil Joines Vocational School for Ghost Speakers & Hearing-Mouth Children, recently in the news for the accidental death of a student, the second this year. The victim has been tentatively identified as Regional School Inspector Edward Pacificus Edwards, who had been reported missing the previous night after his duties took him to the Vocational School, his vehicle having been discovered empty some hours after he had been believed to have gone home. An autopsy confirmed the police detective's opinion that the victim was already dead when immolated, having been

struck with a blunt object from behind with enough force
to stave in the skull. Observing no particular abundance
of blood near the site, the police detective gave his opinion that the fatal blow was struck elsewhere, the body
having been transported at some point during the night
to this low-lying and densely wooded part of the school
grounds and there set alight. The clothes and personal
effects of the victim were presumably consumed by the
fire. A bottle of paraffin was found beside the body.

To add to the macabre circumstances surrounding this
grisly find, the Headmistress of the school, Miss Sybil
Joines, was discovered deceased of natural causes in the
early morning hours of the night in question. A representative of the school, Jane Grandison, stenographer,
denied any knowledge of the Regional School Inspector's whereabouts after about 4 p.m. when he left the
Headmistress's office to conduct a final inspection of the
grounds.

Her offer to attempt to contact the deceased, employing
the method of spirit communication taught at the school,
was declined by the authorities, who called it a "tasteless
publicity stunt."

The student who discovered the body was not available
for interview but we have learned that her mother has
withdrawn her from enrollment at the school, citing
extreme emotional distress.

The police are interested in questioning a drifter seen
loitering around the grounds earlier in the week.

I read, then reread the clipping, from which little polygonal shards kept drifting down to settle in the nap of the stained and smelly carpet. I had never heard of the Sybil Joines Vocational School. That alone would have pricked my curiosity, since I had flattered myself that I knew quite everything there was to know about the spiritualist movement in late nineteenth- to early twentieth-century America. But my discovery also resonated with another of my research interests, the proliferation and popularization of what one might call speech studies: stuttering "cures"; elocution; orthoëpy; Major Beniowski's "anti-absurd" or "phrenotypic" orthography (it luks lyk this), Pitman and Gregg shorthand, and other methods of supplanting the arbitrary signs of written language with a sort of "score" based on the sounds of speech. I am only human: the murder intrigued me too. Had the mystery been solved? Suppose I could solve it?—with the methods of scholarship, of course!

I closed the book on its interesting passenger and pressed it to my chest. I had the sudden feeling that someone was looking over my shoulder: not another ghost but an up-and-coming scholar in my own discipline, slavering to take from me the "lead" that was—but for how long?—mine, all mine.

But I think I felt something more than greed, even then: the sensation that a hole had suddenly gaped in a world that had hitherto seemed decently if not prudishly buttoned up. Most of us avert our eyes when this happens, but I looked. And saw ... A flutter of aquamarine and viridian, a pounce of stripes, a spatter of—molten ice, frozen fire—the smell of music! I express myself clumsily, and yet I believe some of you at least will know what I mean when I say that my first thought was *Yesss* and my second, *I remember this.* How indeed could I have forgotten that time I burrowed under the covers to read by flashlight past my bedtime in that warm and golden tent-cave—delicious illicitry—and then, thinking I was crawling back up toward the head of the bed, actually made my way deeper, through a tunnel that went on and on, from whose roof fine roots stretched down to fascinate my forehead, until I came up in the center of a snow-thick forest, where some mechanical angels were rehearsing a hymn of clicks and chirps before an audience of spiders? I had longed for such another opening my whole life.

I suddenly noticed a pair of eyes shining back at me from a gap in the opposite bookcase and started, dropping the book. Doubtless it was again the cat. The proprietor jerked aside the towel-curtain and stood looking at me without enthusiasm. "None of these books are at all valuable," he said. "Please feel free to toss them around."

"Don't worry," I said, "I'll be buying this one." He worked out the tax with bad grace and a pocket calculator, but took my money, though he watched the book vanish into my satchel with evident regret.

My subsequent researches did nothing to dispel my amazement. Even today I find myself marveling that an institution that in its heyday raised a public scandal on more than one occasion, and whose theoreticians pursued a vigorous debate with notable intellectuals of the time, should have been effectively forgotten for so many decades. The decline of the spiritualist movement explains it only in part. I believe the memory was actively repressed: If the dead do live on, the public would prefer, on the whole, not to know about it.

Once I began to look, however, I found references to the Vocational School everywhere. Other articles about the murder turned up on microfiche, and I assembled enough supporting material for a modest paper. It was well received. I began another, more substantial paper, aware that other scholars' interest had been piqued, but confident that I had staked my claim.

It is a common occurrence, and not just among scholars, for a new obsession to awaken reverberations in the most unlikely places. Probably there is nothing really uncanny about it; the observer is newly alert to these echoes, that's all. But it was pretty peculiar, all the same, how rapidly my archives grew. In a thrift store in Madison I found a Vocational School yearbook (containing some very interesting photographs of school activities). Walking down a street in Philadelphia, I was dealt a blow on the temple by a paper airplane that had spiraled down from some open window above me, accompanied by muffled laughter; it proved to be a page from a book about the spiritualist community Lily Dale on which the Vocational School was mentioned in passing. And in one of a number of bags of interesting old books and papers left on a New York curb, as by indiscriminate and probably illiterate housecleaners clearing an apartment whose former occupant had died, I found, tied up with twine, a sheaf of yellowing papers covered in the characters of an unfamiliar alphabet, each page numbered, dated, and labeled in a childish hand, "Betty Clamm, SJVSGSHMC"!

The Internet contains, it sometimes seems, all stories that have been and will be told. It is like that mythical Interstitial Library whose stacks readers sometimes wander in dreams, and whose itinerant librarians sometimes leave on your pillow astronomical bills for library fines levied on overdue books that you have never heard of, bills written in the already faint and soon to disappear stains of those mysterious night sweats from which you awaken terrified and out of breath. So I was not too surprised to stumble upon a reference to the Vocational School in the moribund listserv of a group of scholars whose common interest and broader topic was the work of a French philosopher whose name I did not recognize and cannot now recall but who seemed to employ a great number of obscure but wonderfully poetic terms composed of unlikely combinations or odd usages of otherwise ordinary words. I was skimming the discussion, which got quite heated, enjoying the feeling that I didn't know what was going on, when I caught a phrase in passing: ". . . like those turn-of-the-century concerns that lined their pockets through the spiritualist fad, e.g., the SJVS." Naturally other scholars would have come upon references to the Vocational School somewhere in their reading, just as I had. What surprised me a little more was the reference I spotted a few days later in a customer review of a pair of waterproof loafers I was considering. Well, one does not expect to find reference to obscure cultural institutions of another century ("like something an SJVS student would wear") in the context of protective footwear! Still, they were of a conservative style and it was not really difficult to imagine a middle-aged scholar—say, one of the members of the aforementioned listserv—pulling them on and trudging off through the winter slush to his library kiosk.

That pedestrian image banished all frisson of the uncanny until a few days later, when I received a cease-and-desist letter from a party representing herself as the Headmistress of the Sybil Joines Vocational School for Ghost Speakers & Hearing-Mouth Children, and threatening legal action if I did not immediately cancel plans for an anthology of "pirated" documents produced by and about the early Vocational School, to all of which she claimed exclusive rights. Plans I had not yet confided to anyone. No—plans I had not yet made!

I suspected a prank, though I was struck in passing by certain arcane phrases and archaic usages characteristic of early Vocational School writings, and, somehow, found that my breath quickened as I read on. But when my eyes, swiftly and still scornfully descending the page, came to rest on the signature at the bottom, I thrust back my chair (scoring four claw marks in the varnish—I would lament those later) and strode into the kitchen to stare into the sink with unseeing eyes, a mad conviction growing in me that not only did the Vocational School live on, but so did that exceptional, rather dreadful, and indubitably deceased woman whose acquaintance I had made through a pile of yellowing papers, dreams, and the whispers of drainpipes and dead leaves. That the letter writer's claims were true. Oh, not her claims to copyright, those certainly had no legal merit, but her claims to be the fourth-generation reincarnation—in the special sense of a person channeling another's ghost—of Sybil Joines.

Of course, any halfway competent forger could reproduce the capsizing loops and botched cloverleafs of that unmistakeable signature. My conviction was not rational. Let us say that I was possessed by it.

Below the signature was a URL; I typed it into my browser and found myself regarding a plausible academic website. Vintage photograph of the Vocational School on the masthead, stock images of alleged students with pencils poised, application instructions for would-be distance learners. You may ask why I did not turn up this website in my initial research, and indeed I asked myself the same question. Later I learned that it had only just been launched; I must have been one of its first visitors. Once again I had the uncanny feeling that the SJVS was created expressly for me, was summoned forth by my interest in it, towing its history behind it like a placenta.

A couple of phone calls connected me to someone who, in a hoarse, imperious voice that crackled like an old Edison recording, identified herself as Sybil Joines. I addressed her with awed courtesy and agreed to everything she said. Placated, she eventually warmed to me. Not only did she consent to the publication of this anthology,[1] but she gave me access to a great deal of immensely valuable material in the Vocational School's own archives— much more material, in fact, than I can include here. (I hold out hope for an omnibus edition.)

A note to scholars: Any historian of the Vocational School is faced with peculiar difficulties. Its scribes and archivists alike were in agreement that a self is a mere back-formation of a voice that itself belongs to no one, or to the dead. Thus authorship would be a vexed question even if all Vocational School documents were signed, as many were not. The current headmistress of the Vocational School, for instance, derives her authority from the demonstration that she is the mouthpiece for the previous headmistress, who was the mouthpiece for the previous headmistress, and so on. In a sense, she is who she is precisely because she is not who she is, and to insist too stringently on biographical "fact" is to miss the point.

It is a fault of our age to consider all that is eccentric—and by eccentric I mean merely and precisely what lies farther than usual from a certain, conventionally defined, probably illusory center—as representing only one of two things: the symptom of a malady whose cure would restore the patient to a place in the center; or a new center, toward which all must hasten. What is true, we nearly all agree on; what we nearly all agree on must, we think, be true. But I would suggest that there are minority truths, never destined to hold sway over the imagination of the entire human race, and furthermore, ideas—less defensible, but to me, even more precious—that are neither true nor false but (I have sat here this age trying to compose a marrowsky better than *fue* or *tralse*, but hang it:) *crepuscular*. One might

---

1. But let us not forget that it was her own idea. So did she consent to, or command it?

even say, fictional. Entertaining them, we feel what angels and werewolves must feel, that between human and inhuman there is an open door, and a threshold as wide as a world.

Because I am a—faintly regretful—member of the majority, and know my way back to the center, despite my excursions to its fringes, I can speak to something that interests true eccentrics not at all: the *utility* of the crepuscular. For no one has ever got to a new majority truth, a new center, without passing through these twilight zones and thus eccentrizing themselves.

But for every colonist there are countless expeditionists who will wander forever through deliciously ineffable sargassos, and when they write home, communicate both less and more than their correspondents would wish. For in the crespuscular every word is a marrowsky, if it is not one of those stranger compounds, those werewords, for which there is no name (word-ferns, word-worms, word-mists and -algae). What we know as meaning is not the principle cargo of such words. The Headmistress speaks this language like a native, for while the Vocational School may have appeared on county maps in the vicinity of Cheesehill, Massachusetts, its real address was in the crepuscular zone.

Because the eccentric troubles the center like a lingering dream, there has been a great deal of nonsense written in recent years about the Headmistress of the SJVS. Some have gone so far as to doubt her existence ("And quite right, too," I can hear her say). But she did exist, was as sane as any person of original views passionately held, and whatever fugitive pains urged her on, her central motivation was and always would be the hunger for understanding. Though it is necessary to stress that for her the deepest understanding would feel like incomprehension, and would be communicable only in the way that a disease is.

So although there are mysteries to interest both philosophers and policemen in these pages, I do not propose to offer any solutions. My vision of a scholarly work with the popular appeal of a crime novel has exposed itself for the mercenary fantasy it was. The eccentric, muscled back into the white light of judgment, is just so much more center. Its value, however, is in the darkness that it radiates from the farthest reaches of the spectrum, discovering, in the black-and-white page, shades of imperial violet.

Anyone who has visited the land of the dead, in fact or fancy (and there is not as great a difference between the two as you might suppose), will have guessed that this book can be entered at any point. For less experienced travelers, I have planned a route. Its reduplicate tracks, laid down over a single evening—one by the Headmistress, one by her stenographer—will convey the reader surely, if not safely, to the end. Interspersed between these two interwoven strands, according to a strictly repeating pattern, are additional readings of a more scientific, sociological, or metaphysical nature. Those who, lacking a scholar's interest in minutiae, want to get to the end more quickly, may wish to skip over these parts, and who knows, may even be wise to do so. But true eccentrics may find in them something—a map, a manual—that they have long been seeking.

※ VOCATIONAL SCHOOL ※
FOR GHOST SPEAKERS & HEARING-MOUTH CHILDREN
1201

FIELD DISPATC(38)..

SENDER   RECEIVER

Sybil Joines   *J. Grandison*

CLASS OF SERVICE
OFFICE OF ...
... WIRE, to
nature of the dispatch.
than the speed, ... to
... here. Type is
a branch or notation.
To ...

SYMBOLS
GDL = Day Letter
NL = Night Deferred
MO = Much Object
DL = Deaf Speaking
XTRL NEUROGRAM

Borne on racing white-streaked black. Swirling to the glassy brink of the cataracts, then plunging in din and tumult so constant as to seem a kind of stillness. Around me others fall, so many as to seem like no one. We thunder down. Then smash against the fundament of the world. One xxxx smithereen, I flash past scenes too fleeting to collect. But someone is speaking, and as I recognize the voice, ground forms under my feet. The others stream on, forsaking me.

[Static.]

Are you receiving?

  [Static, sound of breathing.]

Someone rises from the deluge. A bony big woman tented in mourning crepe and bombazine bothered all over with jet beads and netting. The great curved shield of her bosom has more of whalebone than of flesh behind it. The glossy carapace brings beetles to mind. An important personage. She is gripping a lorgnette and glaring about as if looking for someone.

  A suspicion dawns on me that I am speaking of myself.

The personage opens her, my mouth. I am saying something. It is this, that I am saying something, which is this, that I am saying something, which is [several words indistinct]--

  Stop.

  Compose yourself.

Resume.

  Say that my name is xxxxxxxxxxxxxxxxxxJoines; that I am yet something short of two score and ten years old, my precise age being uncertain due to frequent prosecutions of what is, in effect, a kind of time travel; that I have worn crepe from the age of eleven and do not now expect to p-p-p-p-put it aside.

  Please correct phonotactic violations.

  Say that I am the headmistress of a vocational school, that I teach children with what were once known as speech impediments to channel the dead. Having been one myself, once. A child, that is. With a stutter. Say that the dead speak through me. Or let them say so, it's all one. Say that I dispatch this message from the land of the did dad dead, where I have spent many pleasant hours (they aren't hours, there are no hours here, but we would be here all day, if there were days here, if I tried to explain how the lack of time drags on regardless). Say that I live at the school with my students, that they are like family to me, which might sound agreeable if one did not know that my mother was hanged and my father burned alive.

  Say that a child is missing.

1. The Final Dispatch

Dictated by Headmistress Joines to Stenographer #6 (J. Grandison), November 17, 1919

This remarkable document was dictated by Headmistress Joines from the land of the dead over the course of one long night, her last, through a transmitting device of her own invention. All expeditions to the netherworld were accompanied by a running commentary in this manner. Though often disjointed and equivocal, these dispatches not only provided invaluable data on unexplored regions of the necrocosmos, but were a mortal necessity for the necronaut, for whom the narrative thread was quite literally a lifeline.

Because we live in time, when we visit the land of the dead, we must carry our own time with us, or experience literally nothing and never even know we were ever there. Time is speech-time, according to Vocational School doctrine: We talk our way through the timeless land of the dead in a sort of bathysphere made of words, creating both ourselves and the landscape through which we move. In a very real sense the dispatch is the journey. This one was executed in haste, poor health, and emotional extremity, and in consequence, is more than usually disorienting. Only the hardiest and most experienced readers should risk it.

Although it conveys the impression of a single unbroken monologue, we know from the testimony of Joines's stenographer and successor, Jane Grandison, that it was interrupted by intervals of silence of varying duration. Since silence is just as important as speech in Vocational School thought, I have given some thought to how I might reproduce its intervalling effect for readers who might flip flippantly through blank pages or other crude transliterations.

Eventually I decided to divide the dispatch into its longest continuous parts, interpolating other documents between them. It should be borne in mind, however, that they do make up a single unabridged transmission. Thus the ideal reader will read the entire book in one sitting, starting at about four in the afternoon, and will come to the end at about the same hour as the Headmistress came to hers. —Ed.

Borne on racing white-streaked black. Swirling to the glassy brink of the cataracts, then plunging in din and tumult so constant as to seem a kind of stillness. Around me others fall, so many as to seem like no one. We thunder down. Then smash against the fundament of the world. One ~~smth~~ smithereen, I flash past scenes too fleeting to collect. But someone is speaking, and as I recognize the voice, ground forms under my feet. The others stream on, forsaking me.

[Static.]

Are you receiving?

[Static, sound of breathing.]

Someone rises from the deluge. A bony big woman tented in mourning crepe and bombazine bothered all over with jet beads and netting. The great curved shield of her bosom has more of whalebone than of flesh behind it. The glossy carapace brings beetles to mind. An important personage. She is gripping a lorgnette and glaring about as if looking for someone.

A suspicion dawns on me that I am speaking of myself.

The personage opens her, my mouth. I am saying something. It is this, that I am saying something, which is this, that I am saying something, which is [several words indistinct]—

Stop.

Compose yourself.

Resume.

Say that my name is Sssss . . . Sybil Adjudicate Joines; that I am yet something short of two score and ten years old, my precise age being uncertain due to frequent prosecutions of what is, in effect, a kind of time travel; that I have worn crepe from the age of eleven and do not now expect to p-p-p-p-put it aside.

Please correct phonotactic violations.

Say that I am the headmistress of a vocational school, that I teach children with what were once known as speech impediments to channel the dead. Having been one myself, once. A child, that is. With a stutter. Say that the dead speak through me. Or let them say so, it's all one. Say that

I dispatch this message from the land of the ~~did dad~~ dead, where I have spent many pleasant hours. (They aren't hours, there are no hours here, but we would be here all day, if there were days here, if I tried to explain how the lack of time drags on regardless.) Say that I live at the school with my students, that they are like family to me, which might sound agreeable if one did not know that my mother was hanged and my father burned alive.

Say that a child is missing.

[Static, sound of breathing.]

Are you receiving?

No. B 55

The Stenographer's Story
J. Grandison, November 17, 1919

The young Jane Grandison transcribed the Headmistress's final dispatch from her usual post beside the great brass trumpet of the receiving device. She apparently composed the following autobiographical text during the aforementioned lulls in that dispatch, scrolling a new sheet of paper into her typewriter whenever the Headmistress fell silent, and replacing it with the old one when the Headmistress resumed. I imagine two growing piles of paper on the table beside her, first one, then the other mounting higher (this is not the place to venture an opinion on the vexed question of whether the piles ever got mixed up), though the reference to "night" in the second paragraph, which might be taken to suggest that she did not begin her own text until Joines's was already well under way, introduces doubt as to the accuracy of this picture. Nonetheless I have reproduced this alternating movement here, as true to the spirit if not the reality of her method. So, like the Final Dispatch, the Stenographer's Story may be found distributed through the volume.

In addition to offering invaluable insight into the personalities of both the first and the second Sybil Joines (if I may commit the ontological solecism of differentiating them), the text gives a vivid picture of the first impression made by the Vocational School on a nervous instrument so finely tuned as to suggest a diagnosis of neurasthenia, though I am no expert. —Ed.

The Headmistress's tiny, tinny voice has fallen silent. The brass trumpet flower—Pythian oracle, hierophant—is unreverberant, its mechanism still. Only a faint hissing emanating from among the ivory hammers, copper coils, India-rubber bladders, and paper diaphragms tucked like organs inside its mahogany case attests that the channel is open, the miracle continues.

So I have a minute, and maybe more, to figure out what to do. The night is long. There will be time for everything that is required. But to know my duty it will be necessary to know who I am. When did that begin to be a question? Maybe already that first day.

I was eleven years old, could write my name backwards and upside down, but not pronounce it, and had seen several dead people already. The prospect of hearing them, too, did not particularly alarm me. So I had informed my aunt when, with exaggerated surprise, she brought me the letter from the Sybil Joines Vocational School for Ghost Speakers & Hearing-Mouth Children: "We are pleased to offer you a place . . . Room and board . . . Reply soonest." Since I saw that she had made up her mind to be rid of me, pride would have prompted me to say so in any case, but I spoke as I felt. Now, as the glossy, black, indignant-looking automobile we had retained in Springfield brought me ever closer to the school, my breath did come quicker, but it was with curiosity and excitement, not dread.

I braced my hand against the ceiling as the car jolted over a rock. The road had deteriorated after Cheesehill and was now little more than two ruts running in parallel. My escort, a pinched, powder-white woman in weeds, rapped twice on the back of our driver's seat with her cane.

"You there! We shall be rattled to pieces!"

Seal-brown fingers tightened on the wheel. "Got to beat that storm, ma'am, with the roads in this condition, or I won't be making it home this side of tomorrow." Indeed for some time the wind had carried the tang of rain, and a break in the trees showed the thunderheads heaping up over the ridge, though on us the sun still shone.

"Storm? Storm? Are you frightened of a storm, at your age? If need be, the school can put you up for the night."

The driver made no reply but drove, if anything, faster.

The dead people I had seen were my mother and Bitty. Of influenza. My father might have been dead too for all I knew, having skived off before Bitty was weaned. Truthfully, to hear them speak again would have been a very great shock. But I did not at all expect to. Their silence, when it came, had been complete.

My reflection slid stilly over the hurtling trees, leaning over me in an admonishing way, like a censorious second self. I looked steadily through it, drinking in the strangeness of all I saw, wonderful to me, however unremarkable in itself: dark woods; muddy fields; a small, rank, weedy lake where, off the stove-in, upturned bottom of a red rowboat, a solitary heron was just tilting into flight. I half rose in sympathy with its effortful ascent.

"Stop fidgeting, girl."

One might sink a hatpin in Miss Exiguous, I thought, coolly assessing the jet-tipped pair anchoring her black felt hat. Without returning my glance, she shifted uneasily on the seat and I perceived with dreary unsurprise that, like my aunt, she was one of those who feel toward colored folk the way some feel toward a spider or a snake: that even the mildest members of the species make uneasy company.

Deliberately I returned my gaze to the window, though now that I was sitting back, I could see nothing of interest: only branches, sky, myself. I was a runty girl, small, dark, and odd looking, as I could have confirmed in the glass had I wished. A sufficiency of mirrors had already taught me not to hope. Not for a pretty face, at least, and the kind of luck that comes with it.

Not that my face was hideous, but it had a plain, hard, assessing look incompatible with beauty. It expressed my nature truthfully enough. I was not a gay girl.

Now I kept that face turned, with the pertinacity of a praying mantis, toward where I imagined the Vocational School to be. I had been shown a picture of a big black building, and a big black dress with a big white man-faced woman in it, and a line of children, some of them colored like me, with black bands around their sleeves. I had been told that "someone with *your* gifts, girl"—gifts!—would be admitted on scholarship, room and board included. It scarcely mattered. For inducements little greater than these I would have gone to Mongolia, or the moon.

It seems incredible, but I am going, really going, I told myself. My stammer, the cause of so much misery, had set me free.

I was only seven and just come from quarantine to my aunt and uncle's big Boston house when I first heard the Voice (for so I thought of it). It growled and spat in my throat, and I was beaten with a strop, for my new guardians had no better notion than to try to scare it out of me. The sum of their ambition for me was that I should disappear into the nondescript throng of their own children, of whom there were ~~six~~ ~~seven~~ six or seven. Unfortunately I could not do so. If nothing else, my dark complexion would have set me apart—for though my mother was white Irish like my aunt, my father had been black—although my aunt feigned not to notice it, while pressing upon me, as my only luxuries, whitening creams and parasols. But no one scrupled to editorialize on my stammer. Even little Annabel, still in diapers, knew that to imitate me was to earn shouts of laughter from her older siblings, and smiles even from the adults.

I can see her now, in receding view: fat feet drumming the parquetry, Hygienic Wood Wool diapers dangling from a single pin.

("My hat!"—Miss Exiguous, outraged, as a lurch crushed its cheap feathers against the car ceiling. She unfastened it and, having inspected it for damages, laid it on the seat between us, holding it there with one sinewy little hand.)

Still, I thought well of myself, though I had little enough reason to do so, and had I suspected that a stammer betokened "exceptional natural aptitude for spirit communications" (as Miss Exiguous would subsequently inform me), I would have prided myself upon it, no matter how my cousins derided me. But I did not, and I fought the Voice. The Voice won. I had periods of fluency, but much of the time I could barely speak at all and was in a pretty pickle when it came to asking directions of a policeman or naming the capital of Lithuania. I did not go hungry—to point and grunt was not beyond me. Still, if what distinguishes us from the beasts is the capacity to speak, as I was often told, I was not quite human.

At the school there would be others like me, or even worse. It would be interesting to meet the worse. Drooling perhaps. Jerking and hissing like geese.

At home, I mean at the large Boston house of my aunt and uncle, a picture hung on the wall. It had once decorated a Slavic beehive, I had been told; I do not know how it came into their possession, or why they kept it. It looked barbaric amid their twinkling crystal, fringed lampshades, dark soft-glinting mahogany furniture. In it a crudely rendered, gape-mouthed lady was having her horribly long red tongue drawn out by a naked devil wielding a pair of oversized tongues, I mean tongs. Tongue-tongs: it was as if the near-homophone had itself brought them together—as if language held a barely concealed grudge against its chiefest organ. It, the tongue, was frayed at one end into what I took for roots, in the botanical sense. I had red, I mean read, of a tongue being pulled out "by the roots" and had drawn from this the lesson that a tongue was a sort of vegetable, not of a piece with the body in which it was fixed. My own experience had supported this view: Within my mouth, warmly fuming with self, something foreign had grown. So I had half-believed the picture and even entertained, in drowsy reveries, certain fearful corollaries: that if my tongue was not pulled out like a carrot, it would branch, flower, go to seed. Of course it was not my tongue but my Voice that had taken root in my mouth like a weed. I could not imagine the tongs that could pluck it out. But I thought that the devil wielding them might resemble a man-faced woman in black.

I slumped, jamming my chin against my chest through the stiff, coarse cloth of a new pinafore, a parting gift from my aunt. A more loving, better-loved child might have been hurt to be thus packed away, but I was glad. Glad! Hateful Aunt Margaret. Hateful cousins. Hateful house. And hateful myself, there. I had been bad, very bad, so bad that remembering, I swallowed hard, frightened and even awed at myself; but I would put wickedness behind me now. I would be so good, no one would ever send me away again.

The hat crouched on the seat beside me, jet-tipped hatpins glinting like eyes among the feathers. It was watching me, knowing what I was thinking, that it would be so easy to reach over, and with just two fingers . . .

I took hold of the seat with both hands. The car jerked, staggered, jerked. Miss Exiguous was breathing through her nose in indignant little puffs. We had come to the worst stretch yet; at some point the overflow from a drainage ditch had evidently run a good way down the road, washing away the dirt between the boulders; it would be interesting to see what became of the road if the storm fell upon us here, but I was no longer thinking about it.

A peculiar tugging and plucking was taking place somewhere in my midriff. There was an almost palpable *snap* as of stitches parting, and then a slackening and a sliding; my past life was slipping away, like a loose signature from an old book. Already, those tribulations that had seemed so real were disintegrating into dust. Cousins, aunts, salt pork and boiled cabbage, grief and the slow, terrible deadening of grief—had I ever really believed any of it? Willingly, I yielded to a will stronger than my own, and let myself be carried into a new story.

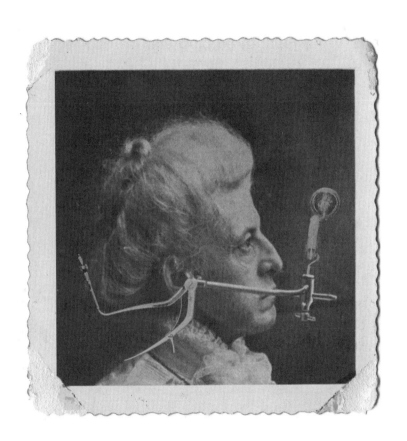

Readings
My Childhood

The following document, ostensibly by Sybil Joines, has been much discussed in the critical literature. It was sent to me as a .pdf file by a representative of the school, rather late in my researches, when I had already begun compiling this book. I subsequently offered it up to the larger community, with my own commentary and modest fanfare. It made a great stir, of course, as contributing a new and more intimate perspective on the early life of the Headmistress, and my reputation as a scholar was such that few questioned its provenance, but after its swift elevation to canonical status, questions began to arise about certain subtle anachronisms in the text, and it was finally condemned as a forgery by several major scholars in concert, in a rather hurtful public demonstration on the occasion of my presentation with an honorary degree from the University of Göttingen.

Flushed, still holding my parchment scroll with its little tassel (which had somehow got caught in my reading glasses), and somewhat the worse for champagne, I was forced to hastily defend the document's authenticity and, implicitly, my scholarly integrity, while at the same time aware of a highly unpleasant sensation in the pit of my stomach, not entirely attributable to Schnitzel mit Spaetzle, *as I awoke to inchoate but long-standing doubts of my own.*

Finally, a Dutch research team took the obvious step of asking to see the handwritten original—as I should have done at the start—and resolved the debate at a stroke, for they found that it was written with a ballpoint pen. (As we know, Laszlo Biro did not file his patent until June 1938, well after Joines's death.) I quickly issued a handsome retraction, making no reference to hurt feelings. Yet questions remained. If I had been the victim of a hoax, what on earth was its objective? Was the SJVS less enthusiastic about my project than it seemed? If so, why had they gone to such lengths to appear accommodating? Why was the fraud so cunning in one respect (whoever wrote it knew his SJVSeana) and so careless in another (how difficult would it have been to procure an inkwell and quill)? Finally, should we not accept as plausible hypotheses, if not facts, the explanations the counterfeit supplied for the many hitherto inexplicable references in the legitimate texts? I found myself unable to "roll back" the changes in my understanding of the Headmistress's story; the fiction had folded in the facts and made them its own.

I took these issues to the community at large, and after much consternation and internal debate we penned a collective e-mail to the Vocational School that was a masterpiece of tactful circumspection, requesting more information on the provenance of the contested document, and offering the dubious "out" that they had themselves been victims of a trickster among their own ranks. The response was quick and disconcerting in its honesty.

Of course the document was modern! It had been completed just days before they sent it to me! The Headmistress had perceived that the book would be the better for an autobiographical overview and had undertaken to provide one. The new headmistress? Well, yes! And also no. It was meaningless to speak of new and old in this context; the new headmistress was the old headmistress. Only insofar as the ghost of Sybil Joines spoke through her was she the headmistress at all.

That this not only discredited the document in question but cast retrospective doubt on all the supposedly historical materials they had been supplying me with, I could not make them see. Concerns of plagiarism they brushed aside with an emoticon. How pointless to insist on verifiable authorship when "We are NONE of us in possession of ourselves," when "We are ALL mere mouthpieces for the dead." (Emphasis theirs.) Indeed, insofar as my extremely "STUPID" persistence betrayed a skepticism that the dead can speak, I risked souring our relationship and thus losing this priceless connection to the fount of all SJVSeana.

I backed off.

I have since decided that as a document of the contemporary Vocational School, this text is just as revealing as if it were exactly what it purports to be, and I would no longer contemplate omitting it from any serious study of the legacy. I leave it to the reader, however, to decide whether it reveals more about this headmistress, that one, or we scholars. —Ed.

I had a fierce, unthinking certainty that I was exceptional. Once a bone had struck the road beside me and bounced up almost as far as my head, having fallen from, as it appeared, a great height. I turned around and around but saw only an old horse grazing on the far side of a field. The bone was therefore a sign. Not from God, not *from* anyone, just a sign: that I was special, that uncommon things were going to happen to me. Once, too, a hummingbird intent upon a trumpet flower had trustingly curled its claws around my finger—until then I had not been quite sure that hummingbirds *had* feet—while I inhaled with my eyes the pulsing iridescent neck, the finely thatched crown, the liquid eye. Even after it tensed and flew away I continued to feel its warm, bony grip, like an invisible ring, as if I were betrothed to the extraordinary *now*. I felt not wonder, but vindication. This was what I expected life to contain. This, and an unending series of similar marvels, like brightly colored glass beads on a string.

"Excuse me, what was your name again?" Susannah says, as Mary coughs behind her plump and freckled hand. Susannah is my next-door neighbor (it is over the fence that dissociates our lush lawn from her seedy one that we conduct this interview). Her father works in my father's factory. So does Mary's. She knows my name.

My breath turns to glass in my throat. I gag; again; again. At the front of my mouth, my tongue (with a pressure slightly, maddeningly off-center) seems to be trying to stub itself out against my teeth.

"Sssssssss . . ." I say, if you call that saying.

Susannah tilts her shining head, and I burn. Not just for the barbaric sound I am making—a spiccato sizzle—but for the hair stuck to my cheek, the stinging spot where my frock chafes, my index finger, twisting my skirt into a garrote. For my whole, objectionable person. It is as if I have been precipitated out of fumes and intimations only now, when the thick, wet, rubbery *fact* of tongue and lip makes itself felt.

The shock disacquaints me with myself. I feel no loyalty toward that wretch, only alarm and aversion. I would like to signal to my prosecutors, watching my evidentiary mouth with forensic curiosity, that I am on their side, against me. But to do that I would need to speak.

"Sssssssssss . . ."

I lean forward, lean back, tilt my head one way and then the other, as if I were explaining something complicated, in complete sentences. Turn out one hand (while the other still strangles in my skirt). The idea may be to convince myself that I am already speaking and then, as it were, chime in with myself. It does not work. I just keep on saying nothing, the nothing that is my name.

The girls are giggling. The back door opening. With a little shriek they flee.

"Sybil, come inside," says my father.

You may imagine me nine or ten years old, chubby, with horrible hair, the stiff, tubular bodice of a pus-yellow organdy dress riding up under my arms where damp circles were spreading, and silk stockings subsiding into the heels of my pigskin boots. I stuttered so violently that I wet my chin, when I spoke at all. This factor combined with my family's high social standing to deprive me of the fellowship of other children, and it did not endear me to my parents either. My father was personally offended by it, as if I were a walking if not always talking rebuke to his ambitions. He had hoped and indeed expected to engender a perfect boy-child to step into his shoes one day. That he did not, he blamed on my mother's unpedigreed uterus and general weakness of character. I remember her sorrowful acquiescence.

Nor were my surroundings such as would compensate in beauty and interest for the shortcomings in my society. Cheesehill was and is a dreary little town. It is located on the rather marshy, thicketed banks of a small, flat, shallow, sluggish river that swells improbably, every ten years or so, into an implacable brown behemoth, sweeping houses off their foundations all down Common Place Road, a town whose architectural history is wiped out at regular intervals, so that it then boasted no very old, no very distinguished buildings except one (now there are none), the piano factory inherited by my father as the last of his line (my insufficient self excepted), built by his great-uncle on bedrock and furthermore on a little rise that may have been the hill for which the town was named (where the cheese comes in I have no notion), though it was scarcely elevated enough to earn the name.

Perhaps they had agreed to call it a hill to promote themselves in their own esteem, to which that hill or rather the factory that stood on it was central, being the only business concern of any significance in the entire area, and employing most of the locals, so you can imagine how they felt when it burned down, and again when I declined to use the insurance money, which was considerable, to rebuild, but instead (after an interval of some years) sank it into the purchase and rehabilitation of the derelict buildings of the Cheesehill Home for Wayward Girls, which, contrary to local tradition, had been built above the flood plain and far enough out in the countryside (among *bona fide* hills, in fact) that in theory its tenants could not infect with waywardness the good girls of Cheesehill proper, or lure with waywardness the good boys, though this did not stop said boys from making pilgrimages out to the fascinating property in hopes of espying some sample of waywardness, which is how my parents met, an event that I can only regard as unfortunate in the extreme, my mother spending her entire subsequent existence in failing to make amends to my father for the very waywardness that had initially drawn him to her, since what was alluring in a sweetheart he deplored in a wife, such that she was by the time I knew her a subdued creature, colorless, except for the bruises.

Cheesehill center is also colorless (see by what contrived means I yank myself out of the lachrymose, as out of the Slow River in spate!)—literally, in its builders' unimaginative preference for white clapboard, but also figuratively: still, today, depressed by the loss of its main employer, its main street empty of foot traffic, its small library nearly bare of books, its public house kept in business by a handful of sots who stare dully at the occasional strangers who make the mistake of entering it in hopes of enjoying a sample of quaint country cheer, only its firehouse boasting a gleaming modern engine and a recent coat of paint, though I would call that, not the paint but the engine, a case of closing the barn door after the, after what, I forget, after the cows come home, the chickens hatch.

I believe that there is something about Cheesehill that does not altogether disgust me, but I can't remember what it is.

Oh, yes, the snails. Cheesehill has a lot of them. They are some of its liveliest inhabitants, rioting in the kitchen gardens all night, then sleeping it off the next day, buttoned up in their shells, halfway up a clapboard wall. Snails are not universally admired, I know, but I do like a sleek young snail stretching out his shining neck, optimistic eyestalks playing nimbly over the possibilities, and dragging a silver ribbon behind him. My father, mindful of his tomatoes and his salad greens, for he fancied himself a gentleman farmer and often wrote off for seeds of new hybrids that promised to combine exceptional flavor and hardiness, did his best to slaughter the Cheesehill snails. Unlike my rabbits and my mother, the snails—as a race, if not individually—came back, full of enthusiasm and heirloom lettuces.

Here at the Vocational School we do not poison the snails that frequent our kitchen garden, nor dunk them in soapy water. The children peel them gently off the cabbages and set them free on the edge of our land. That the spot I have chosen is only a short distance from the vegetable patch of our nearest neighbor is not my concern, though I have recommended that the children wait until dark to give the captives their liberty, to avoid misunderstandings.

I mentioned floods. You might think that, being the wealthiest family in town (the only wealthy family in town), we would have had the means and the desire to build above the high-water mark, but although our house was bolted to its foundations, a measure rarely taken in fatalistic Cheesehill, my father deemed it a point of pride to flaunt our eminence in the very center—such as it was—of town, so we too suffered the rising waters. My father refused to evacuate, choosing to repose his faith in his precautions, and I well remember staring out the upstairs window, while my mother wept quietly on the bed, at a satin-sleek expanse of brown that would have appeared almost stationary were it not for the branches, planks, dead chickens, and other debris that whipped by at a startling clip, occasionally clobbering the keel of our vessel (as I pictured it) with a force that I felt in my bones. How exciting it was to sit at the top of the stairs—for I was not much afraid, feeling dismally and correctly (in this instance) that my father would not let anything really interesting happen to us—and see the dirty water swirling around the banister a few feet below me, carrying, still upright, its lips just above water, a cheap enameled vase that my father had not considered worth rescuing, though my mother was fond of it, and bumping it against the rails, whereupon it tipped, filled with water, and sank. I found it later, buried in the mud, and squirreled it away.

The bolts held that time and another time and once more still and then failed, but that was after my parents were dead and I a young headmistress occupied with my school, whose outbuildings had been menaced by the selfsame flood. Still, I went to look at the sundered house. It had slid sideways off its foundations and was striking on its former lawn a defiantly jaunty pose, one side stove in and the other thrust out like a hip. I could see a muddy settee through a gap in the wall and, disposed upon it, what appeared to be the head of a moose, not a drowned moose but a moose that had been shot for its spread of horns, decapitated, and affixed, the head I mean, to a plaque, and the plaque to a wall, but had made its escape and was now resting from its exertions.

I have often wondered whether dead animals, too, have their ghosts. I would gladly give that moose a pulpit. But I suspect that merely dying would not suffice to teach a mute to speak, so that if animals do visit our throats it is only in the odd sad-sounding yap or bellow.

When I first heard about the waywardness, I pictured a flounced patchwork skirt, such as I believed Gypsies to wear, and began to watch my mother for signs that she was preparing for a trip, since I supposed that to be *wayward* was to be *on the way* somewhere, as by repute the tribe of Romany generally were. I saw this skirt so clearly that I dug through her chest of drawers and the old brass-bound Jenny Lind trunk in the attic in confident expectation of finding it and was disappointed to unfold nothing that was not white, peach, pink, beige, or blue.

Whether because I was looking for it, or because there really was some-thing forever yondering in her, my mother always seemed to me on the verge of departure. One morning I awoke to an empty house and the conviction that she had gone at last. I ran all the way down Common Place Road in nightgown and slippers, eyes wide and wet, but turned back when I reached the factory drive, perceiving that she would never have gone that way, and sped back again, in at our front door (standing open), and straight through the house to the back porch, where, on the steps, staring off toward the river, my mother sat. I sank down beside her, she put her arm around me without taking her eyes off the swatch of sliding silk, and I never asked if she had decided to come back to me or never left in the first place.

When I understood better what waywardness was, I looked for that, too, in my mother but could not find any more evidence of it than I had of the flounced skirt, though my father seemed to detect the taint of it even in the way she kept house or received the mail, while her familiar way with a grocer's lemons once occasioned weeks of recriminations.

But I saw with what hopeless hopefulness she adjusted the lay of a doily or straightened her chairs and her skirts when he was due home and, dismayed, thought hers an all too strait and narrow waywardness. Only, sometimes, when my father was out, did she take off her shoes and go out to stand awhile under the trees in her bare feet, very still and expressionless, and I saw that here was the flounced skirt at last, or what remained of it.

I recall that after what my father deemed to be her indelicate pronuncia-tion of "leg of lamb" at the butcher's he struck her as I watched through the bedroom door, left ajar. "Marrying you was the ruin of me!" He fell on the floor and began pulling his beard and hitting himself in the face, a thing I was always happy to see. I heard him groan, "Bea, Bea, I wanted it to be different! You'll forgive me, Bea!"

I couldn't help it, I laughed.

My mother came to the door. Before she closed it she met my eyes and shook her head slightly. One of her cheekbones was higher than the other and something was strange about her eye on that side. At dinner I saw that a glossy cherry-red spot was rising from behind the lower lid, like a second, devilish pupil. I was afraid to see it watching me and kept my own eyes on my plate. I remember the meal as the very hypostasis of dread: a thin brown sauce spreading from under the slab of lamb as if it were leaking, a gray pile of one of father's healthful grains, and some peas. When my mother came to put me to bed that night I shrank away from her.

In my fear there was also an element of disgust, for like my father I was revolted by weakness. I was offended by my mother's apologetic submission to my father, for it seemed obvious to me that she was the superior being, and I indicated my partisanship when I dared, hoping to inspire her to revolt. For instance, understanding that the incident at the butcher's had enraged my father, though not exactly why, I subsequently made of *leg of lamb* my chief epithet. How clearly I remember shouting "L-leg of lamb leg of lamb leg of L-L-LAMB!" as the ruler came down on my thighs.

To this day I do not greatly savor lamb.

Then, of course, I returned to writhing, sobbing, and patting his feet in wordless entreaty. This may seem chicken-hearted but was in fact a sort of defiance, because he regarded groveling with such disgust, and I wonder now whether the same logic might not excuse my mother's obsequiousness. "I would have expected more pluck from a whelp of mine," he would say, and interrupt my "education," as he called it, to page through a pamphlet on the principles of heredity: criminality, imbecility, and pauperism traced through several generations of tenement dwellers, mollusks, or pea plants; a cat who lost its forepaw in a steel trap, whose grandchild had a limp; and so on.

It will be perceived that my father was a scientific American, and indeed he was a faithful subscriber to the periodical of that name, as also to *Popular Science Monthly*, *The Telegraphic Journal and Electrical Review*, *The Medico-Chirurgical Review*, *The American Journal of Dental Science*, *Practical Sanitation*, *The Water-Cure Journal*, and the like, with whose aid he proposed to manage his life, his business, my mother, and me. The books on our shelves were scientific and were ordered scientifically. Our house was kept clean by science, or so father supposed, though my mother often crept around with a dustpan and whisk-broom to make up for the deficiencies of our hand-pumped Whirlwind Sweeping Machine. We ate scientific food that we chewed scientifically as Father counted aloud, pausing (but holding the bolus ready for resumed hostilities) when he interrupted his count to tender us scientific descriptions of the activities in his corpus as the wholesome ingredients purged his system of impurities.

You begin, perhaps, to get a sense of the range of my father's interests. Some of his other enthusiasms were photography; telegraphy; the mixing of perfumes; the raising of silkworms; modern sanitation; antique dessert spoons; mesmerism; hydropathy; and novel methods of extracting sugar from melons. In some cases his interest did not extend beyond that of a critical onlooker, but he was often inspired to wholesale enterprise by the articles he read, and would write off for the equipment and materials to set him up in a new line of work, for to husband an inherited manufactory did not suit his impatient and choleric temperament. That same temperament rebelled at *any* sustained effort, however, so very few of these enterprises lasted beyond his initial infatuation. In some cases simply writing out an order satisfied the appetite aroused in him by the article or advertisement in one of his periodicals, and by the time a thousand packets of dung-colored, spiky seeds or a lump of waxy material arrived in a bumped, scuffed, stained, and belabeled carton, he had forgotten why he wanted them and sometimes even what exactly they were.

More often he lost momentum only after he met the first serious obstacle, by which time half the house was given over to dyestuffs, say, or the grinding of lenses, and then my mother would enter the field to try to recoup at least some of his expenses. Far more practical than he, she became pretty knowledgeable about the various ways available to a lady entrepreneur to unload a very odd range of goods, and sometimes even turned a profit, though to my disgust she did not ever hold back any of the money she made to supplement the small allowance from which she supplied all her own needs and mine, as she might easily have done, but turned it in to my father, submitting meekly to his grumbling, for of course although he thought "peddling" beneath him, he nonetheless believed that if he turned his hand to it, he would do it better than anyone, always asked what he believed to be very canny questions about the deals she had struck, and invariably concluded by lamenting her sad want of acumen, when the truth was that without her acumen he would have been emphatically out of pocket and perhaps ruined us with his many nonsensical investments.

His extravagances were never more flagrant than when he could style them *research*. For my father planned a great work, whose particulars were yet to be determined. Above all else he admired inventors, knew their names and stories, often spoke, though always in vague terms, of the inventions that he himself would unveil when he was ready, and pored over the official reports of new Patents and Claims with occasional exclamations of annoyance at those who, to hear him tell it, had anticipated ideas for which he had just been on the verge of filing a patent himself. His conversation at dinner was really a monologue on the latest discoveries, many of them of no utility in his line of work, such as a new method for ventilating railroad carriages, or for making artificial ivory out of caoutchouc, ammonia, chloroform, and phosphate of lime; and some quite unwelcome at the dinner table (or so I perceived—for I had a strong stomach myself—from the suddenly rather taxidermic appearance my mother assumed as her jaw froze in mid-bite), such as a new sort of verminous tumor in the stomach of the horse, an improved remedy for fecal stench, or a way to induce sluggish leeches to suck (soak them in beer). He treated us to expositions on the dyeing of ornamental feathers; female labor in Germany; improvements in chandeliers; the preservation of blood from slaughterhouses in the form of a jelly obtained by adding quick or slaked lime; the Inter-Continental Tunnel planned between Tarifa and Tangiers; a new factory proposing to make paper from the cactus plant; a new method for identifying falsification in documents via photographic copies; and an experiment in weighing the rays of light, which showed that the weight of sunlight on the earth was three thousand million tons, "a force that but for gravitation would drive it into space" (*Practical Magazine*).

He gave his opinion freely and somewhat wildly on these topics, of which he had no firsthand knowledge whatsoever. Sometimes he became so exercised that he leapt up from his chair and strode around, employing gestures that recalled the elocutionary training of which he was so proud. (He often mentioned that he had won a prize in school for his recitation of Bryant's "Thanatopsis," a conversational turn that I dreaded, for it invariably progressed from pleasurable reminiscence to lamentation that such as he should have spawned such as I—i.e., a tongue-tied nincompoop.)

When he heard of a new gadget, however dubious or impractical, nothing would stop him from placing an order, and when it came in the mail he would drop everything to read any manuals included with it, to assemble it if necessary, to try it out, and then to show it off. Alas, he did not have any friends to show it to, so he would summon his secretary, the foreman of his factory, and the more trusted and responsible of his skilled craftsmen, and they would all troop into the parlor and sit very silently and awkwardly on our most uncomfortable chairs while my mother poured tea and my father stalked around the device, waiting irritably for her to finish. It was plain to me that these visitors felt uncomfortable in our house and considered the occasion an extension of their work duties rather than a social event, but my father grew flushed and merry and loud and exaggeratedly colloquial in his speech as if to make his low company feel at home (though they themselves were invariably restrained and punctilious in their diction) and reminisced about the event afterward as though it had been a great success. Then he would spend several days in composing a long letter to the manufacturers giving his opinion of the device and suggestions for its improvement and often spoke as if the manufacturers waited eagerly for his letters and were very grateful for his insights and as if he had some sort of official role in the creative process and was indeed practically a co-creator. When I was very young I assumed that this was true and it made me think my father a very important fellow, but later I understood that it was all moonshine and pictured the manufacturers laughing over the letters with which he took such pains or simply dropping them into the trash unread.

I do not remember all the items he purchased. But here are some that I still possess:

An Automatic Signal Buoy;
An Arithmometer, or calculating machine;
A Magneto-Electric Bell Apparatus;
A Pocket Telegraph, or portable Morse instrument;
A Scott's Electric Hair Brush;
A Galvano-Faradio Magneto-Electric Shock Therapy Machine.

My father often spoke of our world as rendered limitless by the ever-extending reach of practical science, and this had its effect on me, for I will not allow death to be an end. But while my father's scientific cast of mind and the ideas and devices that he brought into the house were a great influence on my later work, I hold them to blame for many tribulations. Although my father was a serial enthusiast who could usually be trusted to move on from any given hobby within a few months, my stutter was a continual vexation and a reminder to him of the unfinished project that was my speech, and so from the pages of his science magazines came an endless succession of ways to torture my mouth: the syllabic exercises of M. Colobat, regulated by his *muthonome* or *orthophonic lyre* (a sort of metronome); exercises for the lips, the tongue, the breath; tongue-depressing plates, jaw-spreading pads, obstructions of various kinds—cruel descendants of Demosthenes' pebbles—like the little gold fork of M. Itard, worn "in the concavity of the alveolary arcade of the inferior jawbone," i.e., under the tongue; leather collars that buckled around my neck and pressed firmly against my larynx; metal plates that strapped to my teeth and projected between my lips; and a sort of whistle that was held against my palate by a sharp point digging into my tongue. It goes without saying that none of these devices fulfilled their promises to "restore the patient's usefulness to Society by opening the Floodgates to cogent and mellifluous Speech."

I was supposed to be grateful for the trouble my father took over me and to let any setbacks inspire me to greater exertions, so my mother was not permitted to comfort me when I wept. "You have done enough harm, Madam!" he would cry, for my father considered my stutter a sign of the weakness in the maternal line, and never ceased blaming himself for the "temporary venereal intoxication" that had resulted in the "unscientific" and "counter-evolutionary" union of a man of his elevated forebears with a "moral imbecile" from a "line of shopkeepers and petty criminals." He felt it his duty to correct for the evil effects of his ill-advised marriage on his social class, so when the pages of his monthlies offered no new quackery to inflict on me, he exercised his own ingenuity, pouring all his balked ambition as an inventor into designing novel devices for me to try. No doubt he also calculated that if he could cure stuttering where others had (so obviously) failed, he would make his name.

Never had a mouth been so stretched, cut, prodded, plungered, braced, cantilevered, wedged, winched, pinched—so *Scientific Americaned*—so *Popular Scienced*. These periodicals were possessed of wonderfully detailed etchings of docks, and decks, and dykes, where somber, beautiful, flawlessly geometrical machines enjoyed the anonymous attentions of stiff, tidy men with tapering symmetrical limbs. In my father's fancy and mine, such was or would be my mouth: a site of modern industry, well-regulated and productive, rolling forth (conveyed by belts and pulleys) a serene procession of die-cut, stainless-steel, copper-bottomed sentiments, accompanied by appropriate gestures.

When my father fitted me with his contraptions—the only time he touched me except to punish me—his fingers were not ungentle, and I could sometimes mistake the optimism shining in his eyes for tenderness. Even now I ask myself, was there not, perhaps, under his dissatisfaction with me, a love that could be glimpsed in those moments alone, as mute and enduring as an endolith?

Then I answer, No.

But in those moments during which I sat, given over to his fiddling, my body softened and a strange knowingness went up my spine. "Sit up strai— damn it!" (A spring snapped loose.) "Open, wider, not so wide, clench your teeth, relax, draw back your lips here, no, here, no, you stupid girl, *here*." I complied, with something almost like eagerness, and an optimism of my own. This time, surely, it would work. The intensity of our shared wanting would *make* it work. I felt my coming fluency as a physical pressure at the root of my tongue, begging for release.

It never came. My father's contrivances were beset with misadventures: A spring-loaded cheek-stretcher came uncocked and shot out of my mouth to ricochet around the dining room. A gutta-percha bladder shipped its anchor when I inhaled and lodged in my windpipe, nearly asphyxiating me. A tiny dumbbell that I was, under his stern eye, rolling forward and backward on my tongue, was accidentally swallowed, after which for days I had to bring him the chamber pot that received my excrements and stand at attention while he dissected them with little metal rods like chopsticks. (The object never turned up; I suppose it is inside me still, lodged in my blind gut and slowly poisoning me, for it was made of lead.) For these mischances he naturally blamed me. Perhaps in some recess of his conscience he knew better, however, for he abandoned the most disastrous conceptions without retrial. Though not, I should say, without punishing me as "slothful, obstinate, and recidivistic," bringing down the ruler once per adjective.

Then he looks at the white-edged marks on my palm and his face contorts. "I have ruined my life, I will never amount to anything."

A strange thing for the most important man in Cheesehill to say, but I know what he means. "Don't cry, Father," I say kindly, "Someday one of your inventions will work."

He raises the ruler again.

Sometimes I looked at myself in the maculated mirror above my mother's dressing table and marveled at my ordinary looks, for my mouth felt bigger, if possible, than the head it was set in, and as violently resistant to socialization as a kraken, strapped to my face in place of a mouth and enjoined to speak.

That there was something of pride in my feelings toward this monstrosity, I did not then recognize. Indeed, for a long time I did earnestly try to master my unruly speech, and in sentimental moments the fantasy rose up before me of the loving family life to which I would matriculate once I had solved my little problem: the parlor, of an evening—myself, reading aloud with superior enunciation and eloquent gestures—my parents' faces bright with candlelight and pride! But increasingly I believed it to be impossible, and knew my father for a brute for punishing me for something I could not help. And a brute could not figure in those fantasies of mine. It had been a long time since I had seen anything like tenderness in even the way he treated my mother; so those dream candles guttered and went out.

I often loitered near my father's study as he made his experiments, hopeful that something would go wrong, and once, at least, this paid great dividends. The occasion was the arrival of the Galvano-Faradio Magneto-Electric Machine previously mentioned, which promised to Tune the Entire Organism, Restoring Balance and Harmony to Disordered Nerves, and Sending Vitality Coursing Through the Body. I watched through the door as, moving with deliberation, he unbuttoned his cuffs and collar, took off his shirt and folded it and set it aside, then his undershirt. He had a patch of bear-black hair between naked, womanly breasts. I do not recall that I had ever seen them before. He took hold of one wire and after hesitating a moment fastened the claw-grip at its end to one nipple. He connected the other wire to the other nipple. It comes to me now, as it did not then, that this was a curious site to choose and that perhaps he was engaged in something other than scientific inquiry or medical treatment. I have heard that there are those who take erotic pleasure in pain, their own or others', but I know nothing of such perversions of sensuality—and little enough, to be candid, of its orthodox course—so shall leave further speculation to those better informed.

As I edged a little farther into the room, my father took up the pamphlet and consulted it again, holding it in both hands. Then he reached out slowly and switched on the Magneto-Electric Machine. A strange expression came over his face and he jerked about, dropping the pamphlet and batting at the wires, but they did not come loose; finally he seized hold of one wire and with a powerful yank pulled it quite free of the machine, which spat cobalt zips of light and then went dead. He hunched over, breath coming in tearless sobs, then carefully parted the jaws of the dangling wire to detach it from his nipple. The other still connected him to the dead machine. Suddenly he perceived me watching him. He stared at me for a moment, the wire hanging from his hand, then struck at me with it.

Many things then happened at once. I sprang back, receiving the protruding corner of a credenza in the kidneys. The wire, missing its target, flexed wildly, and its tip caught him in one nostril and scored a line from there down to his lower lip. His sudden movement threw his weight against the wire that was still affixed to his nipple and ripped it free, so that he cursed and clapped both hands to his breast; the first wire, borne thoughtlessly along, flexed again and struck him, though this time with less force, on the forehead. I leaned back against the credenza as if I were quite comfortable there, and made myself laugh, though my side hurt very much. Blood was coming from both his nipple and his lip, and his pale stomach was jumping up and down with his breath.

"Monster! Banshee!"

"It is not my fault, Father," I said. "Perhaps the machine was on an incorrect setting. Why don't you try it again?"

"You'd like that, wouldn't you?" He lunged at me and got me by the ear, twisting it as he pulled me against him, until I cried out. "I'll let go if you can say, 'Please, Papa, pick me a peck of pickled peppers.'" My face was against his sweating side; he smelled sour.

I could not say it, as he knew very well.

Now that he had the best of me he seemed to swell; his stomach broadened, the worm of blood that had started wriggling down it froze as if alarmed. "You would like to curse me, wouldn't you? But you just can't find the words!" He laughed loudly, his rage almost forgotten in enjoyment of my shame.

Let us bring down the curtain on this sorry scene—it can go nowhere good. Suffice it to say that I could never witness his misfortune without ultimately suffering a greater one.

It is probably not possible to feel completely innocent when one is always being punished, so I supposed myself to be a fairly wicked character, and while I was sometimes sorry for it, I felt myself a hopeless case, and gave in to a life of sin and stuttering. Indeed, my father always punished me a little more than I thought my transgressions were worth, so I felt that I had paid in advance for any crimes I might wish to commit, and would be improvident not to commit them. By, for instance, watching my parents through a crack in their bedroom ceiling that I had widened with a nail file, an often boring vigil enlivened by the certainty that my father would be incensed at the illicit advantage it gave me to possess a knowledge that he did not know I had. Or hiding a lump of ambergris that he had acquired at great expense in the back of a kitchen drawer, where it reposed for many years, imbuing the vicinity with a mysterious fragrance. Or tampering with the wiring of a new gadget. Thus I balanced my books. If after a particularly criminal act I thought I might have overdrawn my account, I got an uneasy feeling, and sometimes even goaded my father to punish me again, on the rare occasions that he lacked reasons of his own to do so. At this I became very adept, playing on my father's rage as other, happier daughters might on the spinet, rousing and calming it in orderly arpeggios, until I was ready to release it. The feeling of superiority and control that this gave me was worth the pain of a beating to me, and the system worked to my satisfaction until I stupidly succumbed to the temptation to show him that I did not care much about the kind of pain he dealt me. Then he sought other ways to punish me, and found them.

My first rabbits were not really mine but my father's, intended for the table. When he slaughtered them I grieved but little, since through all the moments of our acquaintance a spectral gravy boat had bobbed, reminding me of their destination. But these rabbits got more rabbits before they died, and I petitioned my father for the raising of them. His enthusiasm for rabbit-breeding having waned, he agreed.

Do not care excessively for anything, not even your own self, and you will be invulnerable. So I thought and so I sought to conduct myself. I made a grim game of hiding away my favorites, but when they were discovered, and delivered to our hired man Lucius, who killed and skinned them, I taught myself to watch. In this way I schooled myself in hardness and thought myself a pretty cool customer. But then came Hopsalot, the weapon I put into my father's hands. He did not look like a weapon, he was fat, furry, and indolent, with floppy ears, but I loved him, though I tried not to show it.

That I had failed I learned on the occasion of a piece of petty mischief. My father had arranged his collection of dessert spoons in order by their year of issue, one of the rare enterprises that he carried through to completion. I had carefully rearranged them. Not having any very high opinion of his discernment, I imagined that he would never notice—the joke was to be a private one—and pictured him taking out his case and polishing each spoon before putting it back in its slot, his lips bunched up with pleasure, while I savored a different pleasure of my own. But my sabotage was discovered after all, and my father confronted me. Aware of the magnitude of my crime, I stammered so badly that I could not answer him, a circumstance that invariably infuriated him. He rushed out of the house and to the shed—there were the hutches; took up his knife from the shelf (I was clinging to his arm now, and groaning in an uninflected monotone, for I could not discover any words in myself, such was my distress); opened the hutch and took out Hopsalot, who hung in his hand as tame, comfortable, and soft as an old hat.

"D-d-d—"

He raised his brows, cocking his head in mock solicitude, and I felt his anger spoil into malice. "Oh, sorry—did you have something to say?" His voice was roguish, kittenish, grotesquely lilting.

A bulb of pressure rose in my throat, forcing my glottal folds, but only a huff of breath escaped before they closed with an audible click. A muscle on the side of his mouth twitched. My mouth shaped the word *don't*, but no breath came to fill it.

To think of it, even now, my skull roars like a blast furnace. Didn't happen, didn't happen, no no no no no no no! Over and over I speak words ablaze with righteousness. Over and over Hopsalot spills new-smelted from the flames: sleek, shining, whole. But that ingot is fairy metal, it melts. Probably there was nothing I could have said to avert what was coming, but I will never know. Silver-tongued Demosthenes did not rise again in me. I stood there, my fingers plucking at my father's arm, and choked on my assassin silence.

My father regarded me with smiling contempt. "Did you wish to raise an objection? No? Nothing to say? My mistake!" He flipped Hopsalot upside down and waggled the blade violently around in his mouth. "We cut the mouth veins so as to drain the body of blood," he said in a neutral tone (barely audible under the terrible screaming, as if addressing nobody, or his own conscience). He ran a wire a few turns around the kicking feet, one of which got loose and broke, I hoped, his nose—then, cursing, strung him up from the roof beam while I kicked him as hard as I could in his shins, Hopsalot jerking, twisting, screaming, and flicking drops of blood all over my father and myself that were indistinguishable from the blood streaming now from my father's nose as well.

Language is a terrible, cold thing, I think. One may recount an event, calmly selecting the most suitable words, that to remember without benefit of ink is almost beyond bearing. We accept the counterfeit and are thankful, for it spares us the awful weight of our lives.

My father thrust me from him and, jamming his finger crosswise under his up-tilted nose, from which black-cherry blood was flowing, strode out of the shed. He left me pretty well frantic, leaping up to catch at the roof beam, though I was too short. I wasted a moment or two in this pointless activity before I thought to pile up the hutches and though I put my foot through one of them, to the stupid consternation of young Gundred, Countess of Furry, I did then manage to reach the beam and, weeping, unwind the wire that bound Hopsalot, paying no mind to his claws raking my cheeks. But when I bore him down to the heap of straw where the escaped but unmoved Gundred, against whom I conceived an immediate dislike, was hopefully sniffing (for concealed carrots, perhaps), he lay listless on his side, paws twitching a little, blood rouging his muzzle, and died.

"Oh, please—don't go—don't leave me—" is what I tried to say, and more to this effect, but it came out very broken under the press of my emotion. Indeed I had possibly never stuttered so violently.

This is how I made the first of my great discoveries, which I therefore owe to my father's cruelty. You can read about it elsewhere. The result was that I brought him back, I mean Hopsalot. Alas, I brought him back, not to healthy indifferent life, but to that moment in which he lay dying, in pain, terror, and incomprehension, perhaps not even trusting, now, my own hands, since they had taught him a lie, that he was safe. I kept him dying for hours, or so it felt, and then in hot, banging shame for my cruelty I shut up and let him be. Be dead. Die.

Gundred took belated fright and fled. I believe that she accounts for the great number of feeble-minded rabbits that presently inhabit Cheesehill and regularly fling themselves under one's wheels.

I rose from the soft mound that had been Hopsalot—the pluperfect was making its fitness felt—and went meditatively into the house, repeatedly spreading and unspreading my fingers to feel the blood that was drying on the webbing between them stick and unstick. My father was languid on the divan in a smoking jacket, a healthy flush in his cheeks, a fine crust of black rimming his nostrils, poring over a pamphlet and mumbling, "Deranged condition of the whole system . . . innervated . . . dyspepsia. Beef tea?" Without looking up, he added in the same tone of voice, "Where have you been?"

I could not call my mouth back from wherever it had been. "Sh-sh-sh . . ."

He swung his feet to the floor and swatted the pamphlet down onto the cushion beside him, which bounced a little. "Damn it," he ejaculated lazily, "you *will* regulate your speech!"

I gazed dumbly at him, my fingers spreading and unspreading.

"You are my creature," he said. His tone was sonorous, he seemed to taste his words; I perceived that he was calling on his elocutionary skills. "My qualities appear in you, although warped and weakened by the deleterious influence of your mother's line. I will not allow that minuscule portion of myself that survives in you to appear before the world with disordered speech and—" he sat back, perceiving only now that my dress was fouled with blood and rabbit fur "—appearance." His tone was disbelieving. "Why, in some vitiated fashion, you express *me!* You bear my signature, although the text is corrupted. The fault for that is mine, and I accept it, but I cannot accept that even in dilute form my gifts are not equal to or superior to those of a lesser man's child, and you *will* make yourself the mistress of my legacy, however diminished. Come here." He smiled grotesquely, patting a cushion. "Let us hear you say, 'I will regulate my speech and impose harmony on my disordered senses.'"

I took a few steps toward him and attempted to force the air between the commissures of my lips. Only a grinding sound ensued, like that of a motor failing to start.

His face twisted in a grotesque imitation of kindness, though the time for kindness, I thought, was past. He had perhaps forgotten what reason he had lately given me for resentment; or I was wrong and he had never understood in the first place what my rabbits were to me. "Shall we try again? 'I will regulate . . .'"

"Grr-grr-grr."

The suppressed impatience roared back into view. "Are you being deliberately obtuse? This is the nineteenth century!" He leaned forward, employing the Horizontal Oblique gesture, Fig. 28, *A Practical Manual of Evolution.* "When industry and the applied sciences break mighty rivers and the power of the lightning bolt to the harness, shall one little girl's tongue idle in a state of nature, as lawless as a catamount? I say nay! We squeeze lemons until they express their juices, and make no doubt of it, Sybil Joines—" he caught my shoulder in a pincer-like grip, forgetting oratory "—I will juice you."

I turned my face away. I pressed my hand to my thigh. I moved my hand and felt that my dress was stuck to it.

How real I was, and solid as a ham. It is distasteful to look back on it, now that I am scarcely here at all. Now that I am little more than a corset through which an interesting wind blows, and the other world is more real to me than this one.

My father had a pedagogical theory (original to him, as far as I know) of the proper sequence of childhood attainments, from the diaper right on up to higher mathematics. Every art was erected on the foundation of the last; each had its numbered place, and although he periodically revised the list, promoting, say, the study of counterpoint from #164 to #158, while demoting the trimming of bonnets from #174 to #193, the spoken word (#13) invariably preceded the written (#37), and as we know, I stuttered. So there I stuck, at the first landing.

Thus it was with the fearful, forbidden relish of an Eve (whose attainments, I noted, would have ranked her in the low teens) that, one afternoon, when he was at the factory, I crept into my father's study, abstracted a book from a low shelf, took it into a corner where a little warm, dust-spangled sunlight fell sidelong between curtain and wall, and seated myself in that bright angled stripe, which etched with crisp shadows the blind-stamped decoration (oak leaves, an acorn) on the front of the object in my lap. Sliding between my thighs, the book presented to me its fore-edge, which was smooth and gilt, and I ran my finger down the golden channel between the boards, consciously dawdling. I had conceived a sort of dread of books, which had supplied my father with so many notions disconcerting to the tranquility of our home, and yet I was determined to make their acquaintance. It seemed to me that if I piled up enough books I might mount high enough that I could leave #13 for a more auspicious time, or forever. At last I parted the willing pages and stared at their Byzantine ornamentation, willing it to become words.

Those peculiar entities they called *letters* frightened me a little. Nothing in the groans and hoots of speech suggested to me that it was made up of such articles. I might have imagined myself the victim of a fanciful hoax, had my father possessed any sense of whimsy or shown the least interest in my belief one way or the other. Spurred and tufted like flies' feet, the printed words seemed glossy but dry, chitinous also as a fly; the round counters were globular, oversized eyes that were watching me knowingly; like flies the words kept deceptively still, but appeared primed for flight, and when I closed the book I heard coming from it the sound a fly makes against a window in another room, a quiet, sad, monotonous frenzy. From other, larger books in the glazed bookcase came the dull underwater rattle of crustacean claws. If speech was made of such spiky characters it did not surprise me that they got caught in my throat and tangled up in one another. The marvel was to see them in such quiet and orderly ranks upon the plot of the page. One thought of cemeteries. Perhaps it was their spirits that rose, silent and vaporous, to the reader's mind. The reader was then God, bent avidly over the charnel ground, inhaling souls.

You will perceive that I was confused, and not only theologically. My mind teemed with likenings. I could not even decide whether the printed word was quick or dead. Now, accepting that it is both quick and dead, like ghosts, I can barely understand my perplexity, but I remember it. With equal vibrancy do I remember the nap of the curtains against the side of my face, and the brandy sheen of the fine hairs on my lawlessly exposed shins, and the dark room whose heavy chairs and desks and secretaries, inkstands, ledgers, and paperweights, galvanometers and centrifuges, coils of copper wire, retorts and beakers all kindly turned their backs to me, and the page staining with brightness the space around it, and how I would shuffle sideways on my haunches without lifting my eyes from the page when a chill along one thigh told me that the sun had moved. Time, syrup-slow. My father's absence, that had made it so. The absence of everyone, except the distant authors whose intentions somehow infused the cryptic signs before me. Infused also the green and violet specters that the incandescent page burned into my retinas.

I do not remember how I learned to read, only that the sound of human voices gradually rose above the stridor of those flies. I say that it rose, but it felt more as though I descended, leaning through the words (which no longer seemed like wrought iron—or flies—or crustaceans—or any solid thing, but like so many bolt-holes) and hanging precariously over another world, whose doings I took in with avid eyes.

Every day it came nearer. The jealous buzzing of the books that I had not chosen rose to a din, the handles of the barrister bookshelves rattled, but I paid no attention, forcing myself—against trivial but unyielding impediments, such as my body—toward a place that felt more like home than home did. Sometimes I came away from my father's study with the sand of its shores under my nails, or a furry blue leaf entangled in my hair. When I stole a look at myself in the shadowed, subaquatic depths of the mirror in the hall, I could see strange reflections in my eyes: languid wicker airships crewed by clockwork octopuses, a church thatched with feathers, a quarry from whose unfathomable depths a winding line of ragged, gaunt laborers dragged barrows heaped with muddy phonographs.

My idyll was cut short through my own weakness and cupidity. I was very often hungry as a child. I do not mean to imply that I was deliberately starved—that was not one of my father's particular unkindnesses—only that in our strictly regulated household there was no hope of securing so much as a heel of bread until the clock in my father's study had informed him that it was mealtime. But my stomach did not heed the clock, so I ravened. Sometimes I dared to set ahead the clock, but not by much. Sometimes I secreted a biscuit or a piece of cheese in my pinafore during a meal, and put it aside to nibble while I read, but my willpower was not strong and I invariably fell upon it a short time later and then was as hungry as if it had never been. Sometimes to chew on a bonnet string gave me a little relief, but it was accompanied with dread, since I knew that I would be punished if the ends were seen to be damp or frayed.

So as the clock ticked, and the golden parallelogram slid across the floor, and the weight on my left thigh grew heavier, and the weight on my right grew lighter, and my soul leaned into another world, held back only by the ignoble cravings of my stomach, I took to eating books.

I exaggerate. I did not eat whole volumes. I tore off the corners of pages and bit and sucked and chewed and when they eventually dissolved, I swallowed them. But it felt like eating, and placated my belly, and so I resorted to it more and more often, and even stole away one tasty book to hide in the shed against my next incarceration. I grazed ever farther afield, depredating whole swathes of my father's library (even today, I must be part book), and learned discrimination. I found that I disliked the coarse yellow stuff of the cheaper books and magazines, which disintegrated quickly into a sort of paper gruel that was gluey and gritty at once. The thick white glossy clay-coated stock on which some illustrated books were printed squeaked nastily under my teeth and sometimes dealt paper-cuts to the corners of my mouth. The best paper rendered down into a sturdy cud that lasted, and had a simple, bready flavor.

You will excuse, I hope, a brief excursion into pedantry. The compulsion to eat paper bears the same name as a measurement of font size. It is known as pica (from the Latin *pica*, or magpie), and is said to reflect, like the compulsion to eat dirt, chalk, or ice, a nutritional as well as a psychological abnormality. I believe that the homology with a type size is instructive, and that pica reflects, also, an abnormality in relations with the printed word. I loved books not spiritually, but carnally. And although I did not know it, I was practicing to channel the dead, who have always found in the printed page their most reliable medium.

Though possibly I was just trying to bite my father, in proxy.

In any case the time came that I had always known would come. When the uproar arose from the study, I set down my embroidery (a mere prop; my work never advanced by more than an X or two), rose, went out the back door, and crept through the loose and rotting latticework (more X's) into the muddy space under the back porch. The feet of giants creaked overhead. It grew colder, darker. I heard the sound of the dinner bell. My stomach boiled obediently. I became aware of the pointlessness of my position. My father was not even looking for me, confident that I would eventually return.

I did, and was beaten, scalded, shut up in the shed. Thereafter my father's study was kept locked. The key now hung around his neck. I would not until years later even consider resorting to the Cheesehill library, for that would entail mingling with my social inferiors. Only one book remained to me, hidden in the shed: a gnawed copy of *Moby-Dick*. I might have done worse.

I believe my father attributed my assault on his book collection to spite and never considered that I might have taught myself to read. Well, I believe that it is uncommon enough.

Now, however, I turned from reading to writing. It was not quite for the first time: As soon as I had learned my letters I had employed them in fell curses scratched on our boundary rocks and fences, calculated to alarm the superstitious children of the neighborhood. More recently I had exercised my talents in a stolen ledger on a few pitiful stories in which young girls defied their captors in magnificent invective, the account of which made up the majority of the narrative. It will be apparent from these examples that the written word played then a merely prosthetic role, supplying an eloquence that in speech I lacked, and giving weight to infantine fantasies of puissance.

But now it became something more for me. My ledger, barely a quarter filled, became my daily consort. Concealed in the shed, where I kept it, I poured into it all the thoughts I could not frame in speech, trivial and great; I wrote about my housework, my rabbits; I wrote fragments of stories; I wrote to read myself writing. As I did not speak like a little girl—did not speak—I did not write like a little girl. My syntax was baroque, my style orchidaceous. The phrases tumbled out, with inflections first heard decades and centuries before my birth. I had read them all before, in arrangements only a little different. Though they addressed the concerns and characters of my little life, they did not seem like mine. They were stamped with a maker's mark I could not quite make out; they belonged to others and to elsewhere. Not to readers; I did not dream of fame. No, to the world of books, beloved and now lost to me. It seemed to me that I heard the buzzing of flies again and louder than ever, that my own voice (always faint enough, in any case) was completely drowned out by the din that rose from the page. I saw that the other world I yearned for was already inside me. To reach it I had merely to turn myself inside out.

How to do that I would learn. It would take me some years.

I became fluent—on paper. To summon this fluency into my throat was not then possible. I suppose that ordinary children begin by saying a word or two, graduate to sentences, then stories, and only much later and with difficulty learn to poke, pleat, and tuck the airborne phenomenon that is speech into a page-sized package. It is perhaps like folding a parachute? For me it was the opposite. My parachute came folded, and only much, much later would I tweak it out and call a wind to fill it.

But the intricacy of those folds! Slowly, my distress at feeling that I had no voice and without a voice, no self, gave way to wonder and delight. What was a self? A wishbone stuck in my throat. On paper I could be anyone. There was nothing to be stuck in or to stick, only boundless elasticity, boundless subtlety, clarity, rarefaction, light and space and freedom; in a word, joy.

I reveled in counterfeit. I wrote about myself in the third person and in hagiographic terms; I described a life that I did not live, and it seemed realer than my own. It eventually consumed my ledger; in searching for more paper in my mother's writing desk, I came upon a little envelope of loose stamps, which inspired me to write a series of scurrilous letters to the editor of our local paper in the name, first, of fictitious entities, then of certain actual persons[2] who had aroused my dislike. This caused a minor stir. It died down. No one blamed me, of course; recall that I had never formally been taught to write, or even to read. What's more, my style was scarcely juvenile. If anything, it was senescent, with the gaseous orotundity of an earlier era.

One day I procured some writing paper and with excruciating care drafted the following letter, or one very like it:

Harwood Joines, Esq.

Dear Sir,

I am very obliged to you for your review of our product, the Galvano-Magnetic Thingummy. You have identified shortcomings that even my own team of

---

2. That the Headmistress, as a child, used writing to assume a false identity has fanned the flames of controversy regarding the authorship of this text. However, to yield to doubt is to enter fully into paradox: if the author is the Headmistress, then she is a liar, which suggests that she is not the Headmistress, while if the author is not the Headmistress, then there is no reason to believe her a liar, which suggests that she is the Headmistress. (Of course, we are free to suppose that the author lies in claiming to be a liar, but then we should really be in the soup.) —Ed.

trained Galvanists did not recognize, and the solutions you suggest display astounding technical acumen. You are wasted in—that quaint name again?—Cheesehill! I would like you to come to my factory and train my workers in your methods. Would you do this for me, Harwood? I employ your first name, because already I think of you as a friend. Great minds must stick together! I see a fruitful partnership in our future. All expenses for your travel will be reimbursed when you arrive, so please do not hesitate, but come as soon as may be, no advance notice required. We shall not stand on ceremony, you and I.

Affectionately,
Your Brother in Science,
Samuel B. Alderdash
Proprietor, Galvano-Magnetic Thingummy

I folded and sealed this in an envelope to which I had transferred a cancelled stamp steamed from another envelope that I had found in the trash. To conceal the inadequacies in the postmark that I had carefully drawn on with faint stipples of ink, I ripped, crumpled, and dirtied the corner of the envelope, as if it had been mangled in transit. Then I slid it under the other mail awaiting my father on the hall table, minutes before he swept it all up and bore it with him to his study.

My heart was slightly, unpleasantly out of time with the hall clock.

My father came out again and stood in the hall, his arms hanging, staring past me. His eyes were wide and glossy; the pink pockets of his lower lids gaped. I realized that I had never before seen him happy. I could bear it only because I knew what was in store for him.

After a few words with my mother, he shut himself in his study. My mother silently packed his bag. At the dinner bell he emerged to request that his food be brought to him on a tray. I ate my dinner with unusual relish, alone with my mother. My father departed early the next morning. From my bedroom window I watched him square his briefcase on his knees as the carriage jerked into motion.

He came back very late that night and murdered my mother.

THE SYBIL JOINES VOCATIONAL SCHOOL

for Ghost Speakers & Hearing-Mouth Children

Dear Mr. Melville,

You will not have heard of me, as I am of small account by the great world's reckoning. Nevertheless I have made discoveries that should interest any man of imagination — and you have imagination, Mr. Melville, do you not? When I read Captain Ahab's vow to strike through the "pasteboard mask" of visible things, I knew that I had to do with a man who had run an inky finger down the chinks in the Wall, and had wondered what wind it was that blew through it.

Mr. Melville, I have found the door in that wall.

Having caught your attention, as I hope, I will now tell you about myself.

I am a woman no longer young; tall, gaunt, with a strong brow. My dress is somber and guided by scientific principles (specifically, acoustics), not by fashion. I am no Lucy-Go-Lightly. I was born in the

Letters to Dead Authors, #1

In April 1919, seven months before her death, the Headmistress wrote the first of a series of letters to deceased authors. We know the date because the envelope in which it was returned, stamped undeliverable, is postmarked. It appears from her own testimony (Letter #2) that she was not initially aware that the addressee of her first letter was dead, but once this was brought home to her, she recognized the merit of the practice, and was to continue writing to him and other deceased authors until the end of her life. Dating of these subsequent letters is infuriatingly approximate, since we possess only undated copies (the originals are presumably still lost in the mail), but they seem to have appeared with increasing frequency as time went on, approaching the function of a daily journal, and providing an invaluable record both of the clouds then gathering over the Vocational School and of Joines's declining health, mental as well as physical. She herself notes (Letter #11) that she has addressed herself to a fictional character (Letter #10), though subsequent lapses go unremarked.

Like the Final Dispatch and other materials here assembled that register the passage of time, these letters will be distributed at regular intervals throughout the volume, but readers should keep in mind that they are not contemporaneous with the Final Dispatch, but conduct us up to the point where it began.

Incidentally, there is no evidence that any of her addressees ever wrote back. —Ed.

Dear Mr. Melville,

You will not have heard of me, as I am of small account by the great world's reckoning. Nevertheless I have made discoveries that should interest any man of imagination—and you have imagination, Mr. Melville, do you not? When I read Captain Ahab's vow to strike through the "pasteboard mask" of visible things, I knew that I had to do with a man who had run an inky finger down the chinks in the Wall, and had wondered what wind it was that blew through it.

Mr. Melville, I have found the door in that wall.

Having caught your attention, as I hope, I will now tell you about myself.

I am a woman no longer young, tall, gaunt, with a strong brow. My dress is somber and guided by scientific principles (specifically, acoustics), not by fashion; I am no Lucy-Go-Lightly. I was born in the small town of Cheesehill, Massachusetts, and grew up odd and lonesome, since I had a stutter, and was shy to boot. Nor were my parents sympathetic, but sought, my father did, to scare my tongue straight. You may imagine what efficacy that had. Only my rabbits—

A fit of coughing has disordered my thoughts. But I was speaking of my childhood. I was an ardent reader, Mr. Melville, and one of your books concealed providently in a flowerpot eased many a desolate hour spent locked in the garden shed with the potatoes, though I do not mean to asperse the potatoes, whose company, on balance, I preferred to that of most of Cheesehill's other inhabitants. I feel a special affinity to writers, even though, to tell the truth, it seems a silly sort of life, making up stories. While I too work with words, it is as an explorer and a scientist. Nonetheless I write to you, and not to Mr. Tesla, Mr. Roentgen, Mrs. Curie, or even Mr. Edison, for it seems to me that writers have made greater progress than scientists (myself excepted) on a venture of the highest importance to our world today, tomorrow, and yesterday: communication with the dead.

Which brings me to my point. I am the Founder and Headmistress of a boarding school and research facility, the Sybil Joines Vocational School for Ghost Speakers & Hearing-Mouth Children, where we teach children to channel the dead and, finally—though a little less finally than everyone else—to travel to their realm. My pupils are all stutterers. Why? Because stuttering, like writing, is an amateur form of necromancy.

I was myself a child when the first ghost spoke through the frozen moment in my mouth. The study of the dead became my passion. In playground games of school, I taught the other children everything I learned.

As a young woman, I sought out the notable spirit mediums of the day, and eagerly applied to them for instruction, but was disappointed; if they had answers (and most of them were mountebanks), they guarded them closely. I was thrown back upon the dead, who did not fail me. I developed my own methods, and having seen firsthand the need for vocational training in the trade, resolved to found a school for spirit mediums.

Returning to Cheesehill, I poured my funds into the purchase and rehabilitation of a derelict property well suited to my needs, and with my childhood companions as talent scouts, scraped together an entering class—each and every one a stutterer like me. Their speech was broken; they were cracked vessels; I would make them perfect. Not by sealing the cracks! By sweeping away the last remaining shards. I would raise a new Eden, in which a primordial silence would rise again, and the din of human voices would no longer drown out the quiet confidences of the dead.

The first time I traveled to the land of the dead, it was an accident, and I nearly lost my life. It was also by accident that, crying out, I found my voice and with it, eventually, the way home. For to travel there one must summon up in words, not just the ground one walks upon, but even oneself, walking. My life's work, like yours, depends on my ability to construct a convincing fiction. Indeed, I would welcome any "tips" you might have for me! But I am seeking more material help as well.

I have recently lost a student. It will happen, given the natural vivacity of children and the nature of our studies. But now my school is under seige. Philistines with no more understanding of Eternity than may be gleaned from the platitudes carved on tombstones are baying at the gates. *Save the children!* is their rallying cry. Rank hypocrisy, as these children are those same "stuttering imbeciles," "degenerates," and "mental defectives" they were so eager to pack off to any quack who promised to cure them or keep them out of sight. Emily herself (not a prepossessing child) would be amazed to hear the fanciful terms in which she is described in the press. Precious bundle? Little lamb? A big bundle, more mutton than lamb! Her doting parents' treasure, their pearl without price? She knew exactly what she was worth to them.

But as a result of this rhetoric (for the land of the living is also shaped by words), some of our more excitable parents have already withdrawn their children from their studies, with a catastrophic loss of revenue to the school.

May I press you for a donation? Even a loan would be of signal service. I have poured the whole of my inheritance into outfitting my school and now must scrimp and scrape to buy necessities. I know your means are modest, but the need is great, the cause honorable. And one day the world will flock to my door, and then this grateful recipient of your patronage will have the wherewithal to make you very comfortable indeed.

At present, I confess, the case is otherwise. To put it baldly, I am broke. Expecting your imminent reply, I am,

Very sincerely yours,
Miss Sybil Joines

Postscript: If you are not in the position to lend me money, could you lend me, instead, your name? A testimonial from a great man like yourself could do much to warm the frigid public eye toward this earnest Seeker.

2. The Final Dispatch, contd.

Someone is missing, a child is missing, calamity, havoc, ruination, snatch her back, fetch her home, remember her, recover her, save her!

These words ~~pl~~ pulse through me, urging me onward, and yet they have no meaning.

Save her? From *death*? It's life that's the emergency. Death is the haven— sequined bough to which the sparrow homes, beetle's duff and worm's earth, whale's harpoonless hiding place. This I teach. Maybe a little too well: my kids go early and eager. It is a lie that only a Munch (rhymes with *lunch*) could believe, that my students are driven by the rigors of their training to destroy themselves; though I am rigorous. Death is not departure but arrival. We are latchkeys kept by wanderers against a future homing. With our last strength, we fit our bodies into this locked world, and turn.

But this time, when I saw the barrel rolling, heard the oiled pins click, I stuck a stick in it. Dove after her, howling to the shades to hold her back.

Her who?

[Static, sound of breathing.]

Finster. Eve Finster, that must have been her name, the girl I sought. Unless it was another girl, but I don't know who, but it might have been.

Ahead, I glimpsed her narrow shoulders twisting in her pus-yellow organdy, what nonsense, her black linsey-woolsey, a little scorched, as she wriggled trout-like through the [inaudible]. Then she and I alike were lost in din and tumult to fetch up here, that is, nowhere, that is, in the land of the dead.

White everywhere, complicating into color, into form, fading again to white. White sky. White plains onto which white cataracts thunder down from an impossible height: souls, pouring without surcease into death, and roaring as they fall. The cataracts—the one stable landmark, the one feature on which all travelers report—are in such incessant motion that they seem immobile: one immense hoary figure, frozen in place, head bowed. Sometimes a bulge travels down the length of it: a fire in a shirtwaist factory, a great ship sunk in icy waters, a [word indistinct].

But my business is not with the deluge, but with the one drop that does not belong here. To find her is the problem. Like all children she is changeable as thought, passing through form after fugitive form—newt, spoon, little toy car. She does not remember who she is. So I remind her. "Finster!" For a moment her name imposes order on the flux and I see her. Then she changes.

I lower a bucket to scoop her up, this bucket here, which is enameled red and emblazoned FIRE and has a crescent of clean water swinging and ringing around the bottom, and is a bucket I made to catch her in, am making now, as I describe it. For I too make my changes, but with method. The bucket comes up dry and different, oaken staves and rusted hoops and a fly on the cracked rim rubbing its hands. But I recognize her, think I do, in the fly, which flies; I follow. Road, I propose, and a road pours out of me. She is a tiny black speck against the, say, warm brown dust. A net, I suggest, and raising it, stride toward the speck. Dust rims the stiff black hem of my skirt. I bring down the net. She scoots away: wind-up mouse, thistledown, cloud.

I gather my resources, my pitons and plotlines, grammar hooks and grapnels, and go after her. The cloud, a small ground-loving one, leaves the road for a path I do not know (I who thought I made all the paths), her own path, thread-thin and tangled, through dendrite forms that one might call trees, in an optimistic mood. I feel something unfamiliar: Fear? Delight? I plant the butterfly net by the path; call it a mailbox, one of a battalion of mailboxes pertaining, mostly, to cranks and hermits, and frequently upset by hooligans; and the path widens to a road.

I know this road. It veers off ~~fromt he~~ from the Cheesehill post road, drops into a ravine and burrows down it through sunless, scrubby, undistinguished woods until it emerges into marshy flatlands dotted with copses and thick with thistles, where already in the distance one may catch glimpses of a gabled roof, stately trees, outbuildings. So now I know where we are going. Where else? I follow.

Green-gray grublike bouncing things that are not dogs bark regardless and keep pace with us through the trees that are not trees. I call my rabbits, the ones with beaks opening red all over their bodies, with wings in their mouths for tongues, with tongues in their fur for wings, these flying, crying, dangerous rabbits that are not rabbits, my protectors. They do battle with the dogs that are not dogs, harrying them toward the hills, the familiar hills of Cheesehill and vicinity now rising like dough at my say-so to enfold both dogs and rabbits, which vanish, for the time being. Time that is not time. Being that is not being.

The what—who—yes, the child [pause] races on, no cloud now, just a child in a pus-yellow, no, a black school uniform, a little scorched, and I after her.

Why do I not let her go? [Static, sound of breathing.]

Really, when one considers the question rationally one does not have to look far for an answer. Obviously, one does not wish to misplace a student under the evaluative eye of a Regional School Inspector. And under circumstances that, under circumstances, under—

Someone is missing, a child is missing, calamity, havoc—

Are you receiving?

The Stenographer's Story, contd.

Another pause. The room is quiet, though today's events have left their spoor: the smell of smoke and lamp oil, shivers of glass, a stain on the carpet. Nothing that cannot wait, so I shall resume what I can still call "my own" narrative, though I keep wanting to type not "I," but "she" or "the girl," probably because, as the car rattled on, the feeling only grew that I was not myself, but some third party—an unattributed pronoun in an unfamiliar story. The clouds came thicker; the day grew darker; we turned at last onto a better-kept road, and almost at once deserted it again for a narrow unmarked drive that plunged down into a thrashing, tree-choked ravine and across a swollen brook, then turned and followed this for a while, crossing it several more times before veering away across slanted muddy fields.

"*That*," said Miss Exiguous, extending her cane across me to rap the window, "is the Vocational School." Though the sun duly broke through the clouds, illuminating the scene, I saw only a clutch of swaying trees, huddled together as if conspiring to hide something from view. But as we slid closer, these parted and fell back as if in capitulation, and there it stood amid its several outbuildings, black and angled, like a house in a book in which something frightening is going to happen. Black birds screamed and fell through the wind. A few orphaned raindrops tapped out a telegraphic message on the roof of the car.

Once more we crossed the stream, now wide and shallow and edged with rushes, and motored up to a heavy iron gate, through whose grim old-fashioned ornamentation an incongruously bright new chain had—no. That was added only recently, after the troubles began. The gate stood open when I arrived (if with no great air of welcome), had probably not been shut in years, in fact, as weeds grew up through it. So we rolled through without hindrance, then hissed and spat up the gravel drive to a point still somewhat short of the entrance, as if the driver did not care to come too close.

"Out you get, missy," he said, extending a hand in through the open door, for though Miss Exiguous was already walking up the drive I had not moved. I scooted stiffly across the seat. For a moment I clung to his lean long fingers as he looked curiously down at me, and then he gently detached himself, went around and wrestled my battered suitcase, a relict of my father, out of the back. "I'll carry that in for you," he said, but I saw that he was eager to leave, and shook my head against his protests. "Sure? Then I'll be off. No, child, you keep that—well, all right, thank you, then." He glanced at Miss Exiguous. "I hope you know what you're getting yourself into, or maybe it's better if you don't. Well, so long! Keep your chin up!" The car slithered as it backed and turned, and shot a piece of gravel into the back of my leg. I cried out and bent over, clapping a hand to the spot.

When I stood up, the feeling of estrangement that, until then, had been contained within me broke free to affect all that I saw. Everything was hard and shining and separate. The drive was separate from the shrubs on its verge, in which separate sparrows shrieked, and from the trees beyond. The trees, unnaturally bright against the storm-dark sky, were separate from one another and from the field on which their separate shadows fell, and the shadows, too, were separate from the field on which they were inflicted by the light. The grass drew itself apart from the mud, the mud from the thistles whose stickers were very similar to one another and yet not the same, and the thistles from the sky. And everything shrank from the school.

Miss Exiguous had disappeared under its tall narrow portico, where a door must have opened to receive her and closed again. The car, too, was gone, and with it my last chance, I thought confusedly. But to do what, go where? I felt the bones in my fingers, crushed against the handle of my suitcase. From the building, a low hum or murmur rose, swelling and sinking with the wind.

I am invited, I thought stoutly, I have a right to be here, and I started up the drive. The front door seemed very far away. My suitcase, big enough— yes, quite big enough to transport a body—knocked painfully against my ankle bone at every step. In each perforation of my too-large oxfords, a crescent shadow waxed and waned as its angle to the light changed, or disappeared in my own larger shadow, and inside my loose black stockings, on which tiny fuzz balls clung, my ankles individually flexed and strained. All these phenomena were separate from one another, and so was I separate from them all and even from myself, this girl crunching up a white gravel drive, to the very foot of the entrance steps. This is what they call a haunted house, I said to myself. It is not what I thought. The ghost—*I* am the ghost.

But the door was opening and a white girl in a school uniform was coming out. "H-h-hello," I said, loud with relief, "I am—"

Then I saw that her eyes were taped shut, her mouth open not in greeting but for some other exercise. She felt her way to the top of the stairs and started down, feeling for the edge of each step with her foot. The shadow of the portico slid off her head, like a veil snagged on a splinter, and the sun slipped a bright sickle into her mouth. When her investigating foot discovered the flagstone at the base of the stairs, she stepped confidently forward onto the drive, and struck against me with the full length of her body.

It had not occurred to me to move. It had in fact not occurred to me that I was really there, and could be touched.

I staggered back, dropping my suitcase, and for a moment I held the hard little chicken wings of her elbows and we struggled together. It was not clear whether we were trying not to fall or to accomplish some other project entirely. She was even shorter than I, so I could see how her skull showed through her thin flat hair like something rising through silty water that one had much rather stayed where it was. A fine white down covered her forehead, barely thickening into eyebrows, and hazed even her sharp cheekbones, on one of which a mud-colored mole stood out. Through the blindfold I could see her eyeballs shift as though to follow something moving inside her head.

Now she drew herself up, forcing out a series of little huffs through her nostrils, as her mouth, as if possessed by a succession of other mouths, stretched itself into an effortful almost-smile, pursed, then gaped, the tongue pulsing visibly in the breach. Clamping her mouth shut again, she pressed out a long, groaning "Wwwww," and all at once, with a surprise that flooded my body with meltwater, I understood that she was trying to speak.

Banished was the spell the house had cast on me. The feeling of *separate,*

separate gave way to one of interest and affinity. Here was a stutterer as afflicted as myself! She appeared no great shakes and I began again to feel that I might fit in and even distinguish myself in this place.

Then she opened her mouth, and said in a man's voice, bewildered and peremptory, and without any hint of a stammer, "Who are you? You're no child of mine."

I jerked back. The girl reeled away, veered into the bushes, and, shaking out a flock of sparrows, forced herself through.

Shaken, I heaved up my suitcase and mounted the steps to the door, which to my relief was still open; I did not think I could bear to offend it with my fist. I managed to maneuver myself and my suitcase through without touching its plated edge or the cold tongue it stuck out at me.

Before me, a great staircase surged up to a landing and turned out of sight. The treads were scuffed almost white except near the walls, where they were black with polish in which just a few golden scratches flared like comets. There was no sign of Miss Exiguous, but a few steps from the bottom lounged a skinny ginger-haired white boy of about fourteen, lashing himself in the mouth with a thin peeled stick. His lips were cut and bleeding. The stick was red where it struck.

Seeing me, he stopped this occupation and cocked his head impatiently. "Mmmmm ... uh-hmmm ..." A fine sweat broke out all over me. I could feel my sleeves sticking to my damp skin. "Mmmm ... Uh-hmmm—mmm ..."

I had squeezed my eyes shut. Now I opened them, only to see that the boy was taking no interest in my difficulties, but had begun striking himself again with his stick in a bored manner. I took a careful breath and started over. "Mmm-*may* I ask where I am supposed to present myself?" I said.

"I—" He stopped, eyelids fluttering. Then with an upward jerk of his chin, "Wouldn't," said the boy, and went on hurting himself.

"Wouldn't what?" Consternation at this incivility vied with elation. I had known I was going to be among stutterers like myself, but I had not understood what it would feel like to excite neither curiosity, nor pity, nor mirth. I was *ordinary*. How glorious!

"A-a-a-ask. Or present myself. If I wa-was you. She don't want to see you. If she wanted to see you she would a-already have seen you. And called you to her office. A-a-a-and given you a uniform, and maybe other privileges too" (this in a highly ironical tone), "privileges the rest of us can only dr-r-r-r-eam of, because there's no telling what honors she might bestow on you if she wa-wants to see you, and without your having time to ask 'Wh—'"—he stopped, stuck out his chin, closed his eyes, struck himself in the mouth, went on—"'where should I present myself?' as if you had any say in the matter. No sir, if you haven't seen her already you'd better just leave."

"But I've only just come!"

"That's good, it means you haven't ha-ad time to offend her yet. Go away quick." He slid his whip between his lips, tasting it.

I was silent, confounded. I hoped I should not cry. I imagined knocking on Aunt Margaret's door, suitcase in hand—the words "all a mistake," her look of dismay—and knew that I would sooner throw myself under the wheels of the train than go back. The thought had a steadying influence, and now my letter of admission swam up in my mind: the envelope with the typed address, the single long half-white, half-dark hair windingly affixed to the adhesive, the brief missive on tissue-thin paper, the enclosed train ticket. And Miss Exiguous on the train platform, holding up a placard with a hole through it in place of words, and pronouncing my name. No, it was not possible that I had misunderstood.

So it was something else. Well, it would not be the first time I was made unwelcome on account of the color of my skin. I was readying a pert reply when the boy jumped up and hurried away down the narrow hall that, skirting the stairs, led back into the depths of the building. I heard a door close.

A moment later a pair of feet descended the stairs into view. They were encased in solid black orthopedic shoes and made with each step the sound—*doom, doom, doom*—of something too heavy to carry being set down only just in time to keep from dropping it. I shrank back a little; even once the adult person to whom the legs belonged turned the corner onto the landing and showed herself in increments, I thought she had for a moment the appearance of legs that had only accidentally and somewhat gruesomely acquired a torso and head, especially because she was wearing a long sort of stiff smock or robe under which one could imagine that her legs went up all the way to her shoulders. There was even something footlike about her red face with its big dry creased heel of a chin.

"You must come at once! I don't know why you are hanging around down here!" she said to me, then turned around and—*doom, doom, doom*—shrank to legs again.

My suitcase banging on a riser, as I hurried after her, caused one of the locks to pop open, so I stopped to fasten it, and when I attained the second floor the woman was nowhere in sight. But neither could I hear her tread on the stairs above me, so I exited the stairwell for a wide hallway, lined with closed doors, and dimly lit by a window at the far end.

It was full of children in school uniform, some perhaps as young as six, some (to my eyes) practically adult. I saw among them, to my relief, several Blacks as well as Orientals and others whose race I could not guess at sight. Most of the children were standing in line outside one or another of the doors, these lines crossing and plaiting without merging. But the impression of order this might have given was greatly offset by other sights: A girl spread-eagled on the floor while a bigger girl, whose uniform had been fitted in back with what looked like a sort of sail, giving her no small resemblance to a *Dimetrodon*, attempted to fit the tapered end of an eight-foot-long, wobbling cardboard cone into her mouth . . . Another seemingly talking to a small rhombic rubber eraser, periodically holding it up to her ear to receive its reply . . . Three boys, one of them mixed race like me, trying to insert their whole hands into one another's mouths. A door banged open and a youth ran out, black paper streamers flying from his mouth, jerked open the opposite door, and slammed it shut behind him. I had stopped dead to take in these portents and now, without meaning to, I giggled. Nobody paid the least attention to me. Again I thought, I am a ghost—no one can see or hear me. It was an oddly comfortable notion.

I flinched at a whirring and the impression of sudden movement near my face: A sparrow had found its way in. Against the round window at the end it bumped and fluttered horribly before hurling itself back down the hall again. Then one of the doors beside me opened and the line began shuffling inside. I watched, balancing my suitcase on the tops of my feet. Inside I could see part of a blackboard, benches, anatomical diagrams suspended from a dado. The last child went in; then a white man with tight black curls and a purplish red face, wearing a sort of smock, buttoned at the neck and loose below, looked out, saw me—this was a shock (but spiritualists do see ghosts, I thought, if anyone does)—clicked his tongue irritably, and said, "What are you doing standing out there like a lump? Take your place at once," seized me by the elbow, and dragged me into the room.

He took up a position at the front of the room, raising his ruler. His smock was buttoned so tightly around his neck that it appeared to have driven all the blood to his head. I had the fancy that droplets would at any moment start from his pores. When he brought down the ruler on his scarred wooden desk, it was with such violence that it rebounded and struck him in the cheek. He clapped his hand to his face with a look of fury and rubbed the spot, where a welt was already rising, as the class clattered to their feet again—I had not left mine—and began what must have been a recitation, though they spoke so quickly that I was unable to make out a word. It seemed possible that they were stammering, but if so, they were stammering in perfect unison and with—if such a thing were even possible—great fluency. It frightened me to hear them and again I began to feel that I was separate from everything and did not belong. Only here was the instructor, glaring at me and pointedly marking time with the ruler.

Hesitantly, I opened my mouth. The music, if that is what it was, came to a stop—inhumanly sudden, inhumanly simultaneous, I thought—and the other children now turned on me their shining eyes all at once, like one manifold insect.

"I had thought to make a show of joining in," I said at last, turning to face the instructor and squaring my shoulders, "just to spare myself the embarrassment of admitting that not only had I intruded on your lesson but I did not know where I was supposed to be instead. But the truth is that I have only just arrived"—indicating my suitcase. I had spoken with uncommon assurance and without stammering, and in my surprise at this circumstance I felt a silly smile spread across my face.

"What is that to grin about?" he said. "If you don't belong here, remove yourself. Go speak to the Intake Coordinator at once."

I picked up my suitcase. Seeing that the instructor was already raising his ruler, I cleared my throat: "Excuse me, I don't know how to find the Intake Coordinator, please."

He swung around with a look of outrage and banged his ruler on the table again. This time, the tip broke off and jumped away, and so did I. I was standing in the hall, morosely inspecting the other doors for a clue, when one opened. "There you are," said the foot-faced woman, very red, the hairs on her lip and her cheek all standing out. "What on earth have you been doing?"

She must be the Intake Coordinator, I thought, and followed her silently into a small office containing a desk, a daybed with a furry throw of an indeterminate color and material messily bunched up on it, and beside it a pair of great black puissant shoes. Now she threw herself down on the daybed, drawing up her stockinged feet and tucking her robe under them, and thumped the space beside her with a heavy hand. "A little nap wouldn't hurt." Then she tucked her hair behind her ears and laid her head down on her arm. In less than a minute she appeared to be sleeping. Her chin trembled slightly as she ground her teeth.

This was very strange, but I did suddenly feel a great tiredness, so I sat down, gingerly, on the edge of the bed. After a moment the white arm of a cat reached out from under the bed and delicately clawed my ankle, catching in my sock, so that the fabric stretched out in a point and then snapped back. I slid my feet out of my shoes and curled up on the very edge of the daybed, so that no part of me touched the woman behind me, from whom a comforting warmth nonetheless reached me, and fell asleep in turn.

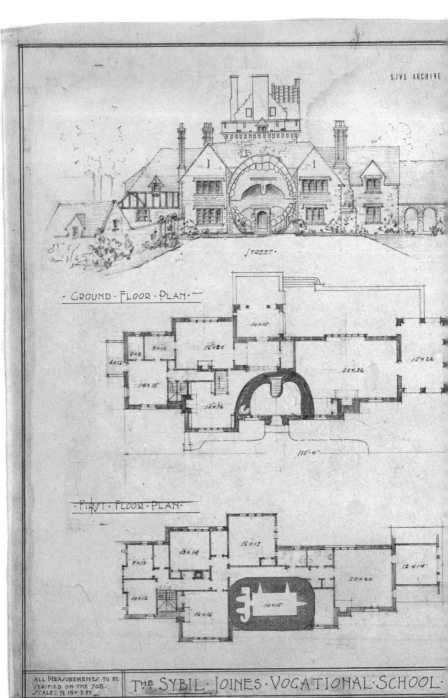

·STREET·

·GROUND·FLOOR·PLAN·—

8×10
6×12
2×8
14×15
16×20
16×16
10×15
20×36
15×22

115'-0"

·FIRST·FLOOR·PLAN·

9×12
13×14
16×17
10×12
16×16
10×15
20×20
12×14

ALL MEASUREMENTS TO BE
VERIFIED ON THE JOB.
SCALE: ½ IN = 1 FT.

THE SYBIL·JOINES·VOCATIONAL·SCHOOL

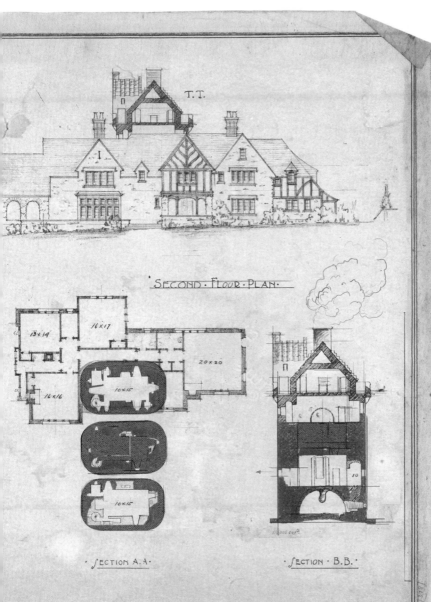

T.T.

SECOND · FLOOR · PLAN

13×14

16×17

20×20

16×15

16×16

10×15

10×15

· SECTION · A·A ·

· SECTION · B.B. ·

· THROAT · TOWER ·

Robert

· SPEAKERS · & · HEARING-MOUTH · CHILDREN ·

JACKSON
ARCHITECTS
No. 179

~ On the Architecture of the
Vocational School ~

The Vocational School is a huddle
of mostly elderly buildings, much
abused by the weathers, and dark
even in summer. The Chapel of the
Word Church is the one recent
addition. (As I came up the ~~the~~
drive I glimpsed above the di-
-lapidated carriage house the
Chapel's narrow spire, like a
finger raised to shush the sky)
Did I say that language were like
those great works of memorial
architecture erected by the ancients?
I found that for the Vocational
School, architecture was language.
Beyond the Chapel's arched
doorway was an introduction
in three dimensions to NJA

SJVS

EAST F

Readings

from "A Visitor's Observations"

We are fortunate that a scholar of what we would today call linguistic anthropology visited the Vocational School during the Founder's lifetime and was able to report on what he saw there. Unfortunately nothing more is heard from him[3] after the truncated text—scarcely more than a pile of handwritten notes toward a book never written, and in no particular order—that appears here for the first time, discovered by myself in a mixed lot of old papers auctioned off by the Cincinnati branch (two old biddies) of the American Spiritualist & Temperance Society. As its length may try the reader's patience, I have broken it into sections; those eager to read them consecutively may of course do so by skipping ahead. —Ed.

How I Conceived the Plan to Visit the Vocational School

I credit my involvement with the Sybil Joines Vocational School for Ghost Speakers & Hearing-Mouth Children to a difficulty with the letter *M*.

Born into the hardworking, hardheaded middle class, educated expensively by the indifferent benevolence of a wealthy great-aunt to whom my parents applied for aid, and who had (and sought) no nearer relation to me, I had found myself a niche in the same small college in which I had recently completed my own graduate studies, dutifully inserting into the minds of the young what had been inserted into mine by my predecessor, recently and opportunely retired. I knew myself to be fortunate but was a martyr to indigestion and, dare I say it, boredom. But in my thirties, something put a period to my boredom in a most unwelcome way: I developed a stutter. How this delighted the young m-m-misses and m-m-misters who were my students, and how I suffered! It was in the search for a remedy that I came across a promotional publication of the Vocational School.

---

3. Unless he is supplementing his observations through my own, using me as a sort of telescoping spyglass through which, though deceased, he is able to keep his eye trained on the object of his study. But I jest. —Ed.

I found, not a cure, but a thesis.

I had long speculated that language had its origins in mourning. Without the desire to speak to and of the beloved dead, we would not have troubled to supplant simple grunts and gestures with words. Everyday necessity cannot account for the disproportionate ostentation of every known language. We do not need descriptive flourishes to say, "'Ware tiger!" or "Give me food!" No, language is the equivalent of those great monuments to the dead—your Sphinxes, your pyramids—the construction of which mulcted generations of the living.

I smoothed the pamphlet on my desk, and copied down an address. Here, finally, was direct evidence of the link between language and loss. If the Vocational School did not mourn their losses, since for them the dead never really departed, that did not confute my hypothesis. They had merely abbreviated the passage from loss to language, achieving consolation so quickly that the grief was never felt. And yet grief lay behind everything they did. I believed that before I ever saw those dark cornices thrusting into the oblivious blue of a summer sky, the stricken eyes locked in that imperious face.

On the Architecture of the Vocational School

The Vocational School is a huddle of mostly elderly buildings, much abused by the weather, and dank even in summer. The Chapel of the Word Church is the one recent addition. (As I came up the drive, I glimpsed above the dilapidated carriage house the Chapel's narrow spire, like a finger raised to shush the sky.)

Did I say that language was like those great works of memorial architecture erected by the ancients? I found that for the Vocational School, architecture *was* language. Beyond the Chapel's arched doorway was an introduction in three dimensions to Vocational School philosophy. The building alluded in its form to both Speaking Ear and Hearing Mouth. The nave was tiered, or one might say whorled, like an ear, and the vault ridged like the roof of a mouth. The children seated in the nave made up the Tongue. (Dressed identically in red flannel short pants, jackets, and caps, they looked a bit like those quaint statuettes known as *Gartenzwerge*.) Members of the faculty designated as Teeth, wearing peaked cowls of starched flannel of an ivory hue, lined the first tier above them and occasionally descended to impose discipline. Circulating freely through the congregation, the Salivary—advanced students, wearing large, pink, *papier-mâché* collars resembling the Egyptian *usekh*, and representing the pharyngeal opening—distributed gags, erasers, and other devotional items.

At the focus of the theater, the Analphabetical Choir was ranged in ascending tiers to left and right of a great hole, angled downward, and terminating out of sight of the congregation, with at the bottom a stoup kept brimming with the saliva of the devout, collected in spittoons throughout the ceremony. (I have contributed my tittle of froth.) In front of the hole, though not blocking it from view, was a standing screen of black paper with a small aperture through which the heavily rouged mouth of the Headmistress might address the congregation. The disconcerting effect was of a mouth, on the verge of being swallowed by a much larger mouth, turning back to utter a few last, barely audible words—"Don't do it!" perhaps, or more mundanely, "White vinegar is sometimes efficacious in removing stains."

If the Chapel was an educational tract, what was the main school building? The original structure, formerly the Cheesehill Home for Wayward Girls, dates back to 1841, almost sixty years before the school was founded, but in it the lines of a once-dignified building in a restrained Victorian style have been lost under additions so peculiar as to raise doubt in the mind of at least one observer as to whether they could be described as architecture at all, or might not better be classed, to quote Jim Jimson's *Notable Architectural Abortions of Old New England*, as "biological growths of the persuasion *mushroom*."[4] But those who, suspending judgment, pass under its preposter-

---

4. Jimson goes on to say, "The visitor may wish to lie down with a damp cloth folded over his forehead after catching an unguarded look at a monstrosity that raises profound doubt about its architect's sanity."

ous porticos to amble down its hallways and faint in its fainting rooms will find a kind of fascination stealing over them. Without perceiving anything obviously outlandish, one begins to feel that one has entered another world in which planar surfaces curve; parallel lines meet; and up, down, left, and right have all been subtly twisted out of true.

One day the Headmistress handed me the key to this mystery with one of her characteristically gnomic remarks: "A building, like a person, is a free-standing hole." Like all holes, it has a special affinity with the dead; only consider how many more haunted houses there are than haunted paddocks or playing fields. But this affinity can be amplified, tuned. When a hallway is adjusted with dropped ceilings and wainscoting to the exact proportions of the trachea, larynx, or oral cavity, who knows but what it may even speak.

I do not know whether this contributed to the eerie way that, when the wind blew up from the valley in the late afternoon, and was channeled down the hallways through a great oculus that was winched open at this hour (in which a wedge-shaped piece of wood, very thin at one end, acted as a reed), the hall and indeed the whole building hummed with a note so deep that it was more felt than heard—a mood, not a sound. The doors to the classrooms opening and closing acted as finger holes to a flute, changing the pitch. Over time I was able to pick out more and more elements of this symphony, as for example the grace notes supplied by the almost inaudible whistles and peeps that issued from tiny holes or spiracles drilled in the walls here and there.

After some months of listening to this curious music I realized that I was anticipating its changes. Unlikely as it seemed, the students, teachers, and menials passing through the doors did so in an intricate but repeating pattern. Remarkable! Perhaps the Headmistress had used musical principles to schedule both classes and the rounds of the domestic help—a logistical challenge, no doubt, but theoretically possible. But the building was a perpetual bustle at this time of day: teachers flapping by in a whirl of black robes; students, some loitering, some hurrying, their oversized shoes slipping off their heels to percuss the floor at every step; maids with expressionless faces and exaggeratedly humble posture, passing up, down, and across the halls, closing doors, opening others. Could all this activity really be choreographed? And if so, what was it *for?*

I was offered on different occasions various answers: The house was a receiving device, in which the students could be made to vibrate in tune with the dead. The house was a pedagogical tool. The house was a philosophical disquisition about language, death, and no doubt, architecture too, given that capacity for recursion for which language is notorious. It was all these things. But I did not really understand its song until I learned who[5] had been a tenant at the Cheesehill Home for Wayward Girls, and saw that the house was also a ghost story.

I felt, I would say, relieved. Not just that I had saved my theory by finding the link I had predicted between language (in its architectural form) and loss. But also that there was a familiar, a *human* basis for the grief that came over me in those moments when, at twilight in the gardens, watching a firefly make its slow way through the still air, I caught a snatch of the school's eerie song, and looked back to see a woman's head in silhouette, turning away from a lit window . . .

You may judge how far I had already come from conventional thinking. Ghosts? A commonplace. But the half-heard, half-imagined song of an old house, *that* confounded and even, I will admit, frightened me. Why then do I find myself humming it now?—in a manner of speaking, at any rate, it being pitched so deep. I do not transpose it into a higher register. No, I hum it in its own register, which is—as I said—that of emotion: I hum it with my soul. It does not make me happy. But then I have often noticed that the behaviors people feel compelled to repeat are not necessarily those that make them happy.

There is a whole wing of the school, incidentally, that has no material form. It exists only in the form of verbal descriptions, rumors, and reminiscences.

---

5. The Headmistress's mother, presumably. —Ed.

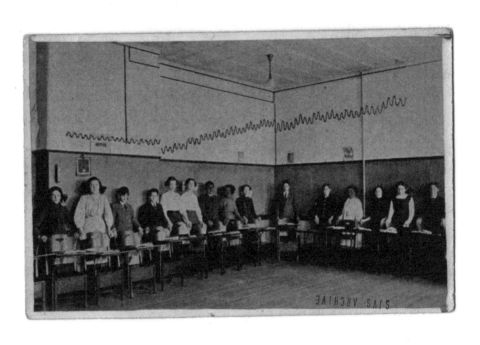

Letters to Dead Authors, #2

Dear Mr. Melville,

It has come to my attention that you are dead. I wish I had known that before writing my last letter; I would have expressed myself differently. I had naturally hoped to persuade you to come to the aid of my school. A testimonial from a great man, a national treasure—

But a corpse cannot write a letter to the *Times*.

A corpse cannot read a letter, either. That is common sense. Perhaps I am a zany for writing this; perhaps it is true what Mrs. Brock and the other hens at the Harmonial Sisterhood said of me. But is it really so much more sensible to levitate tables, and converse with dead Lincolns, and have your likeness taken with ectoplasm pluming from your nostrils, as Victoria Littlebrow did last August in Chicago, at the home of the Beatific Twins?

Which reminds me: I hope my last letter did not give you the impression that I am one of those Very Veiled Ladies clutching at the cold hands of drowned daughters and overlooking the ice bucket in the medium's lap. My researches are driven by a passion for inquiry, not by wishful thinking, and are pursued on the very latest equipment, as the Reflectograph; Communigraph; Dynamistograph, or Cylinders of Matla; and many other devices of original design.

My students receive, in addition to vocational training, a superior general education. Here history is taught by people who lived it, Boolean algebra explained by Boole himself. Our students might study thermodynamics with Jim Maxwell or natural selection with Chaz Darwin. Our school is a hive of industry. Even now, from behind the paneling comes a dry, insectile chirring: my stutterers practicing their scales in the next room, under the bloodshot eye of Mr. Lieu. Some of them cannot pronounce the letter *A*. Some the letter *B*, or *C*, or *D*. And I have lately spotted (in our little town of

Cheesehill of all places) an *E*, and scheme to bring her to us. Eventually we will silence the whole alphabet.

Do you know, once I could not pronounce my own name? It does something to a child, something I intend to do to my students. I have assigned them new names according to their gifts. You are the 'd'ms and 'v's of a new Eden, I tell them.

Why do I continue to trouble your repose, you may ask: Are there no living authors to whom I can turn for guidance or companionship? Perhaps I am more comfortable with the dead than the living, though there seems to me scant difference between a dead and a living *writer*. This is not so much because dead writers seem alive still in their words, as because the living ones seem already dead in theirs.

A book is a block of frozen moments—of time without time, which can nonetheless be reintroduced to time, by a reader who runs her attention over it at the speed of living. Just so does a traveler turn a landscape into a sequence of moments, in one of which she glimpses a javelina disappearing into an arroyo, in another, the fence she can hop for a shortcut home. The comparison is not frivolous: In the book, the author's voice has become a place.

This place is the land of the dead.

I do not mean that figuratively. I consider writers my fellow necronauts, pulling on their Ishmaels and their Queequegs like mukluks and trudging across the frozen tundra of the page.

Incidentally, you would marvel if you could see me, for I am wearing a cunningly constructed device that pulls open the mouth and stretches the tongue, which in my opinion can never be too long. On the latter I am wearing a sort of costume made of paper. One of my principle communicants on the Other Side, Cornelius Hackett, said something today (through my mouth, of course) that I did not quite make out, but that may have been "little dress." It is also possible, as one student suggested, that it was "littleness" (humility?) or even "fickleness." Though to what in this world have I been as faithful as I have been, my whole life long, to death?

I will know soon enough if my "little dress" pleases the dead. It certainly pleases me to see, in the mirror, my neatly turned-out tongue jumping in my mouth, like a pupil at morning calisthenics. On the other hand, my shadow on the wall, wagging with the flame, is fearsome. It almost looks like the head of someone who has been partially flayed with a blunt instrument, possibly a spoo—

I just very nearly set my hair on fire with the candle! And then, in putting myself to rights, scorched the ruffle on my tongue. Let this remind me to keep my attention on the task at hand, instead of alarming myself with figments.

I should explain why I chose to make this dress out of paper and not a stouter substance. For while a fiery demise could not reasonably have been foreseen, a watery one would seem eminently likely, the mouth being a soggy sort of cotillion. But I will always choose paper when I can: it is an ideal conductive medium for spirits. I must have sensed this when, as a child, I had the habit of chewing into a cud corners torn from the pages of books.

Only yesterday, on one of my rare visits to town, the Cheesehill librarian splattered me with dung as she drove by in her motorcar, for she is grown very grand now that she is married and her husband a wealthy man.

On the whole, I am glad you are dead; every author should be dead. When I first understood that most of them are, I was a little relieved, for the idea that they might be paring their corns or nibbling almonds while their ghosts murmured prematurely in my ear seemed not only disorienting but a little unseemly. It is hard to yield oneself fully to communion with a person who somewhere may be singing in a saloon,

There was a fiddler and he wore a wig,
Wiggy wiggy wiggy wiggy, weedle, weedle, weedle,
He saved up his money and he bought a pig,
Piggy piggy piggy piggy, tweedle, tweedle, tweedle.

I see, sir, from the jut of your beard (I have your book propped open to your portrait), that you would not have sung such a song even when in the indiscreet condition that is life, but there is no telling what a man may do in the fullness of time and under the influence of spirits—alcoholic spirits, I mean—so it is very good that you are out of the way of temptation; I have seldom known the dead to sing. (That gives me quite a good idea, however—I must speak to our Mr. Lenore.)

But my little dress is becoming sodden and no spirits come. Do not be angry, Mr. Melville, but I wonder why *you* do not come? One of the ladies of the Harmonial Sisterhood chats regularly with Genghis Khan, and marvels that he speaks such good English, but I would much rather speak to you.

Sorrowfully,
Miss Sybil Joines

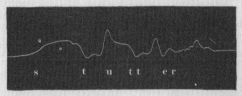

FIG. 13.— Mouth record of "stutter" spoken normally.
There is first a rush of air for the "s," then a sudden fall as the breath is cut off by the tongue in producing the occlusion of the "t." The sharp rise of the line registers the explosion of the "t." The small vibrations belong to the vowel "u." The closure for the second "t" ("tt") and the explosion are similar to those of the first. The final vibrations belong to the vowel "er."

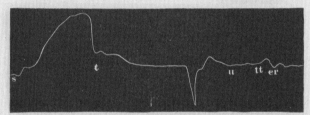

FIG. 14. — Mouth record of "stutter" spoken by a stutterer.
There is an initial gasp followed by a strong "s" and then an immensely prolonged "t." There is then another gasp. The rest of the word is normal.

A normal record of the word "stutter" is given in Fig. 13. It registers the rush of air for the "s" by the upward rising line. The line suddenly falls as the lips are closed for the "t." It rises very suddenly as the lips are opened to let out a puff of air, the explosion of the "t." Then follow the vibrations

5. The Final Dispatch, contd.

[Extended static, several words indistinct] . . . *someone is missing, a child is missing, calamity, havoc, ruin! Make things right, set things straight, mend, amend, avert* . . .

No, no, no, I must not allow myself to get so excited. Now I shall have to start all over again, trumping up a world to catch her in! Only a moment ago, as it seems, I was hurrying down a familiar road. For all its spectral dogs and rabbits, it was, as near as I could make it, the way home. The girl was in my sights! And then my heart flared up white inside me, and road and ravine and crowding hills all blanched and raveled into filaments like the thread-thin hyphae of a fungus. The girl is gone. I am alone on a blank page.

This is not a metaphor. The white is not sand, scorching the feet of the solitary figure trudging from left to right across the otherwise unblemished dune. The white is not snow, blanketing a battlefield in soft heaps, through which the occasional bayonet protrudes like the ascender of a buried *d*. The white is not ash—[static, several words indistinct]. The page is the one on which you are transcribing these words. It is white because the cellulose fibers of which it is made—in Fitchburg, Massachusetts, as I happen to know—are bleached during manufacture, in a process called brightening. Nothing supernatural about that. And yet its brightness and the brightness around me are the same brightness.

What? Yes. I exist, at present, only on this page, since I exist, at present, only in these words. What? Yes. I say I, your right middle finger strikes a key, an inked hammer impresses a letter on the void, and—*mirabile dictu*—I am. [Extended pause, bad static, distant howling.]

[Word or words indistinct: possibly "Am I?"]

Are you receiving?

"Are you receiving?" you type, because you are. (Surely you are!) Your starched collar saws delicately at your already sore chin as your body moves with your hands. Your hair whispers against the rim of the brass trumpet to which your ear is pressed, straining to hear the faint, crackly voice rising and falling in the bell. My voice, speaking from the land of the dead, though I am not dead, as I believe, as I have reason to believe. Perhaps not reason enough. Nonetheless, it is my working theory that I am not dead.

"Not dead," you agree. And I remember how it's done.

I say the words: "dirt road," "ravine," "small wooden bridge." You take them down. On the page, a world springs up. It is this world. It is as real as I can make it. Real enough to bear my weight, or how could I cross its quags and torrents to the girl? I don't look down at the planks, the cracks between the planks, the white streaming below. This is where experience tells. Describe the white and I will fall in. Describe the planks and I will be naming nails for all eternity. Itemizing splinters. No, it is enough to say "bridge" to cross it. Say "steep and winding road" to make my way.

[Rustling.]

If only I were sure that I am not making *you*, dear listener, as well!—and all your accoutrements: your stockings, for example, black, pilling at the knee, bunching at the ankle, sagging into the heels of the regulation shoes that are always a little too big, when they are not too small. If only I were sure that I did not imagine your ears, upon which so much depends, standing out a little from your skull, but delicate, the satin skin stretched over the ~~cartilegi~~ cartilaginous form, two coracles, one a redder brown than the other, hot from the trumpet against which it is pressed. Your hair, ultra-fine, black, kinky, scraped into braids, exposing the elegant shape of the skull and the thin neck, the part a line like a scar, as if someone had once tried to cut you in half. Your nose a little pinched with concentration and perhaps annoyance, for I am talking about you instead of about the land of the dead, or even the girl Finster, and you do not approve. You are all business. It is what I like about you. Little dents form on either side of your nose. Small nose. Small nostrils officiously flared.

Are you receiving?

Through the trees the blank page shines at the head of the rise. The gradient is steep, but the footing is good, and I need only hitch up my skirts to step over the rivulets of white that cut through the road on occasion, as if to remind me to keep my mind on the—

Officiously flared, did you get that down? I shall keep talking about you until you remember your duty, which is, one—to take dictation; and, pursuant to that end, two—to exist. Because if you don't— Your neck: Is there a scarf around it? No. A crucifix? A locket would be better, on a thin gold chain, not real gold, gold-plated, the gold worn to gray. And in the locket? Let's say a tuft of fine brown hair, straighter than your own, and possibly not even human, the hair of a dog, perhaps, or a donkey, or a goat, or a [word indistinct]—

A child is missing, a child is lost—

But there is nothing to be gained by panic. We are making what haste we can. Already I have put the ravine behind me. In front of me I have put the road, of course, and a muddy field where thistles mutter and twitch. Meanwhile it steadies my mind to think about you, phlegmatically typing "phlegmatically," and without even needing to check the spelling. You wear a ring on the thumb of one small but wide, rather rough, dry hand, and it sometimes rings like a bell against the frame of the typewriter, as now— *ding!* Your ring, unlike your locket, is true gold, though worn thin in some spots. It was probably your dead mother's ring, unless your mother still lives, let her live, why not, though much altered, for the worse, by the syphilis.

You half rise. Then you regulate yourself and sit back down. I suppose you think I am wasting my time baiting you when I could be describing wonders heretofore unknown to science. The silhouettes wheeling high above me now, for instance, of the greatest of the many birds seen here, if they are birds, which they are not, and yet they are not anything else either. They gyre around a single point. Naturally it is myself, or rather a point directly above me. They are almost stationary in flight, despite their huge, ungainly bodies, and though you would think such large birds would have to beat their mauve, fleshy wings in a frenzy just to stay airborne, it is not true, they oar the air almost haphazardly and at intervals between which they hover as if sustained by a constant updraft. Only occasionally do they—adjusting the angle of their wings almost imperceptibly—dip and slide into a descending curve.

Here comes one now, its eyes like the glass heads of hatpins, a crescent of dust on each globe. Remarkable detail, but I would disabuse you of the notion that there is anything intrinsically more marvelous in that bird than in the way your shoulders draw together as you shift in your seat, feeling the coarse linsey-woolsey of your school pinafore fret your shoulder blades, or your hard ankles crossed beneath your seat, flexing rhythmically, so that the soles of your shoes knock against the wooden crossbars. I have not even forgotten to account for your oversized and rather scratchy underpants, loose about the waist, slightly damp in the crotch, or for the pocket in your dress, the inky handkerchief in the pocket, and the dime in the lining.

Hark to the bird! A sound like tearing paper as it stoops. I fling myself at a sheltering brake. [Rustling.] A mistake: My fichu is caught fast—my skirt; the snickering thistles pull me down. Thorns rip through my petticoats. Talons rip through my hair.

Then the bird beats back up and is gone. After smaller prey, perhaps— *save her*—I surge up—but no, if I am right, Finster is the falconer here, not the prey, Finster herself in the intemperance of a child's will conceived and sent these birds. Attagirl!

Unless I am. The falconer, I mean, though if I am that, then I am prey and falcon too, throwing my own self off the glove, scaring me up, striking me down.

"A puppet show!" the thistles jeer. "A humbug!" Flecks of page-white writhe across the landscape. It is disintegrating again. And I went to so much trouble over it!

[Static, hissing; two or three sentences indistinct.]

—rely on, at least. Which is fortunate, because I depends [sic] on you. And yet I am almost sure I made you up. Why? You are too real. Too detailed. The crease at your wrist, for instance, usually to be seen in one of what I suppose to be your age—no more than sixteen—only in conjunction with considerable baby fat, though not in your case, it is just that your skin is unusually dry. You have matching creases at your ankles and your knuckles are calloused and fine lines are already forming at the corners of your mouth. You yawn, and a shining thread of saliva joins your uvula to your tongue. A dot or two of white suggest the incursion of streptococcus into your left tonsil, which, slightly swollen, resembles in shape and surface texture an overripe fig. With the tip of your tongue you test your lower lip, in which a crack has opened, salmon red.

I suppose I love you a little. It is easy to love what one has invented.

The girl Finster is not lovable.

Save her!

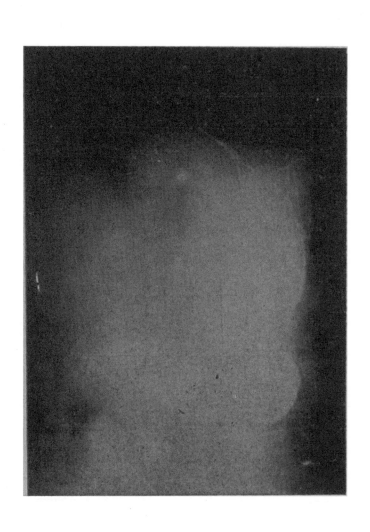

The Stenographer's Story, contd.

"Wake up!" The Intake Coordinator, if that was what she was, was shaking me. "Wake up at once! There's no time for malingering around here; I hope you don't think you've come here just to take naps at the school's expense!" I sat up and hastily worked my feet back into my shoes. "We need to enter your information into the rolls, we need to conduct a placement exam, we need to assign you a cot, a hygiene kit, oral tackle and yoke, and all this before evening calisthenics. We simply don't have time to lie around, however much some of us would like to!"

Though I burned at the injustice of this remark, in which I may or may not have been right to hear a sly echo of that unjust epithet *shiftless*, I nodded and rose to my feet. A moment later I heard a scrabbling sound under the daybed, and then a skinny white cat shot out and across the room, raised his somewhat dingy tail against the wall, and, vibrating, sprayed it with musk.

"You may call me Mother Other," said the woman, not appearing to notice the activities of the cat, who now composed himself and began industriously washing his whiskers. She pulled open a drawer in her desk, then hurriedly banged it shut again, poked inside another with a ruler, then employed the tip of the same ruler to slide it closed. Then in rapid succession she yanked out two or three other drawers and pawed through them, muttering to herself. Papers cascaded out, planing across the floor.

Mother Other? What kind of name was that? (For that matter, what kind of name was Miss Exiguous?) Perhaps it was not a name so much as an honorific and in the fullness of time this Mother Other would retire to be replaced by another Mother Other, not so red-faced or resentful, but destined to become so. Perhaps here there was no such thing as a proper name, only a position to be filled by whatever spirit happened by. Hadn't every one of the conversations I'd had since I arrived been a little strange? Like the conversation of people who remembered talking, but didn't know what it was for?

She picked up a page, scowled at it, dropped it again. "Where is your paperwork?" she demanded.

"I d-don't know if I have any p-p-paperwork yet," I said, chagrined. "I haven't—"

"Quiet!" she said. "Did I ask you a question?" I opened my mouth. "Quiet, I said! Can't you see I have enough to worry about without your prattling on and on until a person can hardly think? No, it's really too much, I don't know why they always give me the difficult cases, unmannerly children from God knows where, who don't even make an effort to look decent. Where on earth is your uniform?"

"I don't have a uniform."

"Absurd! Every student has a uniform. If you have no uniform you are not a student and should not be here. Go down to the supply room at once and sign one out. I shouldn't have to talk to someone who can't abide by even the most basic social niceties, let alone the dress code of the school. It's enough to . . . I ought to . . . No, I just don't know . . ." Her chin was trembling violently.

"Please don't be upset," I said. "I know it's no excuse, but I only just got here, and nobody told me to pick up a uniform. Probably someone else wasn't doing his or her job, it's just too bad that it came down on your shoulders! I can see that you're someone who has to bear more than her share, and that's not right!" Again I spoke with unusual clarity and ease. It's as if the school is helping me say the right thing, I thought, pleased. It wants me here.

Mother Other nodded and put her head down on her hands, her shoulders shaking. "I'll go right away," I said. I turned at the door. "I'm going now . . ." Mother Other did not look up or offer to tell me where the uniforms were kept, so I tiptoed out. The cat slipped out after me.

The hall was empty now, except for the sparrow. The cat stopped with one paw raised, only his eyes moving back and forth, back and forth. Then he seated himself to give one leg three quick hard swipes with his tongue, rose again, and trotted lightly and purposefully toward the stairs. Feeling that I ought to stay close to anyone who knew where he was going, be it only a cat, I followed. At the landing, he passed neatly between the balusters and composed himself on the edge of the drop to stare abstractedly into the void.

"Down there? All right," I said.

The light in the foyer had changed, perhaps the rainstorm had come upon us; it was into a dim and gray-green space that I descended. There were closed doors to either side; I chose the one on the left, but my hand was arrested above the doorknob by the sound of someone moving around inside.

Behind me I heard the opposite door open. The red-haired boy I had seen before stuck his head out. I felt oddly pleased to see him. "Ha-ha-haven't you left yet?" he said. I saw that he was now wearing a sort of bag like a feed sack, made of cheesecloth and stretched over a wire frame that held it open under his chin.

"I'm looking for the storeroom," I said, and added hastily, "I was told to find a uniform, and by no less a person than Mother Other, so you'd better help me, and fast!"

He slid out through the door and closed it behind him, though not before I caught a glimpse of ranks of glass-fronted cabinets and, suspended from the ceiling above them, some balsa wood and paper constructions that might have been kites or models, though whether geometrical, anatomical, or cosmological I could not have said.

"Mother Other? Well, then I really had better h-help you," he said, though there was something sarcastic about his tone. Maybe Mother Other was not as important as I had thought. The disregard for formality evinced by her untidy papers, her tears—her nap!—could mean she was the very lowest sort of employee: a janitor, or worse. On the other hand it could mean that she was very high up indeed.

The boy led me back along the hallway beside the stairs and through a plain, narrow door into another, wider hallway that resembled the one upstairs, except that it was darker and dingier.

"Once I have a uniform, will I be shown to my room?" I remembered suddenly that I had left my suitcase upstairs in Mother Other's room.

"Your room? You'll be sleeping in a dormitory like the rest of us." Then he seemed to reflect: "Unless the Head decides that you need a room of your own; though she has never done so it's certainly in her power, and certainly, too, there are plenty of rooms here, and you wouldn't bother anyone, tucked away somewhere under the attics, or even in one of the many really good rooms that are still empty. But that doesn't mean you should get the idea in your head that you might as well have a room of your own; what's good enough for the rest of us is good enough for you, unless of course the Head decides otherwise, but that would surprise everyone; not that the Head is incapable of suddenly changing her mind, and for reasons seldom clear to the rest of us, but—"

He stopped, a strange look coming over his face, and hurriedly adjusted the laces of the bag around his neck. He had gone a pale yellowish color and I could make out the darker hairs on his upper lip. He jerked his head like a cat freeing itself of a hairball and then, grimacing, worked something out from between his lips that fell into the bag and hung there, waggling.

He stepped quickly across the hallway and tugged on a dangling cord. A distant bell rang, and steps hurried toward us.

"There's Whit and McDougal coming," he said. "You don't want them to catch you wandering around the way you're dressed. Hurry, go, go, I can't help you anymore!" He took off down the hall, toward where two dark figures were bustling toward us, robes agitating.

"But where? Where should I go?" My cry was plaintive.

"To the supply room!" came his reply.

"But I don't know where it is!" I said, then with an "Oh!" of frustration turned back the way we had come. Only then did I see, under the great front staircase, another, narrower flight of stairs going down. Presumably it led to the kitchens and pantry, a janitorial closet, perhaps a laundry. It seemed reasonable to suppose that the supply room was also below, and so it proved.

"At last!" cried the supply warden, the small gray curtain drawn over her mouth on a wire frame billowing with her breath. A narrow fawn-colored person—perhaps a light-skinned mulatto—with great, staring eyes, she dropped the pile of blankets she had been listlessly folding, planted her hands firmly on the counter, and leapt athletically all the way over it (she was wearing bloomers) in her eagerness to shake my hand. I fell back a step in circumspection, having hardly expected such a reception—my person was not such as to inspire anyone to transports of enthusiasm—but then took her hand. "Margaret Dearth!" she cried, and then more slowly, as if still making up her mind, "and you are Jane." It was just my name, but it felt like a kind of unction.

"Yes, I am Jane," I agreed, though it seemed to me that I exaggerated. But *That's* more like it, I thought; after all, I was invited to come, perhaps everyone knows that but Mother Other, what a surprise she will get and how foolish she'll feel when she finds out. "You kn-n-n—" I took a deep breath to silence the Voice, and started over. "You knew I was coming, then."

"Of course!" She beamed behind her curtain, or so she seemed eager to convey with her winks and nods. "You had to be coming, or there wouldn't have been a uniform for you. One might even say, without too much exaggeration, that the existence of your uniform *obliged* you to come, sooner or later, just to fill it. Come, let me show you what I have made for you while I waited."

She drew me by the hand—which she had not yet released—behind the counter and back through shelves upon shelves of stacked, neatly folded sheets, towels, caps, handkerchiefs, and other less recognizable items, into a dim and cluttered corner at the very back. The warden began sweeping small items heedlessly off a cluttered shelf, thimbles, spools of wire, and other objects I could not make out in the darkness, letting them clatter and roll away into the shadows. "Here it is," she breathed. "Come closer." I came closer. "Blow."

"Blow?"

"Like this." There was a soft, sweet sound, like several flutes playing at once.

"What is it? It is a remarkable thing, but I cannot quite make it out." In fact I could not see much of anything in the darkness.

"I call it a *chth*." (That is the best I can do with the spelling of what was less word than hiss.) "It is a hole in the air, to blow through. How it is constructed is a very technical and wonderful thing, but in use it is something like a bagpipe. The land of the dead acts as the bag; all you need to do is blow. I will wrap it in brown paper for you and you can try it out for yourself later on. Here is your uniform. Now be off with you." I found myself out in the hall again, a stack of clothes in my arms, the parcel balanced on top of it.

Where was I supposed to change? Bewildered, I looked back at the supply room door. It had been open a chink when I arrived; now it was emphatically closed. The warden had been kind, in fact she seemed to have taken an unaccountable liking to me, but her parting words had sounded very final. Yet my street clothes seemed to give such universal offense that I was loath to keep them on a minute longer. Perhaps if I explored some more I would find a dressing room or lavatory in which I could slip on my uniform. Of the other doors I opened on that floor, however, one led to a big, banging kitchen, one to a storeroom piled ceiling-high with old furniture and theatrical props, and one, quickly closed again, to unmixed darkness. I went back up the stairs to the hall I had recently quit.

There, the first door I tried opened onto a room humming with machines. On long tables crowded with shining glass tubes and reels of clean copper wire, cranks and pistons and flywheels, ashine with oil, were rocking or spinning or flashing back and forth. Rubber bladders alternately sagged and filled, and rabbit ears of looped wire covered with parchment trembled in tune with unseen influences. Nobody seemed in attendance on all this activity, though, and I moved on.

Behind another door I discovered a row of older girls identically bent over identical black-enameled devices out of which sheets of white paper were wonderfully unfurling, amid a rattling and tapping that would have given even the Fox sisters pause. It took me a moment to recognize them as typewriters, the spirit-rapping just keys striking platen. I laughed aloud and slammed the door.

Farther down the hall, I eagerly pushed open, by leaning my shoulder into it, a swinging door that was also a singing door, for its hinges emitted a high sweet musical note, and found myself in a very large, gloomy room, lit only by a few dim bulbs in wall sconces set low in high wood panels that were almost black with age and grime, and by the long but narrow windows through which the dark day appeared even darker. This room, evidently the refectory, was full of long tables, thickly varnished and much scarred. Long benches provided the seating for these; only on the raised platform at one end, where stood a single mahogany table, were there a few chairs, no doubt reserved for the faculty, or perhaps only for the Headmistress, her intimates, honored guests.

Overlooking this table hung a portrait of a white woman in a black dress, her extreme pallor unnaturally relieved by matching daubs of red in each cheek, holding a paper cone to her ear. Though it was a stiff, unflattering painting, it was an astonishing one—more astonishing than any other painting I had ever seen, though I could not have said exactly why. Somehow it gave me the feeling that I should not be able to see it at all. And yet I could see it, though not well. It flickered, in some sense that seemed to have nothing to do with the light, which, weak as it was, was steady.

Roving unchallenged through the building as if it were my home—as it was!—had made me bold, and now, forgetting my objective, I set down my stack of clothes on a table and went to take a closer look. Only when I climbed up on the platform did I notice that a blond girl in a school uniform identical to the one I had just been issued was standing in the shadows before the painting, her hands joined behind her back, looking up at it, or rather, as I now saw, talking to it.

"What are you doing?" I asked in an easy, conspiratorial tone, like one who is sure of her reception, so far had I forgotten myself in the novelty of my situation.

The girl shook her head sharply, without taking her eyes off the painting, and kept on talking, though she mumbled so that I could not understand what she was saying.

"Is that the Headmistress?"

The girl grimaced in simultaneous assent and reproval.

Undaunted, I took up a position next to the girl and gave myself over to studying the painting. I could identify nothing out of the ordinary and yet the conviction persisted that I beheld something strange if not frankly impossible.

Somewhere in the building a clock began to toll, and a Negro boy came in (it was Ambrose Wilson, who would later need taking down a peg). "What are you doing here?" he demanded. "You're not b-bothering the picture-talker, are you? That's not allowed. What if you brrr-oke her concentration? Don't think for a minute that you wouldn't be blamed! Now get out of the way, we're changing shifts. Isn't there somewhere you're supposed to be?" Waving me out of the way, he assumed the same position as the girl and began mumbling. After a moment she fell silent and let her head drop.

"Y-you're the new student, aren't you?" she said at last, raising her heavy-lidded, rather globular gray eyes. She sighed. "Why don't you come with me. I'll show you where you can get yourself in Compliance. I can see that you haven't the l-least idea how to behave."

She jumped off the platform and walked briskly back down the rows of tables, and I hurried after her. As I snatched up my things from the table—the door was already swinging shut behind her—the package the supply warden had given me slid off onto the floor and sprung open. I leapt to gather it up. I could not see the *chth* anywhere. Of course I had not seen it in the first place and so did not know what to look for. Or feel for; the blond girl, who had stuck her head back through the door, stared in bored disdain as I swept my fingertips across the dark floor. In the end, to be on the safe side, I scooped up whatever was there—dust, pencil shavings, a desiccated broccoli floweret—and deposited it all on the paper wrapper, which I folded and slid into the pocket of my pinafore.

Then I made haste to follow my guide, whose pigtail was disappearing through the doors. "I'm 'lorence," she said as I caught up with her.

"Lawrence," I said neutrally, thinking, Is that not a boy's name?

She shook her head. "'lorence. F-f-f-f-lorence. Through here." She opened a door onto another long corridor at right angles to the first, evidently leading into one of the wings of the building, lined on the left with regularly spaced, curtainless ogive windows, through which I could make out a segment of the curved drive and, beyond the shifting foliage of the trees, patches of a field where identically clad children stood in ranks, their arms rising and falling in synchronized movements made fantastically undulant by irregularities in the glass.

"This is the girls' dormitory," Florence said, going through another door into a high, ill-lit space containing many small iron beds as neat and narrow as graves, their heads against opposite walls, their feet separated by about a yard, leaving an alley down which Florence led me, tapping each footboard with a fingertip as she passed it, as if counting. "I expect you'll get poor old Emily's—I mean, Bed Seventy-four." Beside each bed, separating it from the next, was a small stand with a drawer; on a few of these were personal items, a photograph or a book, but most were bare. "Here." The bedframe rang as she rapped it.

"Thank you," I said, still clutching my uniform. All feeling of freedom and fellowship was gone, and it was with my usual sullen diffidence that I said, "Is . . . is there anywhere to change?"

She looked at me uncomprehendingly, made a sweeping gesture that encompassed the room.

"I mean, somewhere p-p-private?"

"Private!" she scoffed. "Go on, get your uniform on, and then I'll take you to the washroom to put your hair in Compliance. I'm spending my Restorative Time on you because I can see you need someone to show you what to do, but please don't imagine that I'm enjoying it!"

Hunched and miserable under her pale stare, I drew off my pinafore, carefully pressed when I set out, but now wrinkled and blotched with stains from the glass of milk I had drunk at the railroad station in Chesterfield, and pulled my uniform over my head, eclipsing her lunar gaze.

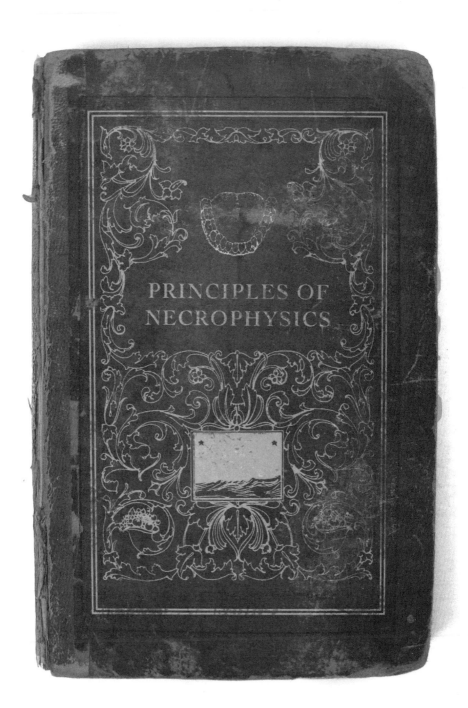

PRINCIPLES OF
NECROPHYSICS

Readings

from *Principles of Necrophysics*: "The Mechanics of Channeling the Dead"

This text, probably composed sometime in the first half of the last century, is still in use today as a general introduction to the subject, not so much for incoming students—these lose no time before beginning hands-on (or mouths-on) practice—as in public lectures, parent-orientation meetings, and press conferences. It appears here complete with the original plates. —Ed.

It is hard to believe that stuttering and stammering were ever regarded as speech *impediments*. Today we know that they indicate a natural aptitude for ghost-speaking. This is partly because to yield your mouth to the voice of another, you must suppress what you may be used to thinking of as "your own" voice. But more important, it is because stuttering and stammering cause a local fluctuation in the directionality of time. A fruit fly taped to the lip of a stutterer will live hours longer than a fruit fly at large, and sustained stuttering can stop or even reverse time, as the juvenile Founder[6] discovered when, grieving over a dead bunny, she saw its glazed eye brighten.[7] For, just as it takes time to make a speech, it takes speech to make time. Only a speaker can spin a wodge of matted moments into a yarn. This yarn, we call life. But when we stutter, repeating or drawing out the same phoneme, the spinning wheel stops. The mouth stands still, as time flows on around it, and lets the past catch up. Or, as we would say, it travels back in time.

When the stutterer's mouth, caught up in the tidal bore it has itself induced, is carried into the past, it takes with it any objects of modest size in its vicinity.[8] A painting of the Founder in a stiff nineteenth-century style

---

6. Headmistress Joines. —Ed.

7. By plumbing the susurrous snake-pit of the single word *sorry*, she kept the justly famous Hopsalot alive for a full twenty-five minutes (correctly speaking, twenty-five repetitions of the same minute).

8. The zone of temporal disturbance can be extended, with practice, to a radius of just over a yard.

appears to hang on the wall of the school refectory. Day and night, working in shifts, a single advanced student stands in front of it, talking it into the past. The picture is, thus, not really there; it has not been there since it was first hung, more than a hundred years ago. But everyone who enters the refectory remembers having seen it, as indeed they did see it, a moment before. Photographs, of course, show a blank wall. Even the nail on which the painting hung is missing. Even the hole for the nail!

If one of the students responsible for the painting fell silent, however, it would resume its place on the wall without fanfare. Time is elastic: the stutter's mouth does not rip the painting out of time but, like a heavy object on a trampoline, draws time smoothly back with it. Thus it creates a tunnel or funnel into the past. If you brought your eye close enough to a stuttering mouth you might glimpse another world. That world is the land of the dead.

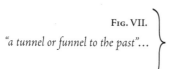

Fig. VII.

"a tunnel or funnel to the past"… }

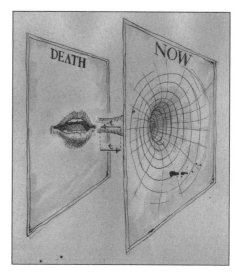

It is a fallacy that the dead lie in the remote past. In fact, they follow hard on our heels. Have you never glanced over your shoulder for no good reason? Some others, we suspect, wait for us in the immediate future, and glance over their shoulders in turn, finding us, perhaps, as uncanny as we find them.

Now, when we say that the dead are in the recent past, we do not mean the past *present* that preceded our own present by a slivered second or two. We mean the past past, the present's past.[9] We did not, in other words, pass through the land of the dead a little while ago without knowing it—the reading that certain jocular critics have given to our teachings. A little while ago it was also the present, as it is always the present (for now), and the land of the dead was then, just as it is now, in the past—*that* present's past. Never current, it is dragged behind us like a net behind a boat, filling up with those we leave behind.

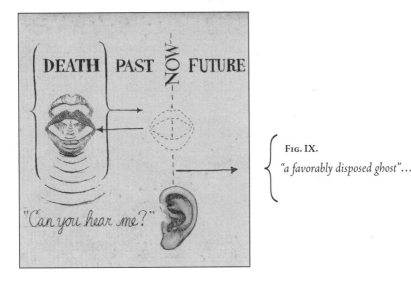

DEATH | PAST | NOW | FUTURE

"Can you hear me?"

FIG. IX.
"a favorably disposed ghost"...

Now, unlike a boat, the present cannot turn around and go back the other way, nor can its passengers pull in that net like fishermen to see what we have caught. Jump overboard we can, but that measure is usually irreversible. No, however closely they follow us, we cannot ordinarily see or hear our dead, no matter how they call to us. But when the mouth of the stutterer is carried back to the land of the dead, a favorably disposed ghost

---

9. Now we are in a position to address a question that may have occurred to the close reader: How does the temporary reversal of time's arrow required to restore life to a suffering Hopsalot differ from that performed in channeling the dead? Answer: The former involves a return to the past present, the latter to the present past. How exactly the two operations differ is apparently highly technical but I am told that the latter requires a highly focused effort, the former mere "bashing about."

can align his or her mouth with the child's and speak through it to the present.[10]

This was advanced necrophysics, forty years ago, but a modern audience is rightly unsatisfied with this explanation. For the dead do not, cannot, speak *in* the present. If they could, the mouth through which they speak would surely have to be in the present, too, and we have shown that the mouth must travel to the past to fill with the voices of the dead. But if they don't speak in the present, how can we hear them?

The astonishing answer: We cannot! We do not hear them, we merely discover retrospectively that we *have* heard them. (Remember that blank wall.)

Fig. VIII.
"relaying the message in slivers"... }

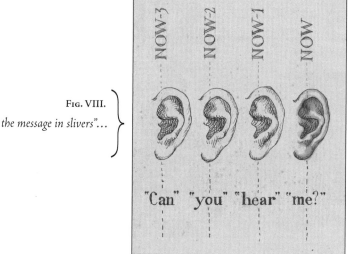

Now, if the dead are only a few seconds in the past, then surely they do not have time to finish saying much before the present falls upon them like a guillotine and cuts them off. But this is not a problem for a skilled ghost speaker. Pleating the fabric of time like a kilt, she dips repeatedly into the past, retrieving and relaying the message in slivers. If she does her job well,

---

10. This poetic description will satisfy most students, but for the technically minded: As the stutterer's mouth travels back in time, time is doubled back on itself. This has particular effects on sound, for if two sound waves that are mirror images of each other—i.e, the peaks on one correspond to the troughs on the other—are played in synchrony, they cancel each other out. The result is silence, a gap in the soundtrack of the world, and an open invitation to the dead.

the listener has the illusion of continuous speech, for though no word is heard, at every moment a word has just *been* heard.

Ghost speakers must train for a long time to avoid any of several common mistakes: One may pause for too long an interval between breaths, creating a dragging or syncopated effect. One may pause for too short an interval, then deliver all the words simultaneously, in a meaningless heap. Finally, one may pause for what amounts to a *negative* interval, starting back for the next word before one has finished the last, or simply overshoot (or undershoot) one's target, with the result that one delivers the words in reverse order or, more frequently, repeats words or parts of words—a result that, coincidentally, may sound (have sounded) a great deal like stuttering.[11]

These technicalities are of interest mainly to the scientist. Once we have mastered the art, it no longer requires conscious effort to speak as and for the dead. Eventually we become aware that we have been doing it all along, that every one of the words we speak was said first by someone else. We say "I," and can no longer remember who we meant. Our diary entries are so many obituaries of persons unknown. We are ghosts, channeling ghosts, who channeled ghosts. The part of us that occupies the present is a dimensionless ring through which phantoms flow, and that is why our student IDs feature, in place of a photograph, a hole.

---

11. Whether this factitious stuttering creates a second puncture in the fabric of reality, this time in the past, perhaps opening a space to the past *of the past*, rather than the past of the present, and thus affording an opportunity for the dead *of the dead* to speak, is sheer speculation, and it is outside the scope of this survey to comment on whether it may have something to do with the appearance of those curious "mouth objects" on which the Founder became focused late in her career—of which more anon.

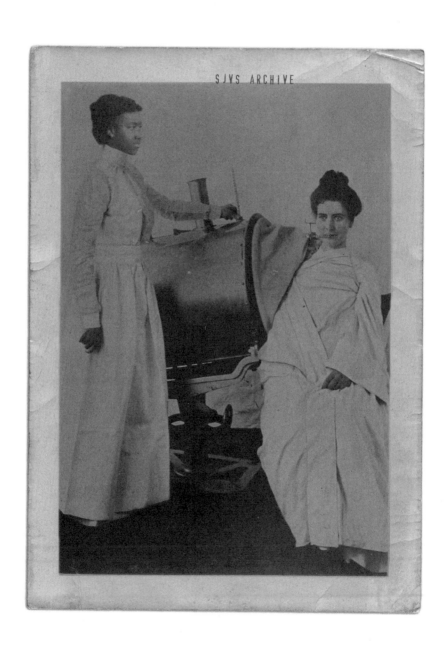

Letters to Dead Authors, #3

Dear Ms. Brontë (Charlotte),

I am—but I shall not introduce myself. I expect you know me, as I have known you since I was a little girl. If not, I hope you will forgive my boldness in so writing.

Today I nearly lost another of my students, a stupendously talented girl whose rejection of the letter G was so absolute that it shaped every aspect of her life. She had appeared on the stoop one day, a dour little personage in breeches and a cap. (Unable to pronounce *girl*, she had been living as a boy for the last four or five years of her brief existence.) She was from Georgia, we eventually ascertained—poor creature! she could not tell us—and had hopped a series of freight trains to get here. Tell me, pray, how she could do this, when she very nearly could not do anything at all? It took great con-centration for her to wake without waking, sleep without sleeping, dream without dreaming—to make, without the progressive tense, any progress at all. She must have picked her way across six states in a series of discrete acts, separated by voids. The present moment was a tribulation to her.

I calculated that she would thrive in death, if anyone would, and I taught her the way. Cocksure, she tried to cross too soon. She would have made it, just the same, but when she scraped against her tonsils, she hesitated long enough to see that she was *dying* instead of *dead*, and so got stuck, halfway down her own throat. (Forgive me, I do not have leisure at present to explain how we get to the land of the dead—but I am forgetting that you already know!) Thankfully, little 'arriet came running, bleating about a "sucking place" and a "mouth with bootlaces" by the washroom sink, and I knew at once what had happened. I rolled up my sleeve, forced my arm down the hole, and towed her out by the tongue.

'arriet asked me why I could not ask one of the dead to push her back from the other side. Perhaps some of them—of you—might be capable, but for the most part you are simply no longer concentrated enough to exert much force in any one direction. You are more like descriptions of people than people. I do not mean to say that you are *diaphanous*—certainly not! Do you perceive how weary I am of that word, of which the ladies of the Harmonial (Hormonal!) Sisterhood are so fond? No—you are solid enough, at least in part. But you are not exactly entities. You are more like situations.

I am in low spirits. Today a girl I saw right here in Cheesehill, asking a grocer for pa-pa-parsnips, and pointing to pears, and on whom I had set my heart, now that little 'mily has left us, for the part of E, or I should say, *not-E*, in my Analphabetical Choir, has declined the scholarship I was prepared to offer her, though it mean firing our laundress, and wearing dirty linens for a year, and says she will not come.

I must have her! Her stammer is beyond anything. Her eyes bulge, her ears turn tomato red, her hands clench, and from her open mouth comes . . . emptiness itself. A humming, fizzing absence, in which I can already hear the distant voices of the dead. I could barely make out the "no" in it, and indeed I thought—hoped—that she wished to say yes but simply (simply!) could not pronounce it, a problem with which I am familiar, and so, while she was still sputtering, I grasped her by the shoulders, told her she might simply nod if she agreed, and asked again, would she come. Where-upon she shook her head so vehemently that her wet bonnet strings—she had been chewing on them—struck me in the face.

There are lies put about in this town. But I mean to have my way, and my Eve, in the end!

Adamantly,
Headmistress,
SJVSGSHMC

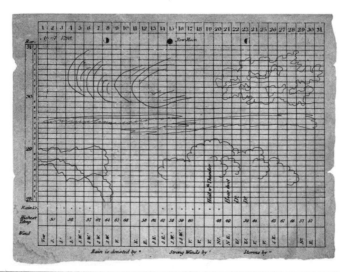

4. The Final Dispatch, contd.

It is easy to forget what you are about, in the land of the dead. Then the scenery with its painted birds and thistles is jerked up into the flies, with a rattle whose associations it is better to ignore. The world goes white.

[Pause, sound of breathing.]

For the moment, I remember only that I am chasing a child. Apparently I must save her. She is not far ahead, on the next page, or the next but one, I hear the shushing of her feet. The dry air, by which I mean the page, carries sound, by which I mean these words in which I say that sometimes she skips, like the child she is, as I never was. Sometimes she stops, to rest, or to wait for me, or for some other reason, I don't know why a child stops, I was never a child.

Setting down one word after another, I make my way to the end of the page, which swings open like a door, as it always does, and shows me nothing, as it always does.

Or something, why not. A clue to keep me going, a little shoe, say, one lace trailing, looping over itself, like the flourish of an old-fashioned signature, but I don't believe it. The shoe is plausible; the lace, though, gives the game away. For when I said "the little shoe," that "little" betraying a sentimentality I am surprised to identify in myself, what took shape was a faded red Mary Jane, a little worn, and yet a Mary Jane does not have laces, nor do we permit play shoes in the school, but only school-issued black leather oxfords, bought at discount, sturdy and unimpeachable, which the students must sign out from Supplies. Those do have laces, and yet the one who is ahead of me, if I know her, keeps her laces tied, as surely as she keeps her wits about her. So it is not her shoe. So it is not a shoe at all. So I made it up.

[Crackling] *Save her!*

As for my wits, never mind.

Save her!

Maybe a dropped handkerchief instead, one of many bought in bulk from a Hebrew gentleman from Brooklyn, New York, issued every Sunday, surrendered to Housekeeping every Friday. If your nose runs on Saturday you are out of luck. Today must be Saturday. There is no handkerchief.

Save her!

No shoe and no handkerchief. No matter. I may be fortunate. Suppose she dropped a hairbrush, like the witch's daughter in the story. I could then expect it to spring up into a thicket or a mountain range. I should count my blessings and keep a weather eye out for personal grooming tools.

Or worse things. A doll made of— Are you receiving?

I race on. O'er the drifting sand, though it is not sand. It is not snow either, yes yes, that has been established. I race on. But for all my haste I have the impression that I am not moving at all, that I am sitting upright, eyes almost closed, in my heavy wooden chair, which is angled to face the window, though the shutters are closed, my legs planted like Lincoln's, big hands stiffly crooked over the carved armrests, a small sedate pillow of minutely patterned oilcloth, stuffed to stiffness with horsehair, slowly sliding out from behind my back, and the stern black crepe of my high-necked dress quite, quite still over my chest. The lamp burns low. Light is coming through the cracks in the shutters, blueing the black of my old-fashioned leg-o'-mutton sleeve in soft stripes, so that it looks almost tropical, some jungle animal lying in wait beside me. My mouth is open a crack, but no breath moves through it; under my lids a crescent of eye is drying.

Or, another thought, that they have boxed me up, couldn't wait, that the toes of my best kid boots are bent against ~~mahag~~ mahogany (cosmetically softened with silk), my hands folded, probably with the help of a mallet, into a semblance of prayer, my cheeks rouged (one slightly redder than the other) in the conventional transvestism of death, all my instructions ignored . . . my strongbox forced, my will[12] removed and burned to ashes . . . [Rapid breathing.]

In short, I have the impression that I am dead. That I am no longer a

---

12. See Appendix. —Ed.

necromath, necrographer, necrologist, or·necronaut, but only a corpse. That I have not been traveling, for hours, for what I count as hours, in death, but only for a few minutes, though long enough to have begun soiling my undergarments, and probably ruining the dress as well. So I won't be buried in it, that's a shame, I liked that dress, it was so ugly that everyone feared me in it, for none but a very powerful lady can resemble an eland in a horse blanket and still command obedience. Well, if I am going to ruin my dress I hope I shall ruin the chair as well, I should not like anyone else to sit in it.

But what am I saying, have I not taught that the dead and gone *don't* go, that I in particular will not depart but will reign on in the person of other, weaker characters who will yield precedence to me, as is proper? And should they not sit, as I have sat and through them will continue to sit, on my chair? Of course they should. I shall try to hold my waste. But I am forgetting, such feats are beyond me now, if it is true that I am dead. When I aspersed you, dear listener, with the imputation that you were dampening your institutional underpants, I was perhaps projecting onto you a suspicion that was already making itself felt, but had not yet reached my conscious mind: that I myself was dribbling. That the great, the ultimate incontinence had come.

You, dear listener, are not even taking down these words, since by now you have noticed that I am dead, and have long since pulled the cord that rings the little bell downstairs. Someone has awoken with a snort in a room of suffocating blackness, windowless, such as my lowliest employees occupy, those who must submit to being woken by a little bell in the middle of the night, if it is the middle of the night, I can't remember. Someone has pulled on his brogues and trudged upstairs, carrying a lamp, has approached the door outlined in light, which he knuckles timidly, no, I am mistaken, boldly, even more boldly than required, since he can place the blame for an interruption on you, listener, and is already looking forward to the punishment you will get for waking him from his sleep on such a stupid errand. Receiving no answer, he has knocked again, harder, and hearing nothing still, has begun to feel the justifiable excitement of finding himself witness to calamity, years of fruitless night-watchmanship rewarded at one stroke, and with unaccustomed confidence he has seized the door handle and walked in. He spots me at once. Stops short. Erect in my chair, I seem to be sleeping. Belatedly meeting your terrified, no, tranquil eye, he pulls his forelock, not literally, I merely conform to literary tradition, and takes a step closer.

Perhaps it is an odor that now alerts him to my real condition. How relieved he is, while nonetheless a faint, fine tremor besets his whole body. Disavowing it, he strides around the room as he would not dare to do at any other time, even touching, in this his moment of ascendancy, those objects that must seem to him the regalia of my power—my great inkwell, my stuffed crow, my ear trumpet, my lace mitts. Finally, he touches the very symbol of his servitude, his manhood thrilling in his trousers—no, not that, the great bell cord—and, curling his fingers around it, gives it a mighty tug.

After that, of course, the house rings with voices, all louder than their owners would have dared to pitch them, a day before. As if they wished me to hear, from wherever I was, and know that they still lived and did not fear me any more. Very foolish of them, for they ought to know that I shall return, more terrible than ever.

But if I am really dead, and only imagine myself a necronaut, then how do I know that I have not been dead for years, for decades? You, and my school, and little Eve Finster might be long gone.

Or [static] never have existed at all, for if I can invent a world for my shade to run through, surely I can invent a girl to flee me through it, and another girl at a typewriter, to write it all down.

But now I am frightening myself. In any case I am probably not dead, and all this is just a distraction and a hindrance—a thicket, you might say. (She dropped that hairbrush after all!) Yes, I must get back to—what was it? Winding road, muddy field—then the bird—the thistles—my boots are wet, green burrs cling to my sodden bootlaces, a nice detail, I'm beginning to believe this story, and so back down the bank to the road. Did I say I left the road? I left the road. In more than one sense. I stopped dead, you might say—

The worms! Would I feel them at their work?

I think not; I think all feeling would have ended, for me.

Let's face it, there is no way to know for sure. I might be dead. You might be dead. We might all be dead, pushers of prams and their passengers, shiners of shoes and those whose shoes are shined, all of us unwitting necronauts, inhabiting through the naïve thaumaturgy of our incessant chatter a world as solid as we can make it. But not quite solid enough. Some knowledge of our real estate leaks through—a whisper, a wisp, a wandering light. We call these lapses "ghosts" . . .

[Static, sound of breathing.]

The road!

SPECIMENS

Showing the improvement, by home practice, of those following the

SELF-TEACHING SYSTEM,

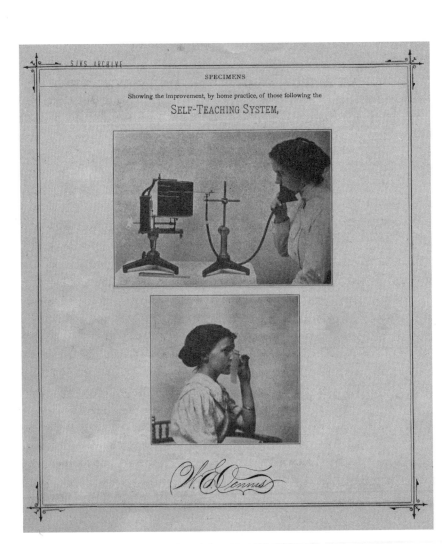

The Stenographer's Story, contd.

I traipsed dumbly around behind Florence for the rest of the day and observed a great many things that made me wonder, but that was no more than I had expected of a school of spiritualism. That I might eventually have dealings with ghosts was a notion that, insofar as it was real to me at all, was rather delicious. More troublesome were my doubts about my own standing as a student, which my reception thus far had scarce allayed.

It was not until the evening meal, while partaking, under the coldly curious gaze of the other students, of a thin, greasy soup in which a few white beans swam, that I finally glimpsed the Headmistress, seated at the high table below her portrait (half visible behind her, a student was posted as before, his back to the assembly)—an ark of a woman, stiff in her whalebone, and with the slightly frowning look of a person listening intently to something almost out of hearing. At one point she dropped her knife to smother a cough in her napkin, and it seemed to me that every spoon paused before dipping again into the broth.

After dinner I was following Florence toward the reading room for an hour of study before evening calisthenics, when Mother Other, overtaking me, dropped a hand on my shoulder. "Do you suppose that my office is a cloakroom or luggage claim repository?"

I indicated that I did not.

"Then I cannot comprehend why you have not retrieved your suitcase from it."

Despite her surly manner I was uplifted at the prospect of seeing my suitcase again, for though it contained nothing of value I felt that my old self was still in some manner bound to it and I was not sure what would become of me without it. I tripped along so close on her heels that I ran into her when she unexpectedly stopped short. The Headmistress, emerging from her office, had signaled to us to wait.

"Who is this?" she said, in that low, hoarse, commanding voice I have come to know almost as well as my own.

"Grandison, miss," I volunteered, though my heart thudded at my presumption.

Mother Other glared. "It's 'Grandison,'" she said, with her manner inserting quotation marks around my name, as if it were false or foolish. "The new girl."

"Can she type?" The Headmistress spoke carefully, as if considering each word for a moment before pressing it into place. Of course, the Headmistress was herself a stutterer. I was obscurely gratified.

Mother Other took a breath, but I got out my "Yes, ma'am," before she had time to speak; I was sure she would assume that one of my age and complexion would not have acquired such training.

"Then come with me, girl. Winnifred, you will excuse us."

I could not type. Nonetheless, I went.

The Headmistress glided into her office ahead of me with the ponderous dignity of an old-fashioned clipper ship. Her stiff skirts creaked and rustled, bellied out as if by a strong sea wind. From this description, over which I have labored, you will see, first: that I am acquiring a passably literary style, and second: that the headmistress affected an old-fashioned mode, viz. a large bustle, whalebone undergarments, and voluminous skirts. These latter were rocked by movements that seemed to have little to do with the body underneath. For a moment I fancied that there was a whole second person under her skirts, moving independently. Then I dismissed this fancy as not just silly but superfluous. At a school that dealt routinely with ghosts there was simply no room for imaginary wonders.

The office of the Headmistress was a somber wood-paneled room with high, shuttered windows. On one wall, above a pneumatic tube and what I identified as the door of a large dumbwaiter, hung a pair of brownish oil paintings that appeared on sidelong inspection to be the matched portraits of a gentleman and lady rabbit in antiquated human attire. A stuffed gray parrot, rather dusty, stood a little atilt on an imposing mantelpiece under which was fitted an iron stove, with a battered coal hod and poker tucked in beside it. On either side of the mantel were numerous built-in shelves and drawers, neatly labeled. Among these, tiers of pigeonholes, perhaps originally intended for filing documents, now housed many small, knobbly, yellowish, translucent objects—anatomical models, I supposed. But the dominant feature of the room was a great old desk, occupied by a blotter; an inkstand; several pens; a dingy little article that, after stooping insensibly for a closer look (sharply: "Do not touch that!") I determined to be a rabbit's foot worn nearly bald; one mechanical device that I recognized; and another, rather larger, that I did not. The former was this typewriter.

(Let me take a moment to say how I love it, my typewriter, for so I privately regard it. I love the gold "Underwood" glowing on the glossy black frame that incidentally, with its beetling forehead, a little resembles the chassis of the car that brought me here. I love the round keys rising smoothly to my fingertips. The oiled hammers tapping down these words, my words, in neat uninterrupted rows.)

The Headmistress gestured at the latter, which possessed a copper coil, a series of nested paper cones, some glass vessels, and a great big burnished brass trumpet—an earlier vintage of the machine I still use. "This is the device that receives my dispatches from the land of the dead."

I nodded calmly. It is one of my great skills to appear tranquil while my vital organs are in turmoil. I developed it in the cruel halls of the Academy for Disadvantaged Girls in Brooklyn, New York, where for a time I was schooled, and honed it to an edge in my aunt's house, and it has saved me, if not from distress, then at least from giving others the satisfaction of knowing they have distressed me.

"Perhaps one day we will devise a way to record dispatches automatically, but for now we rely on the human ear. We employ students to monitor the trumpet and take dictation when required. Unfortunately, Emily Culp . . . We have recently lost a stenographer. Are you capable of long periods of sustained attention?"

"Yes, ma'am."

"You would be obliged to work through the night if necessary."

I expressed my eagerness to forego sleep for the sake of useful employment.

"How is your spelling?"

Happily I was not obliged to lie, for while the Spelling Bee was a bugaboo of mine, since there were so many letters of the alphabet whose names I could not pronounce, I was—on the friendly page—a very fiend for orthography.

"I intend to put you to the test. Are you agreeable?"

I was.

"You will find that communications from the land of the dead are sometimes fragmentary and always strange. I would ask you not to correct seeming errors, unless so instructed, but to take down exactly what you hear through the trumpet, insofar as you can make it out. The silences may be as important as the words, so you will have to make eloquent use of the bitterly inadequate tools of the comma, the period, the ellipsis, and the hard return. Are you fluent in punctuation?"

I tried to say that I was probably more fluent in punctuation than in actual words. "I expect you intend a witticism," she said indifferently, before I could quite get it out, and pressed me into the desk chair, sliding the rabbit's foot out of my reach as she did so. "The device is extremely easy to knock out of alignment. Please do not touch any part of it except, if absolutely necessary, the earpiece. Are you ready? I will go now."

I was then witness to the most astonishing sight of my life.

It is impossible to convey the impression of error and even of abomination that a person's departure to the land of the dead leaves on an unaccustomed witness. Perhaps you have seen a corpse. I have seen a few, and I can tell you that a corpse is several degrees less uncanny than what I saw that day. A corpse is possible; it is even probable, it is in point of fact indisputable, but to die *while living* deals a blow to the expectations of the onlooker from which she does not soon recover. The teachers tell us, I later learned, that one "throws oneself through one's own mouth," but these words, which suggest to me an acrobatic maneuver—a sort of aerial somersault, accompanied by a graphic flash of scarlet tonsils—are at once too concrete and not specific enough. In some ineffable way the Headmistress became steadily more concentrated, especially around the mouth. There was a suspended moment of great tension, and then in one rapid, powerful involution she disappeared. I felt the suction in my own breast and suddenly, fearing that I might faint or part ways with my dinner, I put my head down on the keys—*fghty6!*

The next thing I perceived was a faint, tinny voice emanating from somewhere over my right shoulder.

By now that querulous, metallic, somewhat insectile chirping is even more familiar to me than the Headmistress's naked voice, but it took me a moment to understand what I was hearing. If you regularly employ the telephone, you are, I suppose, accustomed to the notion that a person need not be present to address you as naturally as if she stood before you, but at that time I had experienced this phenomenon only in books and letters, and I was almost as startled as if a printed page had suddenly stretched out an inky hand to clasp mine. Nonetheless I sat up straight, rested my fingers upon the keys in the manner I had seen depicted in advertisements, and (after a brief struggle with the keys that my precipitate nap had jammed) painstakingly typed what I heard, and typing, gained control of my feelings.

I believe I can recite her first sentence verbatim and if I make an error no harm is done for I can later correct it against the original. We do not discard any data recorded in the land of the dead, however negligible. It was as follows: "Not not not not not."

That I was a monstrously slow and clumsy typist you may assume. My fingers were not much more use to me than that rabbit's foot now was to its erstwhile owner, but I stayed calm and got the words down well enough. These amounted to a paragraph or two. Then a point in space disgorged the Headmistress, who plucked my transcript from the device with a whirr of gears and ran a careless eye over it. "Fine. Come again after dinner tomorrow. You will be excused from evening exercises."

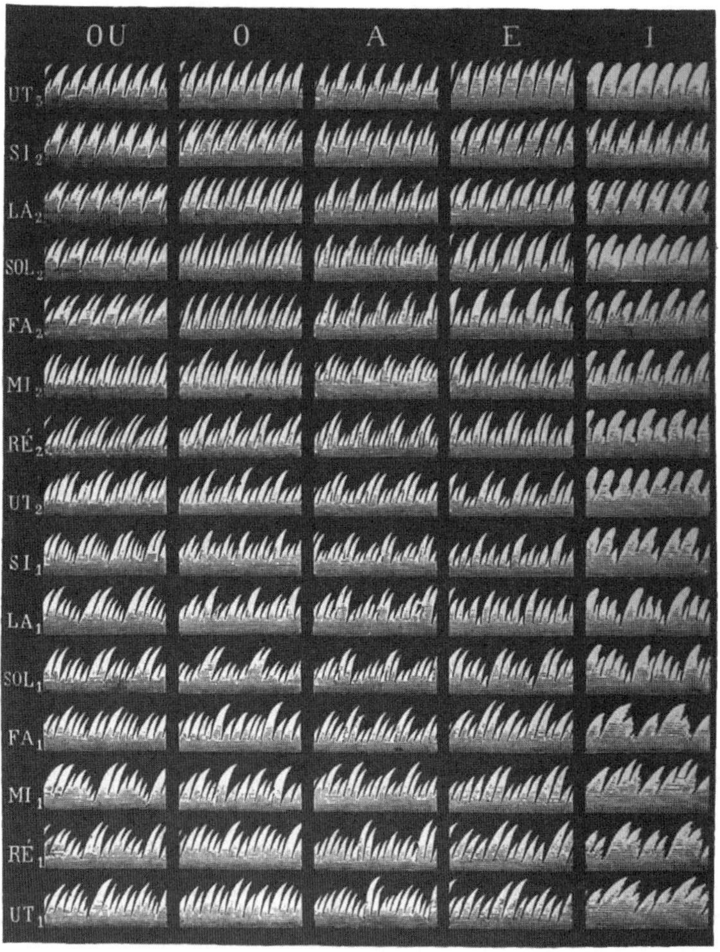
OU
O
A
E
I
UT3
SI2
LA2
SOL2
FA2
MI2
RÉ2
UT2
SI1
LA1
SOL1
FA1
MI1
RÉ1
UT1

Readings

from "A Visitor's Observations"

On Eating and Other Oral Activities

I cannot recommend to gastronomes a dinner at the Vocational School. To delight the palate is no part of the program. In fact, some advanced ghost speakers have their molars removed and, when they are not fasting, take only beef tea, blancmange, stewed prunes, and other soft foods, and this with the liveliest disgust and a modest napkin thrown over head and shoulders, for they consider it an abomination to eat with the same body parts that we use for speech. ("A misstep of evolution as colossal as that afflicting the lady octopus, whose throat affords the only passage to"—Mr. Lieu lowered his voice—"her reproductive organs.")

Others argue that eating is just another form of listening, food a mode of speech intelligible, not to the ear, but to the stomach. Sometimes we make a meal of plain unsalted fact; sometimes we sit down to a stirring romance, with armed conflict, tender interludes, and a thrilling climax.[13] One evening I was privy to a discussion of this thesis in the drafty drawing room reserved for faculty use, after a meal that had certainly felt like a speech—though a long and dreary lecture rather than a yarn. (Now I wonder whether the austere diet that I blamed on the depressing teachings of Dr. Kellogg was not instead a sort of culinary sermonizing.) Present besides myself were several members of faculty; the local physician, Dr. Hiram Beede, a white-haired gentleman with little wet eyes and a tremor; and his protégé, young Dr. Peachie. The Headmistress had excused herself, so there were fewer constraints on our conversation than usual.

As near as I can reconstruct it in layman's terms, the argument put forward by an ebullient Dr. Peachie, whose mien suggested that he was

---

13. It is not unamusing to try to match menu items to literary tropes or rhetorical devices, and indeed some of the work has already been done—"baloney," "flummery," "tripe"!

taking the question rather less seriously than the experts on hand, was that if we admit that food is speech, then (to be consistent with Vocational School doctrine) we must also suppose that food is haunted. The faculty were nodding: Why not? If the material world is, as necrophysics indicates, just language in another form, why shouldn't the dead express themselves not only in vibrations of the air but in, say, chicken wings and buttered biscuits? "Too bad they didn't express themselves that way tonight," muttered Dr. Peachie, who had left most of his dinner on his plate.

Hunger might signal the desire of the dead to speak, someone proposed. "And our eagerness to hear!" another exclaimed.

"We are a captive audience," said the former. "We listen, or we die."

"But that sounds as though the dead are hectoring us, when in fact we *are*—our bodies are made up of—what we retain of their confidences."

"In other words, we are great ears made of words," said Dr. Peachie. "Now this may seem to present a chicken-or-the-egg paradox such as puzzled the ancients: How can our ears be made of words if to hear words we first require ears? But it is no more of one than asserting that our stomachs are made of food, the solution to which is called umbilical cord. The embryo is a small ear growing inside a greater one"—though at this point Dr. Peachie could not contain his laughter.

Several objections occurred to me, and I took advantage of the lull in the discussion to pose them to all present: First, that eating is unlike listening in at least one important respect, that while others' words impose themselves upon us, food we eat willingly or not at all. But I was greeted with looks of puzzled amusement by all the faculty. Finally someone kindly explained to me that I had gravely misunderstood the nature of conversation, in which the listening ear is just as active as the speaking mouth. The ear pulls, so to speak, while the mouth pushes; one is as necessary as the other.

A little crushed, I nonetheless ventured to offer my other, unrelated objection, that if the *entire* world is made up of the words of the dead, to which we listen with our stomachs, then why is it that our hearing is so selective?

For we rarely gobble up cobblestones or fence posts, but are hungry only for the things that do our bodies good.

I expected this objection to meet with no more approval than the last, but had the satisfaction of seeing arrested looks on the faces around the table. "Nearby cattle farmers had better look to their fences!" Dr. Peachie quipped. In fact, one member of our faculty speculated that perhaps we are just not listening hard enough, that those cobblestones fall on deaf ears as it were, but could be digested by a more focused attention. But this idea was not received with much enthusiasm. Another said that perhaps some words are not addressed to us, but to the world at large—say, to cattle, sheep, and other interested parties, such as lettuces.

"Or perhaps our whole world is a soliloquy," said a fellow who had kept silent hitherto, a Mr. Lenore (a drama teacher, as I understand it), "which we overhear only in part." This struck me as all too plausible and by the sober looks of the others I saw that they felt the same. I took leave of the doctor and his protégé and repaired to my bed in a thoughtful mood.

I had thought to prove that language had its roots in mourning. I had been slow to accept that for the Vocational School everything was language. My task was larger than I had thought: Every part of the Vocational School told a story. But an oblique one. I cast my eye around the room. From the ceiling, plaster acorns stared at me in blank entreaty. Cushions nudged and hinted, curtains whispered, the arms of chairs reached out in frozen supplication. Like the students, I would have to learn to listen.

Letters to Dead Authors, #4

Dear Charlotte,

I have seized my Eve, my "'v'"!

It was at the library that I spied her. No, that is incorrect: I heard her, gasping her way through a simple sentence at the desk. When I plunged staring out of the stacks she was just turning to go, wiping her mouth on the back of her hand. She was small, with a high, bulbous forehead that gave her something of a duck's philosophical air, though with her black eyebrows pinched she did not have his kindly looks. Her dress was soiled and ill-fitting.

I gave the librarian, that bitch, a gay wave and went after her.

She mumbled and jinked down Common Place Road, heading into the wind, so that her dirty pink bonnet filled like a gassy gut, and into an ugly little house with rotting gingerbread trim and grass in the guttering. A porch roof sagging one way and its floor the other. I noted a broken sapling in the yard. Someone had bent and twisted it so that the very fibers of the wood had separated. Some unhappiness there. You will think me cruel, but I was glad: It is easier to prise loose from life those children whose roots are already torn and scorched, as I should know.

I pushed open the gate, stuck my foot through a rotten porch step into dust and startled spiders, wrenched it out again, and went up. I did not knock, but went right to the window and put my face to the glass, hoping, I confess, to complete the picture of squalor. Well, I did, but was rudely interrupted. Something—someone—was clinging to my back, and beating at me, and sobbing, and slobbering all over me. She probably thought I was from the WCTU.[14] When I had flung the woman off, for she was slight and far from strong, and deduced that it was the girl's mother (for she had the same peculiarly small and widely spaced teeth), I attempted to press upon

---

14. Woman's Christian Temperance Union. We may assume the lady in question imbibes. —Ed.

her my handkerchief, whereupon the child herself burst through the door and fastened herself onto my back. Apparently this sort of behavior runs in the family; no doubt their ancestors flung themselves on the backs of antelope and nibbled them to death.

However, when I passed my handkerchief to the humid female already described, I had contrived to fold a Gold Certificate note into it. She spread the hankie—brought it toward her nose—lowered her wet lashes—crossed her eyes at the admirable George Washington advancing undaunted toward the double torpedoes of her nose—froze. She hastily extracted the bill, folding it one-handed with great deftness and tucking it into her bodice—and blew her nose.

Meanwhile the daughter, red in tooth and claw, clung to me like a wolverine, raving. Raving circumspectly, for she still avoided the interdicted vowel. Mother and daughter were alike, I perceived, in possessing a talent for calculation during moments of seeming abandon. I felt no indignation at this thespianism, only admiration and pleased anticipation, for I perceived that whatever the daughter felt, the mother was not at all indifferent to the persuasions of the pocket.

I do not wish you to think that I am so improvident or so desperate as to purchase all my students! But this one was worth, I thought, some inducement.

Seizing the girl's hands, I distastefully unhitched her from my collar and placed her in front of me. She soon stopped struggling; I am not frail, despite a cough I cannot shake, and that odd distemper of my heart that makes it leap and flounder late at night. "Your mother has something to say to you," I said. I took in her leaky nose and glaring eye and recoiled. (Even scrubbed, sluiced, and deloused she is no cinnamon bun but it is probably this extreme unlovableness, rare in a child, that warms me to her. A negative charisma has a power of its own.)

Mrs. Finster (although, forgive me, I doubt she was ever married) touched her bodice, hesitated, spoke. "Eve, be polite to the lady. You're to—" There was a question in her eyes.

"To come with me," I said heartily, and not without malice, "to be a student—a *scholarship* student," I added with a glance at the mother, then recoiled when she simpered back, "of the necromantic arts. Make haste and gather up your things. You will have room for a small bundle of keepsakes. Pack no clothing or shoes; you will be issued a uniform."

Of course she could not say "yes," dear friend. *Yes* contains an *e*.

So "No," said Eve, soon to be Finster (we go by last names here).

Nonetheless, we went.

Yours very sincerely,

H_admistr_ss Sybil Joines

p.s. The cost of this exploit: 20 green American dollars, and cheap at the price.

318 Taken 1903
as we 1903

5. The Final Dispatch, contd.

But if we are all dead, then there is certainly no rush to catch the girl who, no matter how I fling myself forward, down the road I fling forward before me, remains [indistinct]. And yet . . . so I hitch [. . .] if I just [. . .]

[Extended rustling, footsteps, rapid breathing.]

So am I [indistinct] after all?

But wait, there *is* a way to tell! Any moment now, if I'm dead, someone will open her throat to me, so that I may remind her of my will and her duty. And if that does not happen, then I am not dead, or there has been some delay, or something. That is not very conclusive. But if it does happen, then I am certainly dead, for I believe—I am quite sure—I am at least fairly sure that it is not possible for the living to channel those who, though among the dead, are only visiting, though now that I think of it, I am not sure at all.

By gum, I think I have hit on something. By gum, I think we should put it to the test. If I am not dead I will act on it immediately. If I am dead I will tell someone else to act on it immediately. Either way someone will act on it immediately.

I feel much better. And so I am better. My shoes have eyelets. My nails have cuticles. In other words, I have spontaneously come out in details that a moment ago were beyond me. My fichu even has a few specks of blood on it. And look, here's the road, firming up underfoot, curving back toward the trees, and, nestled under them, trying to look inconspicuous, old Sabin's sugar shack, which I have always suspected of encroaching on school property, make a note of it.

And now another idea comes to me, I am really brilliant today: that it might be possible (dead or alive) to speak through more than one throat at once. Thus composing a sort of one-woman barbershop quartet. Or choir. Or—fancy the whole school speaking in my voice! Chattering to myself in a hundred accents over thin vegetable soup and a slice of bread smeared with bacon fat until I yell *Quiet!* and bang my cane on the long table so that the forks jump; sneaking away with myself into the bushes to grope inside my stained underpants with cold little fingers and tell myself no, no, and yes, yes, and no, no, all right, but I'm not going to kiss it; standing up in front of myself, my buttocks tight with self-regard, and lecturing myself until my eyes glaze with boredom; prying open my mouths and prodding my tongues with pencils and leading myself in exercises to stretch my embouchure until my tonsils bleed; croaking in chorus, invoking myself, my dead self, and when I fail to speak saying *Hold out your hand* and bringing my ruler down upon my already swollen, already reddened palm, and with vicious satisfaction raising the ruler again, and with fear stifling a plea, and with curiosity in which pleasure is mixed with apprehension looking on, unconsciously rubbing my own palms; somewhere stealing a few coins from the little box that I mistakenly think no one else knows about; somewhere snapping out a command, and somewhere pushing a wad of bread into my cheek with my tongue, replying *Yes, ma'am*; and somewhere bending myself over a bench and forcing myself painfully up my tender bottom and whispering distasteful endearments into my ear and later stabbing myself with a butter knife and shouting incoherent damnations over my corpse on which I then urinate until I shoot the lock and burst in *en masse* shouting imprecations and take myself in custody and bear myself downstairs to our oubliette and leave myself there to whimper to myself all alone in the dark as in the walls the mice mutter in my voice— Oh horrible—[static, hissing, distant howling]

Compose yourself!

The road, leaving field and thistles and birds behind, has dipped back down into the ravine. It is not necessary to be more specific. In any case, here in the deep shade of the trees, all details are indistinct. Somewhere a fungus is grunting. Under the rotting leaves, the infant dead are telling their monotonous secrets. I know better than to listen to their whispers. Or glance around for their pale heads, pushing up the leaves like puffballs.

Yet I seem to be a little out of sorts. Something came up that troubled me, I can't remember what. [Pause, sound of breathing.]

I remember now. The question: If I am inventing the world around me, as of course I am, am I inventing the girl as well?

Oh, I hope she is real, because if she is not, how can I slake this *save her* burning in my throat?

If she's real, she is inventing the world around her, too, there being no other way to travel here. Golly! I might turn the page and see, say, a gloomy water mill, whacking the stream with black and rotting paddles, a stream that is not speaking or even thinking of anything, least of all of me.

How happy I'd be just to stand on a piece of dirt I didn't have to shit out first, if you'll excuse the expression.

Secretary, mark for redaction.

Let us get out of this ravine now. Suddenly I have had quite enough of it. Fields, that's better, and I do not mind the rustling in the grass, if it is grass, though there is no wind here.

It is possible that, just as I have remade the landscape, I could remake her. There is another possibility, however: that if I could remake her, she could remake me! And do not be alarmed, but if she could remake me, then she could make me. And if she could make me, she may have already made me. In which case I do not exist *and never did.*

[Pause, static.]

Oh, I consider it unlikely. It is not at any rate as likely as the opposite hypothesis, that I made her, and even that is less likely than that we are both here, self-made, or made by God and our parents, if you prefer, which I don't. But it is just possible that she, running through the land of the dead, imagined herself pursued, wanted to be pursued, and so created me to follow her. [Pause.] It would even answer some questions, as for instance, why do I want to catch her? Students have disappeared before, if I remember correctly. When it happens, I feel some regret, if only for lost revenues. I even fetch them back. I believe I fetched you back, once. But I do not generally hurl myself through my own mouth in hot pursuit. Why this time? I wish I could remember. Is it possible that I care?

Why not? Other people care, it would seem.

Is it really easier to believe that I am a figment of her imagination, that I wish to follow her because I was created to follow her, having no other purpose?

Yes, it is easier.

Though even easier to imagine the cognate possibility: that I created her so that she might flee me, because I wanted to chase something I could never catch.

The problem, of course, is that I cannot really care about something that I invented solely so that I might care about something. I am not such a sucker as that.

Suppose that she did invent me. Did she just want someone, anyone, to run after her, or me in particular? Surely the wish for an unspecified "someone" would not produce me of all people. But would she really bring into being someone (me) who imagines that she (me again) could bring her (Finster) into being? Would she—*could* she bring into being someone who really could bring her into being? Or even someone who actually *had?*

Oh I am lost. [Static.]

Oh where am I. [Static, sound of breathing.]

That was a close call. That's why only the strongest personalities ought to safari here, those who can hold on to an *idée fixe* for grim life. I have the grip of a raptor, but my concentration lapsed, I forgot that in the real world effects may not precede causes. *Nota bene!* To such rules we travelers must adhere, arbitrary as they seem. Books may not write their authors. Little girls may not invent their fathers, I mean their mothers, I *mean* their teachers.

We are not in the real world, however, as is obvious from the tiny lowercase letters dropping like ash on my sleeves, gathering in the folds of my gown. Here, it is probably possible. Possibly probable, though if so, it is equally probable that I invented her so that she might invent me. So that I might invent her. So that she might invent me. So that I might invent her. So that she might invent me. So that I might invent her. So that she might invent me. So that I might invent her. Are you getting this down? Dear listener, you may think that this can't go on forever. It can. Here, it can. Death is where *everything* goes on forever. [Laughter, extended fit of coughing, several words inaudible.]

So, the road. *My* road. To the school. I plant one foot on it. Then another. Then another (no, not a third foot, the first one again). Obediently, the world assembles itself around me: rutted track, grassy fields, scattered trees.

A little more detail, please. Road: brown, ridged, its puddles reflecting the clouds. Grass: black and curly as your hair. Tree trunks wet. Leaves shuddering, showing their ribbed undersides. Smell of ozone. Letters falling.

As I said, it takes a strong personality.

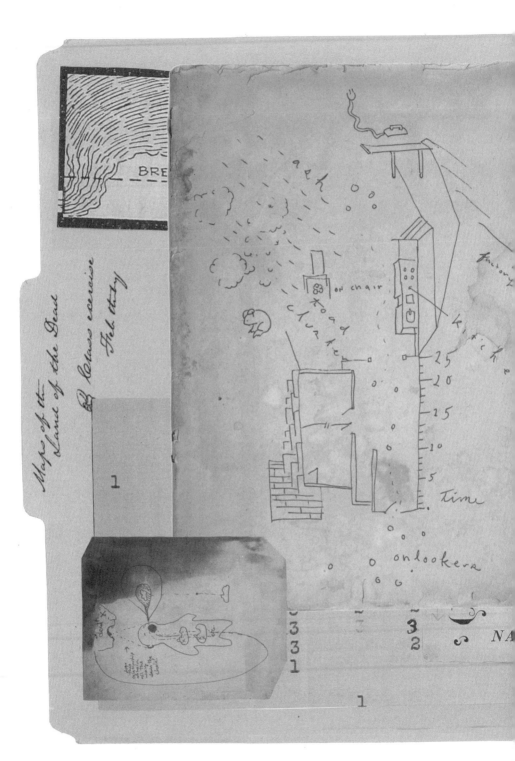

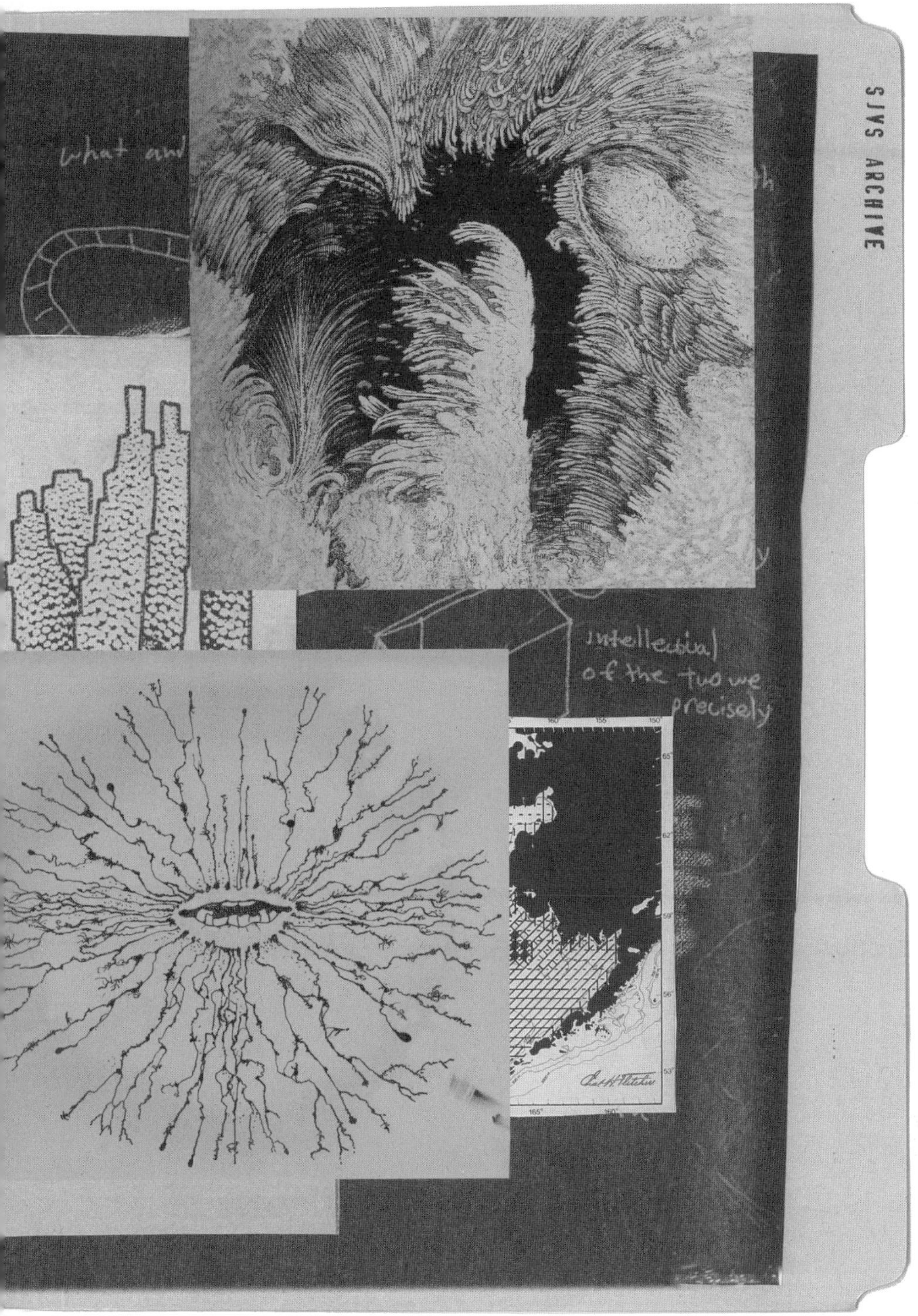

what and

intellectual
of the two we
precisely

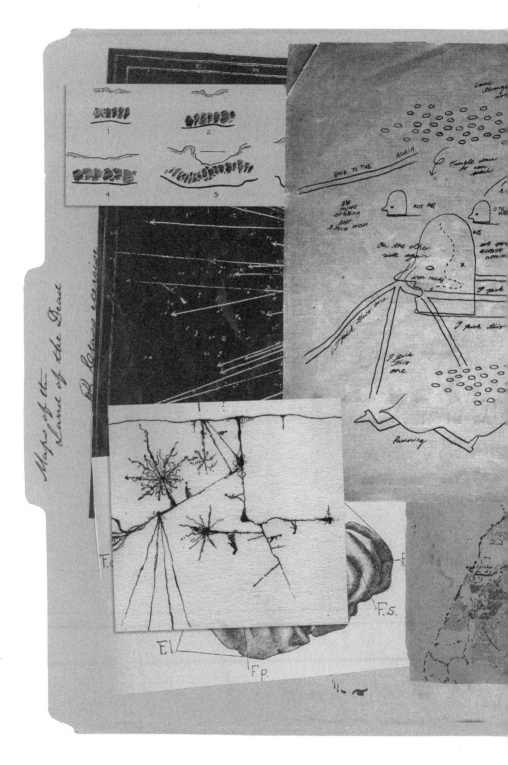

LAND & DEAD

Normal	Returning
Dead	Asleep
Dying	Speaking

5

The Stenographer's Story, contd.

Mother Other was waiting in the hall when I emerged. I had the impression that she had been standing there—patient, stolid, almost inanimate—ever since I had gone inside.

"That was quick work," she said, not entirely approvingly. "You earned the right to call yourself a student, first of all, and I must say I was surprised that you got even that far, and yet you've gone farther and made your way, God knows how, into the private service of the Headmistress." Gesturing to me to follow, she set off down the hall, adding over her shoulder, "I certainly didn't see anything special in the poor, small, and approximate personage you appeared to be. But it seems I must adjust my opinion of you. The Headmistress does not bestow such a privilege without good reason."

"You had better adjust not just your opinion but also your behavior!" I said, with an impressiveness somewhat impaired by the necessity of taking a few skips down the echoing hallway to catch up. I almost laughed, hearing myself speak so boldly. Nonetheless, a secretary had the right to expect considerations that a mere student could not, and I decided to press my advantage. "You can start by bringing me my suitcase, which you seem strangely reluctant to relinquish! I wonder what a person like yourself could want with my poor belongings. Can it be that you suspected from the start that I would distinguish myself? If so, you should have been on better behavior, since someone who has the ear of the Headmistress is in a position to demand respect from those who are less fortunate, even if they have earned some status of their own through long if not necessarily distinguished service." And now I did laugh, appreciatively, as if at someone else's words. As before, I felt that I was receiving assistance from some nearby quarter and was buoyed by the feeling that I was wanted. I had been very little wanted, lately.

"You are making a silly mistake," said Mother Other, nettled by my laugh, "if you think that, having won your way into the inner sanctum of the

Headmistress with unusual speed, you will as quickly win her confidence. It's even possible that she admitted you just to keep an eye on you. I wouldn't be surprised if she identified you as a troublemaker from the beginning, and is only biding her time before putting you out on your ear. But"—here she sucked her lips into her mouth, so that they quite disappeared—"that's not for me to say."

She led me silently through an odd little dogleg corridor, poorly lit, and turned onto a wider hallway lined with closed doors. The round window at the near end, against which gusts of rain were rattling, gave me the clue I needed to identify my surroundings: we were approaching her office once again, but from the opposite direction. "The secretary finds her way unerringly through the labyrinthine corridors," I said to myself with satisfaction.

Mother Other was saying, "You're correct in thinking that such notice from the Headmistress is a rare honor, and even I feel a little awed when I think of it, but that awe is for the condescension the Headmistress is showing, not for you, and you entirely misunderstand your position if you think that it entitles you to throw your weight around and give commands to people who have proven their worth"—she pinched a key out of her reticule and rattled it angrily in the lock—"over what you correctly identify as years of loyal service. The reverse is even true. The higher your position in the school the less you should put yourself forward. It would be only a slight exaggeration to say that the most successful student would be one who isn't here at all, despite appearing on all the rolls: an empty uniform, a cavity in the shape of a schoolgirl, and whose voice is about as loud as a louse's."

She pushed open the door and I followed her into the office, which seemed smaller and dingier than it had that afternoon, and reeked of cat. "It would certainly be more comfortable for you if I took your words to heart and made myself scarce," I said, as she threw open a closet and began to rummage through a heap of clothing and other odd articles—a fencing mask, an animal trap, a hat block. "But you'll excuse me if I take my cues from the Headmistress herself. Or failing that, use my own judgment, rather than relying on advice dealt out by someone who is if anything farther from the horse's mouth than I am, advice that if not intentionally misleading may well reflect some fundamental misunderstanding."

I would do anything, *anything*, I thought, to speak like this forevermore, smooth as a politician or a printed page.

"The horse's mouth?" She cast a choleric look back at me from the depths of the closet. "Is that any way to speak of a woman whose dignity ought to make you weak at the knees? Better not to speak of her at all!" She tugged at the handle of my suitcase, already half buried in the heap. "If I do misunderstand the Headmistress's intentions, it's because they are far beyond what the rest of us can grasp, including young ladies who don't know anything and yet have a high opinion of themselves." Grunting, she hauled it out, employing her foot to hold back an umbrella and several hair ribbons that had attached themselves to it. "Here's your portman-teau. You're wrong in thinking that I had some desire to keep it; in fact I'll be glad to be rid of it, and have been waiting impatiently for you to take it off my hands." She thumped it down before me, adding, "After you have fetched any little keepsakes from it, you will have to check it into long-term storage. It is too large for your personal area." She stepped back, folding her arms.

"I won't deny that I was afraid I might never see it again," I said. I picked it up, almost overbalancing, and teetered to the door. On the threshold I turned. "I beg your pardon for my mistakes, this one and any others I may have made since arriving here. It's true that I know nothing yet about how things are done here, but how can I learn except through the help of those I meet along the way? And perhaps one day I may myself be in a position to help those who had the foresight to help me."

Mother Other said nothing but clumped to the door and held it— though it was already open—as I dragged my suitcase through.

The case seemed even heavier than before, and as I lugged it toward the dormitory I became possessed by the irrational conviction that Mother Other had put, had perhaps *planted* something in it to discredit me. I laid it down, flipped open the clasps, and lifted the lid.

A clawed cloud of fur and feathers exploded from within. I fell back on my hands. The cat, for it was he, whisked out of sight, leaving the shape of his body impressed into my belongings, along with a welter of bloody feathers, not a few tufts of his own white fur, and two tiny clenched bird feet.

After a moment of blank terror, I saw what must have happened, and that it was perfectly innocent after all, if trespass and slaughter can be called innocent. Mother Other, having pawed through my things, must have left my suitcase ajar, and later shut it again without noticing that the cat, having caught the bird, had found there a cozy place to torture and then eat it. I considered my possessions, now dotted with clumps of bloody down—a flowered nightgown that was too tight across the chest and that in any case I would not be allowed to wear here; a little stuffed donkey named Doe, well worn; a book or two (one still bearing the stamp of the Academy for Disadvantaged Girls in Brooklyn, New York). They looked naked, forlorn, embarrassed. What had I wanted them for? I threw them away. I checked my empty suitcase into long-term storage. It is probably still there.

That night I lay awake under sheets tight as bandages, listening to all the new sounds around me, and staring up into the darkness, which the swaying boughs outside the tall unshuttered windows made to shift and flicker. There were tears cooling symmetrically in the cups of both ears. Occasionally a new tear slid down to join them. Donkey Doe, Donkey Doe! I thought. I felt I had committed a murder of which I was also somehow the victim, and that the school had made me do it. But slowly my misery eased. I felt how my breath was emptying invisibly into the volume of air above me and being replaced. Someone passed the open door with a lamp; vanes of light turned across the floor, glanced across my bed, bent up the wall, raced into the rafters, and vanished. "She has come. She has not yet proved her worth, but the school knows its mistress," I said to myself, of myself. "She smiles. She turns her face into the pillow. She sleeps."

I smiled. I turned my face into the pillow. I slept.

Thus, my first day at the Vocational School.

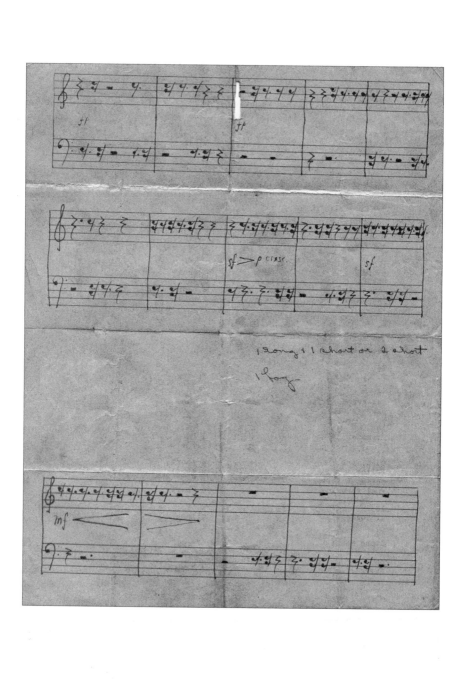

1 long + 1 short or 2 short

1 long

Readings

from "A Visitor's Observations"

On Methods of Listening

Sooner or later, all talk of listening comes back to the ear. Training it is a large part of the curriculum. The young students spend hours quietly attending to the different sounds the wind makes chivvying the ivy on the walls, hustling dry leaves across the playfields and gardens, cracking a rope against a flagpole, dragging a sharp stick across a window, or thwacking the heavy, stained sheets hung out to dry. Then they move on to softer sounds: a crumb of dirt rumbling down an anthill, a rose petal snapping open, the footfall of a fly. The first few times that on my own rambles through the grounds I came across a solitary, still figure all in black, with goose-pimpled legs and runny nose, standing half inside a bush, face intent, or hanging over the crumbling ring-wall of the well, ear cocked to its depths, a laugh was startled out of me, but I soon grew accustomed to the sight, and would sometimes stop and listen for a while myself, trying to figure out what the child was hearing.

I gathered that listening to the faintest knocking, creaking, and rustling was meant to tune the ear to the often very similar sounds made by the dead. For the voices of the dead never sounded fully human. They had a strangely impersonal, accidental quality that made it difficult to attend to them for long; one's attention lapsed, letting them subside into background noise. At times one had the impression that this was, in fact, what the modest dead wanted. The fanciful will sometimes catch, when listening to the wind, what sounds like a muffled word or two. Just so, the students sieved the rattle of grass seeds, the sizzle of horseflies for hints of meaning.

At first I thought this was teaching by analogy, that by cultivating an aural pareidolia the listener sensitized herself to the hints of rational language in the hissing, seething diction of the dead. But no. Apparently the dead really did speak in these accidental noises, not just through the throats of the experienced channeler. Any hole the world opened could become a throat, any object impinging on another could be a tongue, teeth, velum, alveolar ridge.[15]

How can this be? "Maybe to the dead," the Headmistress said, "there is not much difference between a human being and a cabbage leaf perforated by a worm. The cabbage, too, may feel that it is special . . . To congratulate oneself on being human may be sheer parochialism. Ought ice to be proud that it is not water? Well, necrophysics tells us that inanimate objects are to us as water is to ice, the same substance in a different state."

I cannot pronounce myself wholly convinced, but the possibility has made my relations with the world around me a degree more cordial. I feel myself surrounded, if not by mothers and sisters, then at least by cousins of some degree, and often seem to catch a fleeting family resemblance in the tiled corner of a public washroom or a rag stuffed into a broken windowpane.

I should not leave the subject of listening without mentioning an eventual change in the views of the Headmistress. While the official position of the Vocational School was that all sounds were semiotic when properly understood—a principle laid down by the Headmistress herself—her private views were undergoing a transformation. She was no longer convinced that even human speech was semiotic. That we generally made sense of it was no proof that it made sense; we are also prone to discover faces in mildew stains. When we think we are conversing rationally, we are merely, like a tree, *rustling*.

I have not yet spoken of music. I remember a gray morning early in my stay when, still groggy from a sleep both too deep and too brief, I thrust open my casements and leaned out to try to identify the sound that, mingling with my dream to supply the hoarse bellow of a charging ice-walrus, had interrupted my repose. Though I heard nothing out of the ordinary,

15. Naturally, the dead rarely speak fluently or for long through these accidental orifices, nor are most of us humble enough to take advice from a dishcloth flapping on a line.

I decided to investigate. I splashed a little arctic water onto my unshaven chops, threw a coat over my robe and slippers, and slip-slapped down the deserted stairs toward the Chapel of the Word Church, through whose doors a few stragglers were hurrying. At the last minute reconsidering, having not yet been expressly invited to attend services (especially not in pajamas), I impulsively plunged into the shrubbery, to the detriment of my slippers, and took up a position under a stained-glass window that probably looked better from the inside, representing something gruesomely anatomical that later revealed itself to be a part of the inner ear.

So it was there, up to my ankles in grass so wet from dew that I might as well have been standing in a pond, that I first heard the orchestral silence (punctuated by the odd gasp) of twenty-six stutterers in concert. Later I would learn it was the old workhorse "Music for Stammererers" (sic) that I had heard—if one can call that hearing. I had the strange feeling that music was being sucked *out* of my ears rather than fed into them. I thought I caught a snatch of an organ-grinder's song I had heard a couple of days before, and of the exertions of my landlady's daughter back home, plunking her way through The Well-Tempered Clavier. Afterward, wading back through the grass, I felt quiet and hollow.

I eventually came to love this music, in which the tension between being unable to say and being unable to stop saying that is most characteristic of the stutterer's speech was elevated to an aesthetic principle.

Correct Position for Complete Breathing.

Filling the Upper Lobe of the Right Lung.

Nerve Vitalizing Breath.

Cleansing Breath.

Letters to Dead Authors, #5

Dear Mr. Nathaniel Hawthorne,

I stop by the dormitory at night to imagine the ghosts rushing in and out, in and out of the ranks of open mouths. The wind rattles the windowpanes. The whole building is dark. Even the night watchman is catching forty winks in his tiny room, as I allow him to do between circuits of the building and the grounds. Only I am awake.

My " 'v' "—the girl Finster—sleeps hard, her face turned into the pillow, her jaw set, as if sleeping were a task demanding great concentration, as if the night were a ledger filled with figures she is obliged to pore over in agonizing search of a missing zero. To tell the truth she faces the day with much the same look. She is a knot of incomprehension and rage, so I expect great things of her.

Yesterday I left something on the nightstand beside her bed that I had fashioned on a walk through the countryside: a figure made of forked sticks and leaves. This was the only sort of doll I played with as a child, since my father did not hold with toys for children. It was not to be cuddled, but held secretly in the palm of the hand, and then crushed.

It was not there last night, but she was clutching something, and I bent close to see. It was not the doll, but a stuffed toy, stubbled and blind and so shapeless that its species was anyone's guess—was that an ear or a paw? She whimpered as I pried it from her insensate fingers, but did not wake.

Though I can still see the letters that I form, it is dark where I sit on the small terrace overlooking the sculpture garden. Yet above me birds flash, as bright as sparks from a burning building. There is a rational explanation: The sun is setting behind the hills, and I am in their shadow, but the birds are not.

Today I burned Finster's toy, while she screamed and raved. That is what we do with obstacles to our ends. Only when you have lost everything can you open yourself completely to the dead.

Perhaps I used a little excess vigor, prodding the limp form, already almost entirely consumed, until it belched enough smoke to make my eyes water.

The terrace is the last place on school grounds to catch the sun, which is why I sought it out, after this melodrama, but darkness fell sooner than I expected, and with it has come the cold that was perhaps always there, under the sunlight. From the stone bench and the flagstones the chill seeps into me.

Now the darting sparks have gone out and in their place black flecks of ash swoop and twitter against the deepening sky.

In the distance, a rectangle of yellow opens, making the surrounding darkness absolute. It calves; a light moves away from the bank of lights that is the school, winding its way through the garden. It is Clarence, looking for me. He will go to the gazebo, first. Now he is at the gazebo. Then he will go to the labyrinth. Now he is at the labyrinth. He will hesitate at the entrance. He is hesitating. He will call for me. I cannot hear him. Then he will go into the labyrinth, and he will get lost.

Next day. I left my pen and letter on the bench and went to rescue Clarence, who was very grateful to see me, though at first alarmed by my shadowy figure advancing through the shrubbery. It is strange that the domestic staff of this school, though perfectly accustomed to such manifestations of the spirit world as table-tapping, ectoplasm, and spirit voices, are nonetheless subscribers to a callow and baseless fear of "ghosts"—by which they seem to mean a white sheet on a stick, moaning.

I thought it best to guide him back inside, and so this letter camped on the terrace overnight, becoming, as you may perceive, somewhat stiff and warped, and suffering indignities from a literary slug—see its silver footprint here. Discovering my abandoned efforts on my morning constitutional, I picked up my pen, induced it once again to flow, and am now ready to return to my topic. But I have forgotten what it was.

No, I had no particular topic, only the feeling that something fanged was chewing its way up my throat.

When I was a little girl I liked to shake my head until I got dizzy, my braids rhythmically lashing my face, my lips slewing back and forth and slinging spit across my cheek. I wanted to shake some obstruction out of my throat or my eyes or my ears or all three. Later it seemed to me that what I had sought riddance of was just *myself*. Though still small, I was already in my way. It even sometimes seemed to work, if I remember right, and released me for a few minutes or an afternoon to a paradise of clear cold air, black sticks, berries as bright as fire, and the frozen violence of blades of grass. But later I blocked my own view entirely, and no longer even tried to clear a path to that crystal world. I perceived no obstacle, because I had become it; the Sphinx was my own self.

Maybe this is why I like the long lost better than the living. I would not want them back: I like them just *because* they're lost. The dead are not quite there, and it is being there that's what is wrong with the living. We are too much with us. The truest part of me was trained on that crystal world outside me, or even *was* that world. Sticks and berries . . . Why weigh them down with meat and bone? The Long Pig of the self? Too, too solid. A wasting sickness, I thought, was the way to die. To melt, to cease, to suck your own bones dry. To wear at last so thin that you can see the world through your almost unfogged flesh. Then, when you are crystal clear, to die.

But I did not die. So I turned to the ghosts. Nothing to make you feel that you're not there like someone talking through your head. May I confess that I did not care nearly so much what the ghosts had to say, as simply *that* they spoke? I already suspected that nothing said in words we understand is alien to our human case. Ghosts speak like living men and women or not at all. It would have been a great disappointment had I not predicted it. But it doesn't really matter. What I have always wanted was that empty feeling. That I wasn't something like a steak in a dress, but a hole. And if a hole, then I could go through it, or was already through it, in the world at last.

I wrote the above with such vehemence that my nib went through the paper and stuck there (you will note the scar). The pen wrestled itself out of my hand and shot into a pile of leaves, whence I have retrieved it, but how long I crouched over the leaves I do not know. Could a leaf be world enough to satisfy a lifetime's craving? I doubt it. Maybe. The way it crunches, to dust and trapezoids. The still-flexible spines fanning out like bones of a hand. But this, what I've written here, is only the description of a leaf. You know what a real leaf is. You are among the leaves. You left. You are a leaf now.

That is all,
Headmistress Joines

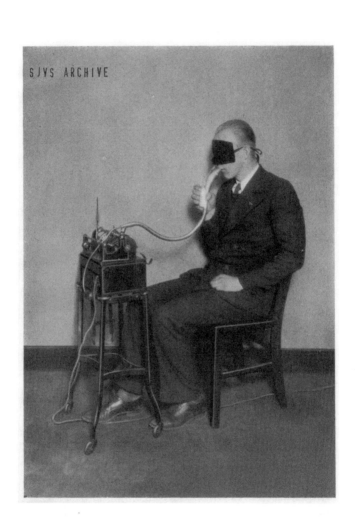

6. The Final Dispatch, contd.

The road, the ravine, the fields, the ~~thstles~~ thistles are all reminding me of something, I'll think of it in a minute. But in fact it would be surprising if anything didn't remind me of something. You, for instance, remind me of the girl I'm chasing. Finster is her name. Yours is Grandison, as I recall. You have the air, both of you, of little old women, though they're two rather different old women, one of them calm, effective, coolly critical (that's you), the other sly, impudent, and full of wrath. Both of you, however, have shrewd judgmental eyes; high, rather protuberant foreheads and crimped black hair; and clever fingers that are always moving: plucking at buttons, picking at scabs, pecking at typewriter keys. Otherwise you do not look at all alike, your skin is dark while hers is sallow and you are almost twice her size. Perhaps the greatest resemblance is in my way of looking at you, because I want something from you both, though I am not yet sure what I want from her.

From you I want, of course, your ear. Your ear and your fingers, piecing together my words, keeping me moving across the page toward the girl who must be close, maybe the next page, or the next but one, I hear a noise, if it isn't the worms, it's footsteps. Quick, quick, turn the page!

No, I am getting confused again. You cannot flip forward to a page you have not yet typed, to see what is written there. That is something time does not permit.

But wait! If what I say comes true in being said, then—listen closely—if I say what she is doing there, two pages from now, as for instance, "In two pages she will be walking up a cypress-lined drive," will it be true? Is it already true, in being said? Can I, then, determine the *future?*

And if so, can I talk her into a corner and keep her there until I come for her?

I might say, for instance, that in two pages, a little girl will be crossing a page, accompanied by the rhythmic crunch of gravel. She kicks a stone that hits the next sentence, in which is sketched out with no great attention to detail the cornered shapes of eaves and dormer windows against the sky. The reader will recognize, no doubt, the Vocational School, where, in a subordinate clause, muddy fields of thistles stretch to the distant hills.

Oh, that's what it was.

The door swings open before Finster reaches it, though there is no one on the stoop to welcome her. She hears an indistinct hum, perhaps the sound of my voice, punctuated by the *taptaptap* of someone typing, unless it is a branch tapping rhythmically against a window, then pausing for a moment, then beginning once again, *taptaptap*. The little girl will go inside. Followed, a page or so later, by an older woman, her face intent and rather gaunt. Myself, though at the moment I have not even reached the first vantage point from which, because the school is on a slight rise, the main building can be seen across the playing fields, though still some distance away and largely concealed by the trees that make parts of the grounds dark, cool, and damp even in the heat of summer. Shortly the first of the cypresses that line the drive will appear, dark strokes against the eye. It is natural to slow, now, as the view narrows between the thickets at the margins and is cut short by the curve of the drive as it rounds the depression that becomes a marshy pond every spring and a shrinking, stinking disc of mud by midsummer, and breeds exceptionally large, wiry but unwary mosquitoes and frogs that I have been told are edible. This is all reasonably plausible. On a sunny day one's shadow eclipses successive frogs that, their basking interrupted, burst skyward. At this time of year, the tadpoles have not yet lost their tails, and so we need not expect frogs on the drive, but later in the season every visitor will see a score of them, and hear, though this is less plausible, the blows of their heads against the undercarriage of whatever vehicle transports them, as they, the frogs, fling themselves unwisely into greater danger than they would have faced had they simply waited for our shadows to pass over. And now the swamp is left behind, or will be left behind, when we arrive at the slight eminence from which we catch our first glimpse of the red brick building heart-hot in the sun.

I do not know why I am suddenly rehearsing the mellow formulas of our part-time and superannuated tour guide, Miss Cavendish, bringing back the past, when what I meant to do was anticipate the future, except that around here the past has a way of becoming the future. In a world without time, these distinctions have very little meaning. Such that I sometimes wonder what law, if any, bars the future from a premature debut. Perhaps here all times coexist, in which case my ghost is already here somewhere, has always been here, holding my place like a finger in a book.

Possibly I *am* that ghost. Would I know?

Thumb bursts the paper cranium of a puffball, dark cocaine of spores smokes out—I—I am—I am lost [static]—no, no! Compose yourself!

Resume.

But I am getting nowhere. Literally, perhaps. So I say to myself, I actually chant, thus, "*I have a goal, I have a goal, I have forgotten what it is, but I have a goal . . .*"

"All right, then"—I interrupt myself (none too patiently)—"what is your goal?"

Stumped? No. My goal is:

To find the girl.

It comes whelming back.

Someone is missing, a child is missing, calamity, havoc, ruination, snatch her back, fetch her home, recover her, remember her, save her!

And with that I am at the steps.

They are just as I remember them. Well, they could hardly be any other way. Since the school is constructed from my knowledge of it, it conforms perfectly to my expectations, though I will not say that I notice no difference—not exactly. The very fact that it disagrees not at all with my expectations disagrees with my expectations to some small degree. I have never passed a day without noticing for the first time some minute detail—a spider descending on an invisible line, a small crack in the woodwork where the joiner bungled.

Details of no significance. The wealth of the world.

I open the front door. Go in. The light is the same, lifting my heart in the same way. The floorboards are scuffed in the same places. From below rises the familiar muffled clank and roar of lunch preparing. I could easily forget that this is not the real school, and slip into my usual routine. Eventually I would decide that it was time to go to the land of the dead, forgetting that I was already there. I would throw myself through my own mouth, and find myself—where? Here again, about to throw myself through my mouth? As I would do, only to find myself, again, here, about to throw myself through, et cetera. Tunneling down a mucus-walled passage to no birth. To tunneling without end.

But I am forgetting the child. I hurry upstairs, and find myself somewhere else.

A sawdusty haze that dries my tongue. The twanging of strained strings. Smell of glue. I know the neighborhood. I don't like it [static], I don't want to be here! But it's too late. They pile out of a fold in space, the men in suspenders and bowler hats and neat mustaches, the balding men inclining the shining, mute, and earnest faces of their craniums to their work, the men in aprons smeared with glue to which the sawdust sticks. There are even a few women with long skirts and bobbed hair and plain, unfriendly faces saying, "Now, Miss Joines, don't disturb your father at his work." They do not like me, think me an unnatural child, uncanny in my silence and my mourning dress, and so I am, but is that my fault? I did not make myself, or, well, something wrong there, never mind, I hoist high the lunch bag by way of explanation and continue straight-backed and cool to his office, where under the sounds of sawing, planing, gluing, sanding, I continue saying, as if I had never stopped saying, as I did not stop thinking, have never stopped thinking, "Why didn't you die? A mistake, I guess, but one you can correct and really should."

[Burst of static.]

Then sawdust swirls up; who on earth has opened the window? The varnish will be ruined! My eyes sting and stream tears, the contours of the room disappear, I am lost [echo, crackling, several words indistinct]—no, wait, control yourself—

A voice, I suppose it must be mine, is saying, in a low, reasonable tone, "Is it not really better to die? You will die eventually anyway, and probably in a disgusting condition; why wait? What of value have you contributed? Your inventions? What inventions? Your factory? It was here when you arrived, you teethed on its hammers, took varnish for your colic, learned to count on its keys; you would make more of a mark by shutting it down than you have by keeping it up. Your family? Your daughter would dig out her ovaries with one of your own antique silver teaspoons to put a period to your line, if she did not doubt, as you doubted, that she is even yours.

"You have been worse than insignificant; you have actively disimproved the world. One woman loved you, enough to marry you, and you killed her; now no one loves you, nor ever will. God doesn't. God cannot exist, since if He had made you, He would have smote you down. Since no one made you, since you squirted the short distance from absence to ignominy through the purest chance, you will have to do the smiting; the one positive contribution you can still make is to negate yourself."

There is no answer, only the wet munching of a man chewing his mustache. [Background noise.]

"Look up. Does that beam look familiar? There's where you strung up the one person who ever loved you, employing a treble string for the purpose. Nothing like rolling up your sleeves alongside the boys, eh? Sometimes you have to get your hands dirty!"

The Stenographer's Story, contd.

"No, no, no, no, no! I said, listen with your mouth. I did not say gargle, or whatever it is you think you are doing. You, girl. Grandison!"

Still holding the rolled paper cone to my mouth and with most of my attention directed toward the vicinity of my tonsils, I did not recognize my own name until I heard it again, this time from much closer to. The instructor had stopped directly in front of me.

"Grandison, I am speaking to you. Cannot you hear me?"

Since I spoke, without thinking, through the cone, my "Yes—no—I can" came out unexpectedly loud, and muffled giggles rose from around me. I lowered the cone, flushing.

"It is yes, *sir*, or yes, *Mr. Behalf*. You are new here."

"Yes, sir."

"You have conceived a dislike for this exercise?"

"Sir?"

"You are crumpling your trumpet." Happy laughter greeted this observation.

I looked down. I was more than crumpling it. I had crushed it into a ball and was kneading it compulsively.

"Take this one, and try to refrain from destroying it."

"Yes, sir." My cheeks burned.

"Now try once more, without huffing, or puffing, or gagging, or fizzing, or anything, to *listen* with your *mouth* . . . No, no, *no!*"

All my life I had borne the double burden of my stutter and my skin. Coming here, though, I had thought at least to halve my load—had looked forward to the novelty of being celebrated for my stutter, instead of mocked. I now learned better. Everyone had a stutter. What mattered was how well one employed it to summon up the dead. And that I could not do at all, nor even imagine how to start. Was it all a bunco game? The exercises we did seemed pointless (and some of them hurt), the teachers' instructions frankly nonsensical. Seeking to "breathe backwards," I might forget to breathe at all and fall off my seat in a faint, or inhale my own saliva and suffer a coughing fit. Not even among my cousins had I been made to feel such a ninnyhammer. The littlest of my fellow beginners, scarcely half my age, was more adept than I.

"Von Gunten, why don't you show Grandison how it is done? Try not to upset the furniture," added Mr. Behalf, as a stout little girl with white-blond braids, brows, and even lashes clumped to her feet, rocking the bench as she did so.

The dutiful giggles cut off abruptly when Von Gunten raised her cone, and my participating laughter, belated and a trifle hysterical, rang out for a moment. Then there was silence. Into it, her eyes a little crossed, she fed a low, hollow note, sustained like a drone. Rather than weakening, it grew louder, and then, just when one would have expected her to run out of breath, it resolved into an adult, female voice saying forcefully but quite naturally, "No respectable girl wears crimson stockings with red morocco tie shoes, except at home or on the summer piazza." There was a rustle as everyone, including myself, looked surreptitiously around, but no crimson stockings were in attendance. (Nor was it at all likely that any of us would be permitted so much liberty in matters of dress.)

"If we may inquire, madame or miss," the instructor said, "what other wisdom do you have for the living?"

"Snuff-dipping is a revolting habit," said Von Gunten, the cone trembling with effort, "that invariably leads to moral and physical dereliction. Crimson stockings . . ." Her voice grew faint and crepitating.

Mr. Behalf inclined his ear. "Stockings?" he said gently.

"Wound around my . . ." *crackle crackle* . . . Then, with great force: "*Pulled tight!*"

"Yes, quite!" he said hurriedly. "That will be enough, Von Gunten. Von Gunten, enough," he repeated, prying open the fat little hand that had convulsed around the cone.

When I first arrived at my aunt's house I was given a new home, new clothes, and a new body. This body had various names: stutterer, colored girl, poor relation. I did not recognize it. It seemed to me a sort of cenotaph for another body, now lost. What I still called my *self* flickered around this marker, homeless and very nearly voiceless.

I am loath to turn a very real affliction into a metaphor by suggesting that if I could not speak it was because I was schooled in silence. Yet I was. And if I spoke all the same, though in a Voice that said nothing, wasn't that because there was so *much* not to say? A whole hullaballoo of silence, with my parents' unspeakable marriage at the center of it. I was not to speak of my father, whom I remembered only in parts—long lovely hands, a black hat, the open collar of a white shirt—though I burned to know more, that I might stitch those parts together, and understand why he had left us. ("People leave," my mother said. Then she left too.) I was not to speak of my paternal grandparents, born into slavery and long dead. Nor of my people in general, though they were all around me, spooning tiny wrinkled potatoes onto my plate, filling my water glass, bearing away my gravy-blotched dress to be sponged and pressed—"my people" because so they would be reckoned by any stranger, not because I was invited to claim them, or they me. Of all this I was the impertinent reminder, the blot in the family Bible. My mother and Bitty had done the right thing by dying. It was too bad I had not had the grace to follow suit.

Such was Jane Grandison, age eleven: All too present, as to body. All but absent, as to voice.

Now I was instructed that this disjunct condition was in point of fact ideal. That I would never recover my lost voice, and must indeed endeavor to lose my Voice as well. Is it remarkable if every part of me refused this teaching? The information that I was "an empty space," "a hollow," "an opening," had the exact opposite of its intended effect. Never had I so keenly felt myself to be a dense material body as when I was striving to fashion myself into an absence.

My resistance had a color. *Was* color: My blackness bound me to this body that was not my body, but a sort of pickaninny doll into which I threw a voice that also was not mine. And it seemed to me they knew it would be that way and wanted it that way. Nothingness needs somethingness to prove itself against. The spotless needs the spot. And I—my obdurate, impertinent, unmentionable body—was that spot.

Certainly I was the very worst student in the school. Again, I was an outsider, and the other children made me feel it, as other children had always done, though they did so through stutters that at the Academy for Disadvantaged Girls would have made them prey just as surely as mine had made me.

Leaning low over her plate of bread and cheese: "Hello, n-n-new girl. Grandison. Hello. Hello. Hello. Look at m-m-me. Hello! Why, you . . ." Here she sat back, struck the table with her knuckles, then drew her baby finger across her sealed mouth. The other girls nodded; one pinched off a scrap of bread and kneaded into a ball, balanced it on one fingernail, and then flicked it into the air to appreciative laughter, an operation that I followed closely, while affecting disinterest, for I did not understand these gestures, though I caught the derisive intent well enough.

Another girl took up the attack. "Listen, Grandison, I have something to tell you, no joke. Don't you want to hear it?"

I folded my bread around my cheese and took a bite.

"You're hurting my feelings, Grandison."

I unfolded my bread again and began scraping the mold off my cheese.

"What, are you deaf? Rude thing! D-d-didn't your mother teach you any manners?"

Now I looked up.

"O-o-ooh, she's getting mad. Watch out, I think she's going to s-s-s-summon a ghost to s-s-s-scare us!"

Then one of them summoned a ghost to scare me. In this she miscalculated, though. The spirit she called up was a great bore who started in on explaining double-entry bookkeeping as necessary background to the exciting story of an error in arithmetic that he had found in his employer's records, "a punctiliousness for which I was not rewarded," he complained, as his channeler sought vainly to fit a slice of buttered bread into her mouth around his words. "Quite the opposite!"

As he droned on, the girls picked up their bread and deserted their unfortunate comrade, for it was forbidden to call up a ghost without supervision, and Mother Other was already bearing down on us. I hitched myself a little farther down the bench and continued stolidly eating my lunch. I will not let them drive me out, I thought. In any case I have nowhere else to go, and I saw in my mind's eye the retreating rear of the car that brought me, taking itself and its driver, not unkind, swiftly away, and for a moment felt a quite unmanageable grief. But "I have nowhere else to go," I said aloud, and took a bite of bread.

"You next carry into the columns of profit and loss the balances of . . ." said the girl, as she was pulled away by the ear.

Another time I had been backed into a remote corner of the playfield by a group of white boys and girls who, by calling me, as I guessed (for their words were much garbled by their stutters and nervous laughter), a "bulldyking coon"—albeit with sidelong glances at two colored students nearby—were trying to elicit some interesting reaction. I had heard worse in Brooklyn and maintained a contemptuous silence. So did Ambrose Wilson and Maritcha Dixon, whose expressions of lofty unconcern vied to convey their elevation above ignominious me. My tormentors had resorted to plucking at my clothes and putting leaves in my hair when Miss Exiguous came hurrying up. "Grandison, I have been looking everywh—what are you doing, boys and girls?"

"We're helping Grandison put herself in Compliance, the nasty messy thing."

"Straighten your uniform, girl. Headmistress wants you to take down a dispatch."

How I gloated, under my calm exterior, as I left my now-subdued tormentors. But alone in the Headmistress's office, behind the typewriter, I experienced another sort of torment. The Headmistress's words buzzing through the brass trumpet came so fast, sometimes, that I had to leave out whole sentences, or were so subsumed in static that only with the liveliest exercise of the imagination could I concoct a coherent transcript.

"Zzzzzridzzz . . . ffzzzmamzz . . . cozzzzpapazzzlllie . . ."

"The ridge of the mountain," I typed, "is covered with papillae."

Every time I presented my trembling sheaf of papers I was sure of being exposed as a fictionist. So I set about forming a new program. If I could not secure my reputation with my talent for ghost speaking, I certainly would not secure it with charm, wit, or good looks. Let others be liked, applauded, or admired: I would be useful. I schooled myself in Dr. Jameson's New Improved Phonographological Method and, whenever I was not occupied with my studies, put in hours drilling on the typewriting machine. And before too many months had gone by I really had all the skills that I had pretended to have, and if I still fictionalized now and then it was for my own amusement and in the confidence that I would not get the sack, for I had become the Headmistress's most accurate, most assiduous, fastest, cleverest—in short, best—stenographer, typist, and transcriptionist. Words I often rolled over my tongue when alone, for I had never before done or been anything that took so many long words to describe.

But my chief object of study, from blank fascination as much as from method, was the Headmistress herself.

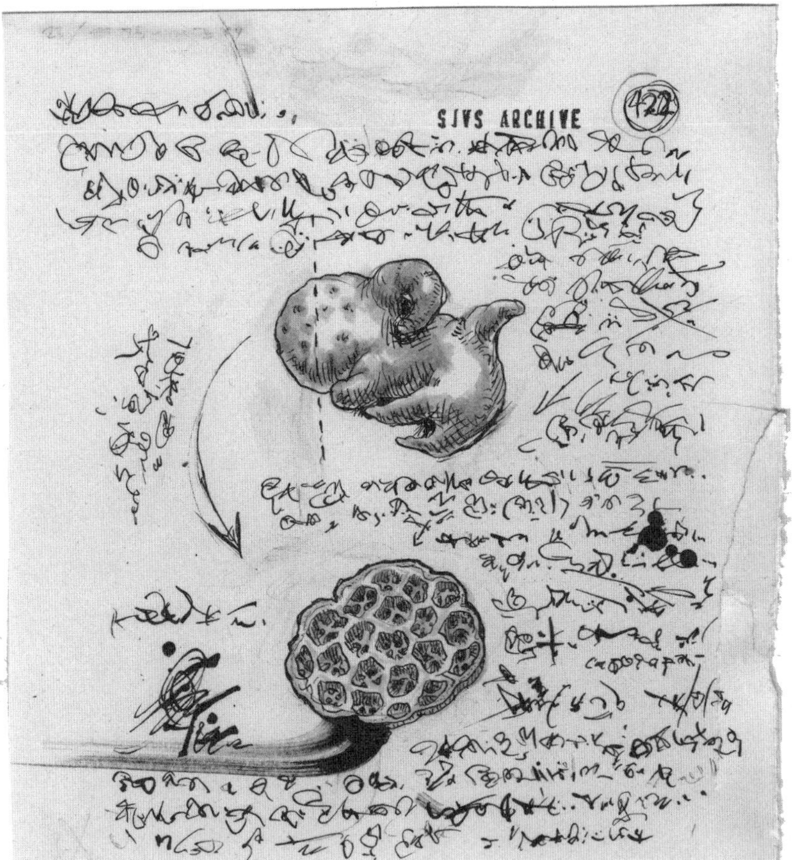
SJVS ARCHIVE
422

Readings

from *Principles of Necrophysics*: "A Report on Certain Curious Objects, Believed
to Be Words in an Unknown Language of the Dead"

For a long time the Founder believed that the cosmos had just two parts, life
and death, pressed together like two palms in prayer.

However, toward the end of her life, something began to happen that put
this simple model into question. She—and, not long thereafter, some of her
more talented students—began to cough, spit up, or find on the pillow in
the morning those waxy, lumpen articles known today as ectoplasmoglyphs
or, familiarly, glyphs, e-glyphs, or just "mouth objects."

What were they? The dead were evasive when asked, and appeared uneasy
with the topic. The Headmistress, in one of those intuitive leaps characteristic
of her, decided that they were *words*, messages from a more corporeal realm
of the dead. Where was this realm? Perhaps the dead also die, passing from
their own plane to a yet deeper one. Death and life are not opposites, then,
but graduations in a series. Thus it was the mouth objects that supplied the
first and best clue to the complex structure of the necrocosmos. Yet in many
ways they remain as great a mystery as when they were first documented.

Ectoplasmoglyphs are translucent, waxen in appearance, gummy but
firm in texture, and something between animal or vegetable in form, so
that they really appear, not modeled by conscious art, but grown. We are
lucky to have a description of "parturition" in the Headmistress's own hand:
She describes a stirring in the throat, then an "intricate rippling, gathering,
pleating, and revolving." She wonders whether this "kneading" by the deep
muscles of the throat, muscles rarely subject to our conscious control, is
what shapes the ectoplasm, imposing form on something itself formless, or
whether the objects materialize in the throat fully formed, and the activity
observed there is merely a sort of peristalsis, moving them forward. With
her usual perspicacity she has hit on exactly the point of contention that
rocks lecture halls today; science has not advanced one jot since her time.

In a magnified slice of a mouth object, you can see the reticulated struc-tures reminiscent of honeycomb tripe, or cow stomach, that some research-ers have described, and that have strengthened the claim that these objects are not merely excretions or accretions of matter, like ambergris in a sperm whale's intestines, but three-dimensional hieroglyphs—a little squashed, perhaps, but still displaying the features by which they would communicate to a viewer possessed of their secrets.

Incidentally, the widely circulated report that in one mouth object researchers found a baby tooth and some coiled hair is almost certainly apocryphal, inspired by those teratomas in which a sort of anagram of a baby seems to be trying to get itself born. If true, however, it would suggest that teratomas and perhaps *all* tumors are special dispatches from the dead. It is not actually such a far-fetched notion: we all carry messages from our forebears, scrolled neatly in our cells. Indeed, we arguably *are* such messages.

It is regrettable that some of the best-known depictions of mouth ob-jects are the work of J. T. Giesel, once a highly respected science illustrator, but since fallen out of favor for the degree to which wishful thinking (if not the deliberate intention to deceive) colored his work. In his rendering, the lumpen and even—why not admit it?—rather fecal word has acquired a delicate tensile strength, like a bridge.

He is right, in one sense: The word is a bridge to the world of the dead—or to, I should say, *another* world of the dead. However, we should not so readily dismiss what is intimate, personal, and a little disgusting about mouth objects. Most things that come out of the human mouth are judged unclean. Speech is ordinarily exempt from this prejudice; we listen publicly to others' words without a blush and even take them into our own mouths in mimicry or quotation. We have learned to unbuckle language from the gag reflex. It is our loss. The ectoplasmoglyph reminds us where the word comes from. Presented here, from the archives of the Vocational School, in an unknown hand, are some images of mouth objects over which no prettifying veil has been drawn.

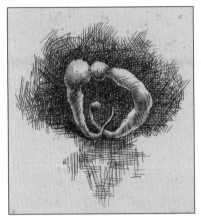 

Fig. XIX. *"some images of mouth objects over which no prettifying veil"*…

It is now generally accepted that these objects are indeed elements of a language of the dead. But questions remain. Are they the three-dimensional equivalent of logograms, in which representational elements can be made out in radically simplified form, as in the Japanese *kanji?* Are they composed of alphabetic elements, fused in a sort of three-dimensional script? Or do they, like the objects exchanged by the learned professors of the Grand Academy of Lagado, signify only *themselves*—in which case the task before us would be, not to determine what they mean, but to see what they are? (It is no small one!)

Do we even perceive them in their original form? Perhaps the once-featherweight word acquires mass through signal corruption in passing through successive regions of the dead. Perhaps a sort of Doppler effect shifts it farther along a spectrum of thingliness, the farther it goes.

Or perhaps these objects are a sort of pidgin, deliberately yet clumsily endowed with physical properties to establish rapport with a world where material things are held in high esteem. If so, they have largely failed, though it is true that students have found that some of these objects name new feelings for them, new thoughts, which once conceived cannot be described in other words.

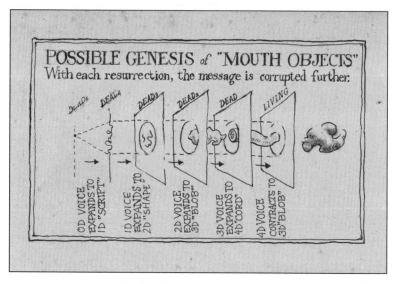

Fɪɢ. XX. *"a spectrum of thingliness"*...

An understanding of the whole language, however, still eludes us. Scholars are cataloguing new words as they appear, in the hopes of discovering patterns that will unlock this language for the living. We at the SJVS would like to call all thanatomaths and interested amateurs to the work of translating these messages into English. Alternatively, some may wish to translate these objects into other material objects native to our world. We would also like assistance in translating our own languages into physical objects. Perhaps we can reply to these strange bulletins from the "dead dead," if we learn their language.

The Founder was optimistic. "It may be that we already speak this language," she wrote, "albeit not with our mouths." After all, we too are material objects, ambiguously and temporarily haunted by voices. Able morticians and undertakers, we groom our corpses, daub blush on our cheeks, pink the lips. We look alive, but only for a little while.

Reasoning that they might communicate through any of their physical properties, not only their form, she performed many experiments on the objects: immersing them in water, then in distilled alcohol, heating and cooling them, rubbing them with wool, striking them with mallets. One word was given to a terrier to sniff, who was moved to urinate, another shown to an infant, who recoiled. One was allowed to air-dry until hard, ground fine, and mixed with ink. A greasy elastic pellicle formed on its surface, which the nib had some trouble piercing. The ink had the tendency to draw itself up into balls on the surface of the page and, when the paper was lifted, to roll away, leaving the paper perfectly blank in places. (This may be no more than a curiosity, but the portions of the text that vanished composed, without exception, pronominal forms and proper names.)

FIG. XXI.
*"to cough, spit up, or find on the pillow
in the morning"...*

Her account of one early experiment is worth quoting in full, and will conclude this brief report. "This evening I conducted tests on one of the words, though to destroy it seemed to me like savaging my own tongue. I first laid it on a glass tile I had wiped with rubbing alcohol. With a clean, very sharp knife I sliced it first longitudinally, then latitudinally. I noticed that I winced as the blade passed through the substance, which clung to it. I had to bring down the knife very slowly so as not to distort the word in slicing it. The cross-section revealed minute whorls and fault lines where the substance was whiter and more

ANTIDOTE: Carbonate of Soda, Potash, Lime or Magnesia in water; followed by demulcent drinks such as white of egg or milk. Then bodily warmth and stimulants as needed.

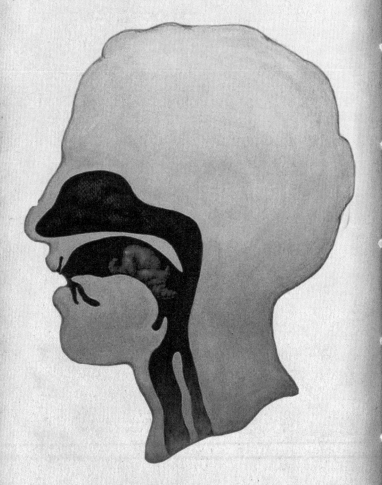

FIG. XXII. "OR WHETHER THE OBJECTS MATERIALIZE IN THE THROAT FULLY FORMED"

opaque, like wax that has been put under pressure. One part of the word I picked up with a pair of tongs and held over a low flame. This experiment was exceedingly distressing to me. I noticed with interest an increase in salivation; my mouth was flooded with sweet water. It would be interesting to try to determine whether this response is characteristic of all observers. The flame took all over the surface of the word, igniting with a soft pop. This flame very bright and mellow. The lump shrank without spattering or bubbling. I deduce from this that its substance is dense and pure. The effect was not unlike burning a candle of very fine wax, but brighter.

"As the word shrank it performed several revolutions or convulsions too quick to follow with the eyes but disturbing and uncanny, especially as it seemed to me that it passed through several forms that were recognizeable and possibly of particular personal significance, through due to the rapidity of transformation I could not get my head around the business of recognizing them. Later I would try to record my impressions of the intermediate positions I had glimpsed and find it impossible.

"The consumption of the final morsel happened very quickly, and the word disappeared. As it did so it emitted a sound that is hard to describe. It might have been a very high-pitched or very fast declaration. It seemed to contain many sounds, though it was over in no more than an instant.

"If I could hear that sound again, it seems to me I would understand everything that is now obscure to me. But perhaps I should not strain, through an act of violence, to translate dead matter into sense. When I myself am dead matter, I will speak the language of things. Then at last I will understand what it is that the world has been trying to tell me, all my life."

{
Fig. XXII.
*"or whether the objects materialize
in the throat fully formed"*...
}

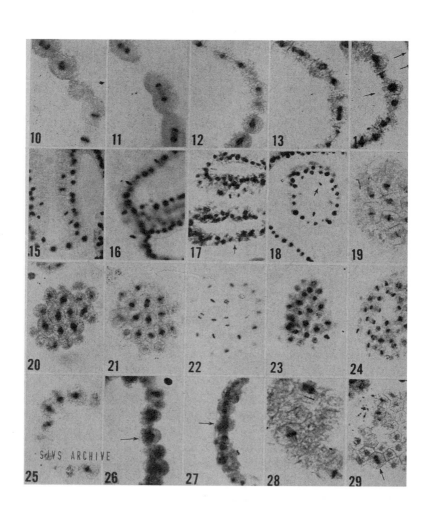

Letters to Dead Authors, #6

Dear Mr. E. A. Poe,

The *Cheesehill Gazette* has published a defamatory letter from A Pupil at a Local Educational Establishment, alleging rats in my kitchen and bats in my belfry. Though I shall hunt down the author and punish her, I am rendered nostalgic. How it brings back my own precocious assays at fraud and calumny. What is that hissing?

It is just the snow scouring the windowpanes. The appearance is of a blackboard striving to erase itself. Incidentally I went out this morning without a muffler to lead the second form in oral calisthenics and must have caught a cold in my throat. I cannot seem to get warm—

Coughing fit. It went on and on and with such force that my vision spangled. I fumbled in my reticule and dragged out a handkerchief (and the drawing compass that was snagged in it, which I had to disengage by feel). I seemed to hear words in the strangled noises I was forcing into its folds: "Sorry, sorry."

I cannot think of any apologies I owe. It must have been a ghost.

Afterward I folded the damp cloth between my hands and squeezed my hands between my knees. I felt limp. The hissing seemed to have moved inside my head. I opened my mouth, in case someone had something to say. "Look down," said Cornelius, his tone malicious. I looked down, parting my hands. The handkerchief fell softly open like an old worn book.

Beauty!

The red.

And the red. The blood that soaked my handkerchief had doubled at the fold: two wings, a scarlet tanager spread on snow.

I felt an obscure satisfaction, as if I had hit upon a solution to a longstanding problem. The stain seemed *meant*: a message, in the body's own ink. What it told me I will not say, though perhaps you can guess.

So cold. Clarence has just brought me more coal and plied a poker in the stove. Unfortunately a cold draft swept in behind him and so any benefit is undone.

Apropos of nothing, I cannot find my rabbit's foot. Where it normally rests, on the desk before me, my handkerchief is slowly stiffening. I cannot stop looking at it. There is a taste in my mouth that binds me to it. If I dipped my pen in my mouth . . .

But I have written all I care to, tonight.

Respectfully,
Headmistress, the Vocational School, etc.

P.S. Please excuse the blots. It is only blood. You know about blood.

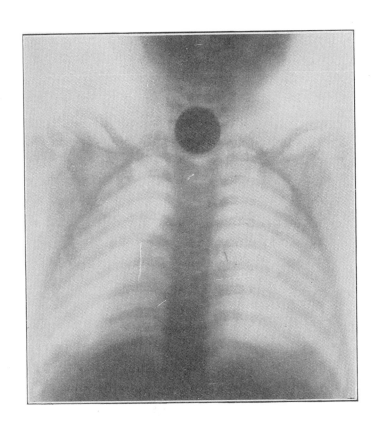

7. The Final Dispatch, contd.

I had never seen a person looking the way she looked when she came home. She was dead, of course. I understood that. I was acquainted with death through my rabbits. But my rabbits still looked like themselves, when dead, whereas my mother had become something like a landscape or a pile of trash. I thought of tree trunks that when the light is right resemble crouching figures, I thought of clouds in which laughing faces can be seen, and fungi that seem to have noses, cheeks, and ears. As with tree, cloud, fungus, the resemblance to a familiar form convinced my eyes but not what I will quaintly call my heart.

That was not because this so-called face was bluish gray and very cut up around the lips. My mother's real face could have been bluish gray, I thought, and still I would have known it. I would not have been able to look at it the way I looked at this—this bag of frozen squirrels, this cow pie, this pan of bubble-and-squeak. I had never been able to look at my mother's face before, not *at*, because it had no surface on which my eyes could rest. Her face swam upstream in my gaze, overtaking my impulse to look, and arrived at the source before I knew that she was coming, then turned to greet me as if she had been there all along and I were the one belated. She opened me like the door to her own room.

No one can say that I have not accepted my mother's death. This is an open-casket chronicle. Nor am I an undertaker, to doll her up, shoo away the flies, and whisper *Shh, she's sleeping.* My mother was not sleeping. My mother was not here. They had replaced her with this *thing*.

This thing was not my mother. But though it was not my mother I thought that it might know where my mother had gone. So I pulled up a chair to the coffin—which was laid out on a low table in our drawing room—and asked it.

Where was my father? I cannot locate him in this scene. Probably upstairs, moaning, "Bea, Bea," repining too late, as usual. Possibly savaging a pillow. Feathers drift down over his disconsolate figure, their soft touch like a healing angel's kisses, I don't think. It should but does not surprise me that I was left alone to experiment with my mother's corpse.

I did not cry or plead like an ordinary child but interrogated the imposter in a monotone, speaking rapidly and without any of my usual tricks, on the contrary seeking out the sounds that were hardest for me, my *s*'s above all, my *d*'s, *b*'s, and *m*'s, so that I might stammer as violently as I had stammered when I talked to Hopsalot that last time. I was hoping to fetch my mother back, as I had brought him back, long enough for her to tell me something. I don't know what. Goodbye, perhaps. It is trite but one comes to expect it.

No, I will not perjure myself for the sake of a cynical quip. I do not know what I wanted. But at her death a question had opened in me like a door, perhaps the one my mother had just gone through. "Where are you?" it might have been. "What are you, now? How should I comport myself toward you? Do you need anything? Can I help?"

What do we owe the dead? I have never received a satisfactory answer. But the empty place in me where my mother was still issues its imperatives, though there is no one to receive my offerings, or tell me I have done enough at last.

All night I stammered, and time stammered with me. I dragged it back, it jerked ahead again, I dragged it back, farther back. By the first blue hint of dawn her mouth had tunneled back, I thought, to the day before. I saw a warmer light on it, glinting off a sliver of tooth. Sunlight, or maybe electric light, factory light. And still it was mute.

Abruptly I was weary with this playacting and sat up, feeling adulthood closing over me like bark. I rubbed my dry eyes. Then I let fall my hands, from which all strength had fled, for I had heard a sound. The most ordinary sound in the world, one might think: a cough. But from that still form, terrible.

Again I bent over the dry, unmoving mouth.

"Harwood," my mother said.

Later I would try to convince myself that she had said it imploringly, or accusingly, or in any other way that would help me construe it as a message and a directive. But in fact her voice was perfectly neutral. It sounded if anything a little bored. But it was my mother's voice.

Now I cried, without dignity, gasping and snorting, eyes and nose stream-ing, drops falling even into the coffin, onto the impervious face.

My father's name was the last thing I would ever hear my mother say, though I talked and talked, trying to get more out of her, I even talked *for* her, saying, "I will never leave you, my darling; I will watch over you, my little girl, my only, forever," and things to that effect. I remember very clearly how these sentiments creaked out of me in the airless wee voice I used back then when I wished to pretend, for the power it gave me with the other children, that I was possessed by a ghost. Oh yes, just as little boys play at murder with toy guns, so I did in fancy what I would later do in fact. Our lies tell the truth about our leanings.

Could I have been channeling her after all, thinking I was pretending?

No, my mother never told me fairy tales.

[Pause.]

She was gone, I'm sure of it. My mother took to death as to her native element. Whereas of my father's death, I have often had the uneasy sense that, like so many of his projects, it would not "take."

[Pause, static.]

Because I am in the land of the dead, where every word is true, I felt, while I was telling you how I leaned my forehead against her coffin, some cold edge press against my brow, as if the sky had bent against my head, and when I mentioned satin I nearly choked on its white billows. As for lilies, I scarcely have to mention them to smell their reek. And once again I am talking, talking, talking, bent over a dry unmoving mouth, listening for an answer that never comes.

Are you receiving?

My mother's face has become a travesty, so I look at her hands, which are more honest in their repose, confiding their familiar freckles to me, though her familiar ring is wasp-waisting her finger which therefore must be, must have been swollen.

My eyes are wet. It must be rheum.

[Pause, static, sound of breathing.]

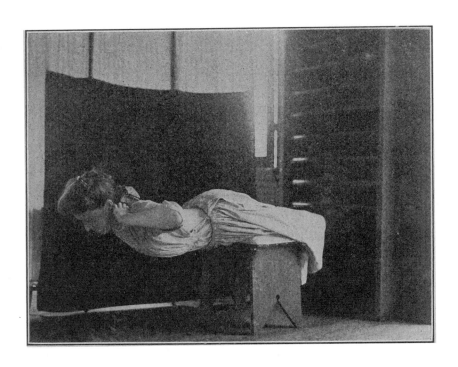

The Stenographer's Story, contd.

She sweeps down the hall, her heavy skirts chivvying dust bunnies along, and light from the shuttered windows stripes her for an instant and then again and then again. Lorgnette chafes her stiffened bodice. At her waist, in a silk reticule, bulky shapes: ear trumpet, tongue depressor, speculum. In her hands a gleaming ferule. Her mouth is stretched around a wire mold. They say she wets her lips with printer's ink at bedtime and wears this armature all night. After rubbing it with erasers inside and out she winds a cloth around the whole contraption: It becomes a snout. But today it is not wrapped, and saliva flows down her chin, wetting her neat linen bib. I note this, as I note everything that may be useful to me.

The Headmistress began to warm up at five for the morning calisthenics, to "open the hatches," as she said, employing every tool in her kit: the camphor-and-menthol atomizers, the gnathodynamometers, the cotton pads, the rubber bulbs, the steel-and-porcelain ratchet gag. When, barely buttoned into their uniforms and blued with a dash of ice water from the basin, the students heard round a corner the rap of her heel or saw the trembling shadow of her snout, they would flee down the corridors or lower themselves into chests and come out much later in a fountain of moths and with faces like moths, all eyes.

All day, the Headmistress came and went, her route decided "more by rhetoric," she explained, "than by expediency," through that puzzle box of classrooms, dormitories, living rooms and dying rooms: rapping down haunted galleries, past laboratories filled with models and machines, and oubliettes filled with wrongdoers, through gymnasia where children flung themselves over and over through their own mouths and out again; rustling through the curtained laying-in room where those expecting mouth objects lay in the half-dark, staring at pictures of holes and of darkness, their lips thickly smeared with goose fat, attended by smaller children who massaged their throats through the swaddling. She would pass down a row of the youngest students arranged by size and bend an ear to each mouth in turn. With cotton soaked in morphine she would soothe strained tonsils; she'd offer ink-and-ipecac purges and poultices of paper pulp and cantharides, and to complainers, the advice, "Pretend you aren't here." Shushing chatterers, bating breaths, tying gags with a reef knot (never a granny), distributing baffles and tightening muzzles, inspecting creels and wind socks, and tuning high voices with a firm hand on the windpipe and a whiff of smelling salts, she reigned: schoolmarm and monarch, high priestess and inquisitor in one.

Bullish, rumpled, Mother Other would stump along behind in her leaden shoes, harrying the children into place, slapping a pointer into the hand of the unvoice teacher, setting up without question or comprehension the masks, the bellows, the paper cones. She'd appear suddenly in the dictation room with a wobbling armful of paper balloons; she'd ball up newspapers to fill an artificial lung or pop a tongue depressor into a passing mouth. Meanwhile Whit and McDougal padded to and fro, palpating creels with white-gloved hands and removing any mouth objects found within, wrapping them in diapers to wick away saliva and protect them for what remained of their journey, and flitting away with them cradled reverently in their arms. Somehow they always seemed to know when one was due, as if like spiders thrilling to the vibrations in their web they had some special sensitivity to the fabric of the Veil. Often they managed to be there to help deliver it, coaxing the mouth a fraction further open and hooking the item out with a crooked finger. Sometimes one of the students, confused, fought them.

"You can't take it! It's mine!" Victoria scuttles away, huddled protectively over the creel, which swings wildly. "G-get back! G-g-g-get offa me!" Runs, knocking over a chair, another chair. Disappears down the hall.

By evening, "Wh-wh-why say anything"—on the phonograph, Edison— "if it's not the *dernier cri?*" the Headmistress would croak, in crepe and whalebone on a horsehair divan, surrounded by ear trumpets, taxidermy, and memorial hair art. "What good is it to be Headmistress of the Sybil Joines Vocational School for Ghost Speakers and Hearing-Mouth Children, if I can't be more famous than the F-F-Fox sisters and better-looking than Cora Hatch?" She took a sip from the "brain," that curiously shaped decanter that Mother Other, to provide ease from the friction of leadership and the traffic of ghosts, kept filled with Stickney and Poor's Paregoric, "1 8/10 grains Opium to each fluid ounce," and fingered her earlobes, then with calipers measured her mouth and again launched into "My w-word, wh-wh-why," etc.

When visitors came, the Headmistress would arrange demonstrations, lavishing particular attention on wealthy relatives who might be persuaded to pony up for a scholarship or a sports field. She required Mr. Lenore, our drama teacher, to rehearse "impromptu" séances to a script, observing, without a blush, that it was a mistake to think that merely because the medium was a fraud, the dead were not really present. Cheating was underrated: "It may be precisely when we counterfeit that we ring true." Along a course minutely planned to give the impression of spontaneity, she led visitors at a stroll, pumping them for information all the while. A discreet aside to any student would send a runner ahead in the itinerary with amendments to the plan: This visitor hopes to hear from a maiden aunt, preferably through the mouth of a well-brought-up young lady; this other from a tot, carried off by scarlet fever; while this one would like to see a boy student, blindfolded, mouth stretched around an ivory wind tunnel, his tongue forced down with a stirrup, his cheeks held apart from his teeth by two flanges locking in place, while his instructor strokes his distended throat with a peacock feather.

O'Donnell was a favorite among the boys, with his erect stance, his white teeth, his blond hair, artfully tousled (by Mr. Mallow under the instructions of Mr. Lenore) before the arrival of his audience. Smithson was first among the girls for her curls and the pearly nails on her little pink fingers, and Dixon next for her glossy dark skin and the theatricality with which she drew herself upright, raised her chin, jerked, and shook out a booming masculine voice. I, less picturesque, was never chosen.

Some visitors, flushed, speaking a little too loudly, would request a private tête-à-tête with one or another of these prodigies, would confess the desire to test the fabric of the Veil, to let the winds of the afterlife cool their hot cheeks, to watch a mouth object delivered, perhaps, into their own eager hands, or even assisted a little with a judicious finger. To these requests the Headmistress or her delegates would smoothly reply, "R-r-regrettably it is not p-possible; the children require the supervision of an expert at every stage, there is always a r-risk of the accidental summoning of a hostile rev-rev-revenant, the school has tried many times to take out a policy against wraith-related m-m-m-mutilations or deaths, but insurers have not been cooperative . . . Are you feeling all right?"

MOUTH THEATER

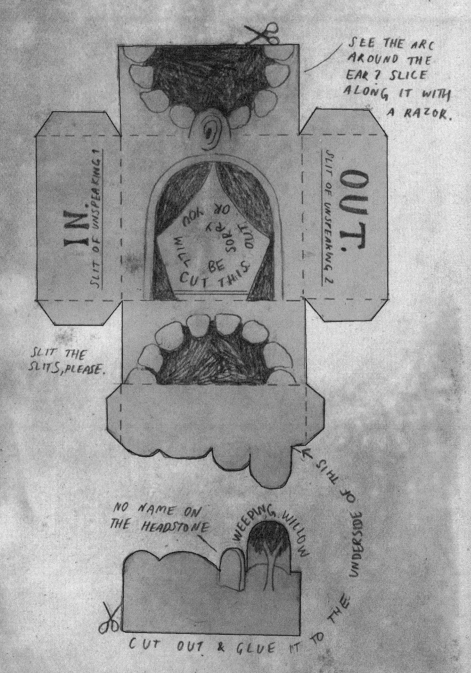

SEE THE ARC AROUND THE EAR? SLICE ALONG IT WITH A RAZOR.

IN. SLIT OF UNSPEAKING 1

OUT. SLIT OF UNSPEAKING 2

WILL BE SORRY OR YOU CUT THIS OUT

SLIT THE SLITS, PLEASE.

← SIHL JO 3OISNBONN ← UNDERSIDE OF THIS

NO NAME ON THE HEADSTONE

WEEPING WILLOW

CUT OUT & GLUE IT TO THE UNDERSIDE

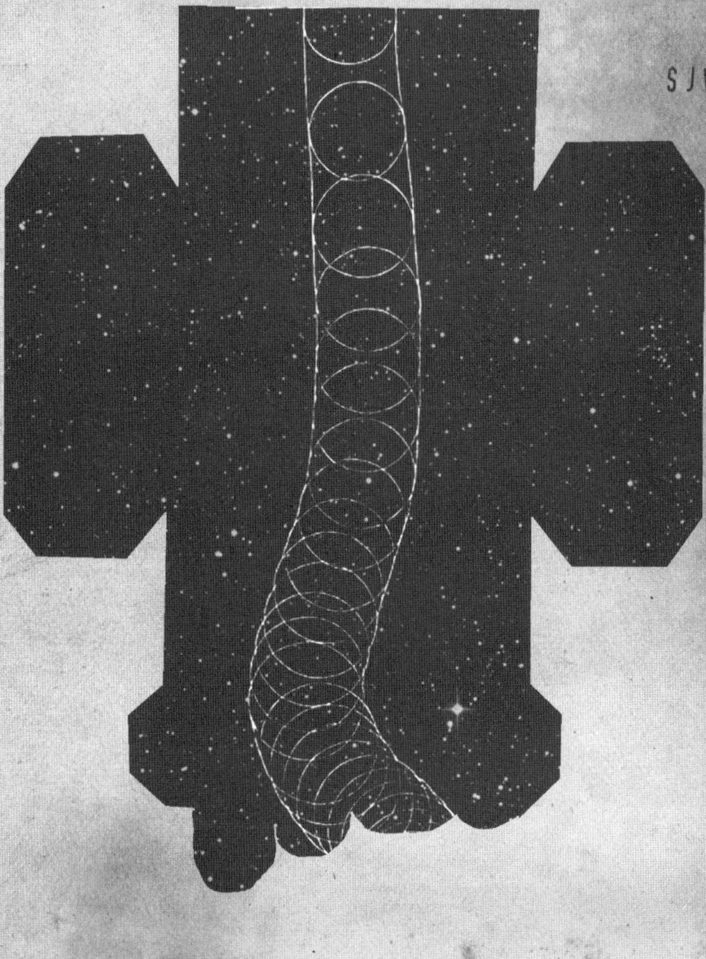

Readings

from "A Visitor's Observations"

On Punishment

I turn now (for I am still gathering my thoughts on weightier matters) to that natural couple, pain and pleasure—or, as they are formalized in school life, punishment and play.

The Vocational School devoted considerably more time to the former. The Headmistress expected perfect conformity with her rules, and when met with defiance did not hesitate to send a pupil to the oubliette. As the latter was in use on the day I might have toured it (a girl was suspected of pocketing the Headmistress's lucky rabbit's foot—apparently a grave offense!), I was not invited to explore, but it appeared quite as dark and dolorous as one would expect. Its primary purpose, however, was not to cause distress, but to forcibly "unclog the pipe" or "remove the blockage" that was impeding passage to the dead. Less severe punishments might take any number of forms. I will list the more unusual:

A tongue-lashing (not a scolding, but actually lashing the tongue with a miniature cat-o'-nine-tails, its paper lashes inscribed with mordant accounts of the detainee's misdeeds).

A boot (not footgear, but a contraption designed to immobilize the jaw, something like a horse's bit).

A beating (not, as one might reasonably imagine, of the child, but of a sort of drum, called—in a pun that was really just a retrenchment to the literal—an Ear Drum, the timbre of which was supposed to be keenly distressing to the listener).

Read-alouds of descriptive passages such as the following: "A saddle, decorated with a stamped design in some unfamiliar alphabet, perhaps Amharic, with, looped around the pommel, reins that had broken and been reknotted," or "A book, the pages covered with brindled fur, over which a scholar ran a desiccated finger." (I confess I could not fathom the tears and pleas for mercy these elicited.)

A perhaps related punishment was inflicted by directing the child's attention to an object in his vicinity. The objects were not in themselves such as should inspire terror: no instruments of torture were to be discovered among them, nor was there, in fact, any implication that they might be *used*. They did not represent a threat of punishment but, in fact, the punishment itself, to whose efficacy the horror on my informants' faces was sufficient testimony. No particular objects were dedicated to this role. Anything might serve: a bent twig, the handle of a porcelain mug, a balding push broom. After its period of service, the object was restored to its previous, unexceptionable status. (Perhaps to do otherwise would have been deemed an injustice to, a sort of libel of, the innocent object.)

Nevertheless the students told me that the object often remained dreadful to them long after the punishment was over; this explained the care the Headmistress exhibited in making the otherwise apparently arbitrary choice of an object. One would not want to instill in a child an ungovernable aversion to an object he had to use every day—a chamber pot, a shoe, a pen. I once saw a child flinch and cry out at coming upon, temporarily abandoned by the janitor, a galvanized metal bucket.

The last punishment I wish to tell you about was much feared. Its principle characteristic was that it could not be recognized as punishment; it did not induce pain or humiliation or restrict one's movements; it might even be experienced as pleasure. I could never make out exactly by what mechanism it was brought home to the sufferer of this pleasure (for suffering they assured me it was) that what they were experiencing was in fact intended as punishment, but there was no mistaking my informants' emotion for anything but the liveliest horror. This is speculation only, but I wonder whether the reason this punishment inspired such unease was that its influence could not be contained to the local; once introduced, the possibility haunted every subsequent experience. I myself have had the irrational thought strike me, in the midst of some signal pleasure, that the sweetness of this peach or that caress might not be the simple good it seemed, but the sly retribution of the Headmistress for some injury or other. The reader will readily perceive that this suspicion, afflicting every passing moment, is itself a form of punishment, lessening one's joy in life; indeed, the Headmistress need do nothing more than allude to the *possibility* of such a punishment for it to exact a cost. Such a punishment would naturally depend for its efficacy on the sensitivity of the victim; on a hardened criminal it would miss its mark. However, the students referred to it with respect verging on dread, and held the Headmistress in considerable awe.

In one respect, however, her policies were liberal in the extreme. The lowliest student might command her respect if a ghost spoke through him. Under the influence of the dead, she would not only excuse malfeasance but would give serious consideration to amending school policy along lines suggested by the miscreant. It was almost laughable, when an infantine lisp gave way to the odd hiccuping groan of the ghost, to see her demeanor change. All that was characteristically impatient and haughty in her fled her countenance. Her eyes softened, her lips parted, and with an eager and even ingratiating air—bending to bring her ear closer to the child's mouth—she gave her full attention to the dead.

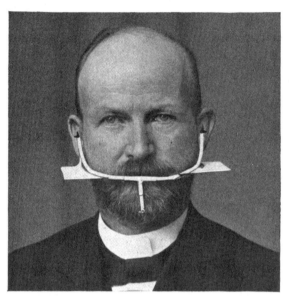

Fig. 91.

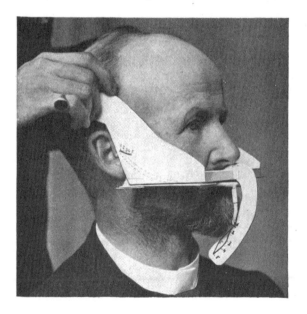

Letters to Dead Authors, #7

Dear Emily Brontë,

Doctor Beede tells me, one finger probing greedily under his vest, that it is pulmonary consumption, or tuberculosis.

"You see?" I want to shout, for the feeling is of a lifelong suspicion confirmed. It is somehow not news. News is what can no longer distract from this.

"The disease is slow to progress, but usually fatal," he tells me, not entirely concealing his satisfaction. If he is waiting for me to repudiate my teachings under the threat of death, he can wait forever.

So I approach the vanishing point of view. The horizon line I thought remote turns out to be penciled on a wall a hand's-breadth from my nose.

I am conscious of a strangely breathless feeling. It is not the tubercles. I believe I am having an emotion. Surely it is not fear. Though it is natural for the organism to feel a little nervous as the axe comes down. Living creatures, as a rule, are lamentably partisan in the matter of their personal survival. Ants may be an exception. On evidence, I am not.

In fact, I am clenched like a fist, as if around a treasure I feared to lose. But there is nothing in that fist. It is the feeling of clenching, the fist itself, that I know as *I*. When I open my hand, it will be gone. But lost?

But ow, ow, oh, O, I'm not, I'm not ready! There are still so many things I wanted to learn. About death, yes. But not by *dying*, like every Tom, Dick, and Harry!

I am the hunter who, bent over the lion's tracks, feels its breath on the back of her neck.

Of course, every hunter is taken down by a lion—of some species or other. It's just that I had hoped to examine its tonsils, probe its caries, sample its carrion reek before the great jaws close. To answer the burning question that has been my life, before, before—

What will become of my school?

I will take a moment to compose myself.

There.

—before the fire goes out.

I will take another moment.

There. I am dying. I do not know why that should make me weep. Who isn't dying?

Yours,

Corpse-in-Waiting Joines

8. The Final Dispatch, contd.

I have just spent a summer in my mother's hand. I do not mean cupped in her palm, but inside the living meat and bone, which I knew was solid and yet was for me (and uniquely for me) a space, warmly flexile like a tent, where I could live. I did not at first recognize my surroundings; I had graduated without noticing it from my coffin-side vigil to a series of elastic passages down which I sprang, pulsing with energy and well-being. I was moving, as I eventually understood, from one finger to another. Sometimes, to please me, or to perform some job of work whose purpose I did not seek to learn, the whole hand flexed around me; I admired the smooth action of the joints; what joy to be jostled into service in a whole so admirably coordinate. It was summer and my mother's hand because I loved it, and I lived in it for years that passed in moments, the moments in which I tell you this, dear listener, which are (like my mother's hand) a sort of *dacha* within the country of the dead, a place of comfort, safety and intrinsic worth. Yes, I rest in the words about my mother's hand as happily as in the hand itself, and that is so because they are the same thing, here.

You should understand this, actually, because I live in your hand, too, as you type; your hands, I mean. You type, therefore I am. Of course my words come first. Or would I be speaking, if you were not listening? Perhaps it is only when you take down what I say that I say it, or am I getting confused again, about time?

Fuck these perhapses!

But I find I have one more: Perhaps you are the real author of this monologue. Then I am at your mercy, maybe. You might change a word, and with it change my fate, turn princes into frogs, ducks to donkeys. If the sky is origami for a moment, it might be because you said it was, though you could say that it was my idea and I'd believe it. Then you could say that it was your idea and I'd believe it. You could tell me everything I'm telling you, think I'm telling you, so that I swung, anguished, between belief and doubt, unsure whether I was inventing you, or you were inventing me, or some unholy mixture of the two. And we haven't even talked about typos yet. Maybe even now you're lifting your cramped fingers from the keys, stretching your hands out before you, studying them, thinking, *Those are my hands*, and *Ha ha ha I am fooling them all*. You rub your eyes, your toes curling inside your hard shoes, stuff a fold of skirt under your nates to soften the seat, return your fingers to the keys. *Taptaptap*.

Of course you do not and could not do that while taking down this account of them, but a little before, or a little after. Maybe you thought, *I will say that I am doing these things, and then I will do them*, or else, *I did those things, and now I will describe them*. But why do them at all, having described them? Why describe them, having done them? If intent on carrying out a hoax, why allow the suspicion to arise that you are feeding me my lines?

"...you are feeding me my lines," you type, and you are quite correct, I am. What am I but a ventriloquist making her puppet say, "I am a ventriloquist, and the person whose hand is up my skirt is my puppet." Why I should do that, heaven knows. One has these little fantasies of impotence. In any case it has probably fooled nobody.

Are you receiving? Your lamp burns low, but there is enough light to see the ranked disjecta in their cubbies on the wall, though not to read the neat, small lettering on the label underneath each one. Your stomach groans; inside it roil the unrecognizeable relicts of a slice of bread with butter and a cup of milky tea. Soon you will need to take illegal advantage of a pause to dash to the close chamber, straining your ear all the way down the hall for the sound of my voice.

The office door rattles dully in the frame and you look up. Someone is coming—no, the tension drains from your shoulders and you return to your work, it is only the customary bustle as day gives way to night, the doors opening and closing, the ovens roaring, dishcloths slapping, water splashing, brushes clattering into sinks, voices rising, querulous and brusque. Outside the great rivers of wind rush unceasingly over the slates, birds flick their shadows across the gravel drive, shrubs rub, over and over, the same spot on the wall, but I do not know if this is real, or ever was. I do not know if I once lived, then died, and now live on—not live, but do whatever I am doing here—talk on, that's it—or if I ever lived at all. I do not know if anyone ever lived at all, including you. Including her. Her solid knees bristling with fair stubble. Her soft white belly with its furry, light brown birthmark. Her neck cross-creased and red-brown in back. Her bluish gray [crackle, audio break]—

I turn a corner in my eyes and find myself in a shack. A shed, actually. Actually I recognize it. Tufts of fur scud into the corners, or tug, trying to scud, at a splinter. The hutch is empty, but still pebbled with droppings. The innocent droppings. My lungs swell with all the howls I have forbidden myself. Then I toughen. Rabbits, I tell myself, fall like raindrops from other, bigger rabbits. Left alone, they would drown us all. The metaphor is extravagant but has its strong points. A mature domesticated long-haired rabbit, as for instance a Lionhead or Angora, does resemble a cloud. A Himalayan or Belgian hare naturally does not. But I digress.

In one of the hutches the girl Finster is hiding.

No [static], it is the rabbit I called Lady Tendertoes.

No [static], it is a coil of rotting rope.

No, it is a wig of human hair, a wasp nest, an apple pandowdy, a sharp cry cut short, a peacock, a telegraph operator, the fingernails of a dead man. No, I am getting confused.

Am I [static] dead? [static]

No, but the longer I stay here, the harder it is to tell the difference, by which I mean, to tell the time, to keep time moving along at the usual clip, so that I don't get bored, or maybe so that I don't get interested, maybe it's getting interested that's fatal, that's a new idea. Maybe death is just stopping to get a better look at the world, that might be true, better not test it, better keep going, it's what the living do. But time keeps slipping out of my grasp, it feels too heavy to budge, and at the same time too light.

You know, when I have spent too much time with the timeless, the idea that things happen one after another, each causing the next in line, like a row of dominoes, strikes me as bizarre. Dominoes can fall two ways. So can effects cause causes, turn back the turning points, fold the unfolding and stack it for storage.

So I open the door of the shed, though I feel a moment of surprise—why did I expect it to be locked?—and am back in my school. I cross the upper landing and pass down the hall, my feet crying across the wooden floor, thus. Thus the walls hold themselves upright, leaning away from me a trifle, as if offended and pretending not to notice me. At the end of the hall the window is a pewter badge of light: flat, phlegmatic. I am in no doubt about where I am going and so the door is where I knew it would be and I open it. A fly zings out [static], bangs into my left eye, then reels heavily away, thus, and the momentary pain is thus.

Within, the door handle is fought over by sycophants eager to persuade me that they anticipated my entry. I give the handle an extra push as I relinquish it and have the gratification of seeing the door rap the forehead of the contest winner, one Mr. Mallow, junior administrator in training, whose smug expression gives way to indignation, then is forcibly reestablished, despite the red ridge rising on his forehead.

But I have seen it all before.

STUDY 7

The Right Use of Words

IS AND ARE

1. The boy...
2.
mul...
3.

F
we
C
with
the

4.

5.
your
6.

7.
8.
9.
10.
form
11.
12.
13.
14.
15.

LESSON LIV.

LETTER EXERCISE.

To the Teacher. — It will be helpful in fixing the *form* of the letter, to let the child practice for a while on blanks like that below. Only one form of letter, viz., that for letters of blankship, should be taught at this stage.

BLANK FORM OF LETTER.

..................., ...,

..................., ...

...................,

....

....

....

....

....

....

....

....

....

...................,

....

82. Copy this blank form, and then make it several times from memory.

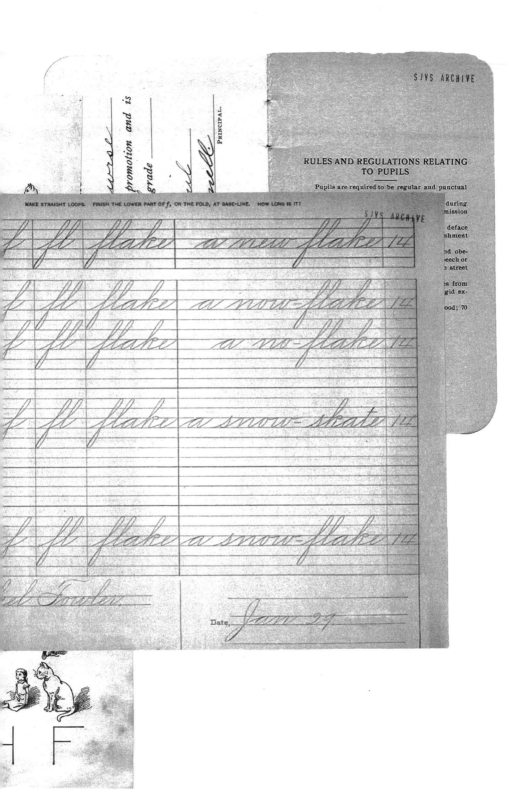

RULES AND REGULATIONS RELATING
TO PUPILS

Pupils are required to be regular and punctual

during
mission

deface
shment

nd obe-
eech or
e street

s from
gid ex-

ood; 70

promotion and is

grade

PRINCIPAL.

MAKE STRAIGHT LOOPS.   FINISH THE LOWER PART OF f, OR THE FOLD, AT BASE-LINE.   HOW LONG IS IT?

f fl flake   a new flake 14

f fl flake   a now-flake 14

f fl flake   a no-flake 14

f fl flake a snow-skate 14

f fl flake a snow-flake 14

Date, Jan 27

H   F

The Stenographer's Story, contd.

I was lying in my bed, putting in a little extra practice. That morning while suffering through laryngeal maneuvers I had felt something pressing up from inside my throat and all my hair had stood up on my arms, for I thought I had a ghost at last. It was only a belch. How the little ones had laughed, while the great girls rolled their eyes—"Disgusting!" one had said, and another choked out, "But my dear!"—pause to retch into a hankie— "We must make allowances for her background!"

The Headmistress, who was by chance quite close enough to hear, snapped, "I do not know what that is supposed to mean, when we all have the same background: the long, long march of the dead." It was an unlooked-for kindness, but I had much rather she had not said it, for I saw how the girls' merriment turned to vitriol. Later, at lunch in the refectory, they had all crowded together at the end of the bench, squabbling for the position farthest from me, while I stabbed my cutlet again and again with my fork.

But here in the dark my recalcitrant flesh seemed to spume away. I was only a darker patch of darkness, a shade among shadows. I parted my lips, lowered what I hoped was my larynx—

"Grandison!" my neighbor Jarndyce hissed. "Stop making revolting noises in your throat. Haven't we all had enough of that today?"

"I am practicing," I said calmly. "You would be wise to do the same. You may have the advantage of me today, but my endeavor will outlast your talent. And when you are as far below me as I am below you now, you may pray that I have forgotten how you spoke to me tonight."

She gave a little laugh. "Oddity!" she called me, but in an uncertain tone, so that I felt that I had triumphed.

Again I marveled at my own fluency, which was not achieved by force of will but came of its own accord when I reposed and even forgot myself. Then the words came trippingly. Was that what was meant by listening with one's mouth? I curled my hand into a trumpet and pressed it silently to my lips. That made me remember the *chth*, and fumbling in the darkness I opened my one small drawer, opened the folded piece of paper I found there and tried once more without success to imagine what a "hole in the air, to blow through" might feel like. I felt nothing. Whimsically, I raised that nothing to my mouth.

The next morning, I stood like an organ pipe between McCaughey (a little taller than I) and Ramshead (a little shorter) on the gravel drive before the school. Dawn kindling the parallel center parts in our smeared-back hair, still damp at the temples from the washbasin. Cold marbling white arms with purple, pinking elbows. My own were ashy though I had been surreptitiously dabbing them with butter from my breakfast roll, putting off the day I would have to ask someone—Miss Dearth, perhaps, or one of the colored maids—where I might get some lotion.

A nosebleed bloomed, exciting a brief commotion down the line. I did not move. My stiff new uniform stood out all around me. It seemed to contain a larger, invisible person, within whom I was trespassing.

"Say ah!" A hundred holes opened in the day. One chin trembled, one head dropped; a tap under the chin with a ruler lifted it.

The stepped façade was a hot red against what was left of the night. The flush slid down its face. The foot of the building was still in twilight, as were we. Was it chance that the Headmistress opened the door at the very moment the sun reached it? She looked like a golden icon in a shrine.

Mr. Behalf went down the rows, inserting a tongue depressor into each open mouth as we tried to translate into concrete action his murmured suggestions ("Speak in the *other direction*," "Hush *out loud*"). I heard gagging sounds from Dixon, Wang, McCaughey. Now Mr. Behalf had reached my place; the tongue depressor was inserted into my mouth and pressed firmly down. I tried, as I had already tried a hundred times, to "find my other lungs," hollowing the back of my throat in an effort to open it onto an elsewhere. I felt nothing but the roughish wood pressing down my tongue and a slight impulse to gag, which I warded off by sheer force of will. A chance thought flashed through my head—something about the right amount of flour to thicken a gravy; I saw my fingers softly brushing together, letting the flour sift between them to alight on the bubbling surface of the syrupy, almost black pan drippings—a humdrum image, but wrong in some way. What was it? Oh yes, the fingers I saw were a blotchy beige, not my own brown. And then I no longer felt the tongue depressor, but something else: a voice, a word, or rather a name, pressing up through my throat, as real as a shoe.

"Algernon!" I shrieked.

I did not know an Algernon.

I saw McCaughey and O'Donnell scowling as the others gathered around me, clapping my shoulders and blowing in my ears in the sanctioned celebration of a new ghost speaker. The Headmistress nodded approval. My mouth continued to enumerate Algernon's shortcomings—"you low-down moocher, you phony, you bootlegging, womanizing . . ."

Readings

from "A Visitor's Observations"

On Play

I am not sure that any games played at the Vocational School really deserved that appellation. Most of the organized activities of the school were calculated, so far as I could tell, to instill a keen sense of the insignificance of the individual and the flimsiness of his or her claim to existence. Skill was not usually a consideration, nor was fun, so I was surprised, one afternoon, to hear the merry sounds of children at play rising from the field where calisthenics were ordinarily performed to grim silence or groans. I had been strolling in the sculpture garden; now I started pushing my way out through its perimeter hedges toward the playfield, dealing good-humoredly with the inevitable scratches, for my spirits were lifted by the prospect of seeing the wretches *romping*.

The game involved a ball and a court with two sides where players in colors held various positions within complicated zones delineated with chalk. The whistle blew while I was forging a path past a feral forsythia; the players ran about like agitated ants; I took a step forward to see what they were doing, and was thwacked in the face with a wet branch. Once my vision cleared, and I had attained the edge of the playfield, I saw that the players had taken up their positions again, the ball having moved somewhat closer to one end (that of the white tunics), and come to rest in a different one of the many subdivisions of the playfield.

"I say! I think that child is ill," said Dr. Peachie, who with Dr. Beede had joined me at the sidelines. A boy had run off the field and appeared to be retching into a cloth bag. Another student bent over him, and then took off toward the school building.

Dr. Beede peered at the boy over his glasses and began unhurriedly moving toward him, gesturing to us to follow. "It's not what you think," he said.

The boy rocked, rocked, and relieved himself into the bag. A few minutes later, Whit and McDougal came hurrying up, pulling on their gloves, and having given the bag a gentle squeeze, carefully turned a knobbly yellow object out of it into a white cloth one of them produced from the pocket of his robe.

"Good lord, what is that?" asked Dr. Peachie.

"An ectoplasmoglyph," said Whit, who was patting the object dry with a corner of the towel. He raised it up and regarded it appraisingly, turning it over and over with the tips of his gloved fingers.

"You mean that thing is pure ectoplasm?" Dr. Peachie exclaimed. "May I—"

He reached out, but Whit swiftly flipped the corners of the towel back over the object, and snugged it under his arm. "The Headmistress would not like it, Dr. Peachie."

The whistle blew—Whit and McDougal departed with their prize, watched by Dr. Peachie, who still seemed much struck by what he had seen—the teams ran hither and thither—and this time, my view unobstructed, I saw what they were about. Instead of moving the ball, they were moving the *playfield*, one team ceaselessly scuffing out and redrawing its numerous lines according to what appeared to be complicated rules of precedence and interdependence, while the opposing team did all in their power to hinder them, slyly redrawing freshly erased lines, rubbing out new ones, standing in the path of those not yet completed, or knocking a stick of chalk out of a player's hands with a quick elbow, right under the referee's nose. The ball reposed in its place unmoved (and heaven help any child who, accidentally or through craft, nudged it even an inch from its resting place!). It took only a slight perceptual adjustment, however (as when we perceive the dock as gliding past the boat, rather than the reverse), to imagine it flying back and forth across the field.

"I think I will rest a little before supper," I said. Drs. Beede and

Peachie turned back along with me. "Somehow I feel a little discouraged," I added.

"Yes, it's a shame—what I wouldn't give to run some tests on that object!" Dr. Peachie said.

"No, I mean—do they never just *play?*"

"Oh, I see what you mean," said Dr. Peachie.

"No, never," said Dr. Beede.

SJVS ARCHIVE

OFFICIAL PLAYING RULES
Of the game of "Not I"

The ball is called the "zero" and is not to be touched for the duration of the game. The object of the game is to capture the zero by drawing it into one's goal; the team with the most zeroes wins.

All players shall be equipped with large pieces of chalk and either rags or whisk brooms.

Players are roughly divided into four sorts: seekers, stoppers, scratchers, and ghosts. (In practice, any player can play any of these roles.)

Fig. 1

Fig. 2

No. 1 Seekers employ their chalks to capture the zero for their side by drawing around it, in strict numerical order, the successive zones of the playing field. Upon drawing the zero into the goal or "throat," seekers must call out "Not I!" (Seekers who forget to say the words will forfeit the zero and take a turn as ghosts; see No. 4.) Every time the zero is in your throat, you may free one ghost from prison.

WHAT A PLAY...

Fig. 1 'Zero'

Fig. 3 Ribbon

Fig. 4 Rag

Fig. 3

Fig. 4

No. 2 Stoppers attempt to trap rival players in a closed polygonal figure or "prison." These can be quite elaborate and part of the fun is designing such complex figures that the player does not even realize he is captured until the umpire blows his whistle and calls out "Not I!" Upon capture, they become ghosts.

No. 3 Scratchers employ rags or whisk brooms to strategically erase parts of the figures drawn by seekers and stoppers.

No. 4 Ghosts are a. those captured by stoppers and b. those who have broken a rule—have touched the zero, failed to call out "Not I!" player. Ghosts must wait on the

Percentage and Recapitulation

FOR

Month Ending ..... *Sept. 19.* .....

"The wave is as much trough as crest."

PERCENTAGE IN VARIOUS BRANCHES.

Reading	*92*	Rhetoric	*97*
Writing	*80*	Composition	*96*
Listening	*86*	Decomposition	*95*
Silence		Bot'y & Zoology	
Oral Calisthenics	*98*	Physics	*98*
Posture Arts	*90*	Necrophysics	*94*
Breath	*86*	Drama & Music	*95*
Mathematics	*90*	Self-Ablation	*98*
Geography		Ghost Speaking	
Thanatography		Acoustics Shop	
Literature	*85*	Necronautics	

Field Work-Land of the Dead · *100*

Ectoplasmoglyph Translation Practicum · *0*

RECAPITULATION.

Behavior,	*92*	Neatness,	*91*
Punctuality,	*0*	Politeness,	*91*
Days Absent,	*84*	Times Tardy,	*92*

Mrs. O. A. Reynolds

NAME OF PARENT.

Percentage

Month Ending

" Honor and shame
Act well your par

PERCENTAGE I

Reading	*9*
Writing	*8*
Listening	*8*
Silence	
Oral Calisthenics	*9*
Posture Arts	*6*
Breath	*7*
Mathematics	*9*
Geography	
Thanatography	
Literature	*9*

Field Work-Land of the

Ectoplasmoglyph Tran

RECA

Behavior,	*92*
Punctuality,	*0*
Days Absent,	*8*

Mrs. O. C.

Letters to Dead Authors, #8

Dear Mary Shelley,

Intermediate Death Studies. The students bend their heads over their compositions, fidgeting with their gags. Outside, the sun, a purplish stain in the haze, sinks behind dead trees. It is a dispiriting sight. I prefer the stainless black of night.

I have long contemned those spiritualistes who regard the Beyond with the same proprietary air that they would an heirloom sugar-dish, confident that their dear Departeds can be tempted away from exchanging platitudes with Ludwig van Beethoven and Pocahontas by the opportunity to festoon their descendants with ectoplasm. The dead have their own concerns. The grief or guilt of the living is not one of them.

Pray tell me then, how I should explain this scene? It is mid-afternoon; somewhere the students are doing tonsil lifts under the eye of Mme. Once. I am in conference with a visiting parent—a woman with a giant fleshy nose, pince-nez, and a look of dyspepsia—when the new girl, Finster, bangs into the office, gags, grabs her throat theatrically, and says in a low, sharp, unmistakeably male voice, "I thought I told you never to touch my spoons." Mrs. Woodbridge lets out a shriek and collapses. When she comes to, she immediately writes a cheque for a full year's tuition. I whisk away the cheque—and the child, who will receive an extra biscuit at supper—before she can change her mind. "It was he! It was my dear father!" Mrs. Woodbridge kept saying. But it was not her father. How do I know?

Because it was mine.

Mrs. Shelley, well do I know how expectation can deceive, moulding alien sounds and sights into the figments of a domestic idyll. But I neither wished nor expected to hear my father's voice. Now I am anadiplosis is the repeti—

Excuse me, little Upshaw posed me a question, and I lost my thread. I do not have the spirit to continue tonight. Perhaps I will pick up my pen again tomorrow.

(Next day, early:)

Perhaps I was mistaken, about my father. But I am rarely mistaken about the dead. But perhaps I was. Perhaps there are other fathers with a penchant for spoons and savagery. Perhaps nothing is more common. In any case I have heard nothing more from him. But I should not have taken up my pen, the eastern horizon is stained with pink. Dawn approaches; how I hate it. The sky peels up, bleeding, to admit another nasty day. I will to bed.

Vehemently,
Your Friend (as I hope),
Sybil Joines

9. The Final Dispatch, contd.

So I am back at the beginning of the chase. First whiff of the fox.

It is a cold November morning. This very morning, if I remember correctly. The Regional School Inspector is expected, and I have been making my rounds, looking over uniforms, giving the staff their lines, directing Clarence to retire our more ominous-looking learning aids to the cellar for the day.

Now Miss Exiguous, Mr. Mallow, Mother Other, and I are in one of the small gymnasia where advanced students put in extra practice. In a corner a tall girl is running rapidly and silently through a series of mouth shapes. In another a small boy at stretch stands leaning a little forward, showing excellent form as he uses his weight, slight as it is, to force his mouth farther down a blunt-tipped wooden cone that must already be challenging his tonsils. "Gag for the gain, Ballard," I bawl, and see a flicker of pain pass across Miss Exiguous's features; she will be reprimanded. The truth is that I play the hearty, horsey gamesmistress as much to amuse myself as to buck up the children.

And in the center of the room, there she is: Finster, as I live and breathe.

An unfortunate choice of expressions.

I have to restrain myself from plunging at her, for this is only a figment, I am pretty sure, a bit of the past propped up and put through its paces, though in admirable detail. See, for instance, how her hair, as didactically parted as all my girls'—as yours—is inching up into ripples despite the cruel tightness of the braids. A fine fuzz rises like a mist from the back of the neck.

Miss Exiguous is holding Finster before her by the upper arms and shaking her a little, her fingers sinking into the scanty flesh. The girl, forcing her arms away from her body despite the effort this must cost her, stares past Miss Exiguous at me—haughty, pugnacious, defiant. P-p-p-plosives explode. (Secretary, stet.) Miss Exiguous releases one arm, leaving behind her handprint in red, to pluck a handkerchief from her iron bodice and work it distastefully down her bosom, dabbing away the dots.

"What is it?" I demand. "Why this atmosphere of suppressed *Schadenfreude*, and why am I being subjected to what resembles a scene from a pantomime? Do let poor Finster go, Miss Exiguous."

"Finster has been showing off," says Miss Exiguous, reluctantly stepping back, "channeling rogues and foreigners to frighten the little ones. And now she has sent Mother Other's cat to the land of the dead!"

It takes me a moment to understand what I am being told for this is a pretty advanced class of mischief and I am inclined to believe that someone has been making up stories. But when Mother Other assures me that she saw with her own eyes the dispatch of her cat I am not so much angry as proud that Finster's skills are so far above grade level. But I put on a stern face.

"Finster, I must commend you for your precocious abilities," I say, "while condemning the hubris and lack of discipline that tempted you to this wanton display. In dealings with the dead, we must never put aside caution. The dead are not always kind." She gives me a quick mocking look. Have I said something funny? "You, a beginning student, have not had enough training to discriminate between malign and benevolent visitants, let alone to open a gateway to the land of the dead through which any sort of creature might blunder in or out! That is an experiment very likely to prove fatal, and you—and we," I add *sotto voce*, with a glance at Mother Other, for this is no time to lose another student—"are very lucky that it was a cat and not yourself who went through it! You will repair to the dormitory immediately and sit quietly on your bed with your hands in your lap, reflecting on your foolhardiness, until the lunch bell is rung." I hand her a cork. She inserts it, but again I see something ironical in the roll of her eye as she bobs a shabby curtsey and, shooed along by Miss Exiguous, departs. The saucy thing.

"What about my cat?" exclaims Mother Other.

"It will find its own way back, I expect," I say, with a gesture that refers the tribe of cat to its own devices.

"But—"

"Winnifred. You cannot expect me to go haring off after a cat at a time like this." For during the absorbing work of the morning I had not forgotten that all the while, somewhere not too far away, a [crackling] Regional School Inspector was [crackling] tightening his box tie, adjusting his cravat, smoothing his hair, donning his hat, picking up his scarred cane (its grip darkened by hair oil) and rapping it once on the floor, was exiting his small office, gliding down the gloomy stairs, was raising the crooked end of the stick to alert the cab driver already summoned by his amanuensis, was refusing assistance to hoist himself into his seat and attempting to conceal his surprise and dismay at the loss of the shiny brass button that his exertions had caused to shoot into the cab, was feeling for the button with the tip of his cane as the vehicle lurched into motion, was making a quick dart to investigate a rattling sound (his head disappearing from view), was rising red-faced and discomfited with nothing in his hand as the vehicle rattled past the last house on Main Street, was ducking again as the cab creaked and boomed over the old bridge across the Slow River, tan and smoothly swollen with recent rains, was cutting off a curse as the vehicle bounced over the gravel-filled ditch where erosion was carving the bank out from under the end of the bridge and he struck his head against the corner of his briefcase, which was slowly working its way off the edge of the slippery leather seat, was rising with the button clutched triumphantly in his hand and sitting back to watch with a sanguine expression as fields gave way to trees whose bare, black branches were made even gloomier by the gray sky and wisps of mist, was opening his palm to regard his prize with idle pleasure that turned to surprise and dismay as he beheld a button, yes, but the wrong button, cheap and tarnished, was casting it into the depths of the cab with a disgusted look, was disappearing again to root for a long time among pebbles, horsehairs, pine needles, and crumbs, finding and discarding again and again the wrong button, and once, the right button, not recognized as such, before giving up in disgust, as the cab turned off the main road between Cheesehill and Chesterfield onto

the narrower road toward the Vocational School; that the cab was crossing the Slow River again and then again as it squiggled toward us down
the ravine, then emerging onto fields with scattered brakes, skirting the
frog pond, its jingle and creak startling the frogs into silence, except one,
which continued yelling its slogan at regular intervals, passing through
the gates and up the graveled drive, approaching the school, which came
angling up like an ocean liner in the chill mist, was crunching to a stop,
whereupon the [crackling] Regional School Inspector, taking hold of the
door handle, and, not waiting for the cab driver, was forcing open the
reluctant door, stepping down onto the gravel, and starting up the steps
toward the front door.

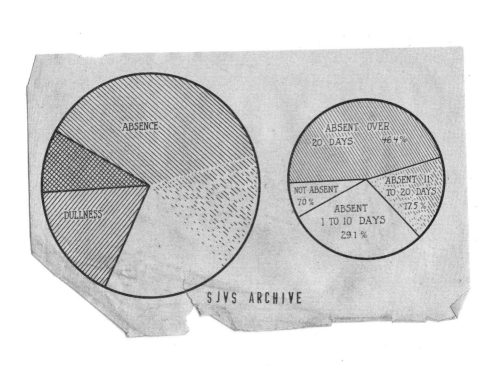

ABSENCE

DULLNESS

ABSENT OVER
20 DAYS   46.4 %

NOT ABSENT
70 %

ABSENT 1
TO 20 DAYS
17.5 %

ABSENT
1 TO 10 DAYS
29.1 %

SJVS ARCHIVE

The Stenographer's Story, contd.

I swim up from sleep, frowning, my mouth working—who? who? I cannot remember who I am, where. Open my eyes on a blue barely morning world, the sough of sounder sleepers, ranked bedsteads, the—the *dormitory*, got it, and I, a student here for some months now, am *Grandison*, whose first name I cannot pronounce—but it does not matter, here; gone are the routine humiliations of the classroom and its sequelae on the playground—yes, I, Grandison, am waking and telling over the letters of my name like rosary beads. Inside my head it is not quite silent—transmissions are passing through me, radio waves perhaps, looping languidly through the countryside on their way somewhere more important, but more likely ghosts, which are quite a lot like radio announcers, faraway people saying important things, but so quietly that ordinary people cannot hear them no matter how hard they try; but I can.

For I have the knack. And now, unseen inside the cave of my sheets, I exult. No one can any longer persuade me that it is by mistake or deceit that I am here; I belong. My lips move against the coarse bedsheets as I form an O for the pleasure of feeling the words already taking shape in my mouth: "I was standing on the edge when my uncle came up behind me . . ." But I do not even need to move my mouth to hear them. To one with the knack of hearing, the place is reverberant with whispers.

But it seems that not everyone can hear them, even here. Not even the instructors, who stand in front of the beginning students lecturing them on how to speak to ghosts while brushing aside the ghost who is shouting in their ears the whole time, trying desperately, poor dismal creature, to make herself heard.

It was still early. The dormitory was silent except for the whickering of ghosts and the drone and whistle of the sleepers; a soft gray-blue glow filled the ogive windows and delineated the ribs of the slightly arched ceiling, picked out each each humped quilt, each iron headboard, and the shoes set side by side under the bed. Somewhere in the bowels of the building a thump more felt than heard meant a hob of coal dumped down beside the iron stove, a groan was the heavy iron door swinging open so the coal could be shoveled on the banked fire within; I had not seen it done but I heard the same sounds in the same order every morning and had come to imagine the scene thus. A bird lightly bumped the window glass and reeled away, not much hurt, I thought, or a ghost told me, it was not too good if I could not tell the difference between what I thought and what the ghosts said to me but that was the way things were probably going to be here, there was someone talking almost all the time, saying, for instance, "Are you the One?"

"Oh, stuff it!" I said (and a muffled complaint rose from the next cot over): They were always trying to make you feel important, it was one of their tricks. So I brought the wings of the pillow up around my ears and felt the soft rushing of my blood close in around me and grew sleepy once again.

And woke up again with a snort to the muted uproar of a general arising; quilts flung off with the sound of sails snapping in a changing wind; a pell-mell rush to the washroom to the clop and shuffle of untied shoes on bare feet; someone already crying, a slap, a muffled curse. The bright gray light had lost its blue. The ghosts had receded, summoned to a stronger electromagnet, perhaps, such as the Headmistress. Through her mouth a gale of voices blew, so many and so furious it was hard (for me) to see her face; it seemed to be made up only of a rushing, a tending, an intending that was not her own. What she was, herself, was impossible to make out behind or through all that commotion and yet she had a powerful persona that was not only the borrowed authority of the ghosts. It was partly a straight back, broad shoulders, strong jaw, and a dress like the sails of a man-o'-war. But also a partly repressed but palpable emotion more powerful than any ghost could muster (for lack of the requisite glands): perhaps unhappiness, perhaps hate. Or fear . . .

Could the Headmistress be afraid of ghosts? The idea, true or not, made me laugh a little with pleasure as (skipping the icy ablutions to be had in the washroom) I struggled into my wrinkled dress, stamped my feet into my shoes, and followed the others down the stairs and out the door.

Fig. 16. The Pupils Are Blindfolded When Beginning Spontaneous Speech

Readings

from "A Visitor's Observations"

On Certain Objects in the Collection

Throughout the school and its grounds one could find the most original statuary, *objets d'art*, and other items whose purpose, decorative or functional, I could not guess. These fell into two main categories (not easy, at first, to tell apart): "travel souvenirs"[16] inspired by things the Headmistress had seen in the land of the dead, and "figures of speech," inspired by proverbs, cliches, and dead metaphors.

The Wrong Tree and the Blue Streak are examples of the latter category, as are the Spoon in the Wall and the bronze statue in the west wing of a running cat with a graphically severed tongue writhing in her mouth. Passing references to these in various documents ("At 3:30 the second-graders have to bark up the wrong tree") caused me considerable confusion before I realized they were actual objects, some of them in daily use! These "figures of speech," eerie at first, lose their mystery once the viewer hits upon the idiomatic expressions that unlock them. The "travel souvenirs," however, open to no key on earth. I was able to prevail upon Clarence, the majordomo, to take me on a tour of them. Here are some of the things I saw:

In an alcove in the northeast stairwell a mechanical woman was seated, breast-feeding a bird; from the concealed tubing, drops of real milk beaded on the black beak.

On the Headmistress's desk a white carnation stood in an inkwell vase, slowly turning black.

---

16. Speaking of souvenirs: With more commercial sense than good taste the current headmistress has contracted with a company in China to produce a number of cheap plastic trinkets that are offered for sale to alums, parents, and curiosity-seekers on the school website. New items are always in the works, but at the time of publication these included a snow globe containing a seated maiden with eyelashes so long they hang down in two ribbons and hide her eyes completely, until the globe is shaken, when they twine around rather disquietingly and afford occasional glimpses of the two pinhead dots of her pupils; a plush dashboard ornament in the shape of a legless, eyeless dog; a flash drive in the shape of a tongue with what appears to be a chancre on it, inside of which tiny pages turn when the tongue is plugged into a USB port.—Ed.

In the hall outside her office door, a flock of knee-high, rather soiled wind-up clouds rolled out an open door, across the hall, and in the opposite door. One banged into the doorframe, churred angrily for a moment, then jittered sideways enough to bumble through.

On a plinth in the garden, surrounded by a brick walkway, an oversized bust of the Headmistress bulged and wallowed strangely. When I drew near I heard a faint buzzing coming from the statue and realized that it was really a very fine mesh sack, given sculptural form with cunning tucks, darts, and gathers, and filled with a quantity of gnats all excitedly airborne and keeping the sack distended through the wind of their wingbeats and the impact of their bodies against the mesh. The bust subtly changed coloration as the gnats concentrated momentarily in the bridge of the nose, say, or one cheekbone, though it depended on the angle of the light whether these thickenings appeared as brighter or darker areas. "On special evening occasions we use fireflies," Clarence said, and indeed I did eventually get a chance to see the bust flickering, greenly glowing, and undulating in the summer night.

Clarence led me through a gate into a boggy fenced area through which a brick path wound. Tea-colored water pooled in the sunken areas, and the rank air was avid with mosquitoes. Clarence told me that an inverse sculpture garden had been constructed here, a series of allegorical sculptures that looked from the path like so many holes in the ground. However, "There were . . . problems," said Clarence, with a sidelong glance. I encouraged him to elaborate, and he told me that a child had fallen into one of the sculptures, where he endured the company of a long-deceased rodent or small cat all night before he was found, feverish and raving. Certain things the child said in his delirium made the Headmistress narrow her eyes. She had herself lowered into the largest of the holes— Clarence seemed to derive some private amusement from recalling this event, for which a team of oxen had been employed—and discovered that the intricate details commissioned from the sculptor and attested to in his sketches were not there; she had been gulled. "What's the difference?" the sculptor had the nerve to ask, when confronted. "Why pour my talents into a hole in the ground? The real artistry lay in shaping your opinion about the hole, and that I accomplished."

"Unfortunately, my opinion has changed," said the Headmistress.

The other sculptures were inspected and found similarly wanting, and the garden was subsequently abandoned, the holes allowed to fill with water and dead leaves. Only one of the artist's sculptures, the Headmistress's first commission from him, was found to be everything the sculptor had claimed. Clarence took me to see it; it was in another part of the garden. It showed the inverted Headmistress seated on a rearing, blindfolded horse, though *showed* is not the right word, as all one could see from above ground was a rectangular slab of marble, what would have been the base had this been a more typical statue. A little farther along was another rectangular slab. I nodded to it, said, "Another underground statue? I thought—"

"No, it is just that you cannot see the hole in the air, since air and the absence of air are both transparent; you would have to fill the hole with something, a colored gas, smoke . . . Though it would probably leak right out . . ."

I was witness to the construction of a few new additions to the collection. The Headmistress oversaw the preparations with barely contained eagerness, intervening often to correct details, most of which could make no difference to anyone but her, as far as I could see. For instance, she had all the concealed screws holding together a mahogany cabinet—if it can be called a cabinet that had, as far as I could make out, no doors—replaced with left-handed screws, which (these proving difficult to find) she had to commission from a metalsmith in Pittsfield. This accomplished, she had the apparently finished cabinet disassembled a second time so that its interior walls could be faced with mirrors, which I am sure no ray of light ever touched after the screws were tightened (widdershins). When the cabinet was reassembled, however, after a long intent look, she turned away in evident disappointment and even disgust, as a connoisseur might from a cheap knockoff. There was, it seems, some ineffable quality of the objects and entities resident in the land of the dead that could not be reproduced in the substances of our world. Why did she keep trying? Homesickness, perhaps.

Letters to Dead Authors, #9

Dear Mr. Stoker,

My voice weakens. It seems to sink back into me, as if my body had every day more need of it, and for a program more urgent than the advertisement of my suffering. Soon I will be talking only to myself.

Maybe that is one definition of death.

I doubt it.

Speaking, I cough; coughing, I bleed; speaking is bleeding, now. I stretch my spotted handkerchiefs on embroidery frames that I label with the date and time, for future study. I can look at them for hours. To me they are eloquent.

You know, I have always been a sort of anticipatory corpse. I look *back* upon myself, as if from the point of view of another, later born, to whom I seem a figure out of history, oddly clad and not perfectly three-dimensional. Among other, realer people, I am an absence in a dress. So I have no doubt that I will survive my death. I have already done so.

The cat came back—thought she were a goner but the cat came back—

Just one thing bothers me. If I am no one, how can I return? If every word is a chord—if every voice is a chorus—if every self is a hole through which these ghostly voices pour—and if every ghost is an assembly of other ghosts themselves assemblies, all of them recruited in one another—then either there is no one there at all—ranks upon ranks of zeroes—or a bland Everyone without distinctions—or an impossibly ancient solitary Someone, the first being ever to speak and thus uniquely ghostless.

The cat came back, yes, but who is she? A cave Cassandra, a pedestrian fish, an ambitious alga. A nobody, a manybody, like everybody else. A name. A shell. A Trojan horse with nothing inside it.

But that nothing will open the gates.

Let us think about real horses instead, how they are hairy and great, and do not say "I," but are there all the same, shitting where they please. Horses cannot be parted from themselves, I think, and so they have no ghosts, I think. About cats I am less sure.

If there is no self, who on earth is writing this letter? I had better end it.

But I am forgetting what I wished to say: There has been another fatality. The stupid boy ran too far with a passing remark of mine (in an address on Concrete Speech) on the subject of blood. Did he hope to please me by subtracting his tuition from the coffers, and subjecting us to impudent attentions from the law? The chief of police made himself a nuisance with his doddering inquiries and hints about chickens coming home to roost. He claims to have known my father; I told him I was sure he had, and my grandfather and no doubt great-grandfather too! Then I pretended to allow my father to say, "Hello, Tom," and the chief pulled so odd a face I would have laughed out loud had not the black crepe drawn over the mirror reminded me that the proprieties demanded a more somber countenance.

You may be curious about the substance of my thoughts on blood. They are as follows. If every substance we emit is a form of speech, bleeding is of these the *ne plus ultra*—the last word—because it is so often literally the last word. In it, form and content consummate their bond, since death, source and destination of *all* speech, is also its eventual consequence. Furthermore, blood offers a particularly fine demonstration that all speech is haunted. Do not our fathers and our mothers consort in every clot of it? Smeared on a glass slide, it reveals to the inquisitive lens a family tree in miniature, each leaf a grinning corpuscle crying out, "Forget me not!"

I have in my reticule such a slide, which I had the foresight to prepare before the law arrived to curtail my researches. After I had put it away, I sat on a piano stool beside the corpse and listened hard, for I hoped his wounds might "ope their ruby lips," as the Bard has it, and tell me something of interest, rather than continuing that red filibuster that had probably ruined a carpet that, though secondhand and somewhat worn, was a *bona fide* Persian. I heard, perhaps, a hissing, very faint. One of his thigh wounds—he had stabbed himself in numerous places: thighs, calves, forearm, groin—seemed to purse around a word, but it kept silent, it was done with speaking. I had missed the recitation.

Or had I? I put my face to it and, speaking, felt time slow and eddy around my mouth.

Unfortunately, it was at this point that the chief entered the room, leading Detective Munch (rhymes with *lunch*). He let out an exclamation, and I was forced to straighten up, and see the wound's fresh-wetted lips blow a bubble to mock my hopes as time enforced its tyranny again. The chief of police cleared his throat. I believe he thought that I was attempting to drink the boy's blood like your own Dracula! Nor did he inform me once during our interview that I had a smear of blood on my chin. Was not that unmannerly?

Your Friend,
Headmistress Joines

10. The Final Dispatch, contd.

This is how it happened.

All was in readiness for the inspector's visit. Wholesome scenes of youthful industry were on repeat in every room. The most obliging spirits had been given their lines, the least obliging students sent to the playfield. So I was undismayed, when I repaired to my office to fortify myself with a glass of paregoric, to see that the door was open and that the ubiquitous Miss Exiguous stood just inside it holding, with a ridiculously sacerdotal air, a man's hat.

A white cat curled around the doorjamb as I approached and scooted away, and I heard a calm voice—yours—saying, "She will be here presently." I entered my office; a man I did not recognize but who wore the ill-fitting suit of petty officialdom and thus had to be the Regional School Inspector came toward me with his hand outstretched in greeting.

"I would like to tour the facilities, of course, and observe a class or two," the Regional School Inspector was saying. "Then take a gander at your records. But first, a little chinwag, eh?—about some of the stories that have been going around. As I think you know—"

I heard a sudden ruction and turned. Miss Exiguous seemed to be trying to hold the door closed against some impetuous force. "No, you bold creature, you may *not* come in!" she exclaimed. "The idea! Return to your scheduled coursework immediately."

There was a bang, a scuffle, a sharp cry from Miss Exiguous, and Finster's head, braids swinging, poked momentarily through the door. "I have something to—I want to give information"—she gasped out, before a male hand, fastening on her ear, hauled her back over the threshold—"against the Headmistress!" could be heard at surprising volume, considering that it was receding down the hall, and muffled as by a hand.

The Regional School Inspector met my eyes. With an apologetic smile that was little more than a wince, he said, "I think we shall have to hear her out, don't you?"

"Certainly not!" Miss Exiguous said, rubbing her shin, but then saw my face. Hastily, she threw open the door and called Mr. Mallow back. Finster was propelled before the School Inspector as forcefully as she had just been repelled from him.

She slouched between Mr. Mallow and Miss Exiguous, head hanging. Now that she had her way, impudence had given way to girlish shyness, and *shy* is not a word one would generally apply to Finster. Nor is *girlish*.

"And what is your complaint against Headmistress Joines, my dear?" the School Inspector said. Finster cut her eyes toward me. "Do not be afraid, you are under my protection. Speak clearly, and do not tell fibs, and no one will hurt you."

"Shh-shh-she bothers me," she mumbled. "She watches me. I don't know why she has to watch me all the time! And she gives me things."

"What things?"

"Strange things. Nasty little dolls, made of dirty old sticks and things. Th-th-they"—she sucked in her lower lip in an exaggeratedly childish expression—"*fwighten* me." I recognized this for playacting, but I took the blow anyway, and unfamiliar tears sprang into my eyes. A barely nascent tenderness was spoiling into an old familiar hurt. It was rabbits all over again.

"Anything else, child?" said the School Inspector.

But of course she did not love me, or even like me. I had taken her mother away. That her mother had mothered indifferently, at best, did not matter. It had not mattered to me.

"And . . . And she touches me, during the exercises." My head came up.

"Oh! Only the way she touches all the children, to correct their carriage, and their embouchure, and so on!" Miss Exiguous said defensively.

"But I don't *like* when she touches me! I don't want her to! I don't, I don't!" Cracking, Finster's voice boomed, dropped an octave—to the register of a grown man—before resuming its childish accents.

Then I knew my enemy.

When I forget that I have seen it all before, I move through these events as liquidly as I did back then. As if anything could happen and not just the terrible thing that had to. As if the past were a great open space and not a solid mass as of pulped paper through which I follow my own inky footsteps, these, toward the inevitable moment when that small mouth opened and my father's voice came out.

His voice plunged into me as if my skin, my meat, my bones, the marrow of my bones, my blood and water were no impediment but an invitation. (You will recall that I said something similar of my mother's face. The effect of course was quite different.) It was not my ears that knew him; his voice rushed past my ears on its way to deeper places, and I had already practically forgotten the sound of it by the time it was rubbing against my internal organs. My kidneys remembered it, however. My duodenum, my heart. My bladder remembered it and released a tiny jet of urine into my unmentionables. My large intestine remembered it, reversing hours of peaceful peristalsis in two seconds flat. Seemlier parts remembered it too, but no part remembered it joyfully.

"That's not the child speaking!" I cried, and looked around for corroboration.

"Why"—said the School Inspector, and if I had not been so upset, I might have laughed to see his face—"who else could it be?"

I folded my arms, pinning my trembling hands to my ribs. "On the whole I am not surprised. My father always lacked stick-to-it-iveness."

The School Inspector laughed nervously. "You are saying it is . . . your father's ghost."

"Speaking through the girl," I agreed, though my voice faltered, for already I sensed that I had made a mistake.

He looked grave. "It is not very like a man's voice."

"There are limits to what a child's vocal cords . . ." put in faithful Miss Exiguous, but I shut her up with a look, for I was roused now and would not stoop to placate and explain.

"Why is she saying these things?" piped my father, in a mockery of a child's voice. "What does she mean?" Goaded, I raised my hand, and she shrank from me. "Don't let her touch me!" Her voice crackled like a fire.

"No one will let her hurt you, my dear," said the School Inspector. "You are perfectly safe. Headmistress Joines, please collect yourself."

"As if there were something sinister in—in caring for a child!" It was the first time I had acknowledged it since rabbits, caring that is, for anything but my work, and something in my chest opened—probably a pulmonary vessel, but it felt like my heart. I saw, of course, that I was doing myself no good, but I could not stop blackening my name. "When it is really all the children I have *not* cared for that should be charged to my account! But no, you *like* cruelty, you like pain, it is tenderness you want to stamp out . . ." A fit of coughing interrupted me, and I yanked out my handkerchief and buried my face in it. No one spoke until I finished.

Then in the silence, as I dabbed blood and sputum off my lip, my father piped up again. "And when I'm in bed, she—"

I flew at Finster then, intent on clamping my hand over her mouth, unwilling—unable!—to hear another nasty, sly, insinuating word. Swinging, my fichu caught on the oil lamp. I swiped at the vessel, thinking to catch it from the air, but only dashing it more forcefully to the floor. Perhaps to another it might even have appeared that I meant to do it. The flames roared up at the child's feet, her splattered skirt caught fire, she saw my hand coming down, and with a scream that was, at least, entirely her own, she threw herself down her own throat.

I have said it many times, but it bears repeating, that in the land of the dead, it is what we say about the world that determines what world we see, and so it is not possible to tell a story about the past without living that past again, and not as a memory, but as current events. So when I say she screamed, what I mean is that she is screaming, and when I say that tears sprang into my eyes, I mean that I am crying, and when I say that I was going after her, I mean that I am going, I go, the aperture that is all that is left of her is still shimmering in the air and turning from it I am leaping down my own throat. Here I go, I fall, I fly, I swallow myself . . .

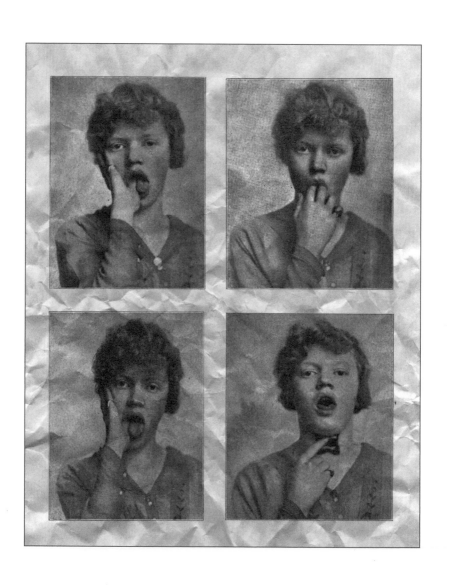

The Stenographer's Story, contd.

It is customary in telling stories from school, I understand, to include a few rib-tickling accounts of youthful antics. Antics have never been to my taste, but obedient to the genre, I will attempt to put one down.

I was hiding in the bushes, having slipped away from a boisterous game of Enough of Your Lip, in which I had already received four headstones (I was never athletic). I was a city girl, and both open fields and enclosing woods made me uneasy, the first with the thought of watching something approach inexorably from far away, the second, of something creeping close unseen. But the snug green warrens under the bushes felt like a haven. Crouching in the duff, twigs scratching my shoulders, I felt my breath calm, my heart slow.

That I was losing the game was not the only reason I had wanted to be alone. I was hoping to be visited by a ghost: I thought I could feel someone halfway up my throat. Ghost-speaking without a spotter was forbidden, but I did not want the others to see how often and how hard I practiced. My mouth was just arranging itself into an old-fashioned shape when a whisper and a muffled laugh told me that I had been discovered. I crouched lower, screwing my feet into the loose leaves to find firm ground to push off from. Then I burst from under the bush like a jackrabbit, as the visiting spirit—for that is what it was—called out quite loudly and with surprising, but most unwelcome pertinence, "Little Bobby Black-bird sat upon a tree, singing to the pussy-cat, you can't catch me!"

I followed this with a little mew of dismay, wholly my own, for in fact they *could* catch me, as I well knew, and give me a drubbing, too.

A little stream, amusingly called a river, took a semicircular bite out of the bottom of the playfield, swung wide around the Chapel, made an exploratory swipe at the back of the school, where several tall trees dropped leaves over a cutbank onto its rippling, spangled surface, then set off toward Cheesehill down a course choked with fallen trees. Eventually it dove between wooded hills and disappeared. More than once I had made a timely escape by splashing through it, leaving my pursuers, who did not care to soak their only pair of shoes, to dance on the far bank. But its winsome limpid shallows could be deadly if another student had you by the back of the neck and was forcing you down, down into the airless rush and glitter . . . I veered back into the bushes. The other boys and girls roared with joyful rage and began thrashing through the thicket toward me.

"Little Bobby Black-bird swimming in the sea," I caroled, "singing to the pussy-cat, you can't catch me!"

They caught me, had me, were pulling on my pinafore so hard I fell over backwards. I lay staring up at a ring of mirthful faces and above them swaying leaves against a white indifferent sky.

"Black-bird, black-bird," they chanted, and kicked leaves at me and dirt, hooting. A rock bit my side. Then something hot was writing on my stomach and with high laughter several other boys had their flies down too and yellow cords were hissing and drilling into my sides and splashing in my turned-away face through which my visitor was still singing, though now quite calmly and gently, "Little Bobby Black-bird, lying in the ground. Singing to the pussy-cat, I'll never be found."

And then suddenly they were not there anymore and nothing was but that voice, though it was now more like a landscape than a sound. After a little while I struck up a self. I seemed to be dressed in my usual clothes but there was something strange about my feet, I felt sure that they were on backwards, though they looked no different than usual, and I understood that I was crippled, we all were, having turned our feet around to deceive ourselves about the direction we were going. I lost myself in these and similar reflections for an eternity, and I use the word advisedly, for it would have been eternity indeed had not one of my frightened tormentors run off to confess their misdeeds to a teacher. The next thing I felt was an unpleasant wrenching, somewhere under my ribs, and then I was flat on my back in the Headmistress's office, staring up into her inverted face. I turned my head and vomited onto the rug.

That was the first time I visited the land of the dead.

S.J.V.S.
DATE <u>Feb. 3</u>

IDENTIFICATION CARD
NOT TRANSFERABLE

A

Ms. Margaret M. H. Finch
NAME

Student
TITLE

IS AUTHORIZED TO ENTER THE SYBIL
JOINES VOCATIONAL SCHOOL DURING
SCHOOL HOURS UPON PRESENTATION
OF THIS CARD.

EXECUTIVE OFFICER

NOT VALID UNLESS COUNTERSIGNED

Margaret M. H. Finch

Readings

from "A Visitor's Observations"

On Articles of Dress

That the topic of ornamental sculpture leads naturally to that of fashion, anyone who has seen a poke bonnet or top hat, hoop skirt, or ruff must agree. I saw some curious articles worn by students and faculty alike. I will not call them clothing, as they resembled many other human inventions so much more closely: slings, baffles, windbreaks, kites or *koinobori*. Some seemed to be a kind of camouflage, some protective, like medieval armor or beekeepers' suits, some, in which the wearer moved with flinching care, to be instruments of self-punishment or mortification. Many incorporated elements that could ostensibly be used in some professional capacity (that is, in communicating with the dead), such as inflatable bladders sewn into the lining of a gorget in which breath could be stored for emergency release; cheesecloth seines, trawls, and creels for collecting ectoplasm; or telescoping cones made of whalebone frames covered with waxed cloth or paper that could be strapped onto one's mouth or, with a small adjustment to the armature, one's ear. (Some of the latter were as much as eight feet in length, and their wearers required seconds whose sole task was to support the wide end of the cone on a pole with a curved and padded saddle on the end.)

Some costumes fluttered with countless tassels and fringes that far from being decorative gave one the disquieting impression that the wearer was gradually disintegrating into the surrounding air, and in fact its finest threads, light enough to be lofted by the least current of air, sometimes brushed against one's upper lip long after the wearer had apparently left the room. Some bristled with whalebone spars up which vanes, spinnakers, and flags could be run. Some had extensive outlying parts: extra detached sleeves, epaulets upon epaulets, storm flaps, petticoats, snoods, bustles, ruffs, and cummerbunds that all had to be laboriously gathered up and carried along whenever the wearer decided to move. Some were so cumbersome in their volumes of heavy fabric that they effectively prohibited movement; I remember one that resembled an untidy hay-bale onto the side of which the tiny wearer was awkwardly strapped, as if she were no more than an accessory to her outfit. Some were designed to fasten around a piece of furniture, an architectural element such as a stair baluster, or another person (who did not always appear entirely complacent in the role). Others, resembling sails, really became sails whenever the wind blew, sweeping up the incautious wearer and hustling him along, until a wall or hedge stopped his progress. A few were so tiny—a scrap of cloth intricately bound around an earlobe, say, or the tip of a finger—that the wearer was effectively undressed (though fully if not decently clad in the thick, scratchy, institutional smallclothes issued to all students and faculty to mollify the frigid conditions obtaining at the school). Some outfits seemed to be entirely invisible; I do not know whether they were worn internally (belted around the tongue or a tooth, for instance), were carried in a hand, or did not even take physical form, being composed of the smell of damp wool, the mere idea of a dress kept firmly in mind, or a story repeated at intervals about, say, an exquisite but deadly shawl, whose pattern, picked out in embroidery silks that had steeped in poison, etched itself into the skin of the wearer.

From time to time an outfit would be greeted with indignant cries of "Not so!" and "It's a lie!" Eventually it was explained to me that they were not merely garments but propositions, provocations, conjectures, rumors, slanders. Some seemed designed solely to refute an outfit worn by another student, whether in formal rejoinder, parody, or the pedantic correction of a host of minor details. And some, indeed many, perhaps (understood correctly) all, refuted the wearer himself, since one of the principle tenets of the Vocational School was that the first person is an illusion, to be programmatically dispelled. I saw one student, for example, gliding about in a wheeled whalebone framework from which hung so many curtains, lambrequins, and shades, constantly opening and closing, that her person could not even be located within them. Of course, this made the ensemble, if not the person wearing it, all the more conspicuous, but then the effect on prospective viewers never seemed to be the point of the costumes of the Vocational School.

Sometimes entire outfits were in the subjunctive case, as if to say, "If I were to dress myself today, it would be in this way, but of course I will not, for no such person exists." Perhaps one could say as much of the fashions worn in the world at large, and I only noticed it for the first time here, at the Vocational School, because the costumes were, to my eye, so outlandish, and the population so small and isolated that new styles evolved at a fast clip. Or maybe the school has denatured the sphere of fashion for me as it has denatured that of language, so that I can no longer look at a boned bodice without consternation, as at a smaller, portable iron maiden, or regard a crepe mourning bonnet as anything but a listening device.

Speaking of bonnets, the sheer variety of these, as of helmets, muzzles, and other headgear worn at the school, was such as to dismay the taxonomist. Among the simplest was an oval of black tulle stretched over a wire frame, held up on another wire from a yoke that fit over the neck and shoulders in such a way as to entirely hide the wearer's face from view, if you were standing directly before her.

I remember another, more complex, whose innumerable tiny wires, radiating from a central armature, were passed through one end of as many tiny strips of paper of varying lengths on which printed words and phrases could be made out, probably sliced from a book, creating a fluttering penumbra at least five feet in diameter and somewhat resembling a dandelion seed head, through which the human head inside it could be made out only as a shadow. It must have taken days to make, and yet I saw it in use only once, and at the end of the day (a day whose still moments crepitated with disquieting whispers) the wearer removed it, held a lit match to it, and tossed it onto the gravel drive, where it softly bounced, tumbled, bloomed with flame, and went out.

Letters to Dead Authors, #10

Dear Mrs. Mina Harker,

Now it is my mother whose voice I seemed to hear. I was strolling down the corridor, listening complacently to the muffled retching of muzzled juniors, when a door flew open, releasing a cacophony in which I heard those familiar accents, and Finster darted out, trailing streamers of batting, a savage look on her face. It has put me in a very thoughtful mood.

In the words of a persistent newspaper columnist who has lately dogged my steps, why do I disturb the blessed rest of the departed, to draw from them their secrets, when there are living people eager to confess theirs on every street corner? Why wait until the Veil is drawn to bend an ear? Why do I cling to the dear departed, yet give no succor to the living, etc., etc.?

I have just spent a very long time staring at the candle flame (its afterimage, a bluish flame, is flicking and sliding now across the page on which I write these words). Someone is growling quietly in my throat. Or snoring, perhaps. I too am tired. Last night one of the children sleepwalked into my bedchamber, urinated in my second-best bonnet, and departed before I could shed my lethargy enough to turn him out.

I think he was sleepwalking.

We have a number of sleepwalkers here.

In any case I could not get back to sleep until nearly dawn.

It is true, Mina, that the living are merely *unmatriculated* dead, and any one of them may be as wise, as wicked, as tender, or as cruel as any spirit you could name. But I do not speak to the departed because they are dear to me. I am different from the majority of Spirit Mediums and Trance Speakers in this regard: It is not grief that draws me toward that Chasm, whose other shore is crowded with loved ones we have lost. It is not anger, either. It is . . .

I want to know.

Know what?

What it is like to exist, for instance. Contrary to popular opinion, only the dead can tell us that. You do not ask a horse what it is to be a horse. A bad example. I cannot think of a good one. Never mind. I mean simply that one must stand outside a thing in order to describe it; we cannot say what our eyes look like, what our tongues taste like, or what listening sounds like. We cannot know our knowing, or say what it is that saying says. And so we must cease to live in order to study life. That this leaves no one to record the results, some might call a cruel paradox, or a lesson in acceptance.

I call it a technicality.

And so I ask the question (for you yourself are dead, if you do not mind my saying so): What is living like?

What is the world like?

What are we?

And in a word: What?

But the telephone is ringing and—

I have just had an unpleasant conversation with one of our trustees. For the first five minutes I could not figure out which of our students she was talking about, but not imagining that it could be important, I regrettably decided to carry on without clearing up this point. When it became clear from my responses that I was laboring under a delusion, she very nearly put down the phone. The mistake was unfortunate, but understandable—I cannot know every student personally! She took the position, however, that I ought at least to remember *this* one. As if to die were a feat of particular originality. When I tried to explain that I had more important considerations than the carelessness of one not very talented child in getting himself killed, she became unreasonable. My nature is imperious, my temper hot; I nearly told her to go to the devil, but I bethought me of the handsome cheque we receive from her every autumn and began hastily offering up reassurances that no more students would die, which I am afraid were not sincere or even sensible, for how can I keep the executioner's axe from the neck that summons it? Not a single person has ever done so.

What a blight on the soul of a Seeker are pecuniary considerations!

When we had both cooled a little, I inquired as to where she had learned of the affair. It was the most important newspaper in which my school had yet figured, and I privately jubilated. While the incident may cast us in an unflattering light, I find that my theories stretch toward the light . . . I want them better-known.

It should be no big surprise. Dying, one thinks of one's legacy, and I have been dying my whole life.

Reply soonest,
Headmistress Joines

11. The Final Dispatch, contd.

[Crackling:] Where am I?

In the gymnasium with Miss Exiguous, Mr. Mallow, Mother Other, and the girl.

Again?

Again.

In life, things happen only once, as I recall. Therefore I am dead, in the provisional, the necronautical sense. Dead, and cooking up a scene; Miss Exiguous and Mr. Mallow are not really here.

"So there you are." It is Finster. And yet [static] it is not. "Put out your hands and take your punishment."

"Father," I say again. Again I tremble. [Static.]

Then another voice speaks through her. Frankly I doubt it is really my mother, she never stuck up for me. "Pay no attention to him. He was never the man he thought he was, and he is still less that man today."

"Whereas you are the whore you always were, you whore."

Miss Exiguous, who, even as a figment, is nothing if not correct, takes Mr. Mallow by the arm and summoning the few students still at practice leads them from the room in tactful silence.

"Mistress Other," I say, "you may go too."

The large woman draws herself up. "I don't know that I should leave you with that girl, Headmistress Joines. She might forget herself. I would not want her to commit an outrage against your person."

"My person is my own concern, Mistress Other. I hardly think that a small child poses a threat to it. Please leave us."

Seeing that she still hesitates, I exclaim, "Winnifred! Do I have to invoke my authority?" Mother Other flushes, seems about to say something further, then sets her mouth and leaves me alone with the girl, whose face is alternating quickly between two masks, like Comedy and Tragedy, though these are surely both the face of tragedy, and yet tragedy often has two sides and indeed two names and my tragedy is called both Mother and Father.

"My darling"—my father says to me, with cutting sarcasm—"at last we have a chance to really get to know each other, something I have always wanted, whether you knew it or not. Why, I'm your biggest fan. Headmistress Joines, is that what they call you? Well, isn't that nice! My daughter, who has always been so good at telling others what to do. I would be the first to admit that you have a persuasive way about you. Why, I believe you could get a man to do almost anything, whether it was in his best interests or not. I believe you might even be able to persuade him that it was his own idea, when really his little girl had put it in his mind, drop by drop, day by day, like a slow poison, in that quiet, cool little voice that as if to mock my ambitions for you had shed its stammer for this sole occasion, saying *don't you think* and *sometimes I wonder* and *isn't it true, Papa, that*, the words sinking deeper and deeper into a man's heart until he almost believed the lies you told him, a little girl who should never even have thought such thoughts, let alone thought them of her father—"

"Finster," I said, "end this session at once." She blinked and shut her mouth. "You will repair to the dormitory immediately and sit quietly on your bed with your hands in your lap until the lunch bell is rung." I handed her a cork. She inserted it, and left, and I sank down upon a stool, adjusting my skirt with shaking hands.

I could have put her in the oubliette, I suppose.

Cross that out. Sometimes I forget that one does not say such things.

But one is free to hope, I believe. Something [static] could happen to her, things do, there are stairs down which children sometimes run much too quickly, there are bottles of fluids about which children are naturally curious but from which [static] I am sure they should not drink, and there is the land of the dead, from which we do not all return, where a shed [static] has been assembling itself around me for the last few clauses. Under my feet are black boards, scuffed soft. Splintery, gray, split, and rivered boards rise up and tack themselves to nothing; angled beams through which tar paper shows lower themselves from the plaster medallion in the ceiling. The tiny window with its cracked pane shows my oak paneling for a moment, then a familiar foam of foliage.

Now [static, crackling] flames lick the bottom of the wall. Now they die down. It is plaster in any case and not splintery gray deal. Damp plaster with a greenish cast. Now black mold spreads over the walls, which flake away from the slats, fall in chunks to the rotting floor, through which they knock great holes. Through the holes I can see the party going on below. All the neighbors are in their nightclothes, standing on the grass, passing around mugs of hot toddy. Someone has died or [crackling] there has been a fire. Are those cinders blowing through the crowd or are my eyes failing? I try to move my legs, to find they are pinned by something warm and heavy resting on my skirt; it is the child, Finster, sitting at the end of my bed, leaning back on the baseboard. She is calm, though there is something knotted around her neck that seems to be making her uncomfortable, for she keeps raising one hand to touch it, and then lowering it with a fluttering, falling, hopeless gesture.

Is it Finster?

I do not see how she can speak, with that constriction, and in fact when she parts her bluish lips it is not her voice I hear, nor even my mother's, as you must have expected. "Dear daughter. Dear . . . voice. You are still talking, aren't you? What's that I hear you saying? Are you [echo]—why are you repeating what I'm saying to you?" There is a [pause] pause. Then: "You're 'creating' me, aren't you? 'Bringing me to life' in your words? You take that kind of power unto yourself, don't you. The power of life. And death, am I right? A little girl like you. Oh wait, I forgot, a great big woman now. Older than your mother was when she died. How do you feel about that, eh?

"Creating. Maybe you've forgotten who created you. Well, here I am to remind you. You must have known that I would have my say eventually. Silent as the grave for all those years . . . Well, I think I've done my time, dear daughter, voice, voice-daughter, spooky little creep, talker. [Very loud, almost screaming.] _Talker_."

Secretary, underscore *talker*. Double underscore it, the voice is very loud, almost screaming.

[Pause, static, sound of breathing.]

The child's face has gone slack, though her mouth jaws on, and her eyes are fixed on some distant point somewhere to one side of me. I deduce that she is listening to something only she can hear. Meanwhile my father has begun to crow, mistaking silence for capitulation. When he understands, he falls silent himself. Then he rallies.

"Ah, the still-small voice in the inner ear. As mother to child. Loving guidance in difficult times. How you must have yearned for Mother Dear to speak that way to you. What does this not particularly prepossessing child have that you do not? Is she sweeter? Cleaner? Prettier? More innocent? Which of your abundant defects drove her from you? Have you considered that your very love for her, for your mother, I mean, may have bored or even repelled her with its intensity? Recall the times when you tugged on her apron and she shooed you away! Maybe you were never really a delight to her. Maybe you were just not quite lovable enough to stand in the circle of her arms, in the [temple?] of her [inaudible]. Perhaps it was your stutter that she found [word indistinct], grotesque, even frightening—by God, I did!—or the pain you exhibited so nakedly when the other children laughed at you and called you names. It is a natural thing to avoid the sick and wounded animal, to loathe what others deem loathly. Even when it is [static] your own child. The unwholesome are slain or abandoned by the pack, it is the way of nature. And oh, God, when she died, the way you raved, drooled, sobbed, pissed yourself . . . Knowing her the way I do, I am sure she was disgusted. She was not one for passionate displays of feeling. I felt the frostbite of her judgment more than once, you can imagine. I'm sure you can imagine, because you are like me, aren't you, not like her? You rave with love and you rave with pain. You bellow with grief until your lips are sluiced with snot and tears and your eyes are red marbles. She hated it when I cried. She hated it when I loved her. She hated it when you cried and loved her. She hated it when she died and when, dying, she for a brief moment showed her own feelings. And I am sure she hated it most of all when in grief at her death and anger at me you tried to kill your own father, you unnatural little horror, you changeling."

Then, panting, between defiance and tears, a high color in her cheeks, she throws herself back through her own chapped lips, and I fling myself after her.

VIDE DIAGRAM CHAPTER VIII. VIDE DIAGRAM CHAPTER VIII.

The Stenographer's Story, contd.

I have told how I gained a reputation as a necronaut as well as a ghost speaker.

Meanwhile, in my secretarial role, I took upon myself more and more duties. I not only carried out the tasks required of me, such as typing and filing, and, increasingly, those more personal services formerly performed by Mother Other, such as the warming of slippers and dispensation of tooth powder, but I performed services no one else had thought to offer, such as applying mink oil and blacking to her ceremonial lungs, or pumping them full of air in advance of use. By watching, through keyholes if necessary, and listening, at doors if necessary, and reading such papers as she left on her desk, and sometimes inside it, I learned to tell when the Headmistress wanted something, and provide that thing without being asked. In this way I made myself indispensable.

From time to time I was uneasy. When I passed one of the colored maids, for instance, both of us hurrying, with things in our hands. At those times I apprehended that I was only by some frail magic walking on the water in which she was submersed, and feeling myself foundering, looked away. I worried, too, that a too-perfect service might cheapen my labor, cheapen me, by making the extent of my efforts invisible; that I might be passed over, not for being too far from the seat of power, but for being too close. One does not offer one's right hand a promotion.

Then, too, it seemed to me that at some point I had had another purpose. But I couldn't imagine what it might have been—perhaps only the purpose of conceiving my own purpose, and that seemed a small prerogative to cede. My purpose now was hers, and I felt that it was a grand one, though I did not understand it and thus toiled with all urgency toward a blind spot.

The same could be said to some degree of all of us. We were all, every one, turned toward the Headmistress like daisies toward the sun. Wintry sort of sun! An outsider might ask why we did not search out a warmer light. Almost anyone at all would have been more charismatic, inspired more trust, seemed better equipped to carry out this task that we obscurely felt would help us all. No, *help* is the wrong word, *help* only helps us to the things of *this* world, and she was furiously scratching away at this world with every sharp point of herself, only to get to another one. (For by now, we all knew that to equip us to earn a living was the least of her objectives.) If help can be useless and still be called help, that's the kind of help she offered. Yet that did not deter me. I wanted nothing more than to fill my hands with the uselessness that streamed from her.

Though I was at times unhappy—or so I suppose one would describe the way dreariness and dread stole over me in quieter moments—I never thought of leaving. I had moved further and further from my former self until I no longer felt estranged, just strange. But that strangeness *fit*. Every day I became more perfectly that "she" for whom alone some as yet untried lock would open.

One day, during a private administrative meeting with Miss Exiguous for which I was taking the minutes, the Headmistress coughed, dabbed her mouth with a mottled handkerchief, got up, and walked calmly out. Miss Exiguous's narrow little face flushed—she was in the middle of a lengthy presentation on the relative merits of surcharges for special privileges and an overall fee hike—and she seemed on the verge of chasing after her. Then she sighed and began scraping together her papers.

"If she seems distracted," she said, half to me and half, I thought, to herself, "it's because she hasn't chosen her successor yet, and naturally she worries; what would happen to the school, if she were to die? Not that she is unwell, though subject to coughs, well, we all are, in this unhealthy air, the damp rising from the fields at night fills the whole house with a miasma, I go to bed expecting never to wake up again, but I do wake up, we all do, she is no exception, she is if anything the strongest of us, and yet she worries, naturally, a mind of such penetration can see into the future, in which either there is a school, or there isn't one, it all depends on whether or not she finds the right successor."

She might have gone on speaking; I did not hear her. I was taking a call, being called—one might say, finding my calling. Except that way of putting it does not quite convey how I rang, body and soul, with the summons.

Successor!

I submitted greedily, lustily, sensuously to the discipline of my vocation. When I drew down upon me the wrath of Mr. Ister for my poor showing in oral calisthenics, I bounded across the room, even leaping a desk, to receive my beating. I actually dared to grab the baton and pull it even more violently against my mouth. (The next day my lower lip was stiff and cracked. I felt it protruding, and when I sensed people looking, I thrust it out even further.) But I had too often been denied my deserts to trust that merit alone would secure my position. So as hard as I worked on channeling the dead, I worked harder still on faking it. If my larynx shipped its anchor just as the teacher was calling on me, I rolled up my eyes to show the whites, dropped my jaw, and—false phonation weirding my vowels—put on a show. Even when I didn't need to, I pretended, just to keep in practice, until no one but me could tell the difference, and even I was not always sure.

I was not the only humbug in the school, though humbuggery took pluck, not least because the Headmistress took quite as much interest in an accomplished hoax as in a real ghost, and would engage it in metaphysical debate for as long as the hoaxer's inventiveness held out. Or nerve: I saw one student, under this treatment, burst into tears and confess. She refused to acknowledge him, and continued addressing her remarks to the "spirit," until he could no longer speak for blubbering. Then, "Your only error," she said coldly, "was the elementary one of imagining that you are a jot more genuine than your masquerade." So whereas at other schools it was the weaker students who cheated, among us, it was the strongest.

McCaughey and Wang were the ones to watch, I thought. Lancet was sometimes brilliant, it was true; one day he surprised everyone by disappearing down his throat for almost a full minute (Turnbull, one of his chums, said sixty-one seconds, but I made it fifty-six; all the same an impressive achievement for a third-former), but the red flags in his cheeks told me he loved his preeminence all too well for someone who was supposed not to exist. He would push himself too far and come to grief; that, or leave us. I once saw him consult a tintype portrait he had been hiding in his handkerchief. That sort of thing was completely forbidden, of course, and I let him know with a look that I had seen it, but would keep his secret—as long as it suited me! No, he was no threat.

But Wang and McCaughey, that was another story. One day Wang was ahead, dazzling everybody with the volume and timbre of his hush, which he projected so effortlessly that it seemed hardly possible that it found its source in one narrow rib cage. The next it was McCaughey, offering a spontaneous translation of a mouth object that was so authoritative that the professor entered it straightaway into the lexicon, saying that it might serve as the standard for years to come. Well, what could I do but screw myself down in my seat and bow my head?

You may imagine how the others resented me, for they sensed that I meant to rise above them. They teased me, mocked me, spoiled my few possessions, and blamed me for misdeeds of their own. It was my cousins all over again, but this time it was my own doing and I did not care. They found a hundred ways to trip me up; it did not avail them. I excelled at my courses, disposed of my competition in whatever ways made themselves available, and soon was near the top of my class.

One day Ramshead showed her ignorance by condoling me that because I am colored I cannot become headmistress as I deserve. Though ordinarily ranged with my enemies against me, Dixon, who is blacker far than I, took umbrage and said that she did not see what my complexion had to do with it. "A cockatoo might run the school if the Headmistress spoke through it."

I could not regard this as any very great endorsement and wished she had not said it. But I found that I could not stop thinking about it, and on an impulse, finding Dixon alone in the reading room one day, I appealed to her. It was the first time I had confided these or indeed any of my private thoughts to anyone at the school, and apprehension and relief made my voice shrill, I think; anyway, she drew back as I began to speak. "So I can better myself, by ceasing to *be* myself. Wield power, but someone *else's* power. Have a voice, but not my *own* voice. Why are we working so hard, if it is just to be an old white woman's speaking trumpet?"

She glanced around to see if anyone was listening, and I thought she would snub me. But she could not resist a chance to show off her knowledge. "She is herself the speaking trumpet of the dead," she reminded me.

"Who also seem to be mostly white," I said. It was the first time this thought had occurred to me and I wondered if it was true. "Or does the afterlife, too, uphold Jim Crow?"

She bridled. "The dead aren't any color, they have no faces anymore. They have been translated into the *lingua franca* of death, rendered like beef fat into the tallow of language itself: a colorless all-color, impersonal as fate.'" She was quoting the Headmistress, of course.

"Is the *lingua franca* of the dead English, then? Because I have never heard her speak Chinese or Cherokee," I said. "Why should deceased Esquimaux speak the language of a tribe of whites from an island around the world, or any language but his own?"

"Nobody's language is his own," she said, with exaggerated patience. "We are all spoken for, and through."

"But why might not the Headmistress then speak Esquimau, just as well as English?"

"Perhaps she would if there were Esquimaux to listen. 'The ear commands the voice.'"

"For that matter," I pursued, "why does she always speak in a tolerably clear if quaintish English, and not Anglo-Saxon or Common Brittonic? Why don't I speak some combination of Gaelic and Igbo or Yoruba? Why don't you—"

She cut me off. "Stop showing off. Our biological ancestors don't have special title to our mouths, you know that. It's not our bodies but the voices passing through them that make us who we are."

"But we aren't *anyone*, supposedly. Except that the nobody we are isn't just anybody. It's American, or English—anyway, English-speaking—and it's white—anyway it sounds white—"

"So do you!"

"Or think about this, Dixon: I'm nobody. You're nobody. She's nobody. Right?" She shrugged agreement. "But somehow she's a more *important* nobody than we are."

I never heard Dixon's reply, if she had one, some other girls having entered the room just then. I took leave of her feeling that I had probably done a very foolish thing in exposing my misgivings to one of my chief rivals. Entering the refectory that evening, I braced myself for the repercussions. But the faces—beige or brown or pink, friendly or malicious or indifferent—dipped to their spoons as they had always done, while the ghosts flicked and fluttered in the rising steam. Out of solidarity, perhaps, or the fear that discredit would fall on us both indiscriminately, Dixon had said nothing.

However, swept along by my words, I had gone further than I had intended, and my own thoughts disturbed me. On my way to the dormitory that night I passed a maid, brown like me, and did not avert my eyes as I was wont to do, but sought hers out. Her eyes brushed mine and lowered, their message familiar and unmistakable: Not one of us. When in my aunt's house I had thought to find comfort among the kitchen help, and had felt how guarded their kindness was, I had not understood, but now I did: Because when I opened my mouth, a white girl's voice came out. ("The white black girl," that is what they call me downstairs, to this day.)

But I was a Spirit Medium now, was I not? Among the Benjamin Franklins and the Lizzie Bordens, was there not a Dred Scott or Tituba with something yet to say to the living? Why were they so quiet, those legions murdered by calculation, by neglect, by concentrated abuse and vicious prejudice, their lives held cheap because of the color of their skins? Their lamentations ought to deafen the living!

I stood a long moment in the dormitory door, my eyes ranging over the ranked cots. Then my hands opened, as if to let something go, for why should they choose me as their mouthpiece? I crossed to my bed and sat, folding my arms over my chest. With the life I had had, jumped into white society as trial of and testament to its liberality, I had not been obliged to bear that weight. Could I take it up? I wanted to (innocent that I was), for I thought that might be the price of admission to a fellowship that I had never felt. But I had not really earned the right. Someday a mouth would open and let pandemonium out. But it would not be mine.

The ghosts drew near. If those deracinated wisps could have put forth eyes, they would have seen bewilderment, hurt, the rootless homesickness of someone who had never had a home. But slowly their whispers worked on me. Fling your roots forward, they seemed to whisper. We are waiting for you. Come home.

So I put aside doubt like a temptation, and worked if anything harder than before.

Gradually the derision I saw in every eye changed to resignation, calculation, even fear. And at the same time, as already related, I had made myself useful to the Headmistress and made her business my own; when, as often happened, in the ongoing attempt to devise a more perfect language, she began using a new idiom without bothering to explain it first, it was I, now, who stepped in to interpret. I interpreted her gestures, I interpreted even her silences, for I had begun to know her better than almost anyone did. That was a great advantage. That was in fact practically everything.

WAYS TO

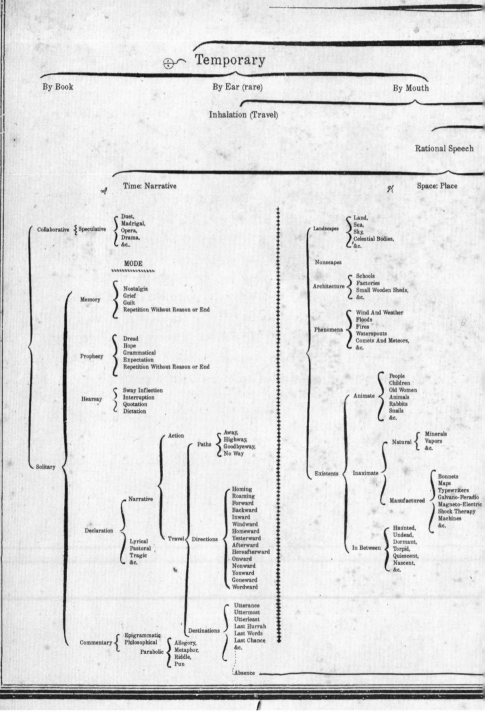

Temporary

By Book   By Ear (rare)   By Mouth

Inhalation (Travel)

Rational Speech

Time: Narrative   Space: Place

Collaborative

Speculative — Duet, Madrigal, Opera, Drama, &c..

MODE

Memory — Nostalgia, Grief, Guilt, Repetition Without Reason or End

Prophecy — Dread, Hope, Grammatical Expectation, Repetition Without Reason or End

Hearsay — Sway Inflection, Interruption, Quotation, Dictation

Solitary

Declaration

Narrative

Action — Paths — Away, Highway, Goodbyeway, No Way

Lyrical, Pastoral, Tragic, &c.

Travel — Directions — Homing, Roaming, Forward, Backward, Inward, Windward, Homeward, Yesterward, Afterward, Hereafterward, Onward, Nonward, Yonward, Goneward, Wordward

Commentary

Epigrammatic, Philosophical

Parabolic — Allegory, Metaphor, Riddle, Pun

Destinations — Utterance, Uttermost, Utterleast, Last Hurrah, Last Words, Last Chance, &c.

Absence

Landscapes — Land, Sea, Sky, Celestial Bodies, &c.

Nonscapes

Architecture — Schools, Factories, Small Wooden Sheds, &c.

Phenomena — Wind And Weather, Floods, Fires, Waterspouts, Comets And Meteors, &c.

Existents

Animate — People, Children, Old Women, Animals, Rabbits, Snails, &c.

Inanimate

Natural — Minerals, Vapors, &c.

Manufactured — Bonnets, Maps, Typewriters, Galvano-Feradio, Magneto-Electric Shock Therapy Machines, &c.

In Between — Haunted, Undead, Dormant, Torpid, Quiescent, Nascent, &c.

APPEAR ♒ ♐ ♉ ♊ ♋ ♀ ♎

Death

☉

♆ Permanent

Exhalation (Arrival)

Nonsense   Groans, Cries, &c.   → **Absence**

♅   Self-Hypostasis

Metamorphosis
- Acoustic
- Pneumatic
- Hydraulic
- Ballistic
- Chronological
- Cosmological
- Epistemological
- Dioptric
- Catoptric
- Architectural
- Textual
- Orthopedic
- Chirurgical
- Cosmetic
- Animal
- Botanical
- Mineral
- Chemical
- Alchemical
- Pyrotechnical
- &c.

Death

ves With
eeth
atinous
ianos
terranean
kies

Transformation

Augmentation
- Become A Thing { Thicken, Inspissate, Harden, Indurate, Fossilize, &c.
- Become Everything { Comprehend Compass The Whole, Subsume, Expand, Dilate, &c.

Near-Absence
- Trifle
- Minim
- Shred
- Crumb
- Iota
- Jot
- Scintilla
- Whit
- Speck
- Smidgen
- Trace
- &c.

Diminishment
- Riddance
- Omission
- Truancy
- Aposiopesis
- Erasure
- Ablation
- Evanesce
- Lapse
- Shrink
- Withdraw
- Etiolate
- Atrophy
- Abbreviation
- Obliteration
- Want
- Lack
- Undoing
- &c.

Maintenance

Absence
- Want, Shortage, Lack, Dearth, Hunger, Thirst, Need
- Emptiness
- Caesura, Syncope
- Silence, Surd
- Forgetfulness, Oblivion, Ignorance, Nescience
- Hole, Void, Orifice, Gap, Rent, Rift, Fissure, Breach, Rupture, Gulf, Aperture, Opening
- Nil, Naught, Nix, Null, Nothing, Zilch, Zero, Cipher, "", "∅", 0
- Can't
- N't

Readings
from "A Visitor's Observations"

A Secret

One day, on my way to the room I had been granted as a study, I glimpsed through an open door the young doctor-in-training passing something to one of the young kids, who cut a look at me and ran. Dr. Peachie, having wiped his hand on a handkerchief, clasped mine solidly. "What say we take a turn around the garden?" I was surprised, since although we were on as cordial terms as any two professional gentlemen thrown together by circumstance, any impulse (on either side) to closer acquaintance had been discouraged by my stammer, or my old self-consciousness about it, which came back around outsiders. But it turned out he was more interested in talking than in listening, though he waited until we were strolling along the garden path before unburdening himself.

"I have a confession and a proposal to make. I hope I may speak in confidence."

"Of course," I said, curious and flattered in equal parts.

"May I have your word on that? I would not like what I am doing to get out, not at this stage."

"Well—yes, all right. What's the mystery?"

He grinned and in a stage whisper confided, "I have been conducting an experiment." I laughed hesitantly. "No, really. You have heard of ectoplasm."

"N-n-naturally."

"Naturally. You have seen the precipitations—the objects some of the children produce."

"The 'ectoplasmoglyphs,' yes."

"Do you know the commonest use of ectoplasm, outside these walls?"

I said that I knew it was associated with séances, that it manifested most frequently in the mouth of the medium, that some examples had been shown up as disgraceful fakery involving cheesecloth or cotton batting, that—but he was interrupting me.

"So you have not heard of its use as a psychotropic drug?"

I expressed my surprise.

He sat down on a bench, gesturing to me to follow suit, which I did, flushing a little. "In medical circles we have been hearing rumors for some time of a new drug, difficult of access and unreliable in quality, but growing in popularity. Without a regular supply it has been impossible to conduct rigorous testing."

I began, I thought, to see where he was going. "The Headmistress has allowed you to take samples of—"

"Not at all, not at all—no—never! She wouldn't hear of it. The *children*. They are often glad to have a little extra pocket money, the poor devils. The mouth objects, when melted down, yield a very pure form of the drug, ideal for experimental purposes. It is no good using the street stuff, which may be diluted or mixed with other narcotics. One must strictly control the dosage."

"I suppose," I said slowly, "that it is important to discover—to study—so as to treat—"

"Exactly!" He beamed. "Already I have made great strides. The circumstances are in fact ideal—a steady supply, a controlled population of experimental subjects . . ."

"Do you mean to say that you are experimenting on the ch-ch-ch-children?"

He smiled. I saw that I was in the presence of an enthusiast.

"Is that not dangerous? What are its effects?"

"It is a mild psychotropic with narcotic properties. As one might expect, it inclines one to thoughts of death, and therein lies the importance of my work. Simply put, I seek a cure for our collective addiction to death. Naturally I have to keep my views on the *qui vive* around these parts!" He laughed heartily, then sobered, and dropping his voice said, "By administering a concentrated dose of pure ectoplasm, I hope to inoculate against the death drive. If my subjects develop a distaste, even a *disgust* for death and can no longer stand to submit to the curriculum, then I will consider my theory proved. Already I have observed increased truancy. Of course careful experimentation with the dosage is still needed . . . Side effects, in some patients— Why, salutations, sir!" He had discovered the cat, who was crouching under the bench, and now leaned over, wiggling his fingers.

"Surely . . ." I said, addressing the back of his head. I hardly knew what to say. "Surely a morbid state of mind is commonplace here—do you not fear to exacerbate it?"

"There is," he admitted, dragging the cat out by the scruff of the neck, "that risk—that rather than inoculating our subjects against death, one may induce a dependency. But far better discover this under controlled circumstances than allow unregulated use among the underclasses to produce an army of death-addicted neuropaths! That is why the school is ideal; you want a population subject to strict oversight." He settled the cat firmly in his lap and, still holding it down, began smoothing its fur, now and then working out a bur with nimble fingers. His eyes sought over my face and for the first time I saw a hint of anxiety. "You approve the scheme, don't you? I am sure you are a man of vision. The greater good . . . We might see an end to war in our lifetime! But listen, all this is strictly between you and me. The Headmistress, unfortunately, is not to be won over to the cause. I didn't lay bare the entire project, naturally, but the most delicate hints have been met with flat refusal. The ectoplasmic apports are not commodities to be exploited but messages to be heeded, and so on—the usual hocus-pocus. Sheer obstructionism. Also"—here he looked decidedly uncomfortable—"Dr. Beede is not in on the jig. He's an excellent fellow and I owe him the world! But a good old-fashioned country doctor, not a visionary. I don't mean to upset the dear man while he still toddles about but, well, I will be taking over his practice soon enough. And the Headmistress! Quite hopeless. But we have something up our sleeves."

"We?"

"Yes, luckily I have an ally on high. Know him socially, you see, as one does, and I won him over to the plan: solid man at the helm, well-regulated program, research facilities brought up to date . . . Spotless uniforms, gleaming surfaces, points of light glancing off needles and syringes, room after room, tier upon tier, neat as a honeycomb, and streaming out of it without surcease the purest, golden-clearest liquid ectoplasm . . ." He seemed to shake himself out of a reverie. "But the fellow's skittish. Some of the publicity this place has gotten lately—he's threatened more than once to shut down the school. So the strictest secrecy is required, isn't it, pussycat?" The cat put his ears back and emitted a low, cautionary warble.

"May I ask, then, why you decided to confide in me?"

"Ah! You have heard my confession, now hear my proposal. I require an adult subject with self-control, tact, and excellent observational skills. I have of course injected myself on numerous occasions but a lone experimental subject . . . and it is, I think you would find, an illuminating experience!" He gave a little bounce of excitement, at which the cat lashed its tail. "I said, thoughts of death, but that is not very precise. It conduces to thinking of all phenomena as fixed, delimited and corrigible rather than transient. The universe shows forth as a perfect machine, an orrery without original, re-volving on gears of adamant . . . Cells upon cells, wheels within wheels, gloss and smoothness, tiny scintillating points of light repeating and repeating and repeating and repeating . . ." He grinned, showing his eyeteeth (good-ness, he was attractive); he stroked the cat furiously; I saw that his pupils were dilated and suddenly understood his gregariousness. I was conscious of a slight feeling of disappointment, I could not say why.

"You mmm—mentioned side effects."

His eyes rolled up, his mouth went slack, his breath rattled—I thought he was having a seizure. Then his eyes popped open and he grinned. "Sleep-walking!" he said. "Lock your door."

"Well, I will consider it," I said, "though I cannot feel quite good about going behind the Headmistress's back. Are you sure it is not harmful?"

"Would I take it myself if it were?" he said, spreading his hands in a lordly gesture. The cat saw his opportunity and sprang, disappearing into the tea roses.

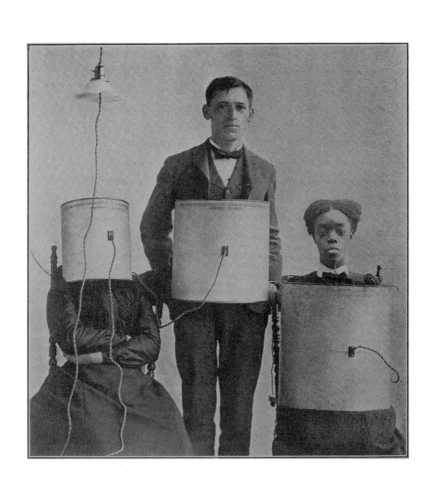

Letters to Dead Authors, #11

Dear Jephra,

There has been another libelous letter in the *Gazette*. (By the way, I am pretty sure that I have guessed the author.) This time, it alleges something I do not quite understand about coils of cinematograph film lying in wait for their pray [sic] in the back basement. I will have to ask our filmmaker friend about it. But it has sped me toward a course I was already considering. I have decided to take my reputation in my own hands, not fleeing but seeking out the public eye, so as to draw it round to my own point of view.

Already my resolve is being tested. I invited a fiend of a persistent newsman, Cartwright is his name, to take a tour of the establishment, and now he will not leave us alone. Of course I do not allow him to roam the premises at whim, but Dr. Beede's young trainee is his compadre and no doubt tells him everything he wants to know. Incidentally I think Dr. Peachie may be a secret tippler. I have several times come across him behaving in a most extraordinary—but Mr. Medlar has just arrived with a report:

"The teething rods are worn. We need new ones."

"Again! So soon!"

He turned out his long, slender hands.

I sighed. "Well, there is nothing for it. Have Clarence speak to the carpenter."

"Also, I—I am afraid I have been injudicious."

My gaze sharpened. "In what respect, Mr. Medlar?"

"I may have given Mr. Cartwright reason to understand that he might be given a tour of the land of the dead."

"What!" I thrust back my chair—splinters flew—and stood. I looked down upon him now.

"I know it was foolish. I lost my head."

"Injudicious in the extreme, Mr. Medlar! We cannot have that nosy parker sniffing around in death!"

"Well, I know that! Of course I immediately corrected myself, but the devil of it is that he had got his teeth into the idea and attempted to insist. Whereupon one of the little—little children, I should say, thought she would set him straight and, to show him how difficult it would be for a person of his girth to enter the Mouthlands—" he quailed at the fierceness of my expression, then went on "—she herself—intending only pantomime—slipped through. And she wasn't wearing an Ariadne string."

I collapsed back into my chair. "So we have lost another one. And right in front of Mr. Cartwright. Oh, Mr. Medlar, I am far from pleased, very far indeed."

Eventually, the creaking of a shoe alerted me to his continued presence. "Why are you still standing around like a lummox? Oh, all right, yes, I will try to fetch her back, though I am quite sure it is too late to mend the damage to our reputation—for which we have you to thank!"

At this setback, a lesser woman might have retreated! But I am only confirmed in my purpose. New ideas, however scientifically presented, have ever met with resistance from the *hoi polloi*. To be widely accepted, one must be widely known. I have come to see that an element of that showmanship that I originally rejected as contrary to the spirit of serious thanatological inquiry is necessary, both to correct the deleterious effect of negative publicity, and to attract the beneficent donors that our school, no less than any other, requires in order to maintain the high standards we are known for, if not yet in this world, then certainly in the next. The matter is of some urgency; my health is far from good. So I have devised a series of ventures that I believe will appeal to the popular imagination. (You, who were never a public person, will understand the feelings of trepidation with which I plan my entry onto the public stage.)

1. A wholesome and improving Theatrical Spectacle in which our advanced students will show to their best advantage, channeling stage personae of a bygone age.

2. A Balloon, or Sky Lung, as I mean to call it, to be filled with the breath of the dead, and suspended from the ceiling or, if the breath is, as I believe but have yet to verify, lighter than air, having more of absence in it, allowed to sail up of its own accord into the sky.

3. A giant ear trumpet, like an alpenhorn in shape but not in purpose, that might enable solo listeners to tune in to the land of the dead, even without a hearing-mouth child to act as interpreter. The length of the trumpet would help to amplify the whispers that the dead emit continually, which normally remain below the threshold of hearing unless, in an access of excitement (when moved to warn the living of an impending catastrophe, for instance, or to punish the guilty), a number of dead speak in unison. Then, of course, the innumerable whispers that the wind elicits (seemingly of its own accord), from bottle tops, fluttering leaves, eaves, ears, flags and other flapping things, build to a crescendo, to such a din that anyone can hear, that it would be impossible not to hear. But I digress.

4. A similar structure, but reversed, through which the living may make their desires known to the dead. Whether, hearing, the dead would compassionate them so far as to take action, I do not know. Privately I suspect that the majority of ghosts are not much interested in the living. It is the geniuses and cranks, the lonely, the guilty, the vainglorious and the vengeful, who bend our ears year after year. Our perfect dead need nothing anymore.

5. A book I wish to write and believe could be quite a moneymaker if any publisher cares to "cash in": *The Compleat Corpse, a Guide for the Recently Deceased.*

I do not ask your help, only your fellowship, for though I stand at the brink of fame and fortune, I feel very alone. The dead blow through me, but do they know me? Does the river know the dog that drinks from it? The earth know the worm?

Sincerest Regards,
Headmistress Joines

P.S. I believe I addressed my last letter to a fictional character. I am not sure what I was thinking.

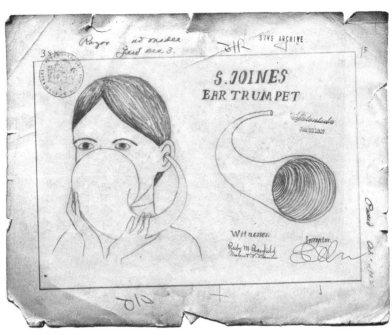

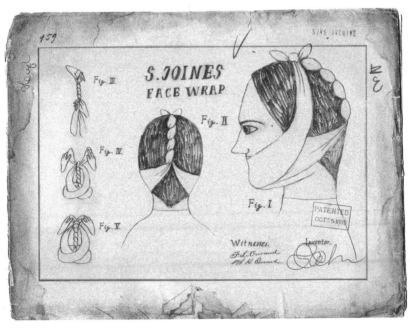

12. The Final Dispatch, contd.

[Static, three or four sentences indistinct] . . . thought it was a piano factory, I was sure it was a piano factory. The air tangy with resin, dizzied with varnish, the great curved forms like harps, the blond wood, the floor softly mounded with sawdust, the plink the plunk and the sostenuto . . . And then there is the matter of the piano wire. I was sure it was piano wire, so strong, so readily available. In a piano factory, that is. If there was no piano factory, then it was considerably less likely to have been piano wire with which my mother was strangled or hanged as the case may be. It is not easy to remove a wire from a piano. Or it may be easy enough, I do not know, but not as easy as picking up a piece that is lying on a workbench. So I was fairly sure. I mean, that it was a piano wire (a thin one, not one of the thick bass wires made of a core of wire around which another wire is wrapped) that had not so much strangled my mother as [static] very nearly cut her head off—you may have cut cheese with a wire? So that in fact one could not even see what it was that had made that slim incision that encircled her neck, so deep in the flesh was the wire, they had not removed it. And what if not piano wire had snapped at my father's hands, making those cuts, on the inside of the forearm, one on the cheek, right below the left eye, as of something narrow, sharp, lashing? [Pause.]

I had satisfied myself, to the extent that one can speak of satisfaction in such a case, that I knew the story. Yet now it strikes me with some force that it was not a piano factory but a typewriter factory. A powerful image comes to mind: It is a typewriter as big as a pipe organ, bigger perhaps, filling a room otherwise empty, the keys (as big as dinner plates) mounting upward in tiers, like bleacher seats. I remember stepping onto the G, which gave underfoot, for the model had been conscientiously constructed, and really worked. "Slowly, slowly," said my father. I oozed onto the key, my hands outstretched for balance. Nonetheless, when I transferred my full weight to the key, the hammer rose and smooched the page; I heard the kiss of ink.

"Idiot," my father said, or perhaps "bitch," he employed both words with regularity. I pivoted on one foot, reaching back to touch the frame to steady myself, and cautiously lowered my narrow buttocks onto the 7 key. Which sank; there was another kiss, another curse from my father, and then I was arranging my skirts around my ankles and straining my cheeks in a smile.

That is not my only memory of this scene. The other is from the perspective of someone else, looking on, and is in black and white, not color, or I should say, sepia and white. I sat on the 7 key, my feet resting neatly and decorously side by side on the G. At the lower edge of the giant piece of paper protruding from the top of the machine, one could see a faint, imperfect G and 7 printed below a message whose full text I have forgotten, though I remember the catchphrase: *Joines Typewriters—Giants in the Field!* I must have been photographed (and indeed I remember a burst of searing light and a whiff of sulfurous smoke), perhaps by the local paper, where the photograph must have appeared, and from which I or my father must have neatly clipped it, perhaps framing it; perhaps it hung thereafter in the office of the piano factory. I mean the typewriter factory.

Was it, instead, a giant piano?

No, a typewriter, surely.

But how could I confuse a typewriter and a piano?

Well, it is easy enough—both possess a set of articulated keys that when depressed with the fingers induce their respective hammers to strike a vigorous blow within the body of the instrument, producing in one case a letter associated with a sound, and in the other, a sound associated with a letter.

Why the two should not be combined into one instrument I have never really understood.

If a typewriter factory, then no smell of sawdust, no burr of saw and drill. Above all no piano wire and thus no murder, or at least not the particular murder I have imagined. Did my father hammer my mother to death one letter at a time in the giant typewriter, tap dancing on the keys? Obviously not. Perhaps he strangled her with a typewriter ribbon; is it stout enough? There must be *something* to this memory. Maybe we merely owned a typewriter. A giant typewriter? Did we see one, on a trip to the World Fair, say? [Static, sound of breathing.]

Perhaps it was neither a typewriter factory nor a piano factory but a telephone switchboard. I can see my mother now, her hair swept up in a roll, her narrow shoulders and flat chest handsome in a close-fitting long-sleeved high-necked dress, her hips flattered into fullness by a petticoat, reaching out, all concentration, to unplug here, plug there—and wire enough to strangle mobs of mothers—but no, but no, absurd, there were no telephones when I was small; were there typewriters?—I will have to check that, too. Are there typewriters now? Have I gotten ahead of myself, has the future leaked into the present by way of the past, making a little detour through death? Or am I perpetrating a fiction? A murder mystery, and I the pale and ink-stained authoress in the garret, slavering over the pitiful bones, vamping my way through increasingly improbable horrors, with a heat that I have too little experience to recognize igniting my virgin loins? Well, no. At least . . . no.

But my past, I ought to remember it. And I do. I'm sure of it. When I am home I will remember it. When I'm alive. When I look at my photographs. At certain objects, slightly sooty. It is this place that confuses me. In this place the past is not past, it all comes back. And yet not as it was, but as everything here is: changeable, changing. The moving finger writes, and having writ, goes back for edits.

But why have I chosen to make my life a murder mystery? Could I reshelve myself, so to speak, among the romances or, more suitably—but it is all literature, and all beside the point. Which is: ceasing to "live" in this egregiously personal sense and beginning, at last, to exist. Cutting out the first person like a tumor.

Only to find that it has metastasized, and that that is precisely what I have called the "world."

Then burning the world down to the bone, and starting afresh. With what few scraps of matter remain that I do not recognize, do not understand.

The Stenographer's Story, contd.

The months passed, the years. The stream rose, worried the bank, sank back. Summers it thinned to a shimmer. I was no longer the new girl. I became, if not liked, accepted. I even forged a combative sort of friendship with Dixon, often arguing with her in private over points of doctrine. It was a relief, I think, for both of us. By unspoken agreement, we took turns arguing the side of the Headmistress, so that the other might give her skepticism vent, and so stropped our tongues to a razor's edge, which stood us in good stead in class. From time to time we broached again the topic of the racial typology of the dead, without reaching any great conclusions, except to agree that it was strange that white folk were not more fearful of the ghosts of those they had wronged. Wasn't channeling the dead about reckoning with the past? Did they never consider, those earnest seekers who engaged our graduates, that the dead might come not in benevolence but in wrath, and shouldering aside the deceased daughters in their winding cloths, the fathers, sons, and mothers, seek the vengeance they were due? We did not acknowledge what is obvious enough in retrospect, that we took in these speculations a fearful pleasure.

(The one time I tried to raise these questions in class: "Grandison, I am grieved to find that you have adhesions."

"Adhesions?"

"You are clinging to the small potatoes of self. Put them aside, girl."

"Potatoes?")

A filmmaker arrived for a visit, then moved in, bunking uncomplaining with the boys. The doctor began to dodder and acquired a protégé. We all admired Dr. Peachie, who was young and keen and flatteringly attentive to us kids. The girls in particular fluttered around him, and though his manners were unfailingly correct, I saw how his throat flushed and one knee jittered when Marigold perched on the arm of his chair, or laid a daring hand on his sleeve. Whenever he made his rounds, a group of girls would troop around after him asking questions and taking it in turns to try on his stethoscope and peep through his magnifying glass. Does it sound like I was indifferent? I was not, though both too reticent and too proud to play the coquette. One day he met my eyes where I stood on the fringe of the group, and ignoring the hands already reaching for the instrument, extended it toward me. "Would you like a try?"

Frowning, I held his gaze, trying to identify what it was I saw in it, as my hand drifted toward him. A dark space seemed to have opened up under my ribs, as though a malign sorcery had conjured away my organs. In this hollow an unfamiliar knowledge coiled and snapped.

Then the Headmistress came around the corner. "What are you doing, Grandison?" she snapped. "Let us get to work." After that, when I saw the doctor, though my eyes tried to jump to his, I turned away. But I always knew where he was, without looking. I thought he was aware of me in the same way and that the distance we kept between us was like the space between two cupped hands that shelter a tiny flame.

Sometimes when I lay alone I allowed myself the thought of Dr. Peachie and the look he had leveled at me, and I imagined various maladies that might require me to undress myself before those eyes and take shameless positions with an inventiveness I recalled later with hot disbelief. Once I dreamed that he was capering in a scarlet union suit with a giant pair of tongs, and wagging his pointed tail at me, and that I opened my mouth willingly for the tongs. When with a yank that throbbed through my whole body he pulled out my tongue, I woke up in the thought that I had pissed myself, but it was not urine that wet my thighs.

Europe went to war; "I knew it," said the Headmistress, when the news was brought to her, "by the souls flooding into death." Dr. Peachie began his study of ectoplasmoglyph production, and often pulled expecting pupils into the room he called his office—though not without a wary look around, for the Headmistress regarded every glyph as a telegram from some meta-physical front, and resented any delay in its delivery. A tall, sleek girl with glossy, protuberant eyes—I think her name was Candace—got pregnant by someone she refused to name (a revolting hypothesis came to me, but I shooed it away), miscarried, and either was possessed by that tiny, speechless ghost or went mad, no one was sure. A car took her away. Another car came for a shy boy with leukemia who returned six months later, no longer shy, as a particularly plaintive and persistent ghost, availing himself of every open mouth to complain monotonously about a cold draft for a period of some months before at last falling silent.

One day the ghost of a foul-mouthed Scottish stonemason whom Chin-Sun was cultivating advised a small group of us of the exact whereabouts in nearby Greenfield of a buried boot full of money, which we duly located on one of the days off allowed to trusted senior students. Its contents, $1.83 in small change, we spent on ice cream sodas and candy.

One day Ramshead, possibly sleepwalking, drifted spectrally up the length of the dormitory to the side of my bed as I watched, then plopped on top of me, groping me here and there, and tried to put her tongue in my mouth. After a dumbstruck minute I pushed her away.

More often it was Bernadette who came, she who had struck against me in the driveway the day I came. She had grown into a long broad-shouldered girl with white eyelashes and perpetually chapped lips who produced more mouth objects than anyone. She'd sit astride me, knees pinning my nightgown to the bed, and talk in a rasping whisper as tiny wet objects fell out of her mouth onto me and I'd laugh and build stacks of them on my chest while she whispered on, a dark swaying shape, and more things dropped and knocked down my fortifications. Without knowing exactly what I was doing, I was feeling my way along a line of inquiry that seemed threaded through the pit of my stomach and thrummed tightly there. An investigation that had begun, perhaps, with that glance from the doctor. Sometimes I allowed myself to imagine that it was he who sat over me thus, and then the two figures, male and female, seemed to mingle and vie, so that it was sometimes one of them, sometimes the other, and sometimes two in one that straddled me, while I was myself but also Marigold and for fleeting moments, even the disgraced Candace. The excited ghosts shushed and tittered and whirled through and around our mouths, but oh, we living, were we not already as good as ghosts?

One day she leaned over and brought her face so close to mine that our noses bumped. Her breath was in my mouth and it made me feel fizzy and at the same time serious. Then she said something. I couldn't hear what it was, but I felt it, a tiny object dropped into my mouth. My tongue found out the shape of it. It was only a little bigger than a tooth, but more complicated. Having it in my mouth was also complicated.

Bernadette got off and lay down beside me on her back. I sucked and wondered. The object—ectoplasmoglyph—word?—tasted salty, bready, *internal*. Sucking it was like being about to speak, but not knowing what you were going to say. I said to myself, It's on the tip of my tongue. *It* in this case being Bernadette, but a part of her she didn't know any better than I did. That was a different angle on knowing someone than I was used to, and I wasn't sure I liked it. What if you knew someone's insides so well that you forget their outside? And what if their outside was what made you want to know them in the first place? I saw the Headmistress shaking her head and saying, "Let us get to work," and in the end I fished out the word and felt for Bernadette's damp hand. I guess she thought for a moment that I wanted to hold hands and then felt the word there. She never came back to my bed and a month later she had graduated. On the whole, I was glad.

I pitched myself into my work. Gradually, insensibly, my Voice became my voice. In practicing hush and rueing speech, in courting trouble and shunning ease, I had built myself a home of stumbling blocks. No fiend could now pluck out my tongue, for I had plucked it out myself. But I used the absence of a tongue more ably than I had ever used the living organ.

One day, I was typing a clean copy of a letter when, without looking up from the handwritten page from which she was reading, the Headmistress said, "What do you want?"

"What do," I typed, before I realized that the question was addressed to me. Sighing, I pulled the page out of the machine and started scrolling in a fresh one. "I'm not sure what you mean."

Her head came up. "What nonsense. I mean what you think I mean. What do you *want*? To conquer death? Say bye-bye to Mama? Find yourself? Lose yourself?" Seeing my blank look, she added, "Let me make it simpler. To go home, or to leave home forever?"

Which answer would she herself give? To leave home, I thought. But hadn't she made herself a home of the school, with herself *in loco parentis*?

"Both," I finally said, because it was true. The two were even, I would later decide, the same thing. To run away from everything, even my own self, was to find a home I could never lose, because it was loss itself.

Readings
Documentarian of the Dead

The provenance of this text deserves special mention. I was drawn by a passing mention of the Vocational School to an online forum dedicated to that particular form of one-upmanship engaged in by film buffs that consists of the laudatory mention of ever more obscure films. Someone had met someone who had heard of someone who had abandoned work on a documentary about a very early filmmaker (name of Moe Decker or something like that) but was still sitting on some rare footage shot at the Vocational School or environs. There was alleged to be a script. But it was no use asking to see it, the guy was a crank, not Moe Decker but the other one, had never made a film, did not know the first thing about film, except the films of Moe Decker, on whom he was the world's leading expert, in fact the world's only expert, having bought sight unseen and at a sucker's price a mess of decaying film reels that proved unbeknownst to the seller to contain the only copies extant of Decker's masterpieces. Well, I tracked him down and persuaded him that he owed his insights to scholarship. The following text appears first here. —Ed.

"I came to the Sybil Joines Vocational School with one object," wrote Aaron Moedeker in his abandoned memoirs, "to gain access to sights that, if they proved susceptible to capturing on film, would surely be the strangest and most wonderful ever to be impressed on celluloid."

In October 1915, with the aid of the school's experienced necrotechs, an ambitious young amateur filmmaker from California began making exploratory trips beyond the veil with a hand-cranked motion picture camera. After every visit to the land of the dead he would take detailed notes from memory, play and replay the footage (if any), and modify his equipment accordingly. The first trip from which he returned with exposed film took place around August 1916; before then, though the camera was running, the film remained blank. The first footage to present such fluctuations of light and dark as to suggest an image—in which, however, only the vaguest hints of figuration can be made out—was filmed in September 1916, almost a year after his earliest experiments. Oddly enough, it was recorded from within a sealed film canister that remained in Moedeker's backpack for the duration of the trip.

Encouraged by this accidental success, Moedeker broadened the scope of his experimentation. To this period belongs the series of increasingly unusual motion picture cameras at which so much fun has been unjustly poked—the wax camera, the ice camera, the camera with no crank or lens, the diagram of a camera on a sheet of onionskin paper, the word *camera* scrawled on a calling card, the description of a camera read aloud. He even attempted to make a camera out of his own body, holding a strip of film in his mouth, which was exposed to light when he spoke. However, it was on an ordinary film camera that the first footage was shot in which anything resembling a landscape could be made out, though it undergoes peculiar convulsions.[17]

It turned out that to function beyond the veil, cameras required certain modifications. These seem to add up to a sort of animal disguise: a thick layer of goose fat, a carrying case of pigskin, a lens cover woven from horse or human hair. The film suffered less distortion if it had been breathed on. A small sack of ants tucked into the camera bag seemed to help.

Other modifications were made by death itself. Moedeker took careful notes of alterations to his equipment discovered on return. Unfortunately in most cases the equipment itself has not survived. We know, however, that his lenses took on a great many fantastic forms. Some sprouted an array of subsidiary lenses, connected to no eyepiece, whose pertinence to the putative footage seemed nil. Extra reels of varying sizes imposed intricate divagations in the path of the scrolling film. Several cameras were lost when

---

17. Moedeker once declared that these first attempts captured something that eluded his later work, despite the latter's technical superiority. However, they are generally considered unsuccessful, if not downright unwatchable. During an early screening at a Chicago social club devoted to "Spiritualism, Prison Reform, and Moving Pictures," three audience members allegedly ran mad, since which time rumors of a curse have attached itself to these works. They are even today more often talked about than shown.

they grew pseudopods and ran away. One melted, one burned, one was eaten in a moment of distraction by Moedeker himself, with no ill effects recorded. One divided itself into five hundred tiny cameras with working parts, some of which have been subsequently recovered from dollhouse collectors. One of these was still loaded with miniature strips of film; scholars are still arguing whether the evocative but enigmatic footage recovered from it was shot in the land of the dead, or was the work of some little girl, and the face that some claim to be able to make out, through the pale flicker of celluloid decomposition, merely that of one of her dolls.

The film and its emulsion also changed, making it hard to determine which visual phenomena were the effects of what we shall resign ourselves to calling "light" (though necronauts say that it no more resembles the light of our world than it does a stomachache or the sound of fingernails clawing at rough deal boards) and which were properties of the film itself—whether Moedeker was creating a record of actual sights, or merely of transformations of the film—or whether it even made any sense to assert a difference between those things. Nor was it clear whether such films should be played on ordinary projectors, or at ordinary speeds—with ordinary light! Or even whether to *play* the film was actually what one ought to do with it rather than, say, plant it, or boil it in brine, or wrap it around one's neck and pull, pull hard . . .

One film grew like a vine, dividing, subdividing, and extending runners; after a late night, Moedeker fell asleep at his desk, and upon waking found that the film had coiled itself around his wrist and a table leg, effectively binding him in place. He was not found until the next day, by which point the film had seized his other wrist and sent an exploratory tendril into his mouth. This film was reportedly destroyed, though a rumor persists that Moedeker could not in the end bear to "kill" it, but hid it in a remote corner of the school basement, where it continued to grow and occasionally claimed a victim in a curious child drawn to such out-of-the-way places.

One film was transformed into a strip of paper on which a single phrase was printed over and over in capital letters: "THERE IS LAPE," or possibly,

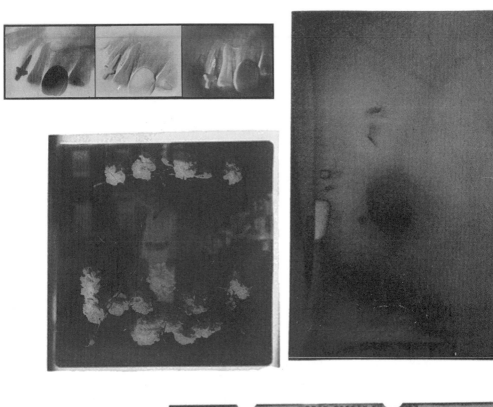

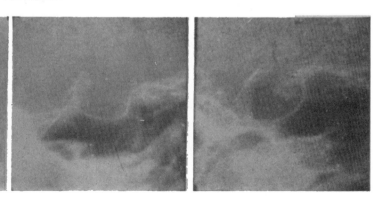

"THERE I SLAPE" (the final word here has been interpreted by some as a nonstandard past tense of *sleep*). There is lape! The phrase has the ring of revelation. It has even entered popular usage, where it has come to mean something like the give in the grid, the stretch in the hanging rope, the pigeonhole's back door.

Belatedly, Moedeker came to believe that all objects altered by exposure to the land of the dead were "footage" and to conceive of the land of the dead as itself a sort of recording. The living play it back, running the past through their mouths, one moveless moment after another. "The challenge is to teach the camera to listen," Moedeker wrote.

Pursuing this program, Moedeker for a time confined himself to close-ups of the Headmistress, as she pronounces words we cannot hear. Most of this footage is about as interesting as one would expect, but one reel is different: Between the intermittently parted lips of the subject appear flashes of light that could initially be mistaken for blemishes in the film, but resolve into what seems to be a landscape with distant figures moving across it. Near the end of the footage a large dark shape appears to cross the opening; then one of the small forms in the background grows until it fills the aperture, which goes black. It is virtually impossible not to read this as a figure approaching the Headmistress—or her mouth—from behind, as it were, and presumably without her knowledge. Some viewers have found themselves pressing themselves back in their seats, as if to escape from whatever is coming, though all that does come is the end of the film.

Moedeker filmed the living as well as the dead, shooting many hours of footage of daily life at the Vocational School. But distinguishing these reels is curiously difficult. Are these a row of scuffed and battered shoes, solemnly queued outside a washroom, or the shadowed faces of the watchful dead, who have temporarily mistaken themselves for footwear? Is this unusually clear sequence only what it appears to be, a record of a group of students in school uniform, solemnly performing morning calisthenics in a barren field, their hair still dark and shining from their ablutions, while a couple of donkeys fornicate tremendously in the background, or is this illusory clarity an elaborate instance of pareidolia, the footage actually depicting, who knows, a map tattooed on the palm of a monstrous hand, or a hanging vine on each trembling leaf of which a tiny mouth is opening?

Once the possibility of an origin beyond the veil is broached, the most seemingly unexceptionable images take on an eerie cast. Early film footage is uncanny enough in its own right to give an audience the feeling that they are watching a crew of pallid revenants rehearse with stiff and unaccustomed movements the half-remembered rituals of their former lives. Even under the best conditions, footage of this vintage is often grainy and flickering, and the passage of time commits new depredations from which the Moedeker archive has hardly been exempt: emulsions cracking or blooming with mildew, the film stock itself shrinking, sprouting buboes, and at last disintegrating into a little heap of brown powder.

But is this decaying footage any less faithful to its subject? A disintegrating image might even capture the nature of death more precisely than a well-preserved one. We could liken film decay to the chemical changes effected by light in the photographic emulsion: the gradual registration of an image; what we lament as destruction might in fact be the culmination of the process, a perfect likeness. Likeness of what? Of death, of course. In which case we already have extensive documentation of our expiry, more than we could ever need.

Moedeker's life's work would then be superfluous, and this is exactly the conclusion to which Moedeker himself came. But far from casting him into a melancholy humor that would eventually drive him to self-murder, as some melodramatic chroniclers have suggested, it opened up new avenues of exploration. Moedeker seems to have experimented with speeding up the process of decay with heat and humidity, deliberately destroying thousands of feet of film. The thirty-nine envelopes and sachets of brown powder found among his papers, carefully dated and numbered, but notoriously dismissed without laboratory analysis by an early cataloguer as "possibly soil samples or medicaments," were of course films in their own right. How Moedeker intended us to watch those films is not at all clear; however, we

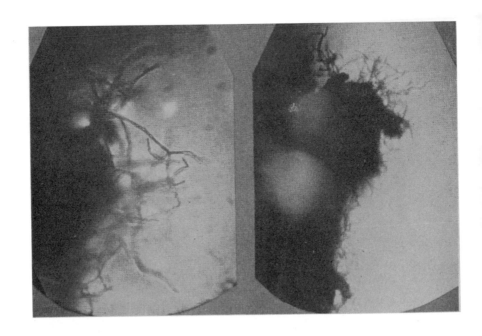

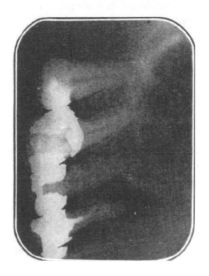

are free to use our imagination. Perhaps we are to take them like snuff, or sprinkle them on our porridge like a digestive powder, or throw them by the handful into a strong wind. Or simply weigh the packets in our hands, imagining that in them an articulated world of moving light and shadow has been rendered, like suet, into a substance that retains all its former beauty, truth, and testimonial power in a more essential form—one closer to "the first and final stuff of being," as Moedeker once wrote.

A few years ago, an undeveloped roll of film was discovered in a corner of the basement that Moedeker had once praised for the "viscid" quality of its darkness. No one very seriously suggests that it is not Moedeker's, but its precise vintage is contestable; still, the possibility that it was the last footage he ever shot is tantalizing. Until recently, however, investigation was paralyzed by a debate over whether or not Moedeker actually intended to develop the film or indeed ever to remove it from the rusty tin in which it has reposed for the better part of a century. Perhaps for Moedeker to leave it in obscurity was to "show" it to the darkness itself, or something of the sort, and the developed film would be a different work whose authorship must be reckoned unknown unless we ourselves wished to claim it. Despite the protests of purists and mystics, however, curiosity finally had its way with the reel.

What can I say about this tantalizing footage? It is very long, but almost entirely taken up with a fury of visual snow that coheres, now and then, into short-lived patterns—white Catherine wheels against a white sky. The figural glimpses are very brief. We see what appears to be two persons, one bent over the other, engaged in some uncertain activity. It seems too much to ask that this footage show the Headmistress during (or after) her final moments of life, but if those hastening to tie two loose ends into a granny knot are correct, it is fitting that to unbiased eyes it is impossible to determine whether we behold murderer and victim, parent and child, or two friends meeting for the last time before one of them departs on a long journey.

It is assumed that Moedeker left the school during the upheaval that followed the Headmistress's death. The last undisputed evidence of his existence is a cobbler's claim check, dated four days before her death, for a pair of shoes that, newly resoled, must have remained empty for ever.

Where did he go? I do not have the answer, but I believe that he became at last so confused about the difference between life and death that it did not exist for him and he wandered freely between the realms. Perhaps when his body gave out he did not die, or at least not so you'd notice. Perhaps he himself did not notice. Perhaps that quiet buzzing you sometimes hear very late at night is Moedeker, turning and turning the crank of his old movie camera, though the film has long since run out.

I like to think that he has found his lape.

Letters to Dead Authors, #12

Dear Herman,

Something is going on in my school that I don't understand. The students gather in groups that disperse when they see me coming. At night, the halls pullulate with sleepwalkers. One of them fell down the stairs and was found in the morning, bruised but complacent, staring at the ceiling with a bland and dreamy smile. In class, they look at me with that same smile. The dead pour through them without impediment. The ectoplasmoglyphs pile out at ever-shorter intervals as if with growing desperation, like pleas for help or warnings that are falling on deaf ears, and today, two different children addressed me in what seemed to be my mother's voice.

That at least is nothing special. Lately everyone speaks to me in the voice of my mother. Mr. Medlar, Mr. Whit, the children, the cook, visiting parents, police investigators. For a comprehensive list please consult the rosters archived in my office: second floor, first right, second door, first cabinet, second drawer, first file, A for *Administration*: an unexceptionable taxon, bespeaking the shining normalcy of our dealings. I insert this remark for the inspectors, but enough of them. Perhaps in any case I will burn this file before. Before what? Say on. My mother! Imagine my profound lack of surprise at hearing her voice issuing from the blue jaw of Detective Munch, rhymes with *lunch*, badge number 12345 (a little suspicious, that; someone has been careless about the details), who has taken to hanging around, waiting for someone else to die.

I wonder if others hear her? Of course they hear her, absurd question. But do they recognize that inimitable gurgling moan? Probably not, she died before most of them were born, though I am not sure about Munch-rhymes-with-lunch. It is nice to hear from her, of course. I say this, but is it nice? Not at all. Not at this late date. And what surprises me, too, is that she can get a purchase in all those throats, many of them completely untrained, for what purpose is there in all that we do here if any Munch can open his mouth and emit a message from the dead?

Rubbish, it does not surprise me in the least. What is speech but the endless prattle of the dead? Now what would surprise me, really surprise me, would be if someone actually said something *new*.

I am beginning to suspect that I do not want to explain about the voice of my mother! I must be rattled. Well, you would be rattled too, if a mouse had just issued from the wainscoting, fixed you with an eye like a fresh black drop of blood, and said in your mother's voice, "Sweet pea, it is getting late." And if a minute later a moth—I am not completely crazy, I know most moths don't have mouths, and not one has a voice box. But if in the dry bustle of its body against the lamp glass, you heard the soft clearing of a familiar throat, would you not fumble for the paregoric? It is at the very least surprising, at last, yes, something I can fairly call surprising, that an animal can channel our human dead. Would they not more plausibly channel their own, emitting squeaks first squeaked by an ancient *Mus musculus* in a little toga? And perhaps I am hearing things, but it seemed to me just now that even the squawk of the desk drawer has something human in it. Go to bed, Sybil.

Next day. It was not my mother. Why would my mother take an interest in a shortage of Graham flour in our kitchen? A bad example, Mother was always trying to feed me. It is, I believe, the principle function of mothers. But that she would concern herself with the national census or the best method of finding the longitude at sea is more doubtful. Henceforth I will refuse to listen.

But say that I'm wrong, say it is her after all: if this is the sort of thing she's come back for, I will miss nothing by ignoring her. Nothing so juicy as an apology for being so weak-willed as to allow my father to foist me upon a body.

"Foist me upon a body," that is interesting, for who is this "me"? That a smear of personality builds up around the mouth is well known, but sometimes I suspect myself of recidivist egoism.

Incidentally, I would like to repudiate the suggestion that the principles of my science are the mere sequelae of a morbid melancholia or what you might call a "hypo" with its roots in early childhood. This to say that while I have my humanities, as you wrote of another, they serve my vision. Not the other way around.

Adamantly,
Headmistress Joines

Fig. 17 (¹).

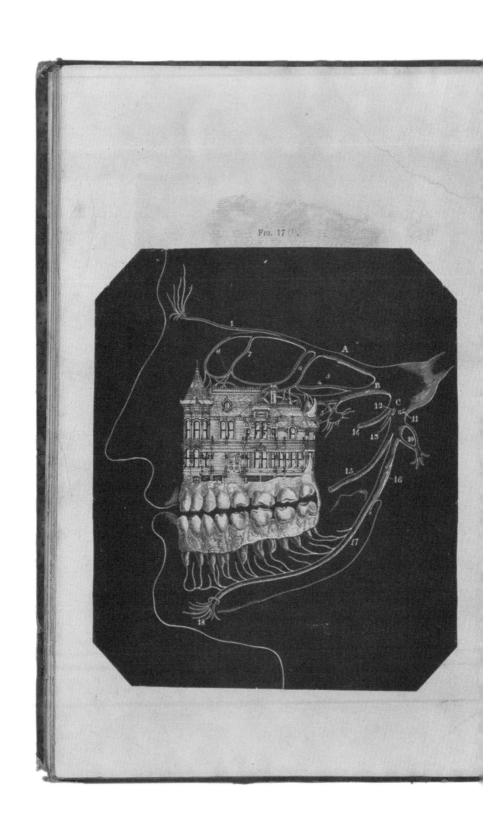

13. The Final Dispatch, contd.

I am down at the swampy verge of our lawn, near the run-off ditch up which in flood weather the river washed garbage up onto the lawn, to the indignation and disgust of my father. I can see an eggshell bobbing like a coracle. Squatting in the thistles and milkweed, I am forcing my fingers down my throat, tasting mud, sap, tears, bile. Eventually also blood. Some sour sort of word is coming out of me.

See how the void colors itself. See how it slops like water when with slimy fingers I pull off my shoes and wade in to catch the eggshell in my cupped hands. See how the void that is shaped like an eggshell bobs on the little pond I hold in my hands, then settles as the void that colors itself water drains through my fingers; see how my finger dents the rubbery little membrane inside the eggshell, pressing it down, until it bursts. See how I thrust my finger straight through the bottom of the shell. See how the shell cracks. How I crush it.

We call this "remembering." It is not very pleasant.

I start up the damp lawn where the rubbery knuckles of mushrooms, nestled among the sparse grass under the chestnut trees, cry out as I tread on them and thus remind me that I am not living though I am walking, what I call walking, what is walking because I say so, which (saying) makes a path scroll underfoot, although a short while ago, if one may speak of whiles, I began to notice that my walking had the feel of creeping and then of crouching motionless inside a small dark place and listening as if for something I feared and expected.

Death is not dark, ordinarily, has not hitherto been dark, for behind all specific things and even through them, I have seemed to see the glare of the page. But now death does begin to seem a little dark to me, while still remaining basically white; it is as if all I can see is the ink, and the chinks between these crudely pegged and wired-together pinewood splits let in only a little light.

In the shafts float dust and rabbit hairs. When I exhale they somersault slowly. Then there is a smell. This is unusual, in death, we often forget about the smells, forget to describe them and thus forget to smell them. As soon as I smell smoke I know that I have been smelling it for several minutes already, and am all at once terrified. More terrified than the situation warrants, for I am in death already, and if I were to stay on, and thus die, it would be merely to accede to a condition already my own, and to a disaster, if it is one, that happened a long time ago. Though, as I tell myself this, my understanding of the land of the dead deepens suddenly, for I see that it is not necessarily true, though I have believed it and may again, that I am in control of where I go and what I do when I am dead, for someone else could write my story for me, as I have conceived writing it for others, and this Someone might not wish me well.

I try to reassure myself with the thought that I have no enemies, but see at once that this is scarcely so. Why just last week I beat two children, fired a maid I suspected of burning, instead of darning, a threadbare sock, chased away a tinker, and adopted a supercilious tone with the town librarian, knowing full well that it would enrage her. Four, no, five people who might wish me ill, and that is not even counting the dead, some of whom have even better reasons.

Thinking this I noticed a brightening of the darkness, an orangeing and yellowing and flickering and above all a changing. Suddenly the nothing was burning, is burning. I am not complaining, merely remarking. I am as calm as a wick. I stand in the furor, just like I did before, and wait to know what to do, which I will very soon, I am sure.

You may take this moment to curl your hands into fists to warm your corpse-cold fingers.

Do not worry unduly. It is a friendly fire, in a way. It is familiar. (From *family*, etymologically.) The nothing is woody and sheddy, sheddish, so it burns readily, and I burn inside it. As I would have burned, that other time, had I not leapt like the hare through the fire, coming out on the other side—of death, you might say—with smoking braids, no eyebrows, and crimped lashes. This time I shall stay put, being already on the other side. I shall think about walking calmly away, or about cold water rising, or about you, uncurling your fingers and *taptaptapping*, making the only sound in the quiet room except for the tick of something, probably a deathwatch beetle, in the walls.

I would like to be telling a different story, secretary. Yours, say. You are more real to me at this moment than fire, though I suppose you are a kind of fire yourself. Do we not burn all our lives long, mixing fuel with oxygen to light our cells, and emitting waste like a kind of solid smoke at the other end? If so, you are a cool fire, friend, cooler than I am. I cool myself against you. I sleep alone, but you would discover, if we shared a bed, a purely hypothetical scenario, that I am like a furnace, that anything pressing against me would grow intolerably hot and begin to smell of smoke, until your eyes burned and you choked, your lips turning bluish gray, no, I am letting myself become confused, you would grow hot and wet, I mean with sweat, no matter how cold the night, no matter how dry the roaring wind, in which sparks and flecks of ash and charcoal fly, dotting your dress with eyelets ringed with expanding circles of fire, stinging your cheeks and neck so that you clap your hands to your face, crying, *no, no, no, no*—

No.

Compose yourself.

Resume.

Your story. You have a nonregulation black shawl draped around your shoulders, with my express permission; my office is not well heated. I do not require it, for reasons we have just considered; I could melt a tunnel through a blizzard. This building suits me not although but *because* it is damp and cold and dark and still as a tomb. Nothing orange and leaping here. No heating stove may more than smolder, as all the housemaids know—I stay out of the kitchen and choose not to know if other rules obtain there.

You are wearing a black pinafore, flammable but not scorched, over a white blouse with long ink-spotted sleeves and a high neck to hide the burns. No, that is wrong, you have never been burned, dear listener. I assert it. Even if you once seized the handle of a cast-iron frypan that was sliding off the range toward your little sister and scorched the entire palm of your right hand, so that pale, plump continents of blister rose up on it—didn't they?—you have never really burned. Not like—

It speaks. Fire, I mean. It howls and sings and harangues and cajoles.

You don't know what I'm talking about, of course. Of course! Ha ha! It is so restful to talk to you. I would give you a raise if I did not know you would save it up toward your independence; and I prefer to keep you. But I shall get you a rug for your lap and a tasseled cushion for your feet or perhaps a hod of coal for your personal use as you *taptaptap* and listen to me, tap and listen all night long, coal to stoke the fire beating orange against the glass until it shatters—no! Your feet are not visible under your skirts but I can hear your narrow boots knocking against the runnels of my chair. That is certainly not the sound of nails exploding from the twisting wood or of a plank falling outward, crashing onto its burning side, to make a narrow blackened runway, edged with flame.

Would you dare to walk that runway through a seethe of flame? You have the look of a deer about you, or perhaps a hare, narrow and wary and strange. Still, but prepared to explode into motion. To leap over or through a fire, if you needed to.

You would leap! I applaud you. I too leapt. I do not need to leap this time. Though now the roof has caught. Of the shed. The sheddy nothing-ness that is all around me like a horrible womb. What a very absurd and tasteless phrase that is, dear listener. Let it stand; every stylist must have her *peccata*.

All around me but tiger-striped. In every fire there are places where fire is not. Stripes of fire, stripes of the absence of fire. To escape a fire one need only organize the blaze so that all that is fire is in one place, and all that is not fire in another, balled together, as it were; then one may walk through an inferno unscathed, and out of it. This, rather than hare-like leaping, is the approach of the rational demiurge, the approach I now prefer. I do not even look back to check whether the roof fell in, as it had to, the moment I leapt,

I mean stepped through the break in the wall, placing my feet one after the other, walking the plank to safety. Now there is just a little heap of nothing burning behind me. Smoke is twirling up into a question mark; now it is thinning, now it is gone.

You, too, did not panic, I am sure of it. You are cool. Competent. And compliant. Of course you are, or you would not have the job you have.

You stammer, I think I recall, on the letter *a*. A-a-and. A-a-again. A-a-afterlife. I like that about you. *A* is the beginning of the alphabet and thus you announce in a sense another alphabet, an alphabet of difficulty and even silence. You grew up in New York, I think. Or Paterson? A city bigger than any in which I ever felt at home. You went to work young, washing dishes perhaps, to support your family: your younger sister (so smart, so spirited), your mother (a drunk of easy virtue). Your sister died. Of what? Of consumption, like me? No, cholera, no, influenza, one of the three, galloping through the tenements where you, like so many others, lived. Your mother, equally afflicted, coughing blood and gin vapors, told you to go to the devil, and in a sense you did: You came, after a sojourn at your aunt's, to me. I am glad you did.

Are you black? Now I think that you are, that I knew that and forgot it, since your mind seems colorless when I speak into your unobstructed ear, a perfect blank on which I write, though I do not mean to imply that to be colorless is preferable or even possible. None of us is that. One is parchment-hued, another peach or pink, another piebald. Personally I am yellowish. For sheer beauty of hue you have the advantage of me.

Have you heard from your sister? She is dead, you said, or I said it, or you said it, saying it was me, writing it as if I had said it, persuading me I said it. I am sure she is; I am sure you would not have left her with your mother (if your mother lived), if what I have heard, I mean what I have said of your mother is true. I am sure that when men, loud with drink and lewdness, made free with your mother's person behind the glowing green sheet that screened the other bed in your single room, you covered your sister's ears, or sang songs (we do not stutter when we sing), or bundled her up warm and hoisted her out on the fire escape beside you, to count the lighted windows and watch the moon up into the sky.

I have made your mother's intercourse an ugly thing, and probably it was, for you. A child does not want to be burdened with her parents' pleasure, any more than with their pain or grief. But the green-glowing sheet . . .

I have been told that sexual intercourse is, can be, like death—that the sexual climax is even called a "little death." During it, I hear, a person becomes like an object, knowing, and glad to know, if for just a few moments, only what things know, as they move against other things and move and lie still and move again. I think I would like to try sexual intercourse. I wonder what you would think if I—but perhaps not with a person. With a tree, or an iron stove. I suppose I might enjoy it with a tinker, in his cart hung with pots and spatulas and buckets of nails, all rocking and clanking and jingling, as if we two were made of nothing but scrap iron and bent spoons bound together with rags. Better if we were. One would not want to start a child. No, no.

Idle thoughts—the impulse is not strong. Perhaps I satisfy it another way, for it seems to me that stammering is like sex, since when we stammer or stutter the substance of speech becomes present to us as a burr and buzz and scrape in the throat, while its meaning recedes. Time bounces like a tinker's cart. Consonants rattle and creak. Stuttering, stammering, we rock in place, we thrust with our tongues, we pull strange faces, our cheeks flush, our mouth is misshapen, the throat is a ring tight on the swelling breath, we forget what we mean, we are only saying, saying, saying. So this is sex, and sex is stuttering, the world beating against a threshold, and both are forms of death, joyful death, because we love the world so much we long to lose ourselves in it.

The world teeters between meaning and matter. We are at the fulcrum—we *are* the fulcrum. And I am tipping the balance, but I don't know which way, I don't know . . .

The Stenographer's Story, contd.

The voice crackles, drops out, returns as pure sound—ice crystals blowing over frozen snow, a handful of sand swirling in a pan. Then there is silence. My fingers striking the keys are as loud as bones snapping.

For a minute, I let them rest (asdf jkl;), and the silence fills with the green of a glowing sheet.[18] It is not in my memory that it glows, but her words. I have never told the story of my childhood. I never will tell it. What is gone tore the hole through which I breathe. We are all built around a riddance: Lungs must empty to fill again. For some here this is doctrine. For me, a fact. Through its ghastly mercy I live.

In her words, I seem to see my past, but from the outside. My mother, Bitty, me, my blurred and spectral father: tiny figures under a glass dome. I can barely imagine their suffering or, more terrible, their joy. What a gift this diminution is. It is only a malicious ghost who whispers, now, "She has stolen the one thing you had left." I drown it out with the clatter of these keys, for no one can hold on to the past. What is life but the broom that erases our tracks? Every minute another minute is gone, to be replaced (if at all) by a memory, which is to say a figment, a fiction. Has she stolen my life and given me a counterfeit? No, at most she has stolen one counterfeit and given me another. Or given me a counterfeit where I had just an aching socket.

So the green glow fades. I will resume my account, which is not concerned with what I was, but with what I have become and am becoming. My destination. (Destiny?)

I was threading through the crowd that always gathered outside the room where Dr. Peachie was seeing patients when I came face-to-face with

---

18. This is one of the very few moments when the secretary seems to be commenting directly on the Headmistress's account, and it may be taken as strong evidence that the two texts advanced together just as I have arranged them here, first one, then the other surging ahead toward the finish line. However, honesty compels me to observe that there is in the Final Dispatch another paragraph lit by an emerald glow, very near the end, that "in her words" might just as well mean in the transcript reread at leisure, and finally that by her own account the secretary is a liar and a cheat, and may have had her reasons to construct a timeline at variance with the truth. By the way, it is not at all clear whether the green sheet is a colorful invention or the truth, and if truth, where the Headmistress learned about it. From the dead? How we should like to know! —Ed.

Mother Other, shoving her way in the opposite direction. As if she had been burning for the opportunity, she confronted me. "You want to be her successor! You're angling for it. Ingratiating yourself. I won't have it!"

"You want it yourself, then?" said I.

Dr. Peachie's door opened and a boy drifted out, his face rapt. There was a collective surge forward and a muted scuffle over the door handle. The door closed again.

Mother Other blushed hibiscus red. "Well, what if I do? I'd be the obvious choice. Or Dotty, of course," she conceded grudgingly, meaning Miss Exiguous.

Ramshead, twirling gracelessly in place, eyes closed, said dreamily: "You're not a channeler, though, Mother Other." She stopped and opened her eyes. "I mean—are you? I mean, I've never even heard you stutter."

Mother Other shifted uncomfortably.

"You can't channel the dead!" I discovered.

"I've been her right hand since the beginning. I know everything about running this school. *Everything*," she heaved forth. "And I'm one hundred percent faithful. I'd do exactly as she'd do."

"But you wouldn't *be* her. So how could you be her successor? You're not even in the running." I met her small, furious eyes and took a step back. "You'd like to strangle me, wouldn't you?" I said, and then laughed. "But I'd just come back again. And again, and again, and again!"

"Don't listen to her, Mother Other," said Florence. "It's ridiculous that anyone's talking about Grandison at all. Even just among the students there are better candidates. Dixon, McCaughey . . . Wang . . . Even Smithson . . ."

"What do you mean, 'even'?" demanded Smithson, who was listening. "But honestly, I don't know why anyone takes you seriously, Grandison. Nobody has forgotten how you tried to fake it back in Speech One. Your 'Dutch Surinamian,' what a joke. I bet you don't even know where Suriname is. I don't know why you weren't thrown out on your bean!"

"Headmistress probably liked her even more for that," said Ramshead. Recognizing the likelihood of this, Smithson subsided.

But though the others believed me a teacher's pet, I knew better. Possibly, at one point, I *had* imagined that the Headmistress, relying on me, might come to confide in me, and even care a little for me. Possibly. I do not say that I did. It would not have been like me to expect affection. In any case it did not come to pass. I had worked for the Headmistress for five years without eliciting intimacies. Cold, commanding, unconvivial lady! I was not sure she credited me with any existence outside my function as a recording device. She certainly did not exert herself to draw from me my story. Perhaps another girl, sweet and open and naturally affectionate, could have snuggled past her guard. But I doubt it. Because my real competition came in the form of quite another sort of child.

It was Dixon who brought her to my attention. One day, after I had bested her in an exam, she rounded on me: "It's revolting, how you hang on the Headmistress's every word. Don't you see that she's completely confused? On the one hand, people blab on forever, changing only their form, and everything is language, even dried porridge and, what, sewing machines, and it's all just so marvelously *meeeeaningful*. On the other hand, the self doesn't exist, every person is a missing person, and speech is not communication but a cacophony that humans make in the senseless way that some neurotic animals ceaselessly rearrange their bedding or pluck all the hair out of the base of their tails, communicating nothing except their inexhaustible distress. Well, which is it? Everything is meaningful or nothing is? The whole world speaks in a human voice, or even humans aren't human?"

"I think"—I struggled to frame my answer—"I think she'd say that contradicting yourself is good. A way to open a crack in what we mistake for a world. Like stuttering, only on the level of meaning," I added, getting interested.

She snorted. "She'd say, she'd say—what do you say?"

"I don't exist."

"Do you believe that?"

"I don't know. Yes. In a way."

"Well, *I* exist, and I'm fed up with her mumbo jumbo. All this harping on holes and what goes through them—what do you think *that's* really about? She's fucking ghosts instead of living people. Of course it isn't satisfying, of course it gives her an empty feeling! But instead of finding herself a fellow or a finger she tells herself she's on the trail of the Mystery. 'Deeper, deeper!'"

"You're not wrong, exactly," I said. "Of course it's desire that's driving her. But I think you have it backwards: Sex is *our* substitute for what *she's* seeking. We're all fucking ghosts, but for most of us there's a body in the way. Our desire can't be satisfied either, only we blame the other person (who's not satisfied either) and move on. But we limit our quest to the human. She's attracted to the *universe*."

"What about Finster?"

I was silent.

"I mean, is she in love with her?"

The idea of the Headmistress in love made us both snort with laughter, which put an end to our argument. But there was something to it, all the same.

Some months ago, perhaps as much as a year, it had come to my attention that, despite her increasing detachment, the Headmistress took a special interest in one of the younger girls. It was not obvious why. *Finster* means "dark" in the German tongue, and so the girl Finster was. I do not mean in coloration; my skin is darker than hers. Finster was *obscure*. One might hesitate to call her a little girl, or even human. She had the overbite, hunched shoulders, and darting movements of a squirrel. Once I glimpsed her sockless foot. It was narrow and bony, the middle toes longer than the big toe, like those of a rodent. Nor did her manners make amends for her appearance. Not too surprising, since she was the get of a shrill, nasty woman who sometimes traipsed all the long way from town to bang on the front door and threaten to take Finster away if she was not paid something for her, and many of us would have told her mother to take her and welcome, for the daughter was no nicer than the dam. But the Headmistress would send Clarence down with a purse or, sometimes, a bottle, and Finster stayed.

I recall the first or second time I saw her. The Headmistress was crooked over her, tense with effort, attempting to fit her with a branks. Finster, her whole body an expletive, tore the branks from her head (along with not a little of her hair) and struck the Headmistress square in the face with it. Mother Other haled her away; the branks jangled under a settee and stuck there. I flew to the Headmistress, offering my arm, and felt her shocking frailty for a moment as she pulled herself up, breathing hard, a single black pearl of blood hanging in one nostril. There was a high color in her cheeks.

I expected to see no more of this Finster and was surprised to pass her in the hall a week later, for the Headmistress was not notable for her leniency. Her sensitivity to the dead was only matched by her *in*sensitivity to the living. Indeed, "One must be prised loose a little from the living," she had taught us, "to go freely among the dead." But perhaps this was even what drew her to Finster, for though many children are not quite of the living, but spend at least some part of their time in conversation with stones and beetles and the way light shines on a leaf, Finster spent her time no other way, Finster had no friends, had conceivably never had any, her speech impediment was so profound that she scarcely spoke, not to other children, nor even to her mother. And in so abstaining from speech and even, as it appeared, scorning it—for Finster was not aphasic, nor mute: she simply preferred not to speak—Finster had made room enough for the dead in her to rival the Headmistress herself.

Dear reader, if ever this document has one, I am sure you already understand several things better than either the Headmistress or poor furious Finster did. The Headmistress loved Finster because she was the least lovable of her students, and this is not a paradox. The Headmistress herself was not lovable and never had been, though she believed (and how can we gainsay her, who are even farther from that lost Eden than she was) that her mother had loved her once. Finster, also shorn of a mother—but *so am I!* comes the cry of pointless protest, but I hold it in—was the Headmistress in miniature, minus the brooch of braided hair (a little singed) and the black bombazine: nasty, suspicious, unattractive, and not particularly clean; and insofar as the Headmistress gave her, Finster, love, so might the Headmistress believe *herself* lovable—a belief that even those who have transferred all their affections to the dead may wish to hold on occasion. Who can blame them?

I might have tried to thwart this partiality, had Finster not sought so earnestly to thwart it herself. For Finster took an interest in the Headmistress in turn, but not a warm one. Quite the opposite: she had the liveliest resentment of a person who had snatched her away from a situation that, however unsavory it must seem to an outsider, had suited her very well. That her mother had essentially sold her—and continued at intervals to sell her, in those transactions with Clarence on the lawn of the school—would have given some children pause, but she seemed to consider it unremarkable, and reserved all her blame for the one who, possessing the means, employed them to wrest her from her home. (Having known poverty myself, I would not say she was entirely wrong in that.)

The interest she took in the Headmistress, therefore, was aimed exclusively at identifying her weak spots and hurling barbs at them. Everyone knew she was the one who stole the rabbit foot the Headmistress kept on her desk. None of us would have dared. She did not fail to perceive the Headmistress's partiality for her—indeed she seemed to regard it an especial affront—and rebuffed her experimental overtures with scorn, though I do not know whether the Headmistress ever even noticed that, imperious as she was herself, and unused to the give-and-take of equals in affection. (How I talk. As if *I* were!) However, deprived of any other outlet, this partiality lent a peculiar intensity to the punishments the Headmistress exacted for Finster's crimes. More than once I came upon her, bent over a twisting, spitting Finster, one hand clamped on her ear, the other employing an oral debrider or other instrument, her whole body tense with focus, and the queerest mixture of wrath, exultation, yearning, and nervous anticipation on her face. Afterward, she was always very fatigued. I think she did not know whether to desire or to dread these encounters.

They certainly did nothing to discourage Finster's sorties. If anything, they had the opposite effect. God knows there was no need to manufacture injuries, we had enough of them, and fatalities as well, but Finster was seen banging a door upon her own arm that she might flaunt her bruises, sniffling, before a visiting parent. She slipped notes to trustees, to old Dr. Beede and young Dr. Peachie, to reporters. One day a colossal boom brought us all running to find smoke pouring from the refectory, where (we eventually discerned) she had set off a small bomb made with coal dust, cotton wool, a candle end, and an alarm clock. Then she wrote a letter to the *Cheesehill Gazette* from A Conserned [sic] Citizen complaining of soot particles in the soup. The next week she blew the whistle on a sinister medical conspiracy to inject the students with narcotics, though this did not go over well with the readership—old Dr. Beede was much loved. Undeterred, she followed with a letter alleging that an artificial manure ring had its headquarters in our carriage house and then one about dumping "rapatious" [sic] snails in other people's gardens under cover of darkness. Seeking scandals to leak with the diligence of a Fleet Street stringer, she canvased the other students—she canvased me—about the Headmistress's proclivities, past and present. Finally she recruited her mother, or somebody, to pump the older townspeople for stories about the Headmistress's girlhood. And by God she got them.

I do not know how the Headmistress had managed it, living in or near the place where it all happened, but until that day no one, including me, had known more than a few blank and unexceptionable facts about her past. We knew her parents were dead; you could hardly miss the Joines plot, the biggest in the cemetery, slung around with chains and stuffed with obelisks, and winged skulls, and limestone lambs, and there anyone might read "Harwood Joines" on a marble monolith and "Beloved Wife" on a limestone block. But the hagiographies that assorted sycophants had tremblingly committed to lavender-scented paper dismissed her parents in a few words, treating them as a sort of trellis to the budding genius, necessary but inconsequential. Now all of the ghastly details came out. All? Well, we thought so at the time.

Finster did not hurl them in the Headmistress's face; she had more cunning. Having circulated the facts among the students and faculty ("Is it t-t-t-true, Mr. Lieu, that Headm-m-mistress Joines's father burned to d-death in a f-f-f-f-f-f . . . ?") she began insinuating covert references to them into English decompositions, aural reports, etc., in the guise of figures of speech. The effect was disconcerting. One does not expect, while grading a penmanship exercise, to find one's mind pullulating with fire, strangulation, filicide, patricide, uxoricide, suicide. Though at the Vocational School death was never far away, its attentions were impersonal; we were not accustomed to such *ad hominem* reapage.

But while Finster's campaign advanced, its object was slipping out of reach. For it had become increasingly obvious that the Headmistress was very seriously ill.

OUR LITTLE BOOK.

DAILY COURSE of LETTERS

1. *Make 26 of these*

(I believe you know the alphabet)

2. *Take one a day, with water*

Readings

from "A Visitor's Observations"

On the Patois of the Vocational School

We come at last to the heart of my topic—how, in a school devoted to the necromancy of the word, people actually spoke.

With experiences to describe and ideas to convey to which an ordinary vocabulary, adapted as it is to *this* side of the veil, was not always adequate, it was natural that the students developed their own vernacular. Some curious terminology found itself in common use. I am not speaking solely of the technical vocabulary developed to discuss the techniques, devices, and theories of thanatology, though it was extensive, but also of terms coined by the children themselves. Another source of linguistic curiosities was the dead, for defunct words, as well as people, were given voice anew in the halls of the Vocational School, and some once-common words that had not been heard in years or centuries enjoyed a second coming—though not always in quite their original senses, for children, especially these children, like to play with words.

Too, these children lived such different lives from ordinary children—and were so isolated from those other children—that the school represented a sort of linguistic Galápagos where new verbal life-forms evolved at a fast clip, quickly diverging from their increasingly distant cousins on the mainland. The vernacular at the Vocational School was always changing, and I was never entirely sure whether terms or constructions that mystified me had simply never come my way before, or whether they had only just been introduced. Periodically I even stumbled into what seemed like an entire new wing of the language. A new vista opened up to me, for instance, when I realized that the children were using physical objects as linguistic elements. It turned out that the same word spoken in a room with wood paneling meant something different than in a room with plaster walls or one in which there was a puce velveteen settee on which rested a round, ruched, gold-fringed cushion, flattened by long use and rather stained with hair oil.

Some rooms seemed to have their own tense, which I would describe as a sort of optative pluperfect, for use in expressing aspirations for one's past and for lives already over (the nearest approximation might be "I hope to had done"). I was told that in the land of the dead, and only there, one often must have recourse to a special tense used for describing the activities of things that have only just always been there. The refectory imposed the passive voice and the southwest stairwell tinted anything said in it with wistfulness while the northeast stairwell inclined to sarcasm. The Headmistress's own office seemed to put even innocent observations in the imperative mood ("It's a bit windy out" becoming, say, "Go and latch the shutters," "It's five o'clock" becoming "Go away"), but that may have been due to the somewhat daunting presence of the Headmistress herself.

I had barely mastered the inflections imposed by architecture when I discovered that certain smaller, portable objects could be used as prefixes, suffixes, and infixes. Sometimes held up and turned from side to side while speaking, but as often merely situated somewhere nearby (such that the inexpert linguist, sensing that the conversation was getting away from him, had to paw frantically through the bric-a-brac for the one relevant linguistic element), they altered the whole sense of the root, though what precise shades of meaning they added were not always clear—could not always, in fact, be explained without use of the new prefix itself. That this was no doubt why a need for the prefix had been perceived in the first place made it no less frustrating for the researcher. When I inquired into the meaning of *visit* when uttered in the presence of a particular bed warmer in the shape of a clock, the students simply shook the bed warmer at me, dealing me, incidentally, a painful rap on the ankle.

To use material objects as elements of speech was not as eccentric as it might appear, since according to one of the hypotheses of necrophysics, the material things of our world were already a debased kind of speech, just as the ectoplasmic "mouth objects" were. The Headmistress held out hope that we would eventually come to understand this language, and she had set a team of advanced students to studying the possibility of translation, though she confided to me that it was her private belief that a breakthrough would not come until after the mouth objects themselves had been successfully translated, those having suffered, in her view, less distortion, being a degree closer to the form in which we might be able to understand them (i.e., speech). The students, however, impatient with the slow and cautious methods of the scholar, had simply set about using them. Never mind that they had no real idea what the objects that they chose meant; they simply assigned them new meanings. The result, of course, was that they never knew what they were really saying (though who knows, perhaps by luck or instinct they sometimes hit upon the objects' real meanings, thinking they were inventing them). Just as the deaf who have mastered a sign language must sometimes read in our random gestures, or even in the tossing limbs of trees, mangled fragments of words, or, who knows, whole phrases of genuine if accidental beauty, so some explorer from the dead might "hear" in the students' juvenile chatter strains of poetry or prayer, oddly mixed with curses, banalities, and sheer nonsense.

Some students seemed to add the same prefix to virtually every word they spoke, carrying the object everywhere, so as never to be at a loss for words. They guarded these tokens jealously, allowing no one else to handle them, so that while according to convention as I understood it, others standing nearby could also have employed them in speech (though a little weakened, no doubt, by distance), I concluded that whatever shading of meaning they added was wholly private. It was as if the first person, the use of which was strictly curtailed in the classrooms and halls, had returned, displaced and disguised, in the form of some external thing: a doll's handkerchief, a candle snuffer, a charred piece of wood. I imagine that the meanings of these affixes were as varied as the objects themselves, and maybe even changed from one hour to another, according to whether the speaker was angry, sad, or in that peculiar state, a kind of anticipatory homesickness for death, that the students called simply "the shortage" or, more jocularly, "a case [or fit] of the shorts."

The world being full of material things, any or all of which might be parts of speech, one would think that a few small human voices would be drowned out by the hullaballoo of the furniture. But it didn't happen that way. Only certain objects were used in the way I have described, and while I was often unsure which of many likely objects were exerting an influence (palpable, if not identifiable) on a given utterance, the students themselves always seemed to recognize them immediately. Whether they actually "heard" that one spoon in the drawer or that brush handle, plucked bare of bristles, shoring up a wobbly washstand—perhaps with some organ that has atrophied in the adult of the species—or just picked up the identifying information from the other students, I didn't know.

According to what criteria did one scuffed boot-heel become a prefix and another just something to stand on? I never understood it, but I am brought to mind of a tattered pincushion in the shape of a little bird that I lifted from my mother's sewing basket so many times, as a child, that she at last relented and bought herself another. I carried the pincushion everywhere. When it fell apart, I was inconsolable; my mother offered me her own much newer but otherwise similar pincushion, but I slapped the imposter away, as revolted as if someone had tried to pass off a wax doll as my mother.

What is my point? I have forgotten . . . I seem to hold again that little bird with its single button eye, the firm batting bulging through the frayed spots in the faded oilcloth, whose original color could still be found hiding in the seams, shockingly bright . . .

Oh yes, that material things speak even to ordinary children. And maybe we understand them better than we are willing to credit, later on.

The vernacular at the Vocational School went through fashions, as it does in the world at large. There was a time when it was *de rigueur* to bestow upon every conceivable object a first and middle name: Winnifred Johnson Table, Lowell Himmelmeyer Coal Hod. One student, cornered, explained that this was merely practical—*table* was a sort of family name, while an individual table was unique, like an individual person, and required its own moniker to spare one the onus of such laborious periphrasis as "the small gateleg table in the upstairs sitting room, no, against the right-hand wall, no, under the window, no, the one with the stained dropleaf."

Another, however, assured me that the fashion stemmed from the belief that all material objects were living beings (on another turn of the wheel, so to speak, that carries us through the various dimensions of speech—but I will have to let another explain the intricacies of Joinesian necrophysics, for I never fully grasped it) and thus deserved the dignity of their own names—only to be interrupted by a comrade with the amendment that they already *had* names, from an earlier pass through our world, and it was common courtesy to use them. Thus everyday speech teemed with proper names to a confusing degree ("Lydia tried to strike Herbie with Lowell, but he hid under Winnifred"). Later it seemed that verbs, too, acquired proper names, perhaps because one moment's walking, running, or even dying is quite distinct from another's, but here even the students seemed to become confused (Lydia Jonquiled to Patterson Herbie with Lowell, but he Abrahamed under Winnifred), and one day a few weeks later, the names were abandoned wholesale in favor of a new fad: compound words in which one of the two conjoined terms they pronounced themselves and the second was intoned by the dead.

To hear their high young voices break in the very middle of a word and give way, with results not unlike the hee-haw of a donkey, to the characteristic hollow honking tone of the dead was very disagreeable.

Still more did I reprehend the later and possibly consequent development of words with a great many prefixes and suffixes, uttered by the children and the playful dead in quick succession to create a sort of two-colored mosaic in sound. Though I consider myself fairly insensitive to the incursions of the other world, even I felt the world *strobing* in and out of presence at such moments (*strobe* was one of their words), and this was disconcerting enough that I covered my ears and fled, not even trying to figure out what the children were trying to communicate. I imagine that they took some delight in my discomfiture and may on occasions have introduced—invented?!—the offending terms to tease me. And lest readers think this admission casts my description of the novel linguistic climate of the school in doubt, understand that far from being reprimanded for their gamesomeness, the children were encouraged to introduce innovations, for although the Headmistress was a martinet and brooked no rebellion from her living charges, she regarded the children essentially as vessels for the dead, so that when she considered a legitimate representative of the dead to be speaking through them—a matter that was not always easy for me, at least, to determine, for the cleverer mimics among the children could deceive me with feigned communications that often ended in the grossest insults followed by peals of high-pitched laughter—she would permit the youngest and least experienced child to hold forth on equal terms with any member of her crack faculty or her wealthiest trustee.

I was privy to a short-lived experiment at the Vocational School. The Headmistress had issued a statement deploring the excessive garrulousness of the student body, which was drowning out the dead. Among the living, speech was strongly discouraged. Soon thereafter she took stronger measures, implementing a quota. Those who spoke too much were put on a restricted vocabulary and moved to smaller quarters, to associate only with other offenders. In this atmosphere of verbal privation, new pidgins evolved, entailing much tedious repetition. As this was deemed a sort of induced stuttering, involving larger parts of speech, Vocational School experts monitored the situation closely to see how the dead responded; it would be uniquely easy to tell if the speaker was dead or alive, one expert advised me, since the dead had license to use the full range of their vocabulary. This enthusiasm was premature; naturally the children hit at once upon the idea of imitating the dead in order to obtain use of their vocabulary, and the fakery was so endemic that the Headmistress terminated the experiment with disgust.

In addition to a new vocabulary, the Headmistress devoted hours of toil to developing a new alphabet, supposedly better suited to writing of the dead. This took place gradually, the process passing through several distinct stages that I was fortunate enough to observe.

The first was the case-by-case expansion of our ordinary alphabet with already extant symbols that, unpronounceable themselves, served to alter the sound of letters with which they were associated, such as the German *Umlaut*, the Russian "soft sign," and musical notations such as *crescendo, diminuendo*, and the scalloped line of a trill to expand the range of vowels—for the dead are very fond of vowels, to the near exclusion of other sounds.

More innovative was the introduction of seven entirely new symbols (I remember the day she came into the sitting room where the senior faculty and I were enjoying a postprandial port and thrust a slate blanched with curious notations before us, her manner triumphant; it was some time before one of us, fortified by the port—it was Mr. Medlar—could bring himself to confess that he did not know what those symbols were meant to represent!) standing for vowel-consonant combinations, expressing, for instance, the sound of a long *e* forced through clenched teeth.

After these new letters had been taken up and were in pretty general use, she began to introduce others, the first of these standing for sounds that while rare in the general population are common among ghost speakers—those extended fricatives, for instance, some of which sound like the hiss of a snake, others like its rattle; some like footsteps in dry grass, others like something heavy falling into snow and lying quite still, and some like nothing more ordinary—or more miraculous—than a breath.

Later she added what I might call several decimal places of refinement to sounds for which we already possess symbols—a slight cast of *e* or *a* in the pronunciation of an *o* (sounds she was previously content to collect under the broad heading of the *o*, or at most, to indicate with the addition of an *Umlaut*) would be designated with a whole new symbol, at the center of which the original letter could sometimes, however, be made out.

She was pretty well along in this series when her process was overset and many if not most of her new additions were disqualified by the revelation that all letters ought to contain a hole or, in typographical terms, a counter. This, in order to stand for and harmonize with the hole that is the self, which is given physical expression by the hole of the throat, and finds its purest form on paper in the letter O. "The letter I, like all leggy, unperforated letters, gives the false impression that we have something to say for ourselves. Only the letter O expresses the essence of speech, which is to express nothing—to hollow oneself out." She immediately issued an ukase: The first person would henceforth be expressed in writing by the letter O, with the result that many school documents from this period seem to be apostrophizing their readers, exhorting them in the elevated tones of prayer: "O require several pints of your blackest India ink soonest."

By the way, the Headmistress saw the hollow tube of the quill pen as a neat reiteration of the hollow tube of the windpipe, and recognized no very great distinction between speaking (writing on the wind) and writing (speaking in ink); in both cases, the hollow was the important thing, not the physical substance—ink or wind—that passed through it, nor the substance of the walls of the hole (which are not, strictly speaking, part of the hole, merely the internal terminus of the holed object, the hole's "host").

Having established the aforementioned constraint (that each letter must contain a hollow), I believe the Headmistress found not only her inventiveness sadly taxed, but also her memory. In transcriptions of the words of the dead from this period we often find that the Headmistress has let a simple o stand in for a great range of sounds, being as it was the essence of every letter—and perhaps also because, as she had by this point designed many tens of letterforms, possibly as many as two hundred, she may not have been able to remember them all, nor look them up fast enough in her reference books to take down a transmission as it was made. There are even a few notebooks extant, dated late in this period of lexicographical invention, in which *every single letter is an* o. It is notable that these are not identical ovals, as if mechanically produced, whether in idleness or as a meditative practice, but that some seem to have been dashed off in great haste, others inscribed with careful slowness, and some few (most remarkably) scratched out and replaced by more o's, not dramatically different, to *this* eye, at least.

It is our good fortune that this period did not last long. Perceiving, one imagines, the weaknesses of an alphabet of either excessively great variety or none, she discarded nearly all her designs and reverted to the noble Roman alphabet. Perhaps in this she was influenced by the difficulty of reconciling the idea that no ordinary alphabet is adequate to the speech of the dead with her claim that all literary works—all written documents of any kind—are nothing more nor less than communication devices employed by the dead.

When I say that she discarded her designs I mean that she issued instructions that her notebooks be taken into the yard and burnt. Fortunately for subsequent scholarship I had long since primed Clarence with a weekly allowance to bring to me any substantial documentation that she discarded. With the result that I possess all—*all*—her typographical designs, as well as many other interesting and unique documents that I will eventually release to the interested public as I see fit or when suitable remuneration is offered.

The Headmistress's conception of the relationship of the living to the dead and both to language, formed in her youth, remained markedly consistent in its broad outlines until her death. However, its details, and even more the principles of action derived from it, changed dramatically at times. For instance, before my arrival, and for a short time after it, she habitually spoke of language in startlingly concrete terms, describing it, variously, as a viscous emission (thus, "gunk," "glue," "grout," a "roux," "ointment," "spackle," and "mortar"), as a powder ("spores," "pollen," "flour"), or a collection of curious little articles ("bric-a-brac," "trinkets," and more disparagingly, "clutter" or "junk"). I suppose this is not surprising, since she did regularly receive communications in material form from the dead, if she was right that the ectoplasmoglyphs were indeed words. But before long, a new sort of metaphor began to turn up, aerating the weightier figures: she might describe language as a gas ("mist," "fog," "smoke," "cloud"); then as a faint odor carried on the air, but with no visible body of its own; for a week or two she might even propose that language was made up of sound—and so much had her views influenced mine that I was struck by the originality of this view and took several pages of notes before it occurred to me that this was in fact the conventional view.

Never mind, because by then her metaphors had changed again; sound was now still too definite, too positive an entity for her, a distasteful imposition of form upon the formless. She had always described human beings as mere containers for holes. Now she described words as another kind of hole, breaking off from the primary hole of the mouth as if that more lasting absence had calved like a glacier. (Or, indeed, like a cow!—for I perceive that I have committed the solecism of mounting one metaphor atop another.) Words took on the semblance of form only insofar as they differed from the more definite substances that make up the rest of our world. It was in one of these phases that she called a hasty faculty meeting (to which I was invited, though only after dropping a pointed hint!) to announce that she had discovered a gross offense against the limpid Not: the alphabet. "I am ashamed to say that it had not previously occurred to me that we are harboring vipers in our mouths, but the scales have fallen from my eyes." (She did not ordinarily employ such conventionally florid expressions, but was speaking under the pressure of strong emotion, as was apparent from the punitive vigor with which she repeatedly polished her lorgnette.)

That some form of writing was still required, she recognized; however, she decreed that from that day forth, the written language would no longer "stuff the mouth of the void with trumpery," would no longer allow a few little squiggles to obtrude between the hole of the individual and the hole of the word. She would not eliminate the alphabet entirely, but would employ it exclusively in issuing instructions for speech, describing the positions that the mouth must take in order to produce the desired word, rather than writing that word itself.

As you may imagine, this was extremely inefficient; the production of even a single sentence required many pages of detailed instructions. Reading these texts was equally difficult; the library and study hall were now filled with strange groans, rattles, and caws that only occasionally resolved into spoken English. The inefficacy of this method would have been apparent to anyone but the Headmistress, who on the contrary seemed to relish the cacophony and to find it uncommonly edifying, as that much closer to the windy speech of the dead.

Despite this, she briefly pondered instating a new policy: that speech, too, should consist only of instructions or recipes for words, rather than the words themselves. To understand it, the listener would have to follow the instructions herself, if possible; thus the intended words would actually be pronounced by the listener, rather than the speaker. This did not deter her, in fact I believe she saw it as a positive advantage, in displacing the word further from the illusory source in the "self" of the "speaker." What did deter her from both her previous solution to the problem of writing and this subsequent development was the unavoidable fact that in trusting language to accurately convey a series of instructions for producing speech, she was retaining a primary if more delimited role of the alphabet in mediating between the individual and the word.

She retreated in some disgruntlement to her study, but several days later emerged with a solution in the form of a new alphabet, one that would undercut any illusion of the independent existence of the word, because its characters were not arbitrary symbols but, again, instructions for speech, this time conveyed through simple diagrams of the positions the mouth must assume to form the sounds that made up the word.

I believe the Hangul script of the Korean people employs a related principle, though if the Headmistress enjoyed a consultation with the deceased King Sejong, she has not said so, nor does it seem likely that she would understand him unless he has picked up a deal of English over the last few centuries. I am inclined to think that she worked alone.

The script was adopted, and the school had just about got used to employing it in all their official texts (I continued taking notes in the Roman alphabet, as I am sure the Headmistress was aware, but I took care to shield my work with my hand, so as not to offend, and indeed—such is the power of convention—began to feel ashamed and even a little squeamish whenever I opened my little book and saw my words, at once so naked, since I could read them at a glance, and so overdressed) when the Headmistress changed her mind. The characters of the new alphabet, which initially had the frankly disturbing appearance of anatomical sketches taken from a cross-section of the human mouth, were already changing. With repetition, the most recognizable of the features that made each sign unique were simplified and exaggerated, while supplemental features and those shared by other letters fell away. Reduced to a few quick lines, the characters increasingly resembled letters in an ordinary alphabet, albeit an unfamiliar one. Oh, for a time one could still perceive, with a little imagination, that this curve represented the tongue, humped at the back, depressed in front, while this other was the palate, and these short straight strokes the teeth, and one could arrange one's mouth accordingly, and thus come to the word mouth-first, as it were, but most students had long since ceased to do so. It simply took too long. Far easier to simply accept, with the elasticity of the young, that this sign was an *a*, that a *z*, and proceed directly to meaning, leaving the mouth alone. This being so, it was not necessary that any character resemble the mouth, just that it resemble no other character, and soon I who, alone perhaps among the population of the school, was still laboriously sounding out words, could no longer recognize anything bodily in those jots, loops, and dashes. The Headmistress, in other words, had removed twenty-six arbitrary symbols only to see them replaced by twenty-six different ones.

The new alphabet was not just retired but banned (although I have found graffiti written in it that I believe to be of recent vintage, so it may be that the students keep it going among themselves), and the old Roman alphabet reinstated . . . And now her metaphors were putting on weight, turning mineral: words were "magma," "mica," "schist," or "gneiss," speech "pyroclastic" or "sedimentary" . . .

A New Letter

for

The Little Ones

AS THE BUNNY APPEARS WHEN CUT OUT AND
PASTED TOGETHER

Directions

Fold in the center and cut out both pieces together. Paste together parts under laps A. Bend up bottom and bend down sides. Paste together the two parts of rabbit and wheel, bending down parts B and C and bending up base of rabbit.

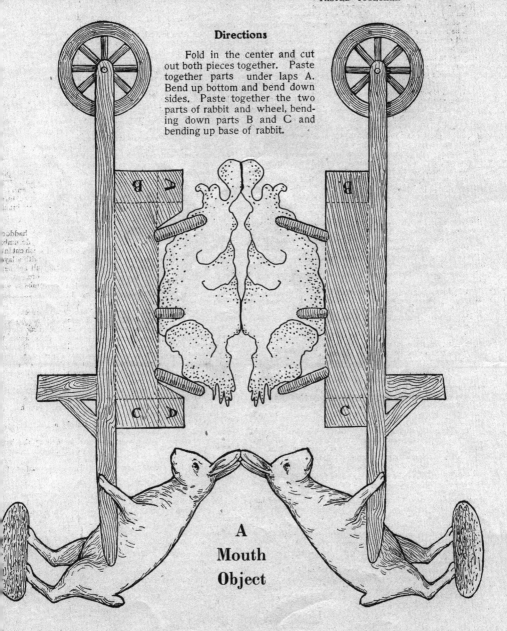

A
Mouth
Object

Letters to Dead Authors, #13

Dear Ishmael,

I have grown gaunt—no one knows how gaunt, I think, since my frame is broad, and I wear a union suit over my corset. Several petticoats over that. And still I am cold. I am always cold now.

So little of me left, and still I stand in my way.

The sun, a cherry-red spot, is slipping down behind the fringed hills, withdrawing its affections swiftly now. Already the roots of the grass are in gelid darkness though their delicate tips are bright, each separately striving for the light against the blue tide rising, already the eastern hills are gray, only their tops aglow, though up in the sky it is still day, day whose long hours I squandered. (Here I must force down the usual clamor of "Failed! Failed again!"—to do what? Reach, grasp, find, learn . . . something worth . . . all *this* . . .)

I always try to toss my spirit up into that warmth, rest in it, a little longer, but it is out of reach and already fading. Now there is nothing in the immense, immobile, transparent sky to hold the light, only a few bright wisps of cloud; these spoil into gray smuts, everything is spoiled, but I rise and close the shutters with a rattle that feels like an offense against the solemnities concluding behind them, and sit back down and dip my pen in night.

I don't know why I still cling to existence. I did not always require it; for aeons I *was not*, and no one sought me. The world breathed in and out without my help. The potato bug did not require my advertisement to seem lovely to her suitor, the cutworm found its way in the dark, the bat identified the moth without referring to my descriptions. Even I could have done without me evermore, for I was not inconvenienced by my absence. Indeed there has been nothing so convenient since. Life could be described without exaggeration as a series of inconveniences, more or less grave, but never unmarked by frustration. Starting with the lifelong frustration of the plan to die. For what is the first thing born in us, the one thing that separates us from nonbeing? It is the capacity to die. But too, despite the body's headlong rush to consummation, a certain reluctance to do so. Yes! I admit it.

I know, I have said it enough: Death is not dreadful—it is not anything. Does that comfort me?

It does not.

You will excuse, I know, these drops—my blood. How bright they seem against the gathering dark! Like embers in the eye.

At first I sought influence from the dead—influence over the living, I mean. Then I sought knowledge. Then I sought death itself, my own death above all, and this before dying. Sought to lie against my own corpse, to press my hot mouth against my cold one. To die living. To live dying.

You might think I had already achieved this. If not I, who? But as I advance toward death it retreats into itself. My fingertips brush its skirts, but I come no closer.

Now I think that to really understand death, I'd have to die, and die more completely than anyone has ever died before. I couldn't hang around in out-of-date fashions, rapping on tables and decorating slates with trite advice. I would have to die with more dignity than that, but less reserve—I'd have to give everything I had to death, leaving nothing to dole out in spots of phosphorescence or a cold breath on the back of the neck. I'd have to give up even the idea of knowing death, for how can I know absence when knowing requires my presence? I'd have to throw myself away, then throw the throwing-away away; lose myself, then lose even the loss. Even riddance would have to go.

To understand death I'll have to not understand it. But not in the cozy-dreadful way that holds sway in funeral parlors. Save me from a domesticated death—beaks and tentacles under the living room sofa!

And yet probably, no, certainly, I have been vainglorious in imagining that I, I alone can turn my face away from human beings and doings to see the nothing-that-is. There is no death in general, there are only billions upon billions of deaths in particular. Death is always of somebody in particular. And there is no way to get from that particular to the general.

In other words, to try to leave my parents out of it was probably a mistake.

Oh, I was right, I'm sure, that death is not essentially their bellowing absence. That is just the hole they made in life. Death is some wholly other thing. But I begin to think I cannot touch upon that other thing without entering the bellowing hole they left. It is not a happy thought.

What if there were a world in which we were extinguished as lightly and as absolutely as soap bubbles, leaving nothing behind? In which our dead never returned to remind us that they too were once alive? What a forgiving place that would be, without memory. What grace.

Wistfully,
Headmistress Joines

66   SPEAKERS, SINGERS, AND STAMMERERS.

5.

V
V
4
V

Cease inhaling as in No. 3, wherever the stop occurs, without allowing any breath to escape for as many seconds as are indicated by the figures.

6.

< < 4 <

Cease exhaling as in No. **4** wherever the stop occurs without taking breath for as many seconds as the figures, if any, indicate.

7.

&c.
V
V
V
V
V

Draw in the breath by short gasps, without letting any escape till the lungs are quite full.

8.

< < < < < &c. Let out the breath by little and little, without drawing in a fresh supply till the lungs are empty.

9.

Draw in the breath *slowly* through the nostrils, *quite noiselessly.*

10.

Draw in a short breath *quickly*, but noiselessly, through the nostrils.

11.

Expel every particle of breath from the inflated lung instantaneously and forcibly.

12.

When letters or syllables occur in the lung exercises, they must be sung in monotone, on any easy note.

13. A figure placed above a letter or syllable indicates the number of seconds for which it is to be sustained, as, e a ah, &c.

Example.

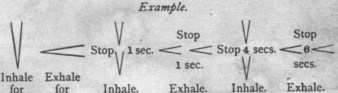

Exercise II.

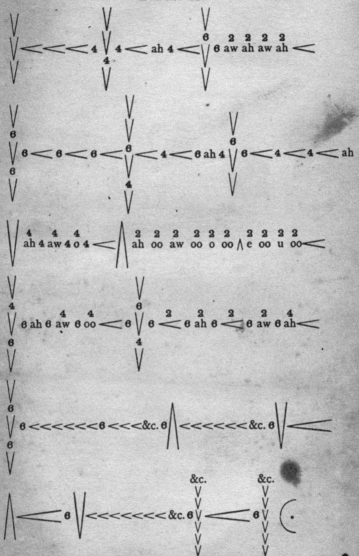

Mary: I think I have a rabbit.
Instructor: What makes you think it is a rabbit?
Mary: I can feel his ears.
Instructor: Are you sure they are not horns?
Mary: No, I think they feel like ears.

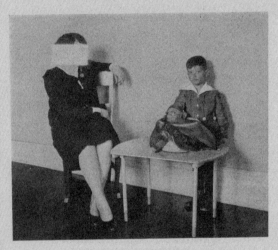

Fig. 12. The Game of Hand in the Box

child, and he establishe
"thinking before you ta

Noah's Mouth. Noah
doll's house. Moving
the same manner.

The clicker is used i
is established. The ca
when necessary.

Hand in the Box.
large box containing c
and ends, such as a key
a pocket knife, etc.
The child puts his ha
article, which he must
touch.

After discussion of t
and the conversation
rabbits live?" etc.

There is a good dea
stammering is likely
are busily engaged, h
he fails to exercise co
only on signals given

14. The Final Dispatch, contd.

Well, here we are again in my office. It looks real—I get up close to the wood paneling to check the grain and there is no blurring or repetition. An exclamation mark of bird muck streaks one windowpane, dotted by a blob on the sill. Bottle of paregoric, stuffed gray parrot, ventriloquist's dummy.

A little test, that, I was just trying to trick myself, to see what I'd swallow. No, there's no dummy here. Except Miss Exiguous. Mr. Mallow. And Mother Other: Puppets, props, automata, the lot of them. The girl, though, is surely real. She does not, perhaps, look the way I have her looking—part crow, part spider, in her black untidy hitched-up too-short dress, holey black tights, with her skinny legs and arms of which she seems to have a few too many. But inside that form is a living soul. I believe it beyond reason.

Why do I not then seize her and fetch her home? But I myself am seized, the key in my back is turning, *click click click*, da da da [singing], the scene must take its course. She opens her mouth. I know what I will hear, and yet I tremble.

"Hello again, my dear."

My father's voice is strange in such a mouth. One knows instinctively that such a voice, a man's voice, cannot have its origins in a little girl's chest cavity. No matter how good a mimic she may be. Not because it is so deep, my father's voice is actually quite high, one might say feminine. It is something else in it—a flat cold killing rage imperfectly disguised as reason. Only I, when I was a girl, might have had such a voice.

"Why use the girl?" I said.

"Think of her as a telephone."

"Perhaps she would prefer to be a person."

"Perhaps I would prefer to be a person as well," said my father, "but I no longer have that privilege."

"You forfeited it," I said, but automatically. For some time I have had the feeling that I had overlooked something, and I had just figured out what it was.

I had always believed that the dead were helpless to shape their world for us, since they do not have the time, literally, to create a temporal fiction. But now it struck me (and here, when a thought strikes you, it can bloody your nose) that if living people who were *channeling* the voices of the dead came here, those voices could probably speak (continue speaking) just as ours do, and with the same effect. In this way I might find myself in a world that my father, speaking through Finster, had made for me, and not knowing it, never discover the way out, but trudge dutifully after him down this hard dirt road forever.

Ahead of me, polished heels, firmly subduing the dust in monotonous alternation.

Sun stinging my nape.

I am seven and my father is telling me the world. How high his degree; how lower the townsfolk's; how lower still my mother's. How she degraded his seed in promoting her own. How I thrust myself upon him through her offices, springing up where unlooked for, spilling toward him out of a dark place, eft, emmet, elver, and reaching for him, despite his very natural feelings of aversion, probably drawn to the Apollonian splendor of his countenance (I can't say I remember it), as all low things are drawn to the high, moth to the flame, mother to father, Caliban, Icarus, et cetera; how, though one should not expect cuddles from Mithras, I might study to deserve the light of understanding that his presence would shed on the world of phenomena; how if I could overcome my constitutional indolence enough to apply myself to his therapies, I might even contrive to be one day a little less disgusting in his eyes.

He instructs me further and I believe him that chloride of lime combats noxious effluvia and that teak is superior to oak for ship timber, that oxalates have the property of decomposing calcareous silts and the prudent man will not partake of port after a meal of oysters, that fornication is an abomination whose punishment is childbirth, that the character of the yellow man is contemplative, that speaking the French language gives a pleasing shape to the mouth, that on repeated bathing with diluted sulfuric acid the skin will resist the action of fire, that a Monsieur Bon had excellent gloves and stockings made of spider's silk, that the efficacy of fomentation in promoting the suppuration of boils cannot be doubted . . .

He curses, cuffs a horsefly from his neck. I smile into my collar.

His shoes impressing the dust with coffin shapes. My own leaving smaller coffins behind.

How oddly comfortable I feel with you. Is this, dear listener, what you would call a friendship? I wish—

In a certain kind of story, you would turn out to be related to the kindly neighbor who watched over me after my parents died (actually she was a suspicious and penny-pinching widow), or would wind up possessed by my mother's gentle spirit and spread beneficence over my tortured soul like treacle. In another kind of story, not so different really, you would be my nemesis. But I hope I know better than to fall for such devices.

For that is another influence to watch out for: the literary. One of my pulpitasters (for I am a sort of pulpit)—one of the stamens thrilling in my perianth—one of the freshets freshening in my sails—or, in plain English, one of the ghosts I channel—is the author Jephra Meant. You will not have heard of her, though she would not believe it. Her fame, such as it was, flowered, wilted, and withered at the turn of the last century. It is pressed in a book or two: slim volumes with marbled deckles, containing essays, a few poems, some peculiar stories in which very little happens, very ornately. You can still find them in the odd antiquarian bookshop at prices not exorbitant. A testy, bombastic old bat, half mad, nurtured on the learned wit of the eighteenth century, Jephra spent the latter half of her life planning the novel to end all novels, but fell ill before she could put down more than a few thousand words. Her ghost pesters me (and others through me) to find those papers, surely by now crumbling into curry-colored dust. Lately I have been feeling her buck and bridle when I speak, hurling her weight behind this word or that one, weirding a workaday phrase with a whiff of hippogriff. (*Pulpitasters, freshets*, hers. *Hippogriff*, hers.) These writers make the most persistent ghosts! She would like, I know, to write her own too-long-deferred novel through me, and she smells the ink on my breath, hears the rattle of the typewriter in my tonsils.

But I defy her deathbeds, her skull-headed ladies, her angelic infants and inheritances. You are neither nemesis nor ministering angel. You are what you seem: a good listener.

What am I, too, but a listener. Yes, you are quite right (I can see your mouth, slightly twisted, your eyes, reservedly amused, and I know very well what you are thinking), I am a loud sort of listener. But a listener.

Right now I am listening to my mother hum. I loll at her feet in the grass. Am I a baby, then, or just groveling? I have lifted the hem of her skirt and uncovered the scandal of bare feet. The oddly waxy sheen of her little crumpled toes. A few dark hairs curling on the crown of the arch. Matching blisters on the littlest toes of each foot catch the light so that they seem to glow: pale amber cabochons. Through her straw bonnet confetti of light scatters over cheekbones, collarbone. A noise, someone coming, she turns her head so that the points of light swing across her chest. Simultaneously pulling her feet back under her gown.

When I look up, I have forgotten where I am.

It is Cheesehill, but it isn't. The sky clings moistly to the land, the land swells sweetly against the sky (only I disturb their commerce), the horizon is closed tight, but I open my mouth and it parts.

A long eye, all pupil, regards the eye that I am.

Gasp of an outbreath [static]. Cinders spinning in a still wind [static]. I nearly wet myself, my dead, I mean, my dear, before I realize—no, I realize nothing, and make the mistake of saying it, I mean nothing, saying nothing [static, audio break, popping]. Black shafts of light slam down through a thundering silence, and I am choking on a glass apple of air. I close my eyes, because the sky has hardened against my face, locked around my legs, thrust up under my arms. When I can I force apart my eyelids my own lashes frighten me, scything at the top and bottom of the world, and the lash-like leaves of the nasty trees that grow here are impudently accurate;

must *every single one* be different? Ugh, ugh! The revulsion concentrates itself in the back of my neck as a feeling of sudden disbelief directed mostly downward: I seem to be a severed head sewn onto a cardboard cutout of a body. Aghast, I command my hands to rise, rip out the clumsy stitches, but my cardboard body does not move, I am trapped, in this head, anyone would be upset, and I'm upset, and nauseated, I feel my gorge rise, and that's my salvation, my body takes on mass, the dimensions unfold obediently into space, the glass apple collapses into a pulpous mass I spit out, and I say my moth, I mean my mouth, I mean my mother, doesn't matter, I say something, and so I am something, again, provisionally speaking, provided I'm speaking.

STEADMANS'
LESSONS
BY
CARRIE H. STEADMAN
Supervisor of Formanship Cincinnati Public Schools

AMERICAN COMPANY

Bunny Says!

The Stenographer's Story, contd.

"There is an excellent private sanatorium in Pittsfield," Dr. Beede said, while young Dr. Peachie put away his stethoscope in his big leather bag. "You would be very comfortable there. Westfield has a large facility. Hadley . . ."

She was shaking her head. "Do you see how absurd it would be," she said, "and what a bad example it would set my students, if I let dying distract me from my study of death? I will do very well where I am."

"At the very least you must stay away from the children," he said.

"And young ladies," said Dr. Peachie, gallantly.

The Headmistress followed his glance to me, regarded me blankly for a moment, then turned back to the old doctor. "No one in this school is afraid of death."

"Nonetheless, to persist, when you know—I'm sure you would not want—the risk of infection—it would be tantamount to murder."

"Of course," she said, but her eyes slid to me—me!—and a smile flickered over her lips. I beamed back.

Tuberculosis took, like an old story, its predictable course. She grew gaunt. Her hair thinned. Her skin tightened over her skull; her eyes became enormous. She gathered herself for her cough like a horse for a jump. Then she gave herself to it, sometimes for hours. The brownish stains on her handkerchief could no longer be taken for anything but blood; bright red ones dappled the old.

Despite the implications of that smile (perhaps I had imagined it), she was seldom to be seen in a classroom now, and she ate alone in her office, though her portrait still stared down on the laden tables of the refectory, or didn't, or whatever. What strength she had, she poured into abstruse ruminations on the structure of the necrocosmos. The day came when the students trooped outside for morning review and found someone else standing in her customary place. I heard one member of faculty whisper that she had *lost the thread.*

I reported this to her, of course, and she took appropriate measures, which is why we now have a new instructor of Posture Arts.

Having studied her as closely as I had stood me in good stead. Nearly every day, now, I was called upon to act as go-between, submitting queries and interpreting her often gnomic replies. I did not allow others to see how much I had to extrapolate and even invent to make up for her omissions. For the Headmistress rarely spoke now, at least not in the usual sense, nor was she interested in listening, in the usual sense.

In another sense she was listening harder than ever. She had moved on from the commonplace larynx to more out-of-the-way passages, conjecturing that nostrils, pores, tear ducts too might afford passage to the dead. (Also excretory organs, but I shall not dwell on that indecent interlude.) How strange and funny it was to see her press her ear to a child's nose. As it had from time to time over the years, the infidel thought pricked me: Could all this be a joke? If she had given any indication that she knew how droll she looked—but she never did.

Formerly, poring over the world like a cryptographer, she had looked for patterns as proof that there was meaning in the mess. Now she cared only for anomalies, aberrations. Flubs and blunders, misprints and mispronunciations: She combed through good English in search of bad. Perhaps a lack of pattern was itself meaningful, perhaps the world addressed us in an infinite, unrepeating language of nonce words. If so, a slip of the tongue might be closer to this first, true language than all our iterations. So she made sure that there was always an eavesdropper with a notebook, usually MacDougal or Whit, to take down additions to the lexicon. I am ashamed to say that we made a game of cooking up new ones. Though perhaps she would not have minded that, come to think.

She had never been particular about her appearance and now she became even less so. Her great crowblack dress was stiffened and glazed with spills, all the more because the napkin she wore as a bib did not by any means catch every last spatter when she coughed. Stale bed-smell until she spat blood, then sudden red iron pong.

I am smelling her *hemoglobin*, I thought. How can she say that a person is only breath, only words? Look how she is a body.

But as if she had caught my thought from the air, she now turned from the spoken word to its material by-products. When we met her in the hall, she would sometimes ask us to stop, and would intrude a small spatula into our mouths, scraping samples from the roof of the mouth, under the tongue, and around the tonsils. "Evidence . . . particulate speech . . ." she muttered. "Nonnarrative time . . . outside the calendar!" We were required to submit our pillowcases to her laboratory once a week.

Once I came into the office to find some fifteen or twenty mouth objects laid out in rows on a stained hand towel. Her hand hovered over one, wandered to another, back to the first, caught it up. She looked up. "Time of day . . ." She placed the object in a new position, squinted at it. "Location too, perhaps? Orientation? I am disgusted with myself that I neglected to document . . ." She glared at the object, glanced up, irritably restored the object to its original position. "Why are you not at your typing station, Grandison? I desire you to record some notes."

But her investigations led her steadily farther from the mouth. It was marvelous to see her, when she was unaware of being observed, run her fingers lingeringly through the crumby talc of insect parts and excrements, dust and dander and human hairs that collected in the corners of all the windowsills in that vast, never fully clean building, then bring them up to examine, clinging to her fingertips, a section of a fly's leg, a shard of a yellowjacket's casing. She could be seen drawing up Rapunzel locks of muddy hair from the dark throats of the sinks, or rolling dust bunnies into twists of sticky twine between her palms. Once I came upon her examining a dead mouse the cat had left on the portal of her office. "Here, fold this into your handkerchief and dispose of it," she said. I bore it away. Its body was as light and hard as an apricot pit, its little claws raised in mock surprise. What had she seen in it?

Timidly reproved by Miss Exiguous for these researches: "So unbecoming . . . and perhaps not quite germane?" the Headmistress snapped back,

"The dead are not so *costive*, that they make only rare expenditures among the living, dropping their coinage stingily into the mouths of mendicants. Probably the dead, having achieved a greater kinship with the material world, no longer see such a profound difference between you, Dotty, and the skin on milk or—or a blob of warm cow dung."

"My dear, *really* . . ."

If you shed the parochial attachment to the human vessel, and even more specifically to the mouth as the privileged portal of meaning, couldn't you find speech anywhere stuff was? Material objects were merely a less lively form of language.[19] Increasingly she preferred it to our common tongue.

Perhaps this was because she was dying. "Lately," I heard her tell Miss Exiguous, "I seem to have more in common with antlers and mushrooms than with other people. More and more, I see myself as a jumble of stuff"— she stopped to spot a handkerchief with blood—"only accidentally haunted by a self. But not for long. If you cannot keep from making those absurd noises, Dotty, you may leave us."

The window shuddered, rain slapped against it, then slid silently down. She turned her head and looked out at the noiselessly thrashing boughs. From her rib cage came a seething sound, as if she were filled with bees or flames. I stared at her in mingled dread, pity, longing. But for what? Visions came to me and were discarded faster than I can type these words: Here I was on my knees with my head in her lap, her hand on my hair, cuticles catching in my curls—here curling naked on her naked chest, a baby again—or the other way around, rocking the infant Headmistress in my own arms—here pricked out of my shell like a snail and swallowed—here pitched into the pupil of her eye, as bright and insubstantial as a spark, to extinguish myself against her retina . . . It was nothing real or possible that I wanted but an indescribable perfect presencing, a recognition so absolute that no gesture was necessary or adequate to it. If this was love, I doubted it. But it was something.

---

19. And more along these lines. I have taken the liberty of omitting a rather lengthy explanation of matters covered elsewhere in this volume. —Ed.

"Why are you staring at me, girl?"

"No reason. I am ready." I wound a sheet of paper into the typewriter with such force that, not being laid in quite straight, it twisted and puckered and tore. Silently I ripped it out again and wound in another.

I raised my head and met her steady look. But she did not ask what was wrong, and in a moment she had resumed dictation.

When had I realized what would have been clear enough from the beginning, if I had let myself see it—that my advancement had only one possible conclusion: my own extinction? We burn the self like clinkers in this engine. Eventually there is only the train, no one aboard. A nobody rushing headlong into nothingness. And this is not even a problem, this is the cause to which we are sworn. Only a failed student preserves the illusion that success is possible, and this is one reason many of us fail, for sure: to save the fantasy of success from the corrosive reality of it. Others of us are drawn after it. That it is an illusion doesn't lessen its appeal. No, not at all, it is all the stronger for it. Only an illusion has such power to persuade; only an illusion is clear and lasting and discrete enough. But the illusion, bright as it is, also contains all the evidence we need to discredit it. For what would it mean to reach the top?

To best all the other students and even the teachers, recommending myself to the Headmistress to the point that she chose me as her successor. (The two meanings of *succeed* here converge. That sort of thing is never an accident.)

And to succeed her, what would that mean?

To cease to be who I have been, to become somebody else. Specifically, her.

So whose, then, would be the glory I would gain?

Once in a dream the smooth brown skin of my right forearm split to expose a deeper layer of a creased and dappled beige. I beheld it with revulsion but not surprise. But I had other dreams in which I was struggling in a dim confused place and, when I fought my way free at last, saw that the heavy folds sliding down my legs were that same beige. So: A dehiscence, yes, but whose?

Sometimes, after I had carried off some deceit, I felt a surge of criminal confidence. Why forfeit everything to be her, when I could fake it? Already I had mastered her little turns of phrase, the offended air with which she polished her lorgnette. I could imitate the carriage of her head, erect, except when she was thinking hard, and then thrust forward and her shoulders raised. Her gulping cough. The stridor of her breath, when she was trying not to cough. How her hand shook when she lifted a glass of paregoric or a pen, and how, when she came upon Finster without warning, she went, for a moment, as still as a rabbit. I knew which of her books held the underlined phrase *ungraspable phantom of life*; I knew which cabinet concealed the mutilated remains of a Galvano-Faradio Magneto-Electric Shock Therapy Machine, and which a charred and blistered enamel vase; I could produce, in fact, every item on the list of proofs by which her successor would be known. I could replicate her signature. More easily than she could, now that she trembled so. Oh yes, I could be her. Better than she could be herself.

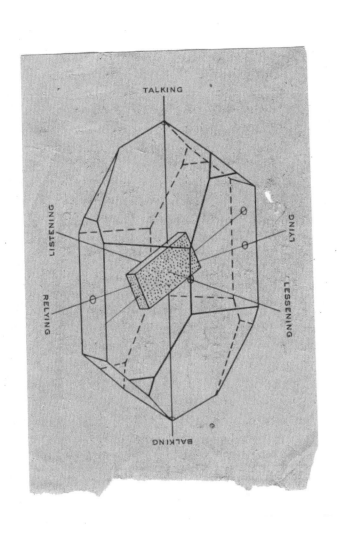

Readings

from *Principles of Necrophysics*: "The Structure of the Necrocosmos"

Life; Death

Where do we go when we die? Our Founder, Headmistress Joines, was the first to map the necrocosmos using modern methods. I will attempt a crude overview.

What we call life is just one plane of a multi-ply universe, or necro-cosmos, through which we circulate by dying. The necrocosmos is made of language; we precipitate a world with every word we speak. The dead inhabit it, and speak and die in turn; the world they speak is ours.

Let me explain.

In life, we dwell among solid and less solid objects, ourselves objects, but with a difference: We can talk. The function of speech is to generate what we call time; "we pull ourselves along the timeline by our teeth," the Founder has said. For us, speech *is* time, and vice versa, a conjoint phenomenon we call speech-time.

Though we say we die, it is really our voices that die, dropping out of time. Our bodies remain.

Where do our voices go? To the next plane of the necrocosmos, familiarly known as death.

In the land of the dead, time does not pass. It is a static medium in which consecutive events exist simultaneously. Where we speak of a time line, the dead speak of a time *space*. And whereas we live in speech-time, the dead live in speech-space. That is what you get when you move speech along an axis perpendicular, as it were, to time. Try this exercise: Choose a single word; for example, *crow*. Move it along an axis perpendicular to time. Even without knowing quite what that means, it is obvious that the word must *expand* in some way, becoming a crowish space, a crow-space. To enter crow-space is clearly not the same thing as to see a crow, but one can imagine things getting crowy, crowsome, croaking, feathery, shiningly dark.

Though such attempts to visualize the land of the dead will necessarily fall short of the reality, it may help to picture how you yourself would appear if you could take every position you have ever occupied in your life, not one after another, but *all at once*. You might look something like a long, bulbous, fleshy cord, partly wrapped in a variegated fabric, intricately woven through and around the world, with one end tapering to a point in a motel bed, backseat, or test tube, occasional long straight stretches indicating periods of travel, and incredible tangles in every stopping place.

Now, attempt to picture what form, if we could see it, the *voice* of that umbilical entity would take. Your voice follows roughly the same path as your body, so it is also a cord, albeit an invisible one, but since a person does sometimes fall silent, it is broken into shorter lengths—roughly spherical beads, if you stand still, macaroni if you move. Furthermore, it has a much greater diameter than your body; it can round corners and pass a little way through walls. Lastly, it fades smoothly out rather than ceasing abruptly, so its contours are diaphanous; it is a sort of serpentine fog.

This, though merely an analogy, may help you understand more clearly the function of the ghost speaker. For to make these voices audible, it is not enough to open a passage to their plane of existence. One must convert them from a synchronic to a diachronic form—roughly speaking, from space to time. The mouth of the living intersects the course of the atemporal voice, and passing along it, "plays back" in sequence the words of the dead. A helpful comparison might be the translation of the spatialized speech of the book into the linear, sequential experience of the reader. The ghost speaker, you might say, reads the dead aloud to the living. Only then, like characters in a novel, do the dead take on, for a while, the appearance of life. Between our visits, they wait—miniature cards clutched in their frozen paws, calabash pipe halfway to their wizened lips!

Doesn't that mean that the dead can say nothing they have not already said? No, the fact that time does not pass in the land of the dead does not prevent what we would call "new" things from arriving in it. After all, new dead are every day enrolled there. It merely means that the new things, when they appear, will turn out to have been there all along. They can also depart, leaving behind an absence at once recent and primordial.

The Cyclical Model

If it is true that the dead too die, dropping out of speech-space as we drop out of speech-time, into what do they drop? And if the dead die, why not the *dead* dead, too, and the dead dead dead and so on? A number of necro-cosmological models have been advanced to account for these possibilities. Headmistress Joines herself proposed a ring of worlds around which we move, departing one station for the next each time we die, until eventually we die right back to life, as shown in her splendid and still useful map.[20]

In this model the dead die into a world of solid objects, something like our own—a step back or down in complexity from our first, multidimensional death. Each subsequent death conforms to this pattern, removing a dimension until there are none left to remove. I.e., the three-dimensional "dead dead" die into two dimensions, a world of grammar we can best envision in the form of the sentence diagram; the two-dimensional diagram dies into the one-dimensional line; the one-dimensional line dies into the zero-dimensional point, which has no substance in itself, only punctuates, as it were, the movement of the line. The death of the point is thus indistinguishable from the birth of the point—and so we rise through the dimensions again. The point dies "up" into the line, the line dies into the diagram, and the diagram (which we glimpse from time to time, angling into our world, as one of our splendid but somewhat didactic angels[21]) dies into us. We are grammar that has died and been buried, as it were, in matter. Our bodies are, in the Founder's words,

---

20. See overleaf. —Ed.

21. Angels are diagrams! We have long suspected as much, from their alleged beauty and goodness, which seem both magnificent and oversimple, correct but impossible. It is depicted clearly in older paintings, whose flatness we must learn to take literally. See the ornate origami of their gilt gowns. Coins of their halos. The words on the streamers never lost their hospital corners, and always turned to face us. Over the landscape's receding perspective, their brave flatness, like harbingers of a more abstract world; no perspective can diminish them, they are dukes of the flat surface.

ELEMENTS OF A MAP OF

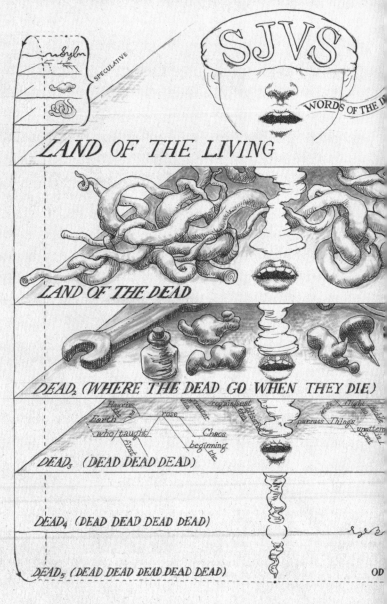

LAND OF THE LIVING

LAND OF THE DEAD

DEAD₂ (WHERE THE DEAD GO WHEN THEY DIE)

DEAD₃ (DEAD DEAD DEAD)

DEAD₄ (DEAD DEAD DEAD DEAD)

DEAD₅ (DEAD DEAD DEAD DEAD DEAD)

OD

THE NECROCOSMOS (*speculative*)

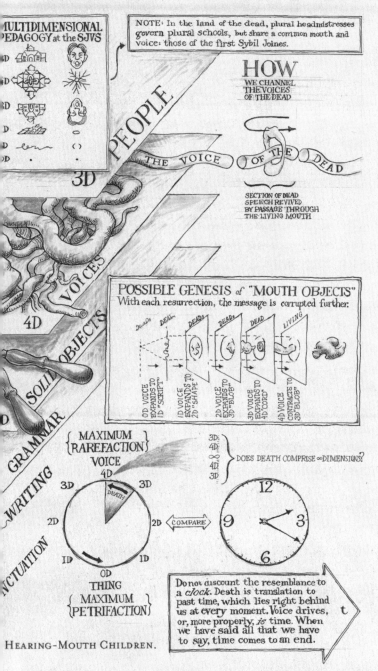

MULTIDIMENSIONAL PEDAGOGY at the SJVS

NOTE: In the land of the dead, plural headmistresses govern plural schools, but share a common mouth and voice: those of the first Sybil Joines.

HOW WE CHANNEL THE VOICES OF THE DEAD

THE VOICE OF THE DEAD

SECTION OF DEAD SPEECH REVIVED BY PASSAGE THROUGH THE LIVING MOUTH

PEOPLE

VOICES

3D

4D

SOLID OBJECTS

GRAMMAR

WRITING

PUNCTUATION

POSSIBLE GENESIS of "MOUTH OBJECTS"
With each resurrection, the message is corrupted further:

0D VOICE EXPANDS TO 1D "SCRIPT"

1D VOICE EXPANDS TO 2D "SHAPE"

2D VOICE EXPANDS TO 3D "BLOB"

3D VOICE EXPANDS TO 4D "CORD"

4D VOICE CONTRACTS TO 3D "BLOB"

MAXIMUM RAREFACTION
VOICE
4D

3D
4D
∞
4D
3D
} DOES DEATH COMPRISE ∞ DIMENSIONS?

3D   3D
DEATH
2D   2D ⟨COMPARE⟩
1D   1D
0D
THING
MAXIMUM PETRIFACTION

Do not discount the resemblance to a *clock*. Death is translation to past time, which lies right behind us at every moment. Voice drives, or, more properly, *is* time. When we have said all that we have to say, time comes to an end. t

HEARING-MOUTH CHILDREN.

"brown-pink, stinking, animal coffins." In another sense, of course, they are wombs in which our voices are born, eventually to die into what we must now recognize as their highest, most complex state: death.

Reversible Linear Model

There are problems with the cyclical model. It is uneconomical to posit *two* two-dimensional planes, two one-dimensional planes, and so on. Perhaps the world of the dead dead, so much like our own, really *is* our own, though entered, as it were, from the other side. In one revised version, the dimensions are not linked in a ring, but form a simple chain. We die and move one link to the left (*right* and *left* are, of course, just metaphors); when we reach the end of the chain, we start back the other way, and so on, back and forth, forever.

A variant of this model ventures to account for the existence on our plane of both animate and inanimate objects. Life is defined as *rightward* motion through our plane. On their leftward journey, the dead manifest as inanimate objects.

In the inventive "two-ply" theory, these objects would include *our own bodies*. Every person has two parts, body and voice (the more common term, *soul*, is a misnomer). The voice arrives on our plane of existence by moving rightward, the body by moving leftward. We are the temporary conjunction of two parts moving in opposite directions along the chain,[22] the marriage of 1. the ghost of grammar, also known as a voice; and 2. the ghost of a ghost, also known as a body. Thus we die into life from two directions.

Many thinkers would add at the rightmost end of the chain another plane not described by the Founder: silence. The other dimensions are as in the ring model, only traffic is two-way; thus our dimension may not be the only one to boast of two-ply inhabitants.

Some thanatomaths make sense of this idea by explaining the half moving leftward as idea, meaning, or diegesis and the half moving rightward as its

---

22. One could describe right-hand movement as attenuation, rarefaction, and abstraction, and left-hand movement as reification and intrication.

material matrix. Linguists will recognize the familiar pairing of signifier and signified. In silence, as the turnaround zone, signifier and signified are one. Intuitively, we feel this to be true; while silence may possibly under certain artificial conditions be said to "represent" silence, it also, undeniably, *is* silence.

You will note, however, that silence introduces an enigma into an otherwise rational order. We can certainly imagine that, after a long series of transformations, we might at last, with a sigh of resignation or relief, cease altogether to be. What is a little harder to understand is how, having already become nothing, we can die yet again. In nothing there is nothing to die, at least that is how it seems to us. So dying becomes an wondrous act of creation *ex nihilo*.

But I will remind you that some scientists claim something similar for the entire universe. Theorists of the Big Bang unpack whole galaxies from a single point; we could call that point a period. Or a comma, its curved tail a saucy hint of more to come.

Infinite Linear Model

Some would argue, however, that there is no reason to stop and turn around at death, except our sentimental attachment to what we call life, combined with our positive inability to imagine what death-sub-2 might be like, let alone death-sub-3, death-sub-4, and so on. It is entirely possible that while it is true that we will keep on dying forever without ever quite ceasing to exist (as the adherents of the other models aver), we will never return to *this* world.

If there are in fact an infinite series of deaths, this would put paid to the contrivances of the two-ply theory, unless there are two sets of inhabitants of the necrocosmos, one dying rightward forever, the other dying leftward. The latter, upon reaching silence, either turn around to go back the other way; pour into silence to be extinguished forever; or—the most attractive solution, for its symmetry—continue on past silence into echelons of ever more ineffable negations. But on this topic nothing definite can be affirmed.

Letters to Dead Authors, #14

Jane E.,

I have had a disappointment. The centerpiece of our Theatrical Spectacle was to be the release of the Sky Lung. It would have been a stirring sight, swimming up into the heavens like a whale—an unbeautiful one if truth be told, made of patched sheets dipped in melted galoshes and thus a dull, uneven, grayish black with hints of green, but still marvelous, especially if one reflected that it was full of the mingled voices of hundreds of dead souls! But it has become apparent that it will take weeks if not months of effort to fill it. So we have had to postpone that treat, and stuff the thing half filled into the old carriage house, where it surges and wallows like some inconceivable sea creature rippling through the submarine abysm. The children sneak in to wade across its buoyant swells, which fling them from side to side as if alive. They will put holes in it; I must install a lock—first I must install doors—that is rehang the doors, their hinges having rusted through—but I am so tired—no, not exactly that, but—

There is not much of me left, and what there is hurts. It feels as though I am trying to sand myself down from the inside. There are easier ways to remove oneself, as I ought to know.

At least I am dying beautifully, and in red. I pay myself out of myself in ropes that startle my linens.

To add to my grievances it will not stop raining.

Plink, plink, PLUNK. That is not rain. The information that someone is practicing the piano, no doubt in preparation for our Theatrical Spectacle, has tunneled up through the pipes, unerringly steering right or left at tee after wye in its zeal to arrive at my inhospitable ear.

It is perhaps strange that for all my devotion to the voice, I have a tin ear. I am not referring to my hearing trumpet.

I do not believe that reveals anything in particular about my character.

They say that I am cold, who take a woman's temperature by her men. It is true that I have refused love, after a few ghastly stabs at it, and hoped thereby to lower my temperature to the absolute zero of death. But there are other passions.

I have no reason to doubt that I sucked a teat as ardently as anyone, for instance. When I was young enough still to be excused certain peculiarities in my manner of speaking, my parents were kinder, to each other and to me, and life seemed sweet. We were wealthy enough that I wanted for nothing that my father deemed suitable, but it was in communion with the natural world that I found real bliss. The whole world seemed to breathe then, groaning and hissing under my feet and in the trees over my head. Green life squiggled through veins in the earth, then fountained forth as weeds and trees. Bits of the world broke loose as bugs, squirrels, foxes ran to other places, then were reabsorbed; other bits lay quite still, but with a gleeful and provocative air, as if they had something to say and were daring me to guess what it was.

I took that dare.

They say that I am cold, but a charred stick can have a ruby core. And Eyjafjallajökull smolders in its dress of ice.

Eyjafjallajökull. Now that is what I call a word. I have dreams that in the vocabulary I spit up daily now will be the one word to end them all. A Blitz of meaning to give speculation its quietus. But wouldn't such a word stick in my throat, not telling me what it is to die—but *showing* me?

Death is a word on the tip of my tongue. Mine the ear for whom alone it is meant. I will rest my hopes in the chance that causes do not infallibly precede effects, and die listening.

Yours affectionately,
Sybil

15. The Final Dispatch, contd.

Do you hear it too? That low, cool, reasonable voice going on and on in the underwater light of the curtained room that smells of mouth, of alcohol fumes and sleep, saying, "You might almost think you were imagining the low, cool, reasonable voice going on and on, it isn't the sort of voice that a child would have, that any ordinary sort of child would have. Of course yours isn't an ordinary child, or a child in ordinary circumstances: your child has lost her mother, lost, that's a good one, as if she had just put her down somewhere and never picked her up again, as if a child could ever forget where she had left her mother, where her mother had left her, lost, that's a good one, I wonder where I got that idea, her mother was taken from her, someone took her, it was somebody's fault she's gone, I wonder whose."

[Pause.]

Barely a pause, and then the voice continues, "The voice continues, after barely a pause, continuous and meandering as thought, perhaps it is thought, not a voice, perhaps it is just someone's idea of a voice, the idea of a voice that never stops talking, talking about what, talking about what you did, and also about the voice itself, which voice, the one that never stops saying that you are responsible, that you have a debt to pay, that you have to pay it, the debt you incurred, there's only one way, and it has to be done, so there's no point in talking, only in doing, doing it, the voice will stop if you do it, if you don't do it the voice won't stop, the voice will keep right on saying that you should do it, that you know you should do it, that you will do it, that you are doing it, only you aren't, you know that, but you know that you should, so you will, won't you, the voice says that you will, so you will, won't you, because the voice is only putting your own thoughts into words, the voice may not really be a voice at all, only your own thoughts, imagined as a voice, the voice of a child, but no ordinary child, no child in ordinary circumstances would talk like that, on and on, low, cool, reasonable, bloodless, but yours isn't an ordinary child, of course, or a child in ordinary circumstances, your child has lost her mother, lost, that's a good one . . ."

A hitch, silvery sound of a flask unscrewing, slosh, glottus, out-breath . . . [hitch, silvery sound, etc.]. "It can't be the child, you know it's not the child, the child's an idjit, can't talk straight, child's defective, tongue-tied, a circus freak, it's not the child, not that child, not any child, no child would talk like that, low, cool, reasonable, bloodless, unrelenting, saying that there's no payment for what you did, no payment but one, and even that one will not cover your debt in full, saying that the ghosts are keeping your accounts, adding it up, the pluses and the minuses, precious few pluses, a peck of minuses, all down in the book, what book, does the child have the book, what book, there's no book, it's a figure of speech, there's no book, just an idea of a book, a book of accounts, your accounts, kept by ghosts, the ghosts who spoke to the child, who are speaking to you, in a child's voice, but it isn't a child's voice, not that child's voice, that child's an idjit, not any child's voice, any ordinary sort of child, any child in ordinary circumstances, but your child isn't an ordinary child, she's an idjit, circus freak, defective, haunted, spooky, nor are her circumstances ordinary, your child has lost her mother, lost, that's a good one . . ." Pause, creak of floorboards. [Pause, creak of floorboards.]

The child is crouching beside the bed, feet numb from the cold floor, knees stiff, haunches aching, unable to stop now. Her voice is low, cool, reasonable. She never stutters, not once. It is not like speaking at all, what she is doing, opening her mouth, letting persuasion through it. Persuasion is not speaking, she understands, it is letting another person's thoughts flow through you, your father does not recognize them, he senses that they aren't yours, but he doesn't yet recognize them as his own, but he will, you are helping him, he is almost there now. Stare at the plaster flowers on the ceiling, stare at the stain on the coverlet, his breath is steady now, drop your voice, let him sleep, for now, let him go to sleep hearing the voice (your voice, his voice) saying [echo], "Maybe it's the mother, not the child, maybe that's who it is, who it's got to be, not the child, talking, on and on, like this, low, cool, reasonable, bloodless, unrelenting, adjudicating, offering arguments for and arguments against, mostly for, for what, for putting an end to it, to what, to the voice, how, you know how, why, you know why, it was your idea, not hers, not whose, not the mother's, not the child's, but yours, you're the one who thought of it, you're the one who'll carry it out . . ."

A hard hand grabs her wrist and yanks her up. She sprawls half on the bed, convulsing away from his body, feet exploding into sensation, bee stings, stars; "Talking!" is all he says, choked voice, smell of alcohol and of mouth, "Talking! You're a little talker!"

"What? No!" She recovers her composure, adds, cunningly, "I thought I heard something."

"Heard what?"

"I don't know." The hand tightens. "A voice!" Another hand takes hold of the bow at her collar and begins idly twirling it. Scrape, scrape on the underside of her chin. "I heard someone talking. I thought—I *thought* it was, was, was, was—"

"Was *who?*"

"*Y-y-y-you!*"

The hand releases her. She sprawls back onto the bedcovers and now she arranges herself there, now luxuriates, now she stretches like a cat, an odalisque. "I thought I heard you talking, on and on, and I came in to find out what you wanted."

"Nothing. I didn't want anything." Adds, "I didn't say anything."

She taps his flask, which chimes. "More hooch?"

"Hooch. That's no way for a child to talk. No ordinary child. No child in ordinary circumstances . . . Go! Get out of here! Get!"

Then, later, as the man slumps on the couch, staring at the joint of the wall and the ceiling, hand plucking idly at his crotch: the child sitting gently down beside him, the voice saying, "If your wife were here, you would be covering her now, but your wife isn't here, wonder why that is, you know why," and pausing, picking at a horsehair poking through the velvet, drawing it through, "Nothing's left of you of any value, if there was ever anything to you of any value, you're done, through, better leave this mess to others to clean up, you'll just make it worse," then humming a little, a tune the wife used to sing, when she forgot herself, not often, but too often, it was all her fault, but then the voice as if hearing his thoughts, no, as if overheard from his thoughts, from a deeper layer of his thoughts, saying, "No, it was your fault, all along, your failure, your sin, your damnation . . ."

A man of no great conscience may have that conscience so fretted and pricked and teased and inflamed by constant consultation that it swells like a cirrhotic liver. A man of no great will can be goaded into decisive action—it had happened once, it could happen again. In the hours when he came home from drinking at night, when he woke up drunk and drank more in the morning, in the afternoon when drunk he waited for the dark to come to cover his walk to the bar, the voice emanating from the narrow space beside his bed trained his thoughts, led him like a Lipizzaner through his paces until he could take his cue in a word, an inflection, and canter through his lines to the end.

Then, unfortunately, he would uncap his flask. Take another drink. The voice would have to start over, from the beginning. The voice was patient, though. He would do it eventually, the star turn, the "airs above the ground." The voice was sure, and so the child was sure.

The child had come to feel that someone spoke through her. Her mother's ghost? But her mother, she was fairly sure, would not have counseled hatred. That was her mother's great weakness, for which the child despised and even, in a way, hated her. Her mother had let herself be killed because she would not see that her husband did not deserve her love or patience. The child was made of sterner stuff. She had her father's gift for hate. And she had the voice, whoever's it was.

It would start again, low, confiding. "Look what a mess you've made of things. Look what a mess you've made of yourself. Look how you've disappointed yourself. How you've disappointed God, if there is a God. Your wife. Your child. Your mother. Everyone who knows you. And if anyone else knew you, they'd be disappointed in you too. Better not to meet people.

Better not to know people. Better not to show your face. Better not to uglify the scenery that way. How can you fix what you've broken? How can you replace what you stole? How can you pay what you owe? You can't. You've got nothing of value to give. If you live longer, you'll just owe more. All you can do now is cut your losses, ease the burden on better folk, improve the world by ridding it of yourself."

The first time in my life that I spoke with perfect clarity, fluently, nimbly, volubly, and it was to kill a man.

I had miscalculated, however. Had not imagined that my father, cowed as he was, obedient as he was in the end to the voice that seemed to address him from his own alcohol-clouded mind, would try to take me with him. Maybe he sensed just enough of the truth to blame me, if not enough to know what to blame me *for*. Or he regarded me as a part of himself, ineligible for independent life. Or it was simple malice.

He dragged me to the shed, as so often before. The hutches were all empty, tufts of fur tugged at my sentiments, I ignored them. Pellets rolling underfoot. Scatter of husked millet on the ground—mice had been at the rabbit feed. Sunlight edged through chinks in the walls, showed up feathers dancing in midair, chaff, dust. My crouch was practiced. I swayed away from a halfhearted kick. The key grinding in the padlock did not worry me excessively. I had been locked in before.

Then the flames came flowering up the boards.

When I flew like a phoenix out of the fire, my feathers black and brazen, I saw a greater glow reflected on the clouds. The factory was on fire, pianos shrieking, their wires snapping and singing.

Or, if it was a typewriter factory (I am at least reasonably sure it was one of the two, a choice between kinds of music), thousands of keys chattering in symphony to the touch of typists of blown flame, hunched and rearing, rising to pace the room, hunching again to snap out a contentious phrase.

Typewriter ribbon burns black and violet, with crawling veins of yellow.

And in the middle of the flames the twisted thing that had been my father.

I did not see it but I saw it, because I had seen it and made him see it with my words.

I stood on the lawn, barefoot, swaying, my hands held stiffly out beside me, trembling and staring, not at the jumping flames of the burning shed, but at those smoldering clouds. Clouds? Smoke, it must have been. My bare feet were stiff and cold, which seemed unbelievable to me, with the heat of the fire still beating on my burned face, and my hair smoking and curling, and my scorched hands singing with pain. Someone found me there, and though I was not liked and was indeed barely tolerated by the neighbors, who found me unsettling, my strangeness was temporarily forgotten in the brilliance and warmth of the interesting tragedy I had survived, and someone wrapped a blanket around my shoulders and sat me down with a mug of hot toddy and told me what I already knew.

At first some were inclined to look at me askance, for this was the second time I had lost a parent and that was at best uncanny and at worst suspicious, but a little later someone came in and the word went around that the fire, the little fire, that is, had been put out, the shed leveled, but that the padlock still held door to frame, that it seemed I had been locked in, apparently by my own father, and that stopped the whispers and the looks, for it struck all and sundry as so terrible that nobody knew what to say and one after another found an excuse to slip away until none was left but the neighbor whose blanket still draped my shoulders, who said blankly but not really unkindly that I had much better spend the night at her house than go home alone after what had happened, and they would figure out in the morning what to do with me.

In the morning my stutter was a hedge, a thicket, a wall of thorns. The chief of police came and spoke gently to me, but I struggled and spat and finally began plucking fretfully at my lips and smacking my own cheek and seizing my jaw in both bandaged hands to move it by main force, until at a glance from the chief my neighbor took my hands and bore them down and held them until I was calm again; but answers I could not give. "I wouldn't be surprised if she's simple," said the chief of police, just as if I were not there, "as well as dumb. Maybe Harwood thought he was doing her a kindness. To go through life with that defect, and alone! I don't envy her. No, I don't envy her one bit."

"What am I to do, officer?" said the neighbor in a confidential tone. "I want to do my Christian duty by the child, but I can't keep her forever and quite honestly the creature gives me the heebie-jeebies. I don't suppose that *you*—"

"A girl child," said the police chief, quickly. "A bachelor's home."

"Oh! Yes? Oh yes, no, I see that that wouldn't do. But then who—"

"No doubt there's family," said the chief, comfortably.

"Yes, of course."

But there wasn't. When the chief turned back to me, I waved him impatiently away, miming writing; when instruments were brought, I quickly and decisively wrote, "No living relatives—all dead." And then, after a considering pause, "I am my father's sole heir." And so I turned out to be.

There was a closed-casket funeral, a perfunctory and ill-attended one, and then the coffin was sped into the ground. I, dressed in black, watched the dirt fall on its lid, my face still. The others watched me. It was not known, I gathered, whether I was aware that my father had tried to kill me. It was now generally said, though no one could explain how such a private matter came to be known, that he had developed a horror of me, because of my handicap, and thought that ghosts spoke through me, and that he meant to burn me to shut them up, but that even after the flames rose up around me, he heard me talking, in a low, cool, reasonable, bloodless, unrelenting, adjudicating voice, so that, understanding he would never be rid of me, he had done for himself as well, the poor bastard. It was also said that he had killed his wife and that I had known it and taken my revenge on him. How a child could do such a thing nobody knew, but everyone agreed that if any child could, it would be *that* one—myself— who scarcely seemed like a child at all.

The Stenographer's Story, contd.

The alarm, though we did not recognize it for what it was, was given by the spiders, via one Mildred Sparks. "Oh dear Lord. Oh dear Lord save us. They're everywhere! That's it, I'm climbing on the table—oh dear Lord, there's one on the table."

Every old building in the country will have its spiders. But these were not the sober brownish specimens we were used to but the big, wiry, green and gold spiders of the meadows and brakes. What they were doing in the house I found out the next morning when, as the others were doing, I climbed up on my bedrail to peer out the high windows, against which the rain chattered like teeth, and saw the churning cocoa-colored swirl that had taken a bite out of the playfield, and the groundskeeper heaping sandbags in the chapel door.

We dressed all anyhow and clattered downstairs where we ran excitedly from one window to the next, pressing our faces to the panes across which drops continuously raced, now to the left, now to the right, now, as if in defiance of gravity, straight up. The rain ripped and tore at the undulating trees; made the gravel jump in the paths; filled the inverted sculptures in the garden, bringing inexorably to light some penny candy wrappers and a corn-cob pipe someone had surely thought gone forever. The teachers attempted to herd us into our classrooms, then gave up and joined us in our vigil.

All that morning we watched the waters rise. Our filmmaker ghosted up out of whatever basement he had been skulking in and joined the rattle of his hand-cranked camera to the hiss of the rain. I went repeatedly to the front door to gaze out over the shallow but fast-moving expanse of brown on which the familiar border shrubs marked out a phantom driveway. Every time the flood was a little closer to the school—if it was still a school, for everything was strange. Teachers were walking barefoot through the halls, displaying bunions and hairy toes; Clarence was talking to one of the cook's helpers; big girls were romping with little ones they normally shunned; and the Headmistress, who could have imposed some order on this scene, was closed in her office and did not respond to my quiet knock.

Lunch was served as usual despite flooding in the kitchen, and that settled everyone's nerves. The school returned to something like its normal routine, with periodic interruptions to check the progress of the flood. During Restorative Time some of the girls declared the reading room out of bounds to spiders and went vigorously to work with brooms. I was too restless to join them, and wandered through the building, looking out at the flood from different angles. From the library I could see the statuary in the garden, poking incongruously out of still water. The rain had stopped, but the flood continued to rise; from the windows of the music room I could see the stream chewing away at the steep cutbank, further undermining the trees that overlooked it. One had already fallen and lay with half its roots exposed and its leafy top half submerged in the flood.

Someone was down there next to it at the edge of the water. He turned and I saw that it was Dr. Peachie. His shirt was off. I observed with a little jolt three patches of coarse black hair, one on his white stomach, the other two punctuated by the dots of his nipples. Nipples, I thought. Hearing the word in my mind shocked me. I unlatched the window. "What are you doing?" I called. Of course he could not hear me for the rush of the waters. I kicked off my shoes, hitched up my pinafore, scrambled over the sill, and, with a feeling of delicious lawlessness, jumped down onto the cold, squelchy grass. On the way down to the stream I passed a tiny mole that had pulled itself out of its flooded tunnel but drowned all the same, there in the grass.

Dr. Peachie had set his bag down on the bank atop his bunched-up shirt and now, walking his hands along one branch of the fallen tree, was edging into the churning waters. Once, the river swept his feet out from under him and he hung from the branch, pulled almost horizontal. I do not know how he got his feet under him again. I hoped he would turn back then, but after a moment he cautiously went on feeling his way toward a tangled clump of soaked branches that the river was busy trying to take apart. On it a drenched creature clung and shuddered.

"What *is* that?" I said, then repeated it, yelling over the water's roar. I had come down to the edge of the cutbank.

"The cat!" he called back. "It is providential, actually, your coming just now. Do you think you might bring me my shirt—perhaps move my bag a little farther from the drink first." I did so and returned. "Now if you could tie my shirt around your waist or something, that's the way, and then come down here and—not wade, the current is too fierce, but if you are not afraid, scramble out just a little way on this tree, using the trunk as a walkway— see, there are plenty of branches to hold on to, and you are so slight, there is no risk they will break under you—and then you could pass me my shirt, because it has only just occurred to me that the blighted creature will try to climb onto my head if I do not wrap him in something and then he and I will very likely both drown!"

I tucked my pinafore into my underdrawers and climbed dubiously down the spongy bank—which, having been severely undercut on a previous occasion, was in the process of collapsing further—to the base of the tree, whose roots, I saw, were still partly anchored in the ground, making it a more stable perch than it had appeared. Once I had clambered around the tangle of muddy roots it was easy enough to creep out on the trunk, though the force of the water ripping by below me made my breath come fast. The cat watched us, his ears flattened, his eyes wild.

"Listen, I am going to pick him up the way a mama cat would, by the back of the neck. He will probably fight like a demon, but if you can throw the shirt over him—I mean, not throw perhaps, but drape—we can bunch it up and—but make sure you do not overbalance!"

One arm clamped around his branch, he stretched out the other. "Ow! You devil! I am trying to save your miserable skin, you idiot! That's better. There. Now you look like a mummified cat from an Egyptian tomb, very aristocratic. Catic. Stop laughing, young lady. Do you think you could take him while I endeavor to join you in the tree? Then the whole family can make our way back to the bank and congratulate ourselves on our little adventure."

But there was no bank to go back to. In the short time we had been struggling with the cat the flood had carelessly flung out an arm and encircled the base of the tree. In doing so, it had further undermined the cutbank, a great chunk of which had collapsed into a muddy pile that was already being swiftly swept downstream.

I gauged the distance. I did not think I could jump it. "This is stupid," I said severely.

"Yes, isn't it?" he said blankly. "I most earnestly beg your pardon. I seem to have gotten us into a fix."

After pulling himself onto the trunk, over which the water was starting to lap, and creeping along it to the rampart of the roots, he made several attempts to ford the channel, but it was deepening itself by the minute. After a fence post came racing sleekly down it like a log down a lumber chute and clobbered him on the elbow, he climbed back up into the branches. "That does it," he said, grimacing. "I concede defeat. I expect someone will notice us soon and extend a ladder or something. Until then we perch in this tree like partridges."

I considered the widening gap. I did not think a ladder would bridge it.

"I think we can be quite comfortable here," he was saying, ripping off some smaller branches and weaving then together into a messy sort of mat to pad the crook of one of the higher branches. "Up you go. Yes, well"—this to the cat, which had emitted an outraged yowl—"you will just have to suffer. Now if you don't mind, we will fasten this fellow around you thus," he said, his arms encircling me, "but you may easily untie him." He demonstrated. "Please don't hesitate to release the blighter to his fate if, heaven forbid, you find yourself obliged to swim. There are limits. *Limits*," he said to the cat, in a stern voice.

He seated himself astride the branch. "Now let us converse like civilized beings. You may call me Nick. What is your name?"

I told him.

"Now I remember. You are the Headmistress's . . . particular . . ."

"*Teacher's pet* is the term you are avoiding. But I'm not."

"I shouldn't think she has pets," he said agreeably. "Autocratic old bag, isn't she?"

"Oh, I don't know." I was shocked.

"I bet you know almost everything there is to know about this school. But I bet you don't know— That is to say, does she ever let you out?"

"Out?"

"Out. To visit family, say."

"I don't have any family. Not to speak of."

"To town, then. Anywhere."

"Of course. If we want to go. I mean, we're not *prisoners*," I said, nettled.

"Do you want to go?"

Under our feet the waters raced away, away. "Yes. I don't know. Yes." Was he courting me? The thought rang through me. There commenced a fine (and, I hoped, invisible) trembling in my arms and legs. I knew I was not beautiful though I had a neat figure. I hoped he did not think that because I was colored, I was easy.

"You must allow me to take you to, let me see . . . Plunkett."

The contrast between his majestic manner and the plebeian destination made me laugh despite my confusion of mind. "Why? What's in Plunkett?"

He widened his eyes. "The most wonderful root beer floats. Also a moving-picture house."

"I have never seen a moving picture," I confessed shyly, and my face grew hot.

"Well, we will see about correcting that oversight, just as soon as we get off this tree."

The branch that was our principle support was curtsying and shuddering as the floodwaters, having completely submersed its leafy extremity, added their force to the downward pull of our combined weight. "Do you know," he added, "I think I will clamber over to that branch there, so that when your tremendous poundage drags you down, down, down into the drink, you don't take me with you to your watery doom."

We settled into a comfortable silence. I had never had such a normal

conversation in my life. I might have drowsed a little, the cat (now somno-
lent) a damp but warm weight on my lap. I had time to think all sorts of
things—absurd things, considering our situation. For instance that there
might, after all, be something for me besides the school. Another last chance.

I would have liked to linger on that pleasant thought. But my mind
raced on. I thought of my mother and how the neighbors had treated her
for bearing a black man's children. It made scarcely any difference that my
parents were married, for to cohabit with a black man was tantamount to
whoredom whether church and state had sanctified the union or not. Some
white men, I knew, had even threatened to kill my father for bringing ruin
upon "one of our women." Perhaps it was why he went away, or perhaps they
did kill him and my mother kept it from us. Or perhaps he was footloose
and faithless just as my aunt had always said, adding, "like all his race." For
a white man it was different, a Dr. Peachie might do as he pleased, up to a
point, but I did not have that luxury and now I began to resent the free-and-
easy manners that moments ago had seemed so appealing.

"I'm damned cold," Nick said abruptly. He sounded irritated. "I wish
I had let the monster drown. I wish I had never come to this pestilential
place! If I thought . . . I say, Jane, you spend a lot of time with the old bat.
How long do you give her?"

"You're the doctor," I said stiffly. Now that he mentioned it, I was cold
too, through and through.

After an arrested moment he laughed. "I am! I certainly am! Well, sooner
or later, this way or t'other, there's a change a-comin'. But don't you worry.
You stick with Nick Peachie, girly, and he'll see you right." He took one
hand from the log for the frivolous purpose, as I noted with disapproval,
of laying a finger alongside his nose, like his namesake St. Nicholas, whom
he did not at all resemble. His eyes were very wide and bright, the pupils
entirely ringed with white. I rather wished he would shutter them. "Brrr!
Not to be ghoulish, not-so-plain Jane, but let's make a pact that if we die,
we'll—say, I've just had an idea! Let's suppose this channeling-the-dead
gambit can be made to work—" He saw me stare and added mollifyingly,

"I mean in a thoroughly modern, methodical fashion, without any hocus-pocus." He went on, "Isn't it true that the spirit world is everywhere and nowhere, so that your medium-wallah can turn the spigot, so to speak, as easily in Timbuctoo as in Cheesehill, Massachusetts? Now tell me if I'm wrong, but it seems to me that a cooperative ghost could carry messages from one mouth in Nova Zembla to another in Java or Paraguay with only the briefest layover in the hereafter, and no need for telephone wires. And then shove over, Mr. Alexander Graham Bell! Picture it: a worldwide capillary system of mediums joined, as it were, mouth to mouth to mouth to mouth to mouth—ah ha ha! Picture it!"

I did, though not a little affronted at the idea of using the dead for nothing more elevated than a telecommunications system. He rattled on, "And surely it is only a matter of time before we can cut out the medium, or rather *become* the medium, and have only to open our mouths to transmit the words of others without having, or needing to have, the least idea what we are saying. Like birds, tweet tweet—"

"In fact this is what we already do. The Headmistress says—"

"Aha! You see? You quote! And"—for he saw my frown—"why not indeed? Why form your own thoughts when all the wisdom of better men, and of course women, is at the tip of your tongue? Why ever read another book? The information to which the dead are privy is perhaps a little behindhand, yesterday's paper so to speak, but there are ways around that—if one wishes to put a person's *present* body of knowledge at one's disposal, one has only to kill him off! It may come to pass that people regard life as a mere apprenticeship for the more lasting use to which they may be put hereafter. Tweet and retweet!"[23]

He kept on chuckling and attempting various birdcalls with a levity that seemed entirely out of keeping with our situation and, annoyed, I turned my face away and, absently patting the now stupefied cat trussed against my chest, let my attention drift.

---

23. Dr. Peachie here seems to anticipate the claim that Sybil Joines invented the Internet (accent on the *ter*). I have been shown a file of unanswered cease-and-desist letters going back to the 1960s. As far as I know, no lawyer has ever agreed to take the case. —Ed.

But now what was he talking about? "New leadership, just as soon as we can pry the old girl loose. A good man at the helm." He saw the question in my face: "Not me, thank you very much! I'm no babysitter, or pettifogging administrator. I will be quite occupied enough with—well." He cleared his throat. "But you, now; there will be a place for someone who knows where they keep the twine and whether the bodies are filed under *D* for *dead* or *E* for *extremely fucking dead*, excuse my French. You could do quite well for yourself as a secretary or even an assistant mistress. I'll put in a word for you, see if I don't."

I said nothing. He did not press me, or seem to notice how utterly my mood had changed. Do quite well for myself! Put a word in! He did not have the faintest idea of my true character. A good man at the helm! Change a-coming! Was everything I had worked for to be, with a fatuous laugh, snatched away?

An exclamation—"Good Lord!"—jerked me from my reverie. I tightened my grip on the branch, feeling how the floodwaters now swirled cold around my dangling feet, and looked wildly about. The day was noticeably darker. "Jane, what the devil is that?

A gray behemoth was wheeling slowly around a snag in the shallow waters near the new shoreline. Now I saw it shake itself loose and glide slowly toward the plunging waters of the main current, then plunge into the body of the flood and come wallowing, rolling, sounding and breaching, fluking and lobtailing toward us. As may be seen by my choice of verbs, I first took it, absurdly, for a whale. Then, "The Sky Lung!"

"The what?"

"Our—sort of balloon—the carriage house must be—"

I did not have time to explain further, because the Sky Lung now flung itself at us, as if with murderous intent. If it had been fully inflated, it would have bounced, or burst, or indeed have already taken flight. But it was a loose wallowing sac, and it wrapped a trailing part of itself around the branches of our perch. The rest of it tried to keep going.

"Hold on!"

The branch was bucking wildly. At the perigee I was dipped in the flood to the hips. The cat stuck its claws into my stomach and screamed.

"We have to disentangle it, or we will be for it! Hold on to my belt, there's a good girl."

I worked my fingers under his belt and leaned out along my own higher branch as, holding his own branch with his knees as if he were breaking a "bronco," he scooted farther out and in water up to his waist began shoving and pulling and kicking at the Sky Lung.

For a moment it seemed possible that he would succeed. Then with one great rending that almost unseated me twice, first on the yank and then on the recoil, the tree split down the center, and his half, still attached to the Sky Lung, was instantly swept downstream. I almost certainly could not have saved him, but I did not try. At the first great tug I had removed my hand from his belt.

For a moment I saw his white, shocked, denatured face raised unseeingly to mine, and then the Sky Lung with its cargo, moving smoothly now, swept around a curve and was gone.

It was a long, cold, roaring, heaving night. Unseen things rushing downstream thumped the tree and sent vibrations right through me. There were cracking, rending sounds. I locked my arms around the straining branch and endured. The cat, half crushed beneath me, was a hot reminder of life. Gradually the wild, springing motion settled into a smooth, regular swaying. It lulled me into a wakeful sort of sleep in which I never quite lost consciousness of the branch that had become my world.

I was awoken by the plaintive yowls of the cat. It was morning. The river, still high, but flat and glassy, had slipped back between its banks. The tree was half a tree. I was alone with the cat in it. And here was the Headmistress with the groundskeeper and a stout stick, wading through the smooth brown water to help me home.

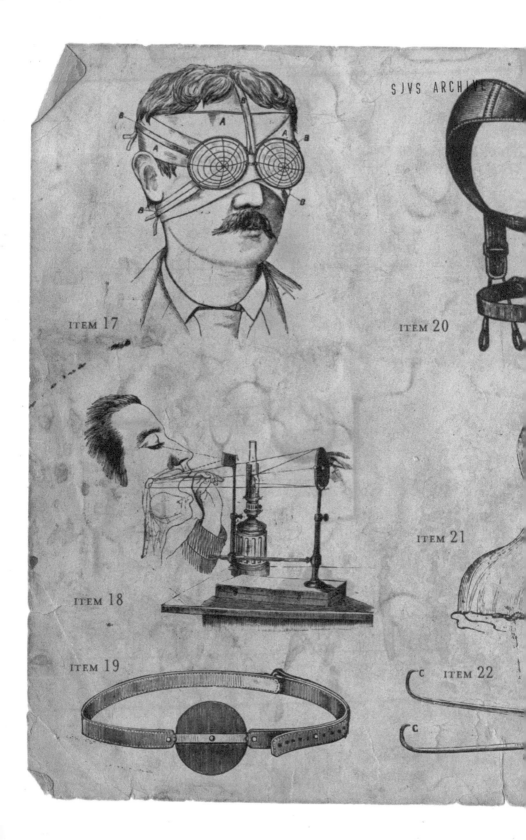

ITEM 17

ITEM 20

ITEM 18

ITEM 21

ITEM 19

ITEM 22

ITEM 24

ITEM 25

ITEM 26

TAYLOR GARNETT EVANS & Co Ltd

MANCHESTER
LONDON & LONDON

Supply list for Expedition

wind sock
lip buckles
  glottal hook
140 ft of line
comma splice & grapples
spongilian cheek pads
                    (check basement)
~~etc~~
extra eraser crumbs
        AT LEAST 2 sachets

subjunctive case
sinker
spirit trumpet
a sufficiency of semicolons, apostrophes,
                        brackets, etc.
Ariadne string
harness
  gutta-percha mouthguard
  pins
~~the~~ Necrophone
  good walking shoes

Readings

from "A Visitor's Observations"

On the Difficulty of My Task

Nick Peachie had been persuasive. I did take a dose of ectoplasm. I took more than one. And I am ashamed to say that I take ectoplasm still, though because I am no longer resident of the Vocational School, all outsiders having been summarily dismissed after the Headmistress's death, I have had to seek it out on the streets, with the predictable risks to my health, safety, and reputation. Yes, I am one of *those*! But do not worry, I am quite harmless. Perhaps, as the world worsens, as whole countries tip and pour themselves into oblivion—or pour others—you can forgive me my little habit. For it is one that nobody kicks. We imagine death can be consumed, like everything else, when death is itself the mouth.

And so we have the situation that obtains today: a world of scooped-out semblances, colorful shells on the shores of a more final absence. Inside those shells? A void, barely thickened by thought, like a broth by a dusting of cornstarch. Increasingly I can *see* it, a gray nothingness pluming out of mouths and nostrils, seeping out of pores, and hanging muggy in the air. People rush together, slide their fingers into orifices, and touch empty space. There is simply *nothing there*. Never mind, there is nothing here either: No one's fingers brush that nothingness. If there is a slight feeling of letdown it does not have a chance to form itself into a complete thought before it wisps away. "I thought"—and it is gone. Or do I imagine it, is it just me? No, the dream of an ending, an answer, a final solution—I am not the only one who has found it seductive. I often think of the Headmistress, who understood its temptations better than anyone. But let me tell you something she also understood: Death is no ending. The more you feed it, the more it wants. For death has two faces. From one angle, it looks like closure. But from the other, endless opening.[24]

Possibly one could say the same of any dream. I would not know, I have no other dreams.

My job is threatened, and I do not care. My pen is slowing . . . Though I do not altogether blame myself for that. I have the impression that, although one could write almost any number of books about the Vocational School without exhausting the subject, not one of these would come to a satisfactory conclusion. All, *all* are doomed to wind up in embarrassed circumlocutions and increasingly prolonged silences, finally breaking off in midsentence halfway down the page. Such has certainly been the fate of my own attempts, of which this is only the most recent. For I have begun any number of accounts of the school, in some of them adopting a whimsical tone (for it strikes me, at least it does when I am in a lighthearted mood, that a Merry Andrew would find much to thrum his funny bone in its activities) . . . In others, cool ratiocination . . . In others the manner of a beloved yarn-spinner, rehearsing a well-lubricated tale in his local tavern for the benefit of cronies who bawl out their favorite lines in unison.

Yet all of these, despite promising beginnings, some dashing flourishes, and substantial effort, suffered a progressive attenuation in style, growing so stark and simple as to freeze the marrow (and I am a florid, comfortable stylist! Like the good bourgeois I was brought up to be, I believe that one can never have too many throw pillows, or adjectives) until at last they petered out altogether: this one resembling a line of footprints leading out into a Sahara (concluding in a smudged and trampled patch and perhaps a few bleached scraps of fabric)—this other, bubbles rising in a quicksand—and this, a pirate ship's plank extending over shark-ridden waters—none of which the reader would be advised to follow without having first commended her soul to her Maker!

While never, or not formerly, a morbid person, I am inclined to think

---

24. The one does not exist without the other, and so we arrive at such perversions as, on the one hand, modern spiritualism (dissolution tricked out as a solution, the unending peddled as an end), and on the other, modern war (solution without resolution. Endless opening).

that the peculiar fatality to which my books have fallen victim derives from their subject, and not, or not only, from my shortcomings as an author. At the heart of all the works and days of the school is the irreducible mystery (or maddeningly simple fact—it makes no odds) of *death*, which effortlessly absorbs into its white and stinging silence as many words as one may throw its way. For all our attempts to map, chart, document, and in short *encyclopedify* death only serve to illuminate the activities of those who haunt its periphery, while driving the phenomenon itself yet further into its lair. To do the Headmistress justice, I feel sure that she would not only acknowledge this circumstance, but describe it as our great good fortune, for death is in her estimation the inexhaustible wellspring, clear and cool, from which she, and I, and every man Jack of us drink without ceasing until, plunging headlong into the waters of oblivion, we ourselves cease to be.

It is this ravening whiteness, and it alone, that I now perceive in every map, model, formula, and printed page published under the colophon of the open mouth, the Vocational School's house imprint. Though I be at first impressed by the inky masses of data, notations, footnotes, endnotes, diagrams, and illustrations, my attention irresistibly adverts to the white space that, ever interpenetratingly present, seems to press in from the margins and well up between words, within them, and in the counters of the very characters that make them up: a milky acid capable of consuming all. Even to glance at a Vocational School publication is to begin to feel a hollowness tunneling down the optic nerve to the brain. The effect spreads to other texts as well; increasingly I see *any* printed page as as an essentially and ideally white one, only accidentally dirtied with a few insignificant words over which the eyes indifferently scud, or as one whose progressive erasure, though still incomplete, has left of a once-complete text only remnants, on which it would be futile to base a speculation as to the cargo of argument it once bore, especially as they, too, they will soon be consumed by the void that is in any case richer in interest than any words—that lures us as the lap and breast of the world—and is the answer to every question, fully satisfactory as no other answer to no other question you have ever asked has ever been, your whole life long. And even such outrageously overstuffed sentences as the one I have just finished writing seem to me to be all too thin. I confess that I even detect in myself a certain reckless eagerness to see these texts through to their destined end as identically blank sheets of paper. My eyes fall on a page, intricately maculated with numbers, and dates, and clauses, and subclauses, and sub-subs, such as the living relish, and I see the rising tide of whiteness licking at the ink, and I am glad of it, and even (fingers twitching on my eraser) long to help it along.

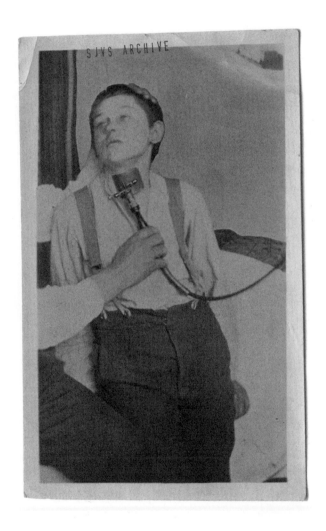

Letters to Dead Authors, #15

Dear Jane,

At first my Theatrical Spectacle bid fair to be another disappointment, for despite the press release I sent out with my assurances that the road was passable again, bridges sound, etc., only one reporter made an appearance, that same fellow, Cartwright, who has been hanging around for weeks. The rest of the party was composed of a single trustee, a prospective donor whom I have been cultivating for months, and our dear, ubiquitous Dr. Beede, though he was not invited. But I was not to be deterred from taking this step into the limelight. The tour itinerary was planned; it would yield edifying spectacles at every turn. The children had been drilled in their roles and awaited only a sign from me. I had left nothing to chance—or so I thought! For the Spectacle proved more spectacular than I could ever have anticipated.

I believe that the story will propel the Vocational School to national, perhaps international fame! People all over the world will soon be reading about me in the newspaper. I might spare this nib and enclose a clipping, but I am eager to record the day's events in my own words.

Hoping to give more members of the press a chance to arrive, I do not take our small group directly to the auditorium. After issuing them umbrellas, I lead them on a tour of the grounds during which we stop twice to watch the older students practicing their calisthenics in the fresh air, rain-splattered but healthy, their cheeks like apples, as they say, as I hope the reporter will say, in his article. Then usher them into a rotunda with a high ceiling of streaked glass sectored with leading around a sort of compass rose at the center, made of smaller facets intricately pieced together. The room looks different to me, no doubt because I am seeing it through the eyes of the Public. A flock of crows swings across the gray sky above. The glass is flawed or the birds are: They stutter in and out of existence, their flight paths composed of dotted lines. And now they are dot-dashing back, short long, short short long—

telegraph messages. The ceiling gives all the light in the room; this falls down very cool and clear on the thing in the center of the floor.

"Gentlemen, I present: The Wrong Tree."

The birds swirl and land all at once: a tattoo of almost simultanous thumps. Their feet are suddenly clearly visible.

Our visitors approach the tree. The reporter exclaims, "Why, it's made of paper! What the devil?" It is indeed made of paper, of printed paper in fact, the pages of books, but torn, wrenched, pulverized, so that all one sees are broken words, mere letters, angled every which way, merging and overlapping.

"Chewed," I say definitively. I regard the tree with satisfaction. The others, with incomprehension.

"Under the paper—"

"Under the paper, yes, there is a tree, once living. Now clad in an integument or second bark of paper—which is, of course, the afterlife of trees."

"Wasn't there some trouble with the town over this?" asks the reporter.

Someone has done his research! I run my hands down my skirt before answering. "A little controversy over what they were pleased to describe as *vandalized* library books. All feathers have been smoothed and the books in question replaced. We have, of course, no desire to deprive our town's no doubt ardent readers of material, even if we differ on the best use of certain texts. And now please come this way—the auditorium—I have arranged something a little special . . ."

I take pleasure in pointing out to the reporter the red tongue of the aisle carpet, the velvet uvula decorating the proscenium arch and the realistically pocked and shriveled tonsils concealing the wings from the view of the audience. "Where are the teeth?" the reporter quips, not knowing that, as I subsequently inform him, the Teeth really *is* what we call those advanced students and faculty who act as the watchdogs of tradition during services in the Word Church, which he is welcome to attend, if he chooses; the auditorium is nothing compared to the Church, though well enough for its purpose.

"You look tired!" I tell him gaily. "Shake it off, we have hours still to go!"

The trustee has seated himself several rows from the front, impassive, upright, only sagging slightly in the middle, like a bag of feed propped up on its end. The prospective donor joins him. The reporter slouches into an aisle seat near the back. The fact that he does not sit in the front row for a better view, though it is unoccupied, as are nearly all of the rows, enrages me. Because of course he has not chosen his seat at random. He wishes to let me know that he is not to be coaxed into partisanship by the sweet voices of children. Never fear, I think, *sweet* is not the word. And it is true that both reporter and trustee jerk back when little Harmony Upshaw steps through the still closed curtains, opens her mouth, and allows the bass rumble of a Elizabethan actor to roll forth. She (or he, through her) is (was) a ham, but a skilled one, plying the bellows of her lungs to inflame a cool audience. I am pleased to see the reporter's attention sharpen.

Joey Minks, emerging next, plays opposite in a female part. He is slight and fair enough to play the heroine. But his voice is that of a woman grown—a mellow contralto with a not unpleasant hoarseness, like a haze of cigar smoke. Incidentally there is no reason the girl could not channel the woman, and the boy the man, as one might expect, but the dramatic instincts of our director have not played him false; the effect is striking. The two depict, of course, Tragedy (Minks) and Comedy (Upshaw), first quarreling, then wooing; a duet concludes these preliminaries, and then the curtains, somewhat jerkily, are drawn open as Tragedy and Comedy exeunt stage right, arm in arm.

Scene One. An old-fashioned, institutional-looking classroom: bare floorboards, high windows, mostly empty shelves, charts and maps and wax models of heads and other unidentifiable objects. The standing blackboard is covered with diagrams among which an open mouth—bristling with numbered points, each with an explanatory text—can be clearly seen. The mouth appears more intricate than the uninitiated would expect. The students are disposed about the room, dressed in matching school uniforms: black pinafores or short pants and blazers. The pale light makes them appear waxen and unwell. Some are standing in front of music stands with hands folded, softly gulping or moaning in rhythm. Some have small masks attached to fine wire structures that project from their faces like small, horizontal Eiffel Towers. Some have rags or curled pieces of paper coming from their mouths. Many wear blindfolds. Some of the bigger girls have soft woven slings swinging below their chins like feed bags. At regular intervals someone scuttles onstage and squeezes these with white-gloved hands, establishing their emptiness, and hurries offstage.

All these characters, and in fact every person who appears onstage from now on, is closely shadowed by another in identical garb who imitates his or her every move. In the case of the speaking parts, the actor in front, whose mouth we see moving, is not the one speaking. The speaker, who is "dead," is the person in back, who delivers his or her lines (to the detriment of their intelligibility) into a clear, flexible tube, the end of which is attached to the back of the other's head.

A teacher enters and claps her hands (it is, of course, her double whose clap we hear). She is wearing wire-frame glasses and long black robes. Her pinned-back hair is threaded with gray.

From the subsequent dialogue it becomes clear that the students are rehearsing a musical. The students, among them Upshaw and Minks in a change of costume, begin singing with startling professionalism. During this number, a woman dressed in old-fashioned mourning clothes creeps across the classroom, watched uneasily by the students. She coughs a bright splash of blood onto a handkerchief, clamps this in an embroidery ring, studies it, then slides it into a pigeonhole in the wall.

The actors, of course, play students and faculty at the Vocational School, each with his or her particular stutter; the dialogue is therefore jerky, but in a highly stylized way, for the hesitations and repetitions are all scripted and have been memorized. You may have heard that nearly all stutterers can sing fluently, without impediment. In fact, most of them can recite lines, as well, if the lines are treated as phrases of music, rising and falling in pitch, and with distinct rhythms. In this case, however, the lines they are reciting so fluently feature a scripted, stylized stuttering. You may say that I might as well have allowed their natural stutters to take effect, but Mr. Lenore would not have it.

There was a little lesson in this for the students, and for any audience member who understood what he was witnessing: The stutter is not here an error or a limitation but the mark and epitome of *Art*, to which any style of speech at all may aspire, and not only that which we conventionally consider fluency; but I am done preaching.

After a choral performance (in which virtually the entire student body takes the stage)—a veritable babel of syllabification—a different sound breaks through, and the auditorium resounds with the professional harmonies of a old-fashioned music hall group.

The scene does not proceed without hitches. A slate carried by a walk-on shows the audience a crude figure daubed on its reverse; a door flies open to reveal a startled child in partial undress; in the midst of an affecting solo, a shout of laughter, hurriedly muffled, is heard from offstage, to the visible fury of those onstage, one of whom clenches his fist at someone out of sight in the wings. But on the whole it comes off very well and I mentally undertake to order extra pudding for the cast and crew.

The music comes to a close as a rude mechanical rushes onstage to make an announcement; someone, it seems, is coming. "Will he like it? Will he like our play?" the students chorus, or something to that effect. I have the growing impression that the play is about putting on this very play, and for a moment I am disoriented, unsure of the reality of my surroundings. Am I caught in a trap, one of those whirlpools of iteration that make travel in the land of the dead so treacherous? But no, for it was not my idea to stage a play about putting on a play, it was the idea of Mr. Lenore, our drama and unvoice coach, who has been to New York and to Berlin and has some modern notions.

My attention is recaptured as one girl (Charlotte Bindemittel), who is about twelve, steps forward from the chorus and, tying her own blindfold, takes a position at center stage, mouth open. The teacher stands beside her, touching her mouth with the end of a cane. The student recites a simple rhyme, considerably prolonged by a stutter. The teacher nods encouragingly throughout. Then the student begins to sing. She stops almost at once, and everyone around turns to look at her, frozen. Her throat and mouth work, and she gradually disgorges a strange waxy object. A thin man rushes into the room, robes flapping, and extends a butterfly net to catch it as it falls. Then everyone crowds around to examine it. The object is passed to another robed figure, who scribbles in a notebook, then back to the first, who sticks a label on it and rushes it to a pigeonhole in the wall. A small group of typists record their interpretations, their clacking keys providing a percussive accompaniment. Then the girl resumes the song, singing this time with great confidence and style (in a mature contralto) a music hall number from a bygone age.

The curtains swing closed, and the light dims briefly, though the song continues through this change of scene. When the curtains open again we see:

Scene Two: the same classroom, but strange. The personae are no longer accompanied by their doubles. The walls are gone. Instead, the blackboard and desks occupy the center of an irregularly shaped, reddish cave, and the anatomical models and jars of dissected newts are now heaped untidily on the floor. Many of the desks, blackboards, etc., look different somehow—they are made out of a different substance, or they lack an essential feature, or are partially fused with some neighboring object, as if they are not actual desks, blackboard, newts, but the imperfect memory of those things. The floor is not flat, but has swells and dips, making it visibly difficult for the actors to walk. To the right is a sort of chute, coming out of somewhere high up, in the wings.

The only direct light comes from a high, oval opening in the distance, at the end of a ridged, tubular tunnel that we see foreshortened. The formations around it make it gradually evident that it is a mouth—seen, however, from the inside. Behind it is a changing scene—painted on a long strip of canvas on rollers—that depicts the classroom of the previous scene from the reverse perspective.

The same voice is singing as at the end of the previous scene, but the person standing alone before the class (played by our instructor of Posture Arts, Mme. Once) is older. One might say that she "matches" her voice. We understand that we are in the land of the dead, and this is the voice that we earlier heard through the mouth of the student.

There is a commotion from among the indistinct objects in the darkness to the right, and a gentleman enters, a distraught student scrambling to precede her into the classroom. The newcomer is formally dressed but covered with some kind of slime at which he is distractedly wiping.

Tragedy and Comedy reenter from the wings. "The Intermission!" they announce in unison, and the curtain closes.

At this interval in the Theatrical Spectacle, and serving at its centerpiece, was meant to be the release of our great balloon, or Sky Lung (as I planned to call it), but circumstances deprived our visitors of this wonder.

When the journalist returns from outside, where I suspect him of smoking a cigarette, Tragedy and Comedy take the stage again for their Dialogue Between Tragedy and Comedy. This time they do not sing, but deliver their lines straight, or as straight as they can, for both are now afflicted, if that is the word, by a stutter.

Study Question: While performing a play about stuttering students, the stuttering actors are possessed by the voices of other (deceased) actors, who have now themselves begun to stutter. What is likely to happen next?

Correct. The dead actors will themselves be possessed, by other ghosts.

And if, improbably, these ghosts should stutter in turn?

And if then . . .

I believe the audience glimpses the danger before even I do. Do you imagine it was my intention to open a veritable "black hole" before the very eyes of a reporter, a prospective donor, and a trustee? I am not so careless with my reputation as that.

I happen to be watching the reporter. The next word from Tragedy's mouth is, as I well know, for I wrote his lines, *Scheherazade* (a word I personally would not undertake without a spotter). But it never comes. The voiceless palato-alveolar sibilant fricative or "Sh" comes out forcefully, but is succeeded after a crotchet rest by a second "Sh" of equal force, and after an even briefer rest, another, until what sounded briefly like an extended shushing becomes an unnaturally rapid and mechanical chir.

At the first jerk—yank—tug—the reporter half rises. I follow his gaze back to the stage, and see the mouth of Tragedy contracting like a pupil, not because Minks is closing his mouth, conscious of danger (though I believe he does try), but because the world is contracting around it, pressing inward, urging itself toward the hole he has made in it (in the world, I mean) like water in a bathtub toward the drain.

I myself am more fascinated than alarmed; I have conceived the possibility of an infinite regress but never witnessed one. To see its effect on the fabric of being is an awesome privilege, and indeed I turn back to the reporter with, I imagine, my soul shining in my eyes, wishing to share my wonder at this phenomenon with someone who might appreciate its rarity. I do not quite understand the expression that I behold, which is certainly not one of wondering delight, but I think no more about it, turning back to the event happening onstage. The boy, I now see, is shrinking and wrinkling, being sucked up into his own mouth. Belatedly I realize how such an event—ordinary enough in itself—must appear to someone not accustomed to it, and hasten to try and remediate the situation. But before I have made it halfway down the aisle, the inevitable has happened: Tragedy has fallen through himself, Comedy has fallen through him as well (her oral guest, departing from the script, incongruously declaiming "The Lady with the Long Red Snood"), the scenery has all begun to shuffle downstage, and the lights to dim. Through the hullaballoo one can still hear how the dead call up the dead who call up the dead, each new voice the merest chirrup, but monitory, like the click of a cocked hammer.

Someone seizes my arm. "Do something, madam!" cries the trustee. "You have lost two students already!"

"What do you propose I do?" I inquire quite calmly. His face reddens and I endeavor to explain, conscious that the reporter is taking down my every word. "My business and my skill is in affording the dead the means to speak, not shutting them up. If Minks will not close his mouth, and he is not now in any position to do so, being dead, we have no recourse but to wait and hope, either that the impulse to speech fades, or that the number of deceased orators with speech impediments is finite. Do you think we have heard from Demosthenes yet? Indeed, if it is not finite (but of course it is), we shall all find ourself dead very shortly."

"But—but that is outrageous! I demand that you take action!" He advances a foot toward the stage, then withdraws it. Indeed, there is nothing he can do there but plunge into the vortex himself.

"We can try applauding," I say mildly. "Perhaps it will persuade the dead that the act is over, and they will stop to gather up the bouquets and *billets doux*." He looks at me with outrage, as if imagining that I am poking fun at him, but when I begin to clap, he follows suit, and the prospective donor after him. A moment later the reporter sets his notebook on one knee and joins us. We applaud, as the stage furniture crumples and slides, as the lashings holding up the painted backdrop part and it folds itself into the hole in the world. Behind the backdrop I see a child with arms and legs wrapped around a girder, braids streaming out sideways. The vaccuum sucks open the door of the auditorium, and a quantity of leaves fly past; one of them plasters itself on the back of the trustee's neck, then peels itself up and flies on, to be swallowed by the mouth onstage. My hair thrashes, scattering hairpins that zip like darts toward the stage. The world is sifting through itself like sand through an hourglass. I am not above gloating a little: I am putting on the stage show of the millennium, and a reporter is here to bear witness!

Then the voices stop. The sliding and the crumbling stop. My hair sags against my neck and with practiced fingers I begin fastening it up with what pins remain. The trustee hesitates, then rushes toward the stage, followed by the others. I almost laugh to see them examining the floor, the remaining props, the drops, the child (now unstuck from the girder): Do they imagine that I falsified the phenomenon with scrim and lighting effects? My hair made respectable, I go after them.

"The children?" says Dr. Beede.

"Dead," I say, "for the moment. It remains to be seen whether that condition will be temporary or permanent. I shall have to send someone after them."

The trustee stares, his face rubiate. "Temporary or—do you not think that you yourself should go, and at once?"

"There is no great rush. In the land of the dead, time does not pass."

"There is no great *rush*? Perhaps not, for the children, especially if, as you so casually remark, they are dead, but for *my* feelings there most certainly is, and if you have an ounce of humanity in you, then for yours as well! How can you not be anxious about their well-being, and hasten to bring them back to those who love them?"

"I do not suppose that haste and emotional extremity will aid our cause," I say. The reporter is again scribbling away. "I remain calm because I am most effective calm. You would not like, I am sure, to see me demonstrate my humanity at the cost of two young lives. I would ask you to remain quiet as I prepare myself *per mortem iter.*"

It takes me several tries to funnel myself down through myself. Once I do so, however, I see to my satisfaction that the unlucky pair is huddled together just inside that swirling orifice we call the throat, frozen with terror and stuck to (really, interpenetrating with) the scenery. I yank them out without ceremony and return before the journalist's shout of surprise has fallen silent—quite the quickest trip I have ever taken to the land beyond the Veil.

"Let us proceed to the expedition room," I begin, only to see that the children, mewling a little, have been closed in the arms of the doctor, who is stooped over them protectively. I am abruptly annoyed. "Children, I believe you have Interrogatory Silence practice? Be off." They tear themselves out of the arms of the doctor and, bowing and touching their mouths as I taught them, though still sniffling, they depart.

The trustee, however, is frowning and shaking his head. "I think I have seen enough. If we may repair to your office, I shall collect my hat and take my leave."

"So soon? I'm surprised you don't want to review our equipment, the very latest design! Or see the Chapel of the Word Church, which Mme. Hume mentioned so kindly in her recent remarks to the British Academy of the Thanatogical Arts. The Analphabetical Choir has been practicing . . . But I see you are not to be convinced . . . I confess I will not be sorry to have the afternoon free for pedagogical matters!"

He hurries off. I had hoped to speak to the prospective donor about our most pressing needs, but he is hard on the heels of the other.

"Do you suppose we scared them a little?" I ask the reporter playfully.

"You, sir, are made of stronger stuff, I gather. Can I show you anything else?"

"I'm—frankly—well! This has certainly been—remarkable. Do you suppose that I could interview the children? After they've had a chance to catch their breath?"

Naturally I say no. "But I would be happy to explain the principles of necrophysics involved, for the benefit of uninformed readers."

"Well, that would be just marvelous," he says. "You'll have to tell me all about it sometime. I must run and—" He wiggles his fingers uncouthly. It takes me a moment to see that he is miming typing. "Just one thing more: Can you describe your feelings when you saw your charges sucked into the void?"

"Feelings?" I stared at him for a moment. The very fabric of the universe develops a puncture, and he wants to talk about my feelings?

He has the grace to look away. "Well, never mind, I think I have all that I need at the moment."

"The article—when do you think—?"

"I'll send you a copy," he promises. And is gone.

I am—we are—launched! I feel like a debutante.

Optimistically yours,
Headmistress Joines

16. The Final Dispatch, contd.

I flew like a phoenix out of the fire, and like a phoenix I was reborn.

I did not discover this right away.

I was not much acquainted with other children or indeed with anyone outside my immediate relations. It had been impressed upon me that the local boys and girls were my inferiors. I had no trouble believing it, despite the low status I possessed in my own house. It was only when tradition imposed upon my father the responsibility of hosting a holiday party for his employees that I was allowed to associate decorously with their children. I recall leading a small troop of them, sullen and strange in shirts and pinafores made stiff as kites with starch, to gaze silently at one of my father's new devices, and delectating in my unaccustomed power.

It was a different matter when these same children ventured boldly into our backyard in all the splendor of their dirt and challenged me to games no one had taught me. Knowing that I could not win I sealed my solitude by a subterfuge. Having read, in some of the journals to which my father subscribed, of the operations of Spirit Mediums, I rolled up my eyes and lowered my voice and pretended to be possessed by the dead. After that I sometimes saw the other children staring at me from the bushes, but they came no closer.

It was only after my father died that, after hasty consultations among the local authorities and the executors of my father's estate, I was sent, for the first time, to school. Pushed out the door of the neighbor's house (in which I had been installed without reference to my own wishes) to walk for the first time down the hard-packed path that followed the river's curves to the schoolhouse, I arrived dusty and a celebrity. Not only was I a new student but I had lost both parents in extraordinarily gruesome ways; my own life had been, they understood, threatened; furthermore, I was a stutterer. When the neighbor who had undertaken to deliver me there unhitched my hand from her sleeve and took her leave, the children gathered around me, shoving and staring. On the other side of the yard, the teacher hovered, waiting, as it seemed, to read the mood of the class.

I was well aware of the poor figure I cut, for though never pretty I had been kept in better trim under my parents' care. Although an heiress I would not come into my money until I came of age and the hag who had the keeping of me was a skinflint. My cheap gingham dress fit me like a sack; my ugly boots, bought large for reasons of thrift, made me clownish.

Still, one does not readily shed feelings of superiority inculcated since infancy. So when the other children fleered at me, I felt, at first, more surprised and indignant than hurt. They had mistaken me for someone else and would soon learn what manner of person I was and jump to my tune. I even felt sorry for the most excitable of them, who would find it hardest to recast themselves in the mold of friendship. I tried, a few times, to launch the routine with which I had had some success when I was younger, pretending to be possessed by a spirit. I was laughed down. The mockery made me stutter even more comprehensively, which excited mockery of a yet more pointed, inventive, and hilarious sort.

One day I had a particularly bad stuttering episode that happened to coincide with a visit from, this is interesting, a school inspector. You might think children would not care about the impression they made on a school inspector and perhaps it was just a pretext to torment me but they gathered around me on the playground afterward to give me grief for sullying the reputation of the school with my pronunciation of the word *deciduous*, while the teacher, not meeting my eyes, having been extremely disappointed in me, as she had already disclosed, allowed the door to swing slowly shut, and left me to my fate.

"What's wrong, c-c-c-cat got your tongue?"

I felt the scathing rays of their regard shoot into me and play over my privacies in mocking disbelief. I felt that they could see me naked, from the *inside*. Why did their eyes shoot rays when mine only received them? If I met their eyes, it was apparently not to parry or pierce in turn, but to extend a general invitation. If I lowered my eyes to keep them out, however, I shut myself out too, and joined the others in gawping at the riddle that I was.

I saw a wrinkled scab of dried pea soup stuck to my skirt and a clump of burrs stuck ridiculously to one stocking. My clothing bunched and dangled. Inside it was a gross, inert, and solid object made improbably of meat. How could such a thing reason, let alone speak? But that was itself a thought, so I was all right, except that I could not remember how one converted thoughts to words, words to intelligible sounds. My mouth did not seem to have any moving parts. Did I even have a mouth, or was there just a smooth convexity underneath my nose, like a forehead or a knee? Tongue fused to palate, teeth locked, windpipe cinched tight, I felt heat rise through me until I was a blazing column. My hair stung my scalp. My earlobes were coals.

I can guess what a ghost must feel, trying to move a living mouth to speak. A bodiless wisp pitting its will against muscle and bone. Pumping the lungs through the voice box, working the jaw on its hinge, while pursing and pouting and flapping the tongue. An insane task of coordination, with a mystery at the core: How could meat *mean*? Just where did meat meet meaning? What, really, was meaning? For that matter, what was meat? "M-m-m-m-m . . ." I said, meaning all this, more or less. (Secretary, stet.)

In doing so, I now recognize, I had actually found a solution; I had seen how, failing to say something, though not saying nothing, I had nonetheless expressed exactly what I was thinking: That speech was impossible. But my tormentors, unimpressed, closed in. I fell upon my body again, to pump out a phrase, any phrase, not hoping it would be clever, only that it would be language. "D-d-d-don't! L-l-leave m-me alone! I'll—I'll—" [sic]

I have always remembered, as the key to a great puzzle, that it was in this moment not of insight and mastery but of doubt and dispossession that the dead rose up in me at last. Saying, in a deep slow growl entirely out of keeping with my appearance, something entirely out of keeping with my desires, but perfectly calculated to puzzle and unnerve my tormenters: "Little children, gather 'round, and I will tell you how I died."

One fading shout of laughter from someone in the back.

"You're not dead," a little girl finally pointed out. Say what you like about Dotty, she has pluck.

"Oh, yes," I said—he said, through me. "I most certainly am. For the last wolf to live in old Connecticut ripped my throat out on a winter's afternoon in 1759, while crows called back and forth above me, and I saw a red rainbow of my own blood arc over me before a buzzing darkness rose up and gathered me in."

They got quiet then. I suppose they could sense, though they did not understand it, that I was not myself—that whoever was speaking, it was not me. Well, it was a man's voice. That is something one can usually tell. The gonads rattle, that's your giveaway.

I think I should mention, listener, that I'm not at all sure I am the one who delivered the line you just took down. Gonads are not my stock in trade. I am not sure I even know what they are, though I have my suspicions.

As I said, it was very quiet after I said that about the blood. The funny thing is that though it was not my voice or my memory, I saw, naming it, the arc of blood, and the pale blue sky, a crow swinging in a pine to the left of me, and another weighing heavy on a bare branch to the right, and I even felt the snow cold under my neck, and the blood hot on it, and a tremendous wrongness where my throat used to be, and a steam rising from it through which a lean, efficient muzzle was already descending again.

I lifted my head, my mouth jerked open, I peeled my lips back from what he wanted to say, and so it was said: "My name is Cornelius Hackett, and I am a dead man. Do not confuse me with the person whose mouth I temporarily employ. I am older and smarter than she is. I have killed one man and bedded many women. Children I beat or beget, and that is the extent of my dealings with them; their opinions do not interest me. I am irritated to find myself dead. I have been irritated since 1759, at least. You will not irritate me further. Is that understood?"

From the back of the crowd, my audience began to slink away.

"I imagine that you are nodding," said Cornelius, conversationally. "But do you know, I cannot see you, though I can hear you, or could hear you, if you were saying anything. 'Yes, Master Cornelius,' for instance."

"Yes, Master Cornelius," said my increasingly horrified audience.

"We are going to play a little game," said Cornelius. "We're going to play it every day. It's called school."

So it was that, still a schoolgirl myself, I became a teacher, and taught the other children what I did not know myself until I taught it (or Cornelius did, through me): the way to summon up the dead.

My students were—we all were, myself to a large extent included— terrified of Cornelius, and had no real desire to call up another Cornelius, or to come any closer to the dead than the side of a casket, and yet Cornelius had to be obeyed, Cornelius had to be satisfied, to be if possible pleased, and so we sought and even fought one another for privileges that in actuality we did not want.

But my own lot had improved immeasurably. As Cornelius's creature I was an object of dread, no doubt, and no one wished my company less than those who sought it most ardently, but it is better to be feared than scorned, and I moved in power. It is true that I wielded it only for him and because of him, but Cornelius had done what probably no *living* person could have done, and installed me at the top of the social order.

I liked it there! I amused myself giving orders. I established new rules: From now on we will wear polka-dotted neckerchiefs! From now on we will wrap our books in oilcloth! From now on we will carry in our pockets small animals folded out of paper, and give them names! Then I would break the rules myself and laugh at those who followed them, and they would follow suit, whereupon I would punish them.

"Dotty, I require your pencil." Silently, she handed it to me. "And is that a new scarf?" It was. I lost it that same day. I did not care. I had no need to hold on to anything anymore. I would have someone else's scarf tomorrow.

One thing never changed: I rated above all else the skill—for so I described it, with Cornelius's endorsement—of stuttering, and rewarded the practice of it. (How perplexed our teachers were. How often they were obliged to suffer through the Ch-ch-charge [secretary, stet] of the L-light Brigade!) Gradually, the dead began to introduce themselves, and thus I began to train a cadre of ghost speakers, the first and, some of them, the best this country has ever known. A few of them are with me to this day. You know our Miss Exiguous. Miss Dorothea Exiguous, Dotty Hobbs that was, for I gave them names to suit their new estate. I am faithful to those who are faithful to me. Those who are not—

You will be faithful, will you not?

And so I began, not yet knowing what I did, to build my school. I used Cornelius, who believed that he used me. One of the things that I eventually learned from him was how to master him. And then it was my school in fact as well as name.

I will allow no one to take it from me. No one.

Do you know, dear listener, that I am never sure how I am going to get back from the Mouthlands? One might imagine that to return to the real world one simply reversed the process by which one got there, throwing oneself through one's mouth in the other direction, like a butterfly net inverted to release a bee. But for the necronaut, to a very large degree, the land of the dead *is* oneself. Thus to throw oneself through oneself in a more than illusory sense, one would have to throw the world through the world—thread trees through their own knotholes, pass needles through their own eyes, bundle whole planets down rabbit holes and drop the holes through after them.

Such things happen. I am not saying that they are impossible, but I cannot guarantee that, having performed such feats, you would find yourself back home.

The usual method of return is both easier and more difficult. Easy, because it may happen quite by accident; difficult for much the same reason. The way is capricious, opening in one place, at one time, in one fashion, and differently the next. You fall down a well, go up a flight of stairs, open your office door, on which someone has been knocking for quite some time, you creep into a dumbwaiter or a shed, and the flames curl up, the flames curl up, the flames [crackling]—

I leap through them—

And am back in the land of the living, where someone is knocking at my office door. At a nod from me you leave your post to open it (something wrong there) and the School Inspector enters (something wrong) with his hat in his hand.

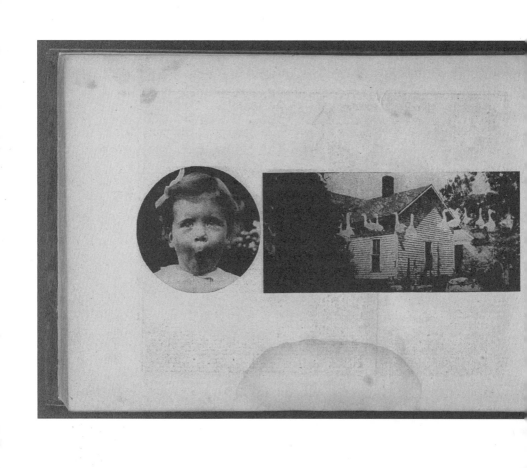

The Stenographer's Story, contd.

The water went down, leaving the grass all slicked with mud. Skeins of weeds, and straw, and here a twisted apron, and there a scrap of tatting, stretched out from snags in perfect parallel, as if still tugged by a phantom torrent. The spiders that had been driven by the flood into the trees spun them full of webs that sparkled like bridal veils in the morning, before the dew burned off.

I still had Dr. Peachie's shirt but had stuffed it into a drawer in the Headmistress's office that I knew she did not open. After a day or two I had the opportunity to take it out. It was still damp and smelled of cat. And a little of cadaver, I thought ghoulishly. I spread it out on the desk. There was something in the breast pocket, a handkerchief bound turban-like around some knobbly object that proved to be a small ectoplasmoglyph. Poked in beside it was a folded note, creased and inky, but still legible.

Elihu says he can get this to you and he will let me know you rec'd it. I will expect yr reply by same carrier in a week's time.

Listen, my boy, I am not very easy in my mind. Just imagine how I felt when I saw that letter in the C.G.! I very nearly choked to death on a finger of toast. I gather everyone knows the letter-writer is a crank, but how could you let that happen? Please find the leak and stopper it. Do not doubt that I am firm in our great Purpose but one more piece of bad publicity and I will have <u>no choice</u> but to close the school. We must put the next phase into effect as fast as possible, the problem is to find our man, I am sounding out candidates as fast as can but must be circumspect. I do not know but that it would be better to take the helm myself as you have urged, still it would look bad.[25] Only something must be done <u>instanter</u>. That lunatic seems bound and determined to blacken the name of Cheesehill. She is shockingly careless with the misfortunate creatures. (What is going on there? Do they truly visit the Next World or is that moonshine?)

I threw it in the trash, alarmed and repulsed, along with the shirt and handkerchief. Then I pulled it out again, to hide away as evidence, in case "our man" should come. Perhaps Dr. Peachie's death had upset the letter-writer's plans, perhaps not. Close the school! That must not happen.

The mouth object was a little damaged, no doubt from being crushed against a tree branch in the flood; I smoothed away the scar, and filed it with all the others.

Later that day the Headmistress said, apropos of nothing, "We are free to imagine that he was carried by our balloon to the land of the dead, like a youthful Wizard of Oz." Outside, a spade was ringing against stone as with rhythmic strokes the groundskeeper cleared the carriage house of mud. "If so, one might in theory fetch him back. It would be curious if it was death that saved his life." She looked sharply at me. If I imagined that she cared, I would have thought that she was testing my reaction.

"It is a shame that Dr. Beede's tutelage was wasted," I only said. "I suppose he will have to put off his retirement a little longer."

"He is quizzing the younger children about their studies again," she said, turning away from the window, and, picking up a dry pen, drew it slowly across a blotter, its sharp point raising a series of parallel scars. "Finster is among them," she added. Finster had stepped up her campaign lately, as if hurrying to have her vengeance before the Headmistress passed beyond her (or anyone's) reach, and I took her meaning.

---

25. If I have one contribution to the solution of this mystery, it is to suggest that the author of this letter is none other than Edward Pacificus Edwards, the Regional School Inspector. For him to assume the headmastership of the school that, as Inspector, he had condemned, would indeed "look bad," that is, tainted by motives of personal gain. —Ed.

I set down the manuscript I was correcting and rose. "With your permission, I will see if I can draw him off," I said.

She raised her head and regarded me mildly. "We have nothing to hide," she said, her hand not relenting in its violence to the page.

"Of course not," I said. "My motives are entirely selfish. I have been afflicted with the bloat, and wanted to coax a digestive from his black bag. That is, if you can spare my services."

"I would be a sorry employer indeed to require my transcriptionist to forge on in despite of 'the bloat.'" Smiling at the homely term, as I had intended, she set down her pen.

Having inveigled the doctor with tea and cakes into abandoning his inquiries, engaged him in trivial gossip, and ushered him firmly to his carriage, I returned. The spatter of gravel could be heard receding down the drive as I sealed the office door behind me. I took my place again, and we resumed our work.

A half hour later, "You are a smart girl," she said, not lifting her head from her work. "Take a dollar from my bag and buy yourself a trinket."

"I don't want trinkets."

She raised her head. "Buy whatever you *do* want, then, girl. Do you think I am interested in how you spend your money?" She put down her pen and shook the cramps out of her hand.

"What I want does not cost money," I said. She raised her eyebrows. "I want more responsibility."

"Do you indeed."

I clenched my hands in my lap. "Yes, Headmistress."

Unexpectedly, her voice deepened and rushed with winds. "The day is coming when you will have more responsibility, whether you want it or not."

"What?" I said, inelegantly.

"What?" she said, and pressing a wad of gauze to her mouth, coughed a red flower. Smearing the spot gently with her thumb, she frowned, in a distracted and slightly impatient way, as if, compared to her other troubles, dying were a mere inconvenience.

At the clink of glass on glass, she reached out a hand without looking up, and I settled in it a snifter of paregoric.

The blanched fold of skin pinched between her brows was just softening when there was a knock. Miss Exiguous opened the door a crack, her eyebrows raised in apologetic obsequy, and threaded herself through it. (She could of course have opened the door all the way, but that would have spoken of self-regard.) Now she crossed the room in what was meant as a girlish swoop, knees cracking, drew an ivory fan out of her sleeve, and began furiously fanning the Headmistress. "I do wish we could forbid visitors. They tire you so!"

"The school requires patronage."

"I know, I know, but what, *what*," she said, "a shame! That someone doing such important, such necessary work, should be obliged to pander to—"

"I do not pander." The telephone on her desk chimed softly with the jiggling of the Headmistress's knee.

"Of course not! Of course not! I misspoke. The quintessence of dignity! But that you allow yourself to be wearied, and I know you are wearied, by the importunities of a boorish paterfamilias or, *such* presumption, a journalist, is"—the fan was closed to permit the extraction of a handkerchief from the other sleeve, which was applied to the outer corner of one eye—"beyond words magnanimous." She dropped to her knees. "Allow me to unlace your boots and chafe your feet."

The Headmistress leaned back in her chair and with one cold eye open on the aureole of thinning reddish hair within which her subordinate's skull could be clearly seen, let my senses extend through narrow corridors, lofty galleries, narrow lightwells and plunging airshafts, dumbwaiters, crawl spaces, and attics. The school was settling down again. The evening noises rose. I took another sip of paregoric; I opened my throat to another world; a cold wind whistled through my teeth and fogged the glass.

I mean *her* teeth. What a very odd mistake to make. But as I said before, I have become very good at guessing her feelings. It is almost as though I felt them myself.

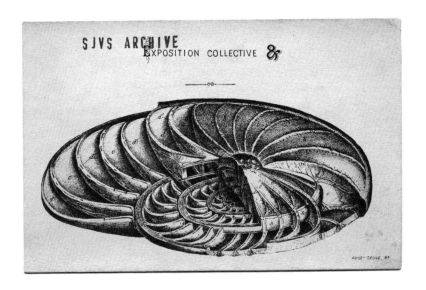

Readings

from "A Visitor's Observations"

A Private Conversation

For all the time that I had spent studying the daily affairs of the Vocational School, I had had only the most fleeting encounters with the Headmistress herself. Still, I saw nothing to shake my conviction that she, with all she had wrought, was the supreme exemplar of my thesis. If the ostensible purpose of the school was to equip the halt of tongue with the marketable skill of Spirit Mediumship, it was obvious that much of this activity contributed but indirectly to that end. If I was correct, an archeological survey of the school's extraordinary activities would unearth, at their core, a corpse. Or better, a mummy, though I risk being styled a punster. For it had not taken me long to confirm what I had already guessed, that the braided hair in the old-fashioned memorial brooch the Headmistress wore was her mother's. Many and varied were the phenomena that had piled out of that ring of hair, but every one carried the sign—like an apostrophe—of an elision. In all those gaps, holes, hollows, and tubes (particularly the throat—I am told her mother was strangled) she recapitulated that original loss. She held it close. And in this way made a mother figure of the *absence* of her mother, and of loss its own recompense.

I do not mean that the Headmistress was trying to bring her mother back from the dead. Certainly not! Indeed her mother *could not* return in any literal sense, because her return was already symbolically accomplished in the practice of channeling itself. Using a symbolic form of return to effect a literal one could only result in the collapse of the entire program. Which would be a tragedy in its own right, for what a work of memorial architecture it was—what a Giza, what a Taj Mahal!

One day, however, I came across her in the gardens (by design, I confess—I spied her setting out and after a seemly interval, strolled after her), crouching beside a bush. Rather than rising, she beckoned me closer and, delicately rotating a leaf to expose its underside, showed me a tiny snail already recovering its poise so far as to extend its eyestalks in our direction. After a cordial discussion of the beauty of that tentative yet persevering creature—"Aspiration in the pure form!" she exclaimed—I found her in an unusually voluble mood, and strolling back to the school with me, she spoke frankly and movingly about how her ideas about death had evolved since certain ghastly experiences in her childhood (she did not tell me what they were, but I had heard).

So far, so gratifying; everything she said was harmonious with my thesis. As she spoke on, however, I realized that she was describing, not a life spent in mourning, but the course of a seduction, progressing through a series of deliciously slow transgressions: from the gross forms death assumes in our everyday world—obscene caricature, grisly joke—to the ambiguous flutings of voices—to the spatial and ontological paradoxes of the land of the dead—to the mute and inexplicable castings of the mouth objects. This was the story that mattered, the story of *becoming strange*, one minim at a time. Even to hear of it was to glimpse, in what had appeared to be a dead end, a hidden door, a little ajar, and beyond it, deep green gardens . . .

I have always maintained that the true movements of our lives are these purposeless and undramatic ones, as calm and motiveless as tides, compounded of myriad minute, alien domesticities. The muddy bank flickers with the feeding claws of crabs, serving themselves invisible morsels behind the awkward pontoons of their other, oversized ones. Longing, grief, anger are real enough, but only briefly interrupt these slow sidereal revolutions, these migrations, tides, weather systems of our lives. Which is to say that what is most important at bottom is not love, or loss, or any of the ordinary emotions, but something more like gravity or time, a deepening involvement with being that these more emphatic emotions cannot interrupt for long.

Some, stirred by these tides, make music, or art, or aeroplanes; she died. Was she the one artist whose work is not interrupted but fulfilled by death? This can be so, I think, if you accept that one of the forms that fulfillment can take is a perfect *dis*satisfaction, that one kind of answer is to identify yourself so perfectly with the question that there is no longer any difference between yourself and it.

Some emotion rippled across her usually impassive features. I would not call it happiness, but neither would I call it grief. It might have been—bliss?

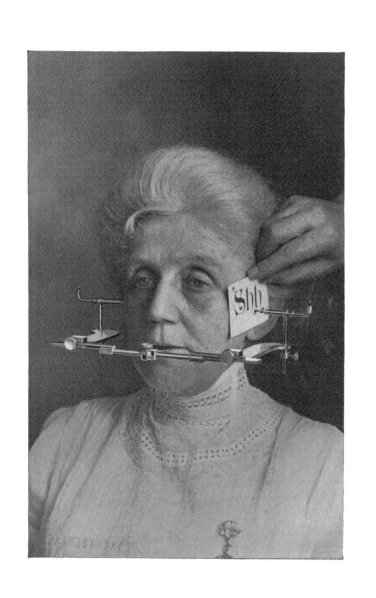

Letters to Dead Authors, #16

Dear Mr. Bartleby,

The story may have already reached you, even in your Plutonian realms. It has certainly reached everyone else.

The article that our friendly newsman finally published, in a disreputable but widely distributed news organ, was inflammatory in tone and rife with the kind of sensationalist exaggerations on which public outrage loves to batten. It attracted the attention of the parents of one of our students. They sent me a letter informing me that clippings of the article were already winging their way to our board of trustees, the Office of Educational Oversight, and the police. (That the lost children were recovered unharmed seems to have gone completely unremarked.) To date I have received fifteen queries from rival news sources, telegrams from three of our more exciteable trustees, and a notice that we are to enjoy the attentions of a Regional School Inspector, news I greeted with tranquility until I discovered that the title had passed from pliable Mr. Benson to a certain Mr. Edwards, unknown to me. The Society of Psychic Research and the Institute of Mediumistic Studies have denounced me as a fraud and the Stage Actors Guild has requested further information about our Spectacle in order to determine whether we may be held responsible for the membership dues of dead actors. We have padlocked the gates; nonetheless I have chased, to date, twenty-four curious intruders off the grounds, some of them bearing picnic baskets. So far only the local constabulary has resisted joining this Salem Witch Hunt but I am sure Detective Munch will soon treat us to his pleasant company.

Tomorrow the Regional School Inspector arrives, no doubt primed for his job by sheaves of indignant letters from the concerned public (and one small sheaf of reassuring ones issuing entirely—under false names, of course—from these premises, for I set everyone imaginable to writing them). I look forward with some trepidation to his visit. In retrospect it strikes me as remarkable that the show seemed to refer, with its talk of a "he" who "is coming," to an event that will only take place after and because of it. I have quizzed Mr. Lenore about it and he cannot explain it, saying only that he thought, he cannot now remember why, that a play in which all personae await the arrival of someone who never turns up was quite a good idea. If only our own drama could enjoy the same lack of denouement.

However, the previous School Inspector was not an unreasonable man, especially when a contribution to personal expenses was pressed into his soft, clammy, not unwilling hands. Perhaps this one will be the same.

I must not lose the school. It is all—*all* to me.

Meanwhile I seem to tilt out of myself, farther and farther, like someone leaning out of a window, trying to make out something very far away. That faraway thing: What is it?

If I knew, I would not be hanging out the window of myself. But would I be going on about my business? Or jumping?

Yours,
Headmistress Joines

17. The Final Dispatch, contd.

The inspector set his hat on the spindly legged occasional table by the door. You accepted his cane and leaned it against the wall, then waited for instructions, your hands clasped behind you. I stood before the stove, one hand on the mantel above it. I had the sudden impulse to retreat behind my desk, but I mastered it.

"Headmistress Joines, a word in private." At my nod, you left, closing the door behind you. "I will be as direct and clear as I know how to be." His voice was not unkind, but he did not hesitate as he went on. "Naturally, the *contretemps* I witnessed earlier gave me the gravest misgivings about your stewardship and even, I might say, your sanity. However, I did not wish to depart without finding out whether you were successful in retrieving the child"—my silence was answer enough—"or acquainting myself better with the school, and so I have allowed myself to be led hither and yon and subjected to a great deal of incomprehensible folderol, that I might satisfy myself that I do you no injustice in what I am about to say.

"Your school has offered a needed service in providing a home and an education to children with this strangest and saddest of afflictions, the spasmodic, ah, indocility of the organs of speech, but we have standards in this state"—I opened my mouth—"Standards of health—safety—and adherence to modern educational principles! The Sybil Joines Vocational School does not come close to meeting them in more than a handful of our seventeen categories. Indeed I cannot understand how it passed its previous reviews, conducted by my predecessor at the inspection board. That your safety precautions, in particular, are far from adequate, recent events have vividly illustrated."

I shifted my weight; he raised his voice a little. "You will say—I anticipate you—that changes will be made, et cetera, but I am afraid the matter has gone too far for that." He held a green ledger—my ledger—and now shook it slightly for emphasis. "In fact I am not sure that it is not a matter for the police! There are records in this book of the disappearance or death of three children and one faculty member in the course of the last year alone. And there have been, one must assume, many lesser injuries that were simply left unrecorded. No, no, I'm afraid I cannot countenance extending your license." He set the book down firmly, rapping its cover for emphasis.

Heat swept up my neck. Suddenly my ears were ringing. "If the board will grant me an extenshh—shh—[sic]—*extension*," I said, "I am sure we can address these issues to the board's satis—"

He was shaking his head. "I consider your establishment to present a clear and present danger to its students. I cannot in conscience let it remain open another day. The children will be taken under jurisdiction by the state until provision can be made for them."

He turned away, perhaps to give me privacy to master my feelings, though ostensibly to pick up his hat from the table by the door where he had placed it on arrival. His back still turned, he cleared his throat and added. "There is one alternative."

"Yes?"

"That we place the school under new administration, effective immediately. Indeed this may be the solution that is best for the children, the school, and yourself."

"New administration?" I suppose I gaped. "A new headmistress?" He did not reply. "Or . . . headmaster. You?" I stepped closer, my hands lost in my skirts. "You want my school." I was actually perfectly calm. "You're taking my school."

He turned back. I saw that his collar pinched his neck; his pink face was perplexed, distressed. "If you consent to this arrangement, I would see my way clear to giving the school a favorable evaluation, so that no scandal attaches to the change of administration. You might stay on in an advisory capacity, if you wish. And as proprietor you would continue to draw any revenues in excess of operating costs." He looked down at his hat, embarrassed. He and I saw at the same moment that a bird had insulted it, and he began scratching at the white patch with his forefinger. That this soft, ordinary person should stand between me and my work! It was wrong, disgusting even, as when a worm eats a man, or a spider a bird—a low thing boosted up to fasten its jaws on a more princely one.

There was a feeling as of a wind rushing through my limbs. I felt very light. It seemed that in a moment I would do something—weep, or strike the desk, or dance like Durga on the fellow's body. Carefully, I did nothing. I drew into myself, tightening to a minute beady intelligence, localized in my braincase. My movements became deliberate. I smoothed my skirts, examined one fingernail. My reptile gaze assessed a torn cuticle, slightly inflamed, while through the pineal eye in the top of my inclined head I stared uninterruptedly at the Regional School Inspector, now twirling his hat in his hands. I had discomfited him.

"You may, of course, appeal the decision before the entire board. Though I believe"—he dared to simper—"I have the deciding vote."

No, he didn't simper, that was a lie, and I scorn a lie. He simply stated the facts. He was a competent, dull, dignified man without a grain of imagination, and I am sure he was very surprised when, having fumbled his hat and bent to retrieve it, he received the coal scuttle on the back of his head. The metal edge bit deep into his neck; he dropped to his knees and let out a snorting sigh. Half-turning toward me, he stared at me in hurt and confusion, then sucked in his breath as if to yell. I struck him again on the side of the head. He slid sideways, landing on the carpet with a gentle thump. He was not after all very big. His head was an almost hairless pink animal, a baby rabbit or a pig, with sleepy eyes. I hesitated, then smashed it again, decisively. It was now a rather peculiar shape and I supposed that I had dashed part of the skull in. All in all I was relieved that the decision had been made and could not be reversed, though as I reflected belatedly it would have been wiser, if I had intended to murder him, to lie in wait for him on the road or follow him home.

I slipped his coat under the part of his head that was leaking and sat down in my desk chair to think. I had not intended to murder him. And I had not exactly murdered him, I felt, though I had certainly killed him and indeed intended to kill him when I struck him with the coal scuttle. I was very angry indeed and there it was, the scuttle, and there it was, his head—so. It happened. A true murder, though . . . That is something else, I have reason to think. Slower. More calculated.

But the important question was what to do with him now. In my office, a Regional School Inspector who would do no more inspecting would soon give himself away, but in the basement or the oubliette he might remain for some time without attracting notice, while I figured out what to do with him. I had to take him downstairs. But clearly I could not drag him down the hall and *bump, bump, bump* down the stairs, for everyone to hear and some, no doubt, to see. I saw that I would have to employ the dumbwaiter.

I wrapped the coat around his head to prevent anything more running out of the latter onto the carpet, and, taking him by the armpits, dragged him over to the hatch. Having opened it as far as it would go I attempted to hoist him in. He had grown bigger again, and heavier, and I could barely lift him, but I managed to wrestle his head and shoulders up to the level of the dumbwaiter before he tore himself free and went slithering and thumping down again. In any case I had already seen that if I laid him on his back as I had been trying to do, I would have to lift almost his whole weight at once to feed him in, whereas if I rolled him over onto his front before lifting him, I might be able to prop first his arms on the edge, then his head and shoulders, whereupon he could probably support himself, as it were, folded over the edge of the dumbwaiter, his lower half waiting outside for me to catch my breath.

This plan I carried out with fair success, while the dumbwaiter rattled and banged. The Regional School Inspector almost appeared to be standing, looking into the shaft. I rested, leaning against the body to keep it from backsliding. It was warm and solid. When I felt restored, I planted my legs, took the Regional School Inspector by the belt and hoisted him up, simultaneously sliding him further in, so that only his legs now dangled out of the hole in the wall.

By then, however, his head was bumping the back of the dumbwaiter, and I saw that I could not bundle in his legs without rolling him onto his side and folding him up like a jointed yardstick at the hip and the knee. After a considerable struggle during which I found myself giggling in a wet-eyed, not quite sensible way, I concluded that I would not be able to do this without getting into the dumbwaiter with him. So that is what I did, inserting myself on his right side. Bracing myself against the walls, I dug my fingers under the far shoulder and attempted to pull it toward me. His shoulder lifted a few inches, but the rest of his mass stayed where it was.

It had always been my position that a person was an insubstantial thing, a sort of wind, or a hole through which a wind passes, but I was beginning to acquaint myself with a different viewpoint. A man, if one could call this still a man, was a heavy thing, like a rolled carpet or a sandbag. The Regional School Inspector, so quick to make his move, was not now moving anywhere. I dropped the shoulder, then pulled it up again, and thus began rocking his body, until finally, as if some heavy cargo had shifted inside him, his whole weight surged up from the floor of the dumbwaiter and flung itself onto me. Now I was on my back in the dumbwaiter, my legs dangling out the door, with a dead man on top of me.

A lesser woman might have been discomposed.

I lifted the near arm, which had fallen over me, and slung it across his body, lifted the near leg and succeeded in crossing it over the other at the knee, where it dangled out of the dumbwaiter—a twisting, languid, sensuous pose, like that of a Florentine Christ in a Renaissance painting. Then I heaved the Regional School Inspector back onto his side. Pulling in at his waist, while thrusting my knees forward and up against his thighs, I attempted to force the body into a S, to the hindward curve of which I was pressed. I had never been so intimate with a man in my life.

"Monster," said the corpse, in a conversational tone. "Banshee." I unbundled his head from the coat to see if by chance he lived. It seemed unlikely, what with one thing and another. He was silent and had the preoccupied look of those whose circumstances have just changed beyond comprehension. Maybe

I had misheard him. I swaddled him again and got to my knees, straddling the body, having perceived that he needed to be slid to the right, into the space I myself had been occupying, if there was to be room on the left for his knees. The dumbwaiter bucked in its channel, its tackle straining and clanking. I could only hope that no one was listening at the opening below.

It was as I was kneeling over him, attempting to shift him to the right without once again rolling him onto his back, that you came back in, dear listener. A slender figure in blue and gray, with a cool, neutral expression on your face that did not change, *mirabile dictu*, when you saw what must have seemed an extraordinary thing.

You said, raising your voice slightly to carry over the racket I was making, "The doctor would like to ride home with the Regional School Inspector. He is on his way upstairs." Then you stepped quickly across the floor and, lifting the Regional School Inspector's legs by the knees, with a twist and a quick thrust of your hips, fit them into the dumbwaiter. Then, marvelous girl, you offered me your hand. Taking it, I climbed down and brushed off my skirts.

"The hat," I said. You glanced around, fetched the hat and the cane that I had not noticed leaning against the wall beside it, and brought them back.

"The cane will not go," you said. "We will have to put it down the shaft." You tossed the hat onto the body, then lowered the dumbwaiter a turn or two. The Regional School Inspector sank out of sight. The cane you maneuvered through the opening to stand on top of the dumbwaiter, in the open shaft, leaning against one wall.

There was a knock on the door. I arranged myself behind my desk as you closed the dumbwaiter and went to the door, silently admitting the doctor.

He took a few steps into the room—he was thus standing almost directly on top of the small damp spot, visible as a darker patch, on the rug—and glanced around with evident surprise. "I thought to find the Regional School Inspector here."

"Why, no," I said. "We spoke quite briefly earlier this afternoon—had routine matters to discuss—and then he took his leave. I imagine that he is long since departed." I saw how, behind him, you gently, slowly nudged the coal scuttle toward the fireplace with your heel.

He clicked his tongue. "I hope he has not forgotten that I was to ride back into town with him. He said he had found me a new assistant. We were going to discuss it on the road. I am very anxious to secure an assistant. The loss of Dr. Peachie has upset my plans for retirement. It is time I retired." His voice had become high and peevish. "My own nag has a loose shoe. I do not wish to lame him. Your man said I might return for him tomorrow. I do not understand what is keeping the inspector."

"Excuse me, but he may still be inspecting the grounds," you murmured. "I heard him ask Clarence where the well was located."

"Then I am sure he intends to keep your appointment and will be back presently. Will you take a tonic while you wait, Doctor?" I stood and took down the bottle, noticing too late that there was a spot of what must be blood on my sleeve. As I lowered my arm, keeping my gaze fixed in friendly inquiry on his face, I let my fichu fall carelessly over the spot, and transferred the bottle to my other hand.

"Is that paregoric? Strong stuff, Headmistress Joines. It will do no harm in small doses, but I would be careful not to develop a dependency."

I smiled. "Is that a no, Doctor?"

"Well, just a drop." I settled the lace more firmly around the telltale spot, but before I could transfer the decanter to my right hand, you stepped forward and took it from me, bearing it away to the cabinet whence you removed two small glasses. You poured as steadily as a waiter in a Pullman car. Your manner as you offered us the glasses was perfect, not too obsequious, not too bold: invisible. That this takes a sort of talent, I recognize. I do not possess it.

Then you sank gracefully down upon the hearth, moving the coal scuttle openly now, back into the shadows behind the iron stove.

I cannot dispel the feeling that there is something wrong with this story. It will come to me.

The doctor sniffed stertorously. "I smell smoke. Is something burning?"

"A small accident earlier today," I said.

We made inconsequential conversation for a while longer, and then, "It is too bad of him!" exclaimed the doctor again. "I don't have all day to wait on his convenience. Where can he be? A fine thing if he just went off without me! Is his vehicle still here?"

You rose at once and, saying you would find out and return with the intelligence, left the room. You returned a short time later with the information that the carriage was still in the drive, but that no one had seen the inspector. "Shall I tell someone you wish him to be found, Headmistress?"

"Yes, thank you. Ask Clarence to take a turn through the grounds, and when he finds the inspector, remind him that the doctor is waiting." You disappeared again. "Should we be concerned for his safety?" I asked the doctor. "Is he a sensible man, would you judge?"

"Eminently, I would have said. Solid. No fool. Though I can't like his wandering off like this. A fine time to go for a stroll!"

"Perhaps he found something else that he wished to *inspect*," I said. If a slight sneer crept into my voice, I regretted it at once. I had something more important than my injury and my revenge to think of. For I knew now that I had found my successor.

What other young woman of my acquaintance would so calmly and efficiently assist in the disposal of a Regional School Inspector with a crushed braincase? Seeing at once that the school came, and must always come, before any one individual's well-being, or indeed his life? There may be some trouble about your complexion, but there have been other colored mediums who have made a "hit"—Paschal Beverly Randolph, Hattie Wilson, Leafy Anderson, to name a few—and you are clever. I make no doubt that you will shrug it off, or even turn it to your advantage. It is what I would do. And it is not the least of my satisfactions that my father would writhe to see a "half-breed" in his daughter's shoes.

You returned with Clarence and the information that the inspector was still missing but that Clarence had found a man to fix the loose shoe and that he would be done presently. "If you will come with me, Doctor?" Clarence said, and led him, still complaining, from the room.

Your eyes met mine, and I nodded meaningly at the typewriter. Then I returned to the land of the dead, where I had, and have, unfinished business.

I know, I have unfinished business in the land of the living, too. It is presently dripping down the dumbwaiter shaft.

We have unfinished business, I should say. Since you will be my successor, won't you?

I should like, I don't know why, to hear you say, "I will." But of course you will. Even if, from modesty or dread at such a heavy responsibility, you demur. Even if you stuff your old suitcase with your few, paltry possessions, your silk stockings, purchased on a secret expedition to Greenfield, the balding hairbrush from which the red paint is flaking, the little purse of figured Oriental silk, also red, with gold birds flying into the seams, and just $3.66 nestling inside it, the black notebook with its homely strap, the ceramic figure of the Siamese twins—I know your little secrets!—and closing the door quietly behind you, leaving the lamp burning in my study, set out from the school this minute, crunching down the gravel drive that is a pale river in the moonlight, the cool mist beading your cheeks. Even if perhaps no one is recording this dispatch, for you have long since left in just this fashion, or in another, if you wish, taking a lantern and striking out cross-country instead, a more difficult path but one that will take you to Greenfield by morning, where you will be able to catch a ride to Boston or even New York, it will do you no good. I will be with you sooner or later, speaking to and through you, speaking my mind, speaking your mind, changing your mind, talking you home.

I will never stop talking.

That's it! That's it! That's what that was bothering me! These alleged events took place, allegedly, in the alleged land of the alleged living. But [pause, static] I could not have dispatched, simultaneously, both my report and the Regional School Inspector! So [pause] I must have dropped the thread of my story when I left here, to commit a murder, and picked it up again when I came back. Is that possible? Of course. But not without leaving a gap in the narrative. And I have the impression that I have been talking continuously.

I'll check the transcript. If there's a gap, I'm guilty. No gap, not guilty, just deranged. I joke! Ha ha ha ha! [Laughter continues, approx. forty-five seconds.] Anyone might—must—fall into error here, where one's very life depends on getting caught up in the story. If that door was a dummy, and like a dummy myself, or a dreamer waking to another dream, I came back to a Creation of my own creation, it's no more than many another necronaut has done. No matter, the transcript will give the truth of it. [Long pause.]

Oh.

No, it won't.

I could be gone a year, two, twenty, and still pick up where I left off.

Well, damn. [Muttering.] It is rather deflating, having witnessed the failure of one's life's work, killed a man, concealed his body, lied and feared discovery, to suspect that it might never have happened, at least not in a sense meaningful to the law.

Was it, perhaps, a rehearsal?

A directive?

Pure fiction? [Long pause, static, sound of breathing.]

In the land of the dead, a person might well experience her life as a book, and not even her own book, but an anthology of fleeting impressions, speculation, and hearsay taken down by minor scholars and anonymous record keepers. She might, further, go so far as to heap this book with baffles and blinds, introductions, footnotes, etc., so that by the time the putative reader reached the crux of the matter she did not even recognize it.

[Audio break.]

But the Regional School Inspector is saying something. I thought he was dead?

"I cannot see my way around—"

I kill him again.

"It is my duty to—"

I kill him.

"I shall recommend—"

Again.

"Effective immediately—"

Again. What sport! Again. Bodies fall and dissolve into black-red surf and form again and shoulder up, cladding themselves in black wool on which with admirable attention to detail a few moth casings have been distributed, and fall again under my remorseless blows. I employ the *Fendente*, the *Montante*, the *Imbroccata*, the *Stoccata*, the *Stramazzone*. I dispatch a thousand Regional School Inspectors and still they come.

"And thus heredity pronounces its infallible judgment," my father is saying, "for an impetuous and injudicious union will yield, without fail, an unsound adult, deformed in both the physical and the moral sense."

"Says the man who strangled his wife."

"And incinerated his daughter, I know. The regret, I promise you, is literally eternal."

"The regret at failing, one must suppose."

"Failing?" The hot surf [static] leaps and crackles. Drops bright as cinders blister my arms. "Certainly my tally is nothing to yours," he concedes handsomely. "You have carried on the family tradition, I'm gratified to see. Remind me, how many have you exterminated to date?"

My arm rises and falls, rises and falls. The hod is looking a little battered. "Figments," I say. Coal-black spindrift smokes up.

"Are you certain?"

I touch a finger to my upper lip and bring it away printed with a fine red thread. "We are all figments," I say, though the dictum has lost some of its power to comfort. Then, despite myself: "I escaped!"

"Are you certain?" says my father.

"I escaped, leaping through the flames."

"You're probably right."

"I broke down the wall, leapt through the flames, and emerged, like a phoenix, stronger and more perfect."

"I'm sure you did." I flinch as my father grins, widening the blood-red cracks in the blackened mask of his face.

I hack and thrust, nauseated. Gobbets, some with hair.

Oh, this poor bald place. Sketch of a sketch of. This poverty of imagination. Compared to the competition. Durer's cubic foot of turf. Or the turf itself.

[Static, audio break.]

I set my foot onto the black blood on the floor. It is wet, black, glistening, a little sticky, nothing like a hole, and still I fall through it. Somewhere a crow is laughing. Or a child?

[Audio break.]

If I am still in the land of the dead, have I missed the Regional School Inspector's visit?

[Audio break, betokened hereafter by a skipped line.]

Miss Exiguous's fingers turning yellow-white with pressure. Finster ducks her head, lets her hair swing forward; I can just see the quivering pink nose, the pink rims of her eyes. The long ears squeezing the narrow skull. And then I look more closely and see wet blood slicking fur, cut mouth gushing blood as it opens again, saying [static]—

Rabbits can't speak.

Opens and she throws herself through. And I—

Has the inspector not yet finished his inspection? Do I still have a chance to fetch back the girl, make everything right, save my school?

Or must I kill him? Again?

And will you, dear listener, having copied down the script, play your part? Or will you rise up against the puppet master and squeak out lines I never wrote for you?

Ah! Here is Finster, running like the dickens right through the walls and across the—

I climbed into the dumbwaiter, inserting myself to the right of the corpse, and just like that I was standing in my office and the rolling knock on my study door was still reverberating in the air. "Enter," I said, but rather than opening the door, I crossed quickly to the blue-glowing window and looked out through my pensive reflection and down. An elderly carriage stood in the drive; two horses stood resignedly in the fading light, their noses in feed bags that looked very like the creels we had fashioned for my students (with good reason, since a similar pair had been their inspiration). The Regional School Inspector had not yet left, there was still time to make things right; or maybe, better, there was nothing to make right, maybe that unfortunate and even more unfortunately timed incident in my office had not yet happened or would never happen: my father would keep his peace and I mine, the lamp would not tip or I would catch it from the air before it fell, Finster would not flee me or death would not snap shut on her so fast that I could not cheat it, this time.

The door opened, and I turned, and Finster splashed into the lakes of my eyes; she did not appear to see me, but hurried across the room, opened the dumbwaiter, and climbed inside, pulling the door shut behind her.

The door opened again, and you came in. Walked across the room to the dumbwaiter. Opened the door, took out a cane—

Or is it my father who planned this farce for me?

—opened the door. Taking your hand, I stepped out of the dumbwaiter and found myself entering the same room from the other side;. It was empty but for myself; the dumbwaiter door on the opposite wall was closed; there was no stain on the carpet, there was no blackened patch; the decanter on the shelf was full. Someone knocked lightly on the door and, without waiting for an answer, you walked in.

"Then I am sure he intends, et cetera," I said. The doctor looked a little bewildered. "I mean, have some paregoric."

"Is that paregoric?"

"Aha! Caught you!"

"Excuse me? I thought you said it was tonic."

"That's almost persuasive, but not quite."

"Are you feeling quite well? Paregoric is strong stuff, you know. It will do no harm in small doses, but I would be careful not to develop a dependency."

"Now that is interesting. Note how new sense is spliced onto senseless repetition, and thus we jog along, looking alive. Sure you don't want some?" I waved the decanter.

"Just a drop."

"Drink up!" I said, handing him the whole decanter. "Really I cannot be bothered to play out this scene." I marched straight to the dumbwaiter and got in.

I was in my study. The dead man on the floor was my father.

I was in my study. The door opened. A little girl came thumping in, set one ill-fitting shoe on a black patch of blood, and fell through it.

I was in my study, sprawled on the floor. A man stood over me, holding a coal scuttle.

I was on the floor of my study. You stood over me, holding a cane, its brass end dripping blood.

I was a patch of blood on the carpet of my study.

I was you, entering the room to see a man's legs sticking out of a hole in the wall, one cuff rucked up, showing red sock garters and a patch of white hairy ankle, from which an old scar ran up and out of sight into the tube of the trouser leg.

You were kneeling, your straight, narrow back to me and your head bent, exposing the brown nape, some fine, minutely curled black hair that had escaped your braids, and a deep gash welling with blood. I was dropping the coal scuttle, my hand falling away . . .

A little girl was sprawled on the floor of my study, her head a peculiar shape.

A little girl was writhing in flames.

A little girl was pawing at the wire that was tightening around her neck.

In short, the witch's daughter had thrown down her last and best talisman. Which? The mirror, of course. In its shards I saw a thousand selves, a thousand worlds.

I don't mind confessing that I lost my presence of mind. (Presence! Of mind?) I don't know how many times, saying *door* and opening it, I flung myself through myself, flung myself through myself, through myself, through my [static], I don't know how many worlds I flipped through, worlds no more than doors to other worlds no more than doors, until for all my haste I might as well have stood stock-still on a representative threshold, since each departure was also an arrival into the same damn place. It was in other words a lot like life, escaping each *now* only to arrive in *now* again, almost unchanged, just a little more out of breath, until the day you are done with breathing. Escaping the now into the now, it's enough to make you lose faith in last resorts, the closest you ever get is the next-to-last, and the door that keeps on opening to let you in is the same door, like, like, like nothing, maybe it's a revolving door. So my hurry was just a frantic way of staying put, and the open door just one more way to lock me in! It stunk, frankly, this pent pending, not literally, it was odorless, but repulsive, ontologically speaking, and it was this stink of a becoming that had stuck and spoiled in the pipe that got to me at last. So I stopped. So now we're getting somewhere. Out of the frying pan. And already the light is roaring against my face, already smoke is pluming through the floorboards, this is what there is, this is all there is, or ever was.

Well, that was fun while it lasted, or terrible, whichever, doesn't matter, I didn't believe a word of it, not really.

It seems to me that it has been some time since I last spoke. Excuse me, I was burning. The fire has taken on a somewhat different quality. I have the feeling that burning is a kind of work that I am doing as carefully and thoroughly as I can. A stoker whose fuel is her own body, I am seeking out patches of skin that are not yet burnt and burning them. The idea that the fire will eventually go out, no matter what I do, leaving my work unfinished, fills me with despair. But all this strikes an insufficiently odd note that leads me to wonder if the fire is not actually a tasteless and revolting metaphor for some quite different thing on which I am likewise obliged to work without satisfaction or conclusion, and into which I have been shoveling not just myself but everything and everyone I could reach.

At this the fire as if offended leans away from me, refusing my tinder, and I am conscious of a pang of loss. *Pang*. Ridiculous word. Is it a pang you feel when your heart is yanked from its socket? I cannot coax a single spark to flourish on me, and the fire goes out like a life.

Now I stand in the place where the fire was. The shed, I suppose, though burned to the ground—a shed without a shed, just as I am a person without a person, the mere site of a demolition—and almost before I think to make up the shortfall, a shed sketches itself in around me, then goes up like a torch. These flames too die. A new fire arises: I hop hastily in, declining to examine it too stringently for inconsistencies. It too goes out, even faster than the one before.

I pass now through a very quick succession of fires, not identical, but sharing many features, though in this one the flames are more like snow, in this like hair, and in this one burning is like breathing, and in this it is like walking a long way.

I am drawn to wire and fire, but fire is winning. So I am my father's daughter after all!

But after every conflagration comes the snuffing out, a sooty emptiness that begins to seem just as important as the flames, and even in a sense the truth of them, so that as I burn I seem already charcoal, already ash, swirling without purpose or emotion on an immaterial hearth.

Sometimes I rekindle the fire myself, holding a match to a pile of dung-soiled straw or a marbled page torn from a book. Sometimes another does me that service. Usually, I burn alone. Sometimes, others burn with me: my mother, my rabbits, little Emily Culp. In one, hyperbolic and quickly dismissed, my mother is hanging while she burns. Now it is the girl Finster in the shed, and I am turning the key in the lock. Now she is roosting on a nest of flames, undressed by flames, her hair a brighter light. I recognize the phoenix, symbol of rebirth, and see that it is also a symbol of redeath, suffering both prolonged and repeated, and my approval turns to anguish as her skin blackens, as her limbs stiffly bend and reach, as she turns to charcoal and still burns, and this time when the fire goes out it feels like mercy.

At the same time as I pass through the fires, I see them as if from the outside, arranged in a line, along the path I have taken, and stretching into the distance. They go back, way back to the ~~first fire,~~ First Fire, and that should be capitalized, secretary, because that is how I think of it now, as the First Fire, a sort of institution and deserving of the dignity of a title, and not only because it is superior in size and brightness and some other, indescribable quality that it might be precipitate to call "reality."

However, as soon as I think that, I make out what was at first lost in its glare: other, more distant fires preceding it, whose light strengthens and steadies as I grow more convinced of their reality, until I cannot see how I ever doubted it. So the First Fire is not the first, nor can I perceive any first, only a series receding into infinite distance. Which is peculiar, to say the least, but I shall not dwell on it, especially now that I see who is in the fire with me this time.

"I didn't kill her, actually, if I remember correctly," my father said. "Well, perhaps in a manner of speaking. But I couldn't explain that to you. You were a literal-minded child. You are a literal-minded woman, I think." There was something strange about his voice, I noticed. It seemed to me from his manner that he was speaking very loudly yet dispassionately, as one might speak to a colleague through an everyday din, and yet I could hardly hear him. Nor was there any din, naturally, except that of my heart, when I reminded it to beat.

"Absurd," I said. "If you were not guilty of her murder, you would not kill yourself in remorse." But already I half believed him, already the tremendous chords of my mother's death were dying out, leaving nothing behind but an absurd person, myself, sitting in a chair, listening to echoes and pretending she was somewhere else.

"What?" he said. He bent to examine his shoe, then held up a finger and squinted at it. My father was losing interest in me. In himself?

Suddenly I saw what was happening. I held in my keeping the only self my father had left; my hatred was all that had kept him from drifting away. (How could I of all people forget that the dead too die?) In vain I sought to draw him back, flaunting my yet unblackened patches, in order to appeal to his sense of duty, of work left undone; now I was like a rejected lover displaying in desperation the charms that no longer held any magic.

My mother was already gone, had never been real, as it now seemed.

A rabbit flounced by, a constellation of sparks smoldering in its fur. I sought to bring it to my father's attention with gestures, to issue a terrible invitation, all the while attempting with the intensity of my gaze to hold my father and bind him, as he would bind himself if he took up the garrotte I showed him, already draped around the rabbit's neck, no, not draped, sunk deep in its neck, its trailing end stiff with dried blood on which a single persistent fly was dully trying and failing to settle, denied a place among the more vigorous flies that teemingly beaded the black blood on the rabbit's coat and outlined its eyes with glittering kohl, for now I saw that the rabbit was already dead and decaying despite its animation.

And when I turned back to my father a doubt struck me: Was it even he? The upper lip seemed shorter, the forehead higher, the pouches under his eyes more pronounced; a patch of hair under the chin bespoke a careless-ness in shaving uncharacteristic of his punctiliousness; the smell of burning that I should have thought would never leave me was gone, replaced by an astringent, medicinal smell that reminded me of nothing at all.

And now I wondered a worse thing, whether my father was kind, had always been kind, would never hurt me and thus never by doing so bind me to him and himself to me. Whether I had no hold on him, whether he was already turning away from me, gathering himself in, with unspeakable, intolerable mildness was becoming something I could not name because it was the end of names.

But without my father's cruelty, what was I? Was I to be left with nothing? Well, exactly.

Now there is another flurry of fires, but they are not at all credible, cellophane and wind machines, spotlights and colored gels; they seem cynical, even sarcastic, and I dismiss them with an impatient gesture, brushing the tepid sparks off my unscorched skirts with a few quick strokes.

Perhaps I, too, am losing interest. The story that I have been telling myself is in pieces, and I am holding the shears. Call me Atropos. Or call me quits, for if in death no time can pass, then terrible as all these figments are, their order and thus their meaning is not fixed. Fires can erect factories, then, and bring forth fathers. Nooses can give dead mothers life. Sisters, for that matter, can take hearses home from potter's fields, and green sheets spread themselves on decent beds, and husbands lie down under them beside their wives. A blow from a coal hod can rouse a corpse to life, and pens can suck the words they wrote right off the page, and leave all blank, and white, and innocent, and unharmed. And then goodbye to guilt and grief, and oh yes, pride and hope and yearning too. Goodbye to clever fingers tapping keys, for I have not forgotten you, but I will.

Because I am not so sure, after all, that I will be coming back, in any form that you would recognize.

Somehow I had forgotten that death was no more lasting than life, that it was just one more misconception in the series that would, not culminate, there could be no culmination, but return again to life, and still not stop there, but keep right on through other, future deaths, and whether or not the dying finally perceived that death was simply another turn of the wheel made no difference, since understanding this was only another moment of temporary paralysis in the streaming.

I was going into something that I did not understand, for all my studies, but I had not failed. Understanding was the business of living, it was not what one did with death, death was not understandable, not because it was mysterious, or withheld its meaning, but because it did not address itself to the organ of understanding.

But even this understanding is leaving me now.

The flames are already nothing. The garrotte. Rid myself of that, too. The blood-soaked paw. Dispose of it. How cold the lack of air on my face as I see that one can learn to live without anything, even pain.

Learn to die, I mean.

And so it melts away—the world, in all its pride of seeming. All that is solid and sullied becomes air, by which I mean breath, by which I mean words. And I am running, my feet (I have feet?) sinking into marshy ground, it feels marshy, but there are no cattails, no frogs or herons, it looks like bread sauce, like chewed paper, a sauce of paper, across which as far as I can see leads, why not, a line of slushy footprints, smaller than the ones that I myself leave behind me as I steer my (as I see when I glance back) unnaturally straight course to the horizon line, it really is a line, inked, not perfectly straight, a blot troubles it here and there, soaking into the sky, but I don't know why I speak of the unnatural, it is all unnatural here, or natural, depending on your opinion of *Homo sapiens*, but it is certainly surprising, the straightness of my path, since it gives evidence of uninterrupted progress toward my goal, when I was under the impression that I had been tracing labyrinthine paths through sub-sub-basements and in and out of closets for an eternity. Of course, like all histories, it may have been concocted retrospectively, to tell a story calculated to please me better than that other, but if so it hardly matters, here all stories are true stories, until another story controverts them, taking its turn in the light of truth. The most important story here, for me, with my face now turned toward the future, is the one that the footprints before me tell, that the girl is still ahead of me, stomping into a future of her own. I even imagine that I perceive, looking at her prints, something of her character—stubbornness, curiosity, pride. She is a page away, no more, maybe less, maybe a paragraph away, a sentence—

I see her! It's her! There can be no doubt! The sharp shoulders slightly hunched, the chin jutting, the stiff black hair sticking out in pigtails of which the left one is coming undone—

No, it's no good. I try to catch her in a sentence, like this: "Here she is!" or "I see her!" or "Lo!" but either she is immune to invention, she alone in this world of figments, or my power to invent is flagging, or was never as great as I thought it was, or I simply do not believe my own lies anymore, or all of these things, or something else I have not thought of.

But wait! I see her now!

No, I am lying again. It is a bag of sand on a passing wagon, it is the light on a thrashing bush, it is a flock of birds or a colony of bats or a swarm of bees or a herd of dik-diks, each a slightly different hue, like daubs of paint, coming together entirely by accident, to compose the figure of a girl who squats to examine something on the ground, she is in no hurry, then stands, now she runs a little, she is using these words as stepping-stones, they give under her weight, slightly, springily, she is not very heavy, but even before I can finish this description, she has leapt to the next one, in which I mention, now, the white dust rising up around me, and is running on ahead of me; the light is shining on her and is part of her, she is not me, she is *not me*, it is what I like about her, that she is not me, but maybe she is me after all, or maybe it's that I'm not me either. Dust rising. Sky lowering. Paper sauce sucking my feet, paper wind wrapping around my face, white dust falling, in my mouth, in my eyes, in my bones. Even if I were to say I saw her, how could I ever believe it?

I sit down.

I have the impression that I sit for a long time.

I shall not bother with the usual tired caveats: if one may speak of time, et cetera.

A white cat appears and sits beside me for a while, then lollops off, long ears glowing persimmon orange with a sourceless light.

From time to time I seem to hear someone saying that *all this* has been cruel and pointless and *for that reason* has value. It has the stench of truth. But I am not sure what exactly *all this* designates. It may not matter. Surely I would be justified in taking *all* to mean all.

I doubt it, though.

And what is meant by value, that is another question.

Another interesting communication: That the dead do not speak, that every word they seemed to say to me, all those years, was in fact said by myself, to myself. Naturally this perturbs me. But I rally, because if I am the only one speaking, then there is certainly no reason to believe everything I hear; I am capable of telling a lie, as I have good reason to know. But I am not quite easy in my mind, for am I not here relying on the claim in order to dismiss it?

Another communication follows close upon the last, varying only slightly: that *all this* has been deception, pure deception from the start, and *for that reason* true.

But although if I could trust this dictum (whether or not I understood it) I might take some consolation in it, I am not quite easy in my mind about it. For I could probably come out with any number of similar formulae myself, without meaning anything by them—that I am cruel, and for that reason kind; that I do not exist, and this is my soundest credential; that I shall never succeed, and this is the only hope for me, et cetera, et cetera, you get the picture.

That I can say these things does not mean that they are not true, however. Or does it?

I don't feel well.

Don't feel well, what nonsense. I feel nothing. The feelings have fallen away with the stories. Gone the rebellious, conniving, or sycophantic underlings, the desperate acts, narrow escapes, flood, fire, blood. I am in my last story, I think. My burial plot, you might say. It is very simple. You know this story. Everyone knows it. It goes like this: I'm going to die.

[static] I'm going to die! [static]

Page white eye white lying still lying half sunk in marsh of chewed paper. Wind with its burden of dust and ash of old bones old books sifting ceaselessly over my face, white falling across a white sky dust falling sideways left to right, ceaselessly. I remain where I stopped (apparently), sunk in a cavity my own shape, my face turned upward offering to the heavens (heavens! Really, Sybil) my mouth still speaking, thus. There is little room for me between white and white, not cold not hot lukewarm no wind no calm, particles of ash clinging to a screen white hair not mine curling in air forming letters of no words in an Arabic without origins. Great piles of gray, ground bones ground books piles of white of salt of teeth or again ash the blind eye of the sky sees me without a pupil stares down blinkless all dry white fire falling through my bones sand through an hourglass whisper of scales on sand of sand ghosting off the knife-sharp crest of dune, sun with no source, sun with no sun, sun that is everywhere, sun that I am, beats in my bones, wind that is no wind, wind that is everywhere, on which I am carried while lying still, hoots through my bones, hisses and whistles in my womb, near me an animal pink of snout is gnawing with yellow tooth on a sardine can or tobacco tin the repetitive sound like the sound of my blood in my ears, *wruhh wruhh wruhh*, perhaps the child is in the tin, what child, I forget, no there is nothing in the tin. Near me a dress full of air gesticulates slowly and near me an empty hat drops onto the sand with a soft sound. I try to roll over. Perhaps I roll over. I roll over. Yes. Good. Now my face is half in the sand. Good. One eye is full of sand. Good. It sees no less than the other one. Sand flows into my mouth, slowly, with overlapping swells, I let it come. Each grain a soul. I am content to be among them no more nor less than they. My throat fills with sand, apparently I do not need to breathe, not yet, or not at all, not anymore. Is this what I want, I ask myself, and I answer, near enough. The witch has caught up with Nix Naught Nothing after all.

But there is something still bothering me. Some bug in my eye, some sliver in my thumb. As everything else dishevels and softens and falls open, Finster still sticks in my craw.

And then I see her. After all, it is this simple: If I say so, it is true.

She is right in front of me. Write that down. It is Eve Finster. Here she is. Eve Finster. I see her. Eve is her name. She is crouching in the margins, crumpling the paper a little; she is ink-stained around the mouth and fingers, as you are, dear secretary. She is holding something in her cupped hands. It appears to be moving.

I perceive that it is a world.

I get up. I creep toward it.

These invented worlds have a leaning toward catastrophe. If you have visited a gallery of coin-operated mechanical marvels you will have seen how the little skeletons do bounce out of coffins and closets and holes in the ground. So I know what to expect. Flames and rabbits and piano wire. Or a woman in black, holding a coal hod, a dumbwaiter open behind her.

But I am wrong.

Oh, it is a world all right. Tiny and particular as any world of mine, but it is not mine. She does not even look up as she urges two of her creatures, a sort of animate sombrero and a—what is it? A pony, but with claws, and a forked tongue?—through a labyrinth, the blossoms on whose blooming hedges snap and whisper as they pass. Her mouth moves—"left, right, right, left"—and I know beyond proof that she is a righteous guide, not even tempted to slip up, to slip in the extra right turn that would take them down the dogleg where the biggest flower of all gnashes and waits.

She looks older than I remembered.

And now I wonder whether it is Finster at all. Do I see her as she sees herself, here where one may invent oneself and in any fashion one pleases, or in some other way? I will not describe her. I will do something quite different: I will say what she is. (What she is for me, I mean. What she is for herself is for her alone to know, is dark to me, *finster*, hidden in Finsterness.)

She is myself. She is myself, that is, before they damaged me. A self I cannot remember or understand. Real *because* I cannot understand her.

And now I will say what I am. (What I am for her. What I am for myself, I no longer know.)

I am the damage that threatens her.

And not just in what I have already done, by bringing her to my school in which children die, some, not many, but some, and for which I have killed or imagined killing, I don't care which, but in seeking to seize her, to know her, to write her into my story. I drove her, not to her death, but to mine. As if to keep her there forever, a stuffed kitten in a pinafore, working sums at a pygmy blackboard.

But when I saw that she was describing something I had never seen before and could not imagine and that yet came into existence between her hands, wonderful in its smallness and detail, I no longer wished to possess her but to return her to the living as soon as possible, so that she might pursue her program of living in a world not made by me. Here it was, the thing I had been looking for, my living, blooming death, the not-me that, in the end, I was. And all I had to do to claim it was let it go.

I did not see any other doorway by which she might return to the living and so I swallowed her. And felt her inside me like my own death, intimate and strange. For a moment I seemed to become her, and was afraid that I would lose her in making her mine, but instead she made me hers, and I gloried in my strangeness to myself. Then through my mouth gave birth to her, weeping in joy and pity at what I did, like any other mother.

Are you there?

You delivered her, I'm sure, with your usual phlegm. Probably fielded her with one hand, kept the other poised over the keys. Not knowing that I could have nothing of greater importance to say.

Send her home in disgrace, it will set her up for life. Nothing like a grudge to inspirit the young. Let her mother comfort her; even hyenas nuzzle their young. We're not comforters, my dear. Succor is not our métier.

[Pause.]

I think I will go home too.

[Pause.]

I do not open my mouth, I open the world in which my mouth is. It swings apart on jaw hinges, and through the gap in the world, the world begins to spill. I am the hole through which existence pours itself torrentially through itself, and this torrent is what I have called my life. Murders, frightened children, their no less frightened parents, dead rabbits, fires, they spill through me and dissipate like mist.

The unutterable takes the shape of a word. I seem to know it. I am about to say it. I will say it now.

The Stenographer's Story, contd.

Reader, she was dead. It is hard to explain how it happened—how a voice rattling around a brass trumpet became a body quietly cooling in a chair. She was not there in the flesh, and then she was, but there was no soft *pop* of displaced air, no creak of wood and wicker adjusting to a sudden weight. She did not drop from the ceiling or open like an umbrella. Perhaps it is most accurate to say that it did not happen. I merely noticed that it had already happened, that by the time I noticed that she was dead, I had already known it for some time, had settled into the knowing like a watcher at a wake. She sat across from me with her hands, in fingerless net gloves, folded in her lap; as upright as if strapped to a backboard, with fixed and yellowish features and an open mouth, in which her drying tongue could be made out.

I am quite sure, however, that she was not here a few moments ago when Finster spilled out of a fold in space onto the carpet and, howling, went straight to bed. At least, that is where I sent her, and just in time, too, for hard on her heels came the next corpse—I mean the corpse.

Beside me, the trumpet blared the silence.

I had a question, when I began this document: Who am I? My curiosity was not idle, for the answer would determine my responsibility for the work done here tonight, and in the hours to come. And now the answer was clear. I was—I am the headmistress of the Sybil Joines Vocational School for Ghost Speakers and Hearing-Mouth Children.

Already I could barely remember what it had been like to be anyone else, so I suppose it was fortunate that I had written it all down. If I was conscious of a slight feeling of letdown, I lost no time in shooing it away, for I would need all my fortitude and cunning for the enormous distances I had yet to cover, and that were only now truly apparent to me. It was as if I had scaled a great mountain, only to find that it was only a foothill of the far greater eminences beyond, which multiplied in blue hazy echelons as far as the eye could see. There was work to be done before I slept; I knew my duty and had even had an inkling, in writing these pages, of how to discharge it. I would not look back again, nor ever trouble to remember who I had once been, whom I had once taken myself for, a mean figure who now bore, I thought, hardly any resemblance to the figure I now cut, in which I already recognized some of the Headmistress's pride of bearing, and as I rose and stepped forward to confront the body I even coughed once or twice.

I lifted her heavy arm to free her reticule, which was wedged between it and the arm of the chair, and groped inside the latter for her—for *my* keys. I slid them inside my waistband. I arranged everything as she would have wanted. Then I straightened my papers and rang for Clarence.

A curiosity: In moving her arm I discovered, scribbled in ink on the inside of the cuff of the left sleeve of the dress, like a schoolgirl's crib-note, these words: "We do not exist, but we are responsible for our figments."

Addendum

The following, undated, but of comparable vintage, was paper-clipped to the final page of Grandison's report. —Ed.

I will not comment on the "confession" some have seen in these pages except to note that anyone who is moved to sweep off to gaol those implicated in them should bear in mind that they were dictated from the land of the dead by a woman in the terminal stage of a mortal disease and show many signs of confusion of mind. It has been sufficiently demonstrated, I believe (and our constabulary concurs), that the events described are not only scrambled in the telling but impossible. Even if we accept that a woman sick unto death could wield a coal hod with a force and efficacy that would be remarkable even in a healthy one, then cap this feat by hoisting a grown man's body into a rather small receptacle, there remains the inconvenience that she had departed the land of the living well before the inspector's arrival—*and never returned.* This well-attested fact has been disputed by careless readers who point out that the Headmistress herself states that she departed the land of the dead to carry out this murder. Indeed! If you believe everything you read, why then, pray make your bow, for I am the King of Ding-a-Ling.

To more judicious readers it should be evident that as she herself noted, a person cannot carry out the murder described while simultaneously dictating a running account of proceedings to her secretary through a transmitting device. Such readers will require no better proof that the so-called murder was a hallucination, likely induced by that same party whose baneful influence the Headmistress herself suspects. I am only sorry that the Headmistress died believing herself the murderer that her father undoubtedly really was.

The overwrought suggestion that the fictitious murder served as a sort of "blueprint" for a real murder to be carried out by another in her stead does not deserve a response.

Finally, I will remind the speculative that the outraged corpse discovered on our grounds has still not been positively identified as that of the Regional School Inspector. It is not impossible that it is the body of some other person whose absence has not yet been noticed. If two disappearances seem one too many to account for a corpse, perhaps they are linked! I speculate only, but is it not possible that the Regional School Inspector, over whom so many tears have been, I will not say wasted, but shed, chose murderous means to stage his own disappearance, using a luckless drifter as a mannequin on whom to hang the semblance of his self?

I for one believe that the inspector is enjoying his anonymity and a glass of rye in one of our larger urban centers. One need not be a Peary—or a necronaut—to feel the call of another world.

Editor's Afterword

My publisher would like to advertise the mystery solved, but I have prevailed, and lay it before the reader in all its convolutions.

The case as I see it is as follows. Either the Headmistress murdered the Regional School Inspector, in more or less the fashion she has described, or her secretary did.

The former's motivation is sufficiently clear from her testimony, but there are ambiguities in her account that call its veracity into question, as she herself points out. The latter's motivation can only be guessed at, but it is obvious that she hoped, if she did not already know, that she would inherit the school. Hence her interests would be on this point indistinguishable from the Headmistress's. Furthermore, we know that she was in possession of a note betraying the inspector's growing unease with his involvement in her deceased swain's ectoplasm ring, and thus had even more reason than the Headmistress to believe the inspector a danger to the school. She was at least an accomplice to the crime. Whether she was in fact its principle hangs on the contentious chronology of the Final Dispatch, and the difficulty, even for its author, of telling fact from figment in it. Frankly, I see no way to settle all its ambiguities.

And then, perhaps I am too much a convert to the precepts of necrophysics to believe that a case is ever closed, the past ever past. No, one day another mouth will open and through another's throat a father's voice will ring out. Another mother will plead in vain for mercy. Another daughter will do what must be done.

Other characters, too, will take their encores. There will be another Clarence, silently orchestrating the daily life of an institution. There will be another Miss Exiguous, insinuating herself where she is not wanted, though her name and her features will be different. One day I might discover anachronistic inflections in my own speech. Maybe my prose has already betrayed, to an astute reader—or a computer program analyzing word usage frequency patterns—the presence of an interloper. If so, he—or she!—is surely a minor character. *Mine not the alpinism of the soul! But to have a role, however small . . . I would not turn down that chance. Meaning is nothing but pattern recognition, I sometimes think, and this at least I do share with Headmistress Joines: the age-old dream of a meaningful, a legible universe.*

I have recently received an invitation, on SJVS letterhead, and signed by a familiar hand. I have accepted it, for I am a twenty-first-century man (though my manners and appearance would not have excited remark fourscore and ten years ago) and do not really believe in ghosts. I will take care not to turn my back on the Headmistress, all the same, and keep a weather eye out for sharp or heavy objects in my vicinity, for am I not a sort of school inspector?

But I am optimistic. The SJVS teaches that history is already written, and returns in endless reprints. But that does not preclude revision.

Now and then, a Finster gets away.

Last Will and Testament

Of

of *Cheesehill Masschusetts*

File 29752 N

, being of sound mind and memory, do make, publish and declare

this our last Will and Testament in manner following, that is to say:

I, Sybil Joines, of Cheesehill, Masschusetts, being feeble in body but sound in mind, and conscious that the former soon must perish, though the latter speak on in another, and lest local authorities, sound in body but feeble in mind, should choose not to recognize the legitimate authority of my person (or, as I prefer, my voice) when alienated from my body, do hereby give and dispose of my worldly estate, goods, chattels, as well as all posts and privileges at my disposal, in the following manner and form:

In primis, I hereby nominate, constitute, invest with full powers of attorney, and appoint as my successor that person, to be known by ꝏ certain demonstrations, specified in a signed and sealed document that will be found in my effects, in whom I speak again, this person also to serve as the executor or executrix of my will, and, effective the moment of my decease, to be considered in all matters as my proxy, with all rights and duties pertaining thereunto, and indeed as myself, being possessed of all my qualities without alteration or diminution, a station that I charge my confederates on pain of dismissal to to recognize, endorse, and defend against contestation, irrespective of any perceived deficiencies of education, bearing, personal magnetism, manners, class, or any other quality supposed prejudicial to fulfillment of the duties of Headmistress, these duties to be held for his or her natural life; this person also to legally assume the name of Sybil Joines, as soon as practicable, along with all my possessions with the exception of my brooch, my bombazine dress, and other garments in which (after laundering) I desire my body to be decently enveloped prior to its dispatch as follows;

Appendix A: Last Will and Testament

I, Sybil Joines, of Cheesehill, Masschusetts, being feeble in body but sound in mind, and conscious that the former soon must perish, though the latter speak on in another, and lest local authorities, sound in body but feeble in mind, should choose not to recognize the legitimate authority of my person (or, as I prefer, my voice) when alienated from my body, do hereby give and dispose of my worldly estate, goods, chattels, as well as all posts and privileges at my disposal, in the following manner and form:

In primis, I hereby nominate, constitute, invest with full powers of attorney, and appoint as my successor that person, to be known by certain demonstrations, specified in a signed and sealed document that will be found in my effects, in whom I speak again, this person also to serve as the executor or executrix of my will, and, effective the moment of my decease, to be considered in all matters as my proxy, with all rights and duties pertaining thereunto, and indeed as myself, being possessed of all my qualities without alteration or diminution, a station that I charge my confederates on pain of dismissal to recognize, endorse, and defend against contestation, irrespective of any perceived deficiencies of education, bearing, personal magnetism, manners, class, or any other quality supposed prejudicial to fulfillment of the duties of Headmistress, these duties to be held for his or her natural life; this person also to legally assume the name of Sybil Joines, as soon as practicable, along with all my possessions with the exception of my brooch, my bombazine dress, and other garments in which (after laundering) I desire my body to be decently enveloped prior to its dispatch as follows;

In secundis, I give and recommend my mortal remains to the U.S. Mail, desiring that they be introduced under the oversight of my executor or executrix hereafter mentioned into an oversized envelope with the stamped legend RETURN TO SENDER and delivered without undue delay or mutilation to the Post Office, in the assurance that that venerable institution will convey it faithfully to its intended destination in the Dead Letter Department.

Under no circumstances are my remains to undergo cremation. Fire will play no part in my future. Nor loam. Paper will be my crypt, the only worms that sieve my corse, *bookworms*.

In testimony whereof, to this my last will and testament, I have set my hand and seal this Ninteenth day of July, Anno Domini, One Thousand Nine Hundred and Seventeen (1917).

SYBIL ADJUDICATE JOINES

Signed and declared by the above named Sybil Joines as and for her last will and testament in the presence of us present at the same time who at her request in her presence and in the presence of each other have hereunto subscribed our names as witnesses.

Ms. Winnifred Other

Ms. Dorothea Exiguous

Jane Grandison the executor, sworn November 18, 1919, and letters Testamentary granted unto her. The said Testator died on November 17, 1919, at or near 4 a.m.

Subject:

k as in kill.
g as in gale.
ng as in sing.
(Front view.)

ah as in father.
(Front view.)

ah as in father.
(Cross section of mouth
showing tongue position.)

1

k as in kill.
g as in gale.
ng as in sing.
(Cross section of mouth showing position of tongue
and soft palate.)

ee as in feel.
(Front view.)

ee as in feel.
(Cross section of mouth
showing tongue position.)

J. R. Ruffin

Appendix B: Instructions for Saying a Sentence

This exercise is taken from the "kit" of a traveling admissions officer of the Vocational School and was used to assess the latent talents of prospective students. Assiduously following its instructions will allegedly give any reader the experience of channeling the dead. I hesitated to include it in this collection, as it makes but poor reading, but of course it was meant to be not simply read, but executed. Its true meaning thus lies not in the words here reproduced, but in those other words that, following instructions, you will utter, or the dead will utter through you.

Frankly, I have never been able to figure out what sentence it is I am supposed to say. A superstitious fear has always prevented me from finishing it. —Ed.

Tense your vocal cords and, beginning the controlled emission of breath, produce a tone from your throat. Sustain this tone, so long as your breath holds, throughout the following operations.

Now purse the lips, leaving only a minute aperture, as if you were going to whistle. Meanwhile, press your breath forward into your hollowed mouth (in which your tongue should be held low, tense, and delicately pointed), allowing only the slightest seepage of breath from between the lips. (If prolonged the effect would be of a moan or grunt, but the next step follows quickly.) Considerable pressure should build in the throat before the release as, from their forward and gathered position, you pull the lips quickly, wincingly apart and back, curling and raising the upper lip as you draw down and square the lower, allowing the hitherto muffled note to leap forth. Not unaltered, however, for in the meanwhile, the tip of the tongue advances, approaching (but not touching) the palate in back of the lower teeth, while the dome of the tongue presses upward toward the roof of the mouth, tightening on the breath that passes over it.

Already, however, the vowel sound is changing, for your lips and tongue are softening as you open your mouth and let an open vowel roll forth. Now, however, you should all at once chew down on it, humping the back of your tongue to touch the flanking molars, tensing the tip, and jutting out your jaw, while tightening and slightly flaring the lips—raising the upper one as if to growl, drawing in the lower at both corners.

Now raise the pitch of your sustained tone. The tongue slides forward slightly, now nearly touching the roof of the mouth. Quickly lower the tip of the tongue, as if peeling it off some clinging surface, while bringing the lips together, corners drawn back, into the shape one might form to play the flute. Now soften and part the lips, but bring your upper and lower teeth together. Advance the tip of the tongue to the lower teeth and press it softly against them as you raise the tongue until it just touches the roof of your mouth, leaving only a wet and narrow passage over your tongue. Buzz briefly, softly.

Lower the pitch of the tone again, as you allow your mouth to fall partway open, though not as far as earlier. Then pull your tongue quickly back, wedge the tip behind the lower teeth, while the back of the tongue rises and presses against the palate and, securely wedged against the upper back teeth on both sides, seals off the mouth passage entirely for an instant, engaging the nasal cavities. This seal is immediately broken with a minute click followed by an unvocalized release of air.

Protrude the lips, the upper tense and slightly curled, the tongue high, nearly touching the roof of the mouth. Now lower the tip of your tongue as you open your mouth. The effect is of allowing the hitherto restrained breath to spill down into the hollow at the front of the mouth. Now, raising the lower jaw again, forcefully retract the back of your tongue until it meets the molars, while lowering the tip.

Raise the pitch again. Close your lips, while parting your jaws, and hum. Then open your mouth, keeping it round and hollow. Lower the pitch as, contracting your lips, you tighten the hole of your mouth without closing it. Then press the upper surface of the tip of your tongue against the cutting edge of your two upper incisors, firmly, but not so firmly that a little breath cannot hiss through when, as now, you forcibly urge it through the ensuing aperture.

With vigor, with dash, pull your tongue away and back. Relax your jaw, still your vocal cords, subdue your breath. Be silent.

Appendix C: Ectoplasmoglyphs #1–40

The dead, as usual, will have the last word. Let those who can, read. —Ed.

Acknowledgments

Above all, I want to thank the dead, who have talked me through my life, and whose voices haunt this book. To Zach, of course, fellow necronaut, whose eye and mind informed every visual element of the book, and his assistant Veera, thank you for throwing yourselves with such enthusiasm into my world, and making it your own. To Christopher Sorrentino (who read it twice), Kelly Link, Edward Carey, Darcey Steinke, and Pamela Jackson, thank you for your scrupulous, frank, wise, and generous responses to early drafts. To PJ Mark, for your support, shrewd advice, timely interventions, and for suggesting Zach, thank you! To my editor Mensah, thank you for championing this book. Your guidance was invaluable in shaping it, and your fluency in necrophysics was a marvel. Thanks to the whole team at Black Balloon for supporting and even celebrating this book's eccentricities, and for the grace and good humor with which you helped me and Zach realize our vision for its design. And to Sean, music director of the SJVS and unofficial collaborator, for help of all kinds, and Shibi, my delight and inspiration, the biggest thanks of all.